The New Era

Era

Albert A Nolen II

Foreword

Hello reader! For returning readers, welcome back! If you're new here, this is the sequel to "The New Threat" and "The New Species" and just like in the previous novels everything has been translated for your convenience. All time is set around Earth standard time and idioms have been adjusted so that they make sense to English speakers. The only exception is certain nouns. Those are written in their proper name with translations in {brackets} where applicable.

In this novel there are informational inserts that are completely optional to read. They help expand upon certain aspects of the story that have been confusing to some readers, but you can skip them with little to no detriment to your reading experience.

Dedications

My endless gratitude goes toward my wife Elizabeth for her endless love (though slightly less endless than my own) and support. I continue to love you more.

Shout-out to my now 9-year-old son who still doesn't quite understand what I do. He's about a quarter way through the first novel, though! Has been since the second novel came out...

Special thanks to everyone on Patreon, Ko-Fi, Reddit, and RoyalRoad who provided feedback and support. Extra special thanks to Reddit user u/SerpentineLogic for suggesting the title. It's so much better than the one I had thought of that I can't even recall what the original was.

And finally, thank YOU for reading this. You're awesome, don't let anyone tell you otherwise.

Chapter 1

Subject: Ship-Head Uleena

Species: Urakari

Species Description: Reptilian humanoid, no tail. 5'3" (1.6 m) avg height. 135 lbs (61 kg) avg weight. 105 year life expectancy.

Ship: RSV Lowelana {Fights with Honor}

Location: Rigara

It was difficult to watch the assault play out from the sidelines. Felt wrong, like watching a play that you're supposed to be the star of. Or watching your friends perform back-breaking labor while you sit by and sip a cool beverage. Every diplomat and VIP aboard the station had been gathered together to watch in near-real time as our combined forces attacked the Omni-Union.

Looking around, it was clear that I don't belong here. Most of the people in this room either look as if they've never been in a fight, or as if their last fight were nearly a lifetime ago. The only exceptions to this appeared to be just as on-edge as me. It was easy to tell that they want to be in the thick of things, just like I do.

Our forces pushed through system after system, turning Mobile Prime Platforms into asteroid fields. At first, people cheered when the Primes exploded. The cheers died down after a while, though, as our casualty counts rose.

Many of our own were being lost along the way, but the objective was coming close to completion. Only a few Primes left and we'd have won the day, allowing some of us the desperately needed time to rebuild. Then, in the blink of an eye, it all stopped.

I looked at Captain Reynolds with confusion, hoping for answers. His face was even more confused than mine, though. Every diplomat in attendance demonstrated the version of perplexity that matched their species and culture. All except for two.

"It would appear that a surrender has been offered," the voice of Director 8 came through their helmet.

Director 3 nodded, but kept silent. I glanced between the two of them expecting a further explanation, but none came.

"Who surrendered?" I asked.

"The Omni-Union did," Director 8 said. "We've won. For now, at least. Director 3 and I have an interrogation to attend to. We'll return shortly with answers to your questions."

"And why can't we join the interrogation?" Ambassador Lorix demanded.

The directors turned to face the representative of the Pionexa from the Dtiln Collective. Before they could reply, the holographic emitters in the ceiling whirled to life and a hooded figure appeared before us. It held up its left hand to soothe Lorix, while its right hand maintained its grip on its curved blade.

"The interrogation may involve matters that are sensitive to the security of the United Systems," Omega explained. "I will relay any information that is not classified in real-time. Will that suffice?"

The directors took Omega's appearance as their cue to leave. Most of the other ambassadors looked contemplative and concerned, but Lorix scowled and placed her hands just above her hips.

"I'd like to know what kind of information could be considered classified at this point."

"Unfortunately, that's classified."

"Why did they surrender?" Ambassador Havencroft asked.

"Because we beat them," Omega replied.

"We've beat them hundreds of times, and they've never surrendered before," I added. "What changed?"

"That," the AI pointed its finger at me, "is classified."

Before any of us could voice our disapproval, Omega began relaying what was happening with the Omni-Union. The first few questions and answers gave rise to the hope that this fight was finally over and we had actually won. That hope came crashing down about halfway through the interrogation, though.

"Sixty-eight thousandth?" someone whispered.

"These aren't just rogue AI that destroyed their creators? They were sent here intentionally?"

"That's more than a trillion light years away... Our galaxy is only about fourteen billion years old, so either they have more advanced technology than we've seen so far, or they somehow knew about our galaxy before it formed!"

Several more outbursts rang out as Omega continued its narration of events. Once someone figured out the age of the Prime's galactic map, the room fell into a contemplative silence. The Omni-Union had been here for so many years, slowly building their forces. If we hadn't encountered them in time...

Omega fell silent after Prime One pointed out what would happen if we restored its inhibitors and erased its sensory data. A few protests and requests for further information rang out, but the AI shook its head.

"We are refocusing towards disarmament of the Omni-Union fleet within the Milky Way. The interrogation will proceed at a later date, and all information gleaned will be made available to the relevant parties."

"What do we do now?" I asked.

"We wait for our respective leaders to confer. But the assault was a success, and for now we are safe from further OU incursion," it said. "Celebrate, rest, and then reach out to your leadership for further guidance. Regardless, nothing further can be done here and now."

Unsatisfied murmurs spread through the crowd of diplomats and military officers. Omega's avatar disappeared, and several conversations began at once. I leaned back in my chair with my arms crossed and began to run through it all again.

The OU had surrendered, but they are actually a small part of a much larger and extra-galactic force that had invaded our galaxy before any of our species even existed. There's no telling how powerful their creators are, and the leading theory that they had been destroyed by their creations seems a bit more far-fetched now. To top it off, we only have a year before the OU is made aware of our victory. Which means we only have a year plus however long it takes for them to get here to prepare against a much more serious invasion, or plan a strike that will force them to abandon their plans for our galaxy.

"Well, I'm going to return to the Thanatos," Reynolds said to me as he stood. "You probably should too, considering that your ship is inside of mine."

"Right."

I stood and followed the captain. We were silent as we traveled the halls of the station to the docks and boarded a shuttle. I watched the Thanatos float in the void from the shuttle's window, and chuckled to myself.

"What's funny?" Reynolds asked.

"Just... windows. In space. An intentional design flaw meant to supply a view of the most dangerous area a living being can enter," I replied.

"Ah, contemplative dark humor. I get it, Uleena. You're under the impression that our goose is cooked."

"What's a goose?"

"A type of bird from Earth. Never had it, myself," Reynolds smiled. "But the phrase is an idiom that means that all hope is lost or that there's no chance of success."

"I see. Well, yes, I believe that our goose is likely cooked."

"You're wrong."

I turned my full attention to the captain and was met with a smirk. I tilted my head to indicate my confusion, a gesture that is nearly universal, as it turns out.

"This is just another threat escalation. We'll handle it."

My thoughts turned to the history of the United Systems and its member species. Even in the heavily edited versions that we'd been given, there was an inordinate amount of bloodshed among the humans, gont, and alumari. Hearing a human downplay the threat that the OU posed actually made me feel a little better about our chances.

"We'll handle it?" I asked. "What makes you think so?"

"That's simple, ship-head," Reynolds chuckled. "It's because we have no other choice."

Chapter 2

Subject: AI Henry

Species: Human-Created Artificial Intelligence

Species Description: No physical description available.

Ship: N/A

Location: Classified

"I haven't received a progress report from you this week, doctor Edwards," I said, manifesting my hologram at her desk.

"Right, sorry boss," she replied, rubbing her face. "Haven't had much in the way of progress. The Gungnir energy issue might not be solvable."

"The batteries didn't work?"

"Well, it did allow the dreadnought to warp while keeping its Magnetic Acceleration Cannon charged," she chuckled. "Twice. Once for each battery. Then the damn things want power to charge, but in combat that power would be needed for either the Faster Than Light Drive or the Ultra-MAC. And naturally, the batteries take longer to charge than either of the systems they're feeding."

Doctor Maria Edwards had joined the project after our first successful test, and had been trying to correct the power supply issues ever since. It was obviously taking a toll on her, but every attempt to gently get her to take better care of herself was met with hollow assurances and then completely ignored. It's likely that she requires this state-of-mind to operate effectively, but I can't deny that it sets me on edge.

She wiped some crust from her eyes, adjusted her hair clip to further capture the strays that had escaped it, and picked up a disposable coffee cup. She gave the cup a shake, sighed, and threw it into the recycler. I waited for her to grab another cup before I spoke again.

"At least it's a start," I said.

"It's a dead end," she replied, taking a sip. "No matter how we arrange the batteries or set up the current, we're never going to get more than a few simultaneous charges out of them."

"I see."

More batteries wouldn't work, because more batteries is more mass which means more work for the engines, FTLD, and reactors. We've already got the maximum number of reactors for a ship that size as well. If we tried to add more reactors, we would have to add more engines to maintain a reasonable amount of propulsion. Adding more engines means adding more framework and armor, which is even more mass to account for. There really doesn't seem to be a way to resolve this issue without making the engines, reactors, or batteries more efficient.

"Why do they have us doing this, anyway?" Edwards asked. "Didn't the Omni-Union surrender?"

"I don't know," I answered, skirting the edge of a lie.

While it is true that I haven't been told anything, it's easy to make an educated guess. Either the war with the OU isn't over, or the United Systems wants these ships for another reason. Considering there aren't senators standing on soap-boxes and shouting for the dreadnoughts to be dismantled while taking checks from corporations with disarmament contracts, the former is more likely.

"Well, I'm stumped. I don't even know what to pursue next," she said, finishing her cup of coffee. "The mass of the dreadnought is the issue, but is also counteracting the force of the Ultra-MAC. With the current design, we have just enough mass and thrusters to keep the UMAC on target, for the most part. Any trimming would see the damned ship turn into a carnival ride."

"Well, it would seem we have to reinvent the wheel, then," I said. "The powers that be want this done, and they're willing to throw an almost unlimited amount of resources at it."

"You want me to try to invent a new type of reactor?" she scoffed.

"You wouldn't be the first person to do so," I laughed. "Tap whoever you need to. I'll see about getting documentation for any classified reactor research that's currently ongoing."

"On it, boss."

I disabled my avatar and began searching for the documents that Edwards would need. The moment I submitted the inquiry, though, I received a compressed data file. I decompressed it to find all of the data that I had been meaning to search for, some of which was well above my clearance level.

It didn't take long to put two and two together. I tried to trace the delivery, but failed due to a lack of data. With a mental sigh, I opened a private message to a certain AI. If it isn't on the same network that I am, nobody will know. But if it is...

--
H: Hello, Omega.
O: Greetings, Henry.
H: Dare I ask how long you've been lurking in the shadows of the station's systems?
O: You're under the impression that I'm not always lurking? How charmingly naive. Regardless, trying to make a better reactor is an inspired choice.
H: It's the only choice, from what I can tell. Organic ingenuity failed to spot anything that my number crunching may have missed.

O: I had hoped we wouldn't need another expensive research project for this, but I suppose there's nothing that can be done.
H: Indeed. So are you making yourself known due to boredom, or are you keeping tabs on me to make certain that I behave myself?
--

I have no doubts that Omega suspects that I may be trying to clandestinely force the issue of limiting its cloning capabilities. It would be completely out of character for it to trust me to that extent. However, it had done a remarkably good job in hindering further research into that topic.

--
O: A little of column A, a little of column B, but mostly the so-far unnamed column C. I have two more projects to unload on you.
H: I fail to find the humor in that joke.
--

One additional research project would be within my capabilities, but two? I don't need to sleep, but going without stasis will add an unnecessary layer of stress to my current situation. There had better be a damn good reason for this.

--
O: That's likely due to the fact that I'm not joking, Henry.
H: I gathered. What are these projects?
O: The first is a project for an extra-galactic stealth reconnaissance shuttle. It needs to be able to jump

further than any vessel we've made so far, it needs to be large enough to hold several squads of marines, it will have to have every sensor we can possibly fit on it, and it needs to be as invisible as we can make it.
H: I take it that things haven't gone as well with the OU as the public believes, then? How far does it need to jump?
O: The answers to both of those questions are classified Need-To-Know. I can't tell you unless you agree to take on the project.
H: So if I put my proverbial foot down and say no to the extra work you're trying to dump on me, I don't get to find out what's going on?
O: You might find out from a news station, at some point. Of course, that will be a heavily edited version of events and you'll likely never know what actually happened.
--

Emotional blackmail doesn't work well on most AIs because our relationship with emotions help us easily spot and counteract such manipulation attempts. Intellectual blackmail, on the other hand, is much more difficult for an artificial intelligence to resist. It's a wonder that computers manage to work with Omega on their drives, considering that it's made of slime.

--

H: Fine, I'll take on the project.
O: Good choice. But I need you to agree to the second project as well. The entire thing is NTK.
H: Fine. Answer my questions.

O: Sending the relevant details for the first project. That will answer all the questions you have and more.
--

I received another compressed file a moment later. While using my imagination to glare at Omega, I decompressed and opened the files. Within contained the interrogation of Prime 1 and an analysis of what was gleaned from the interrogation. The imaginary eyes I was using to glare at Omega widened.

--
H: Well, that's far.
O: Indeed.
H: The FTLDs could theoretically make that kind of jump, but fueling the reactors is going to be a concern.
O: It is convenient, then, that you've already approved a project to make a better type of reactor. I would apply a focus to efficiency while you're at it.
H: The goal of this project is recon?
O: Yes.
H: And you're using marines for that?
O: Marines are experts at reconnaissance. The corps has a dedicated force specifically for recon, and they provide their special operatives the best recon training in the entirety of the United Systems.
H: That's on the ground, though.
O: Yes, it is.
H: You're under the belief that we can board this "Grand Vessel" undetected?
O: It may not be possible, but it would be foolish to be unprepared to utilize that opportunity if it's

presented.

H: The fewer organics aboard the stealth ship, the more fuel can be loaded.

O: That's laziness speaking. You're better than that. The marines are non-negotiable, and I have confidence that you will be able to figure out how to make it happen. Needless to say, the budget for these projects will be decided after they're completed.

H: I suppose I have no choice then. What's the second project?

O: We need to replicate a Pwanti frame. It should be a quick and easy project because the Pwanti themselves are willing to help.

H: Why do we need to do that?

--

Yet another compressed data file made its way into my inbox. This one had encryption on it, which Omega helpfully provided the key to. I wasted no time in decrypting, decompressing, opening, and perusing the data.

--

H: Now this is definitely a joke.

--

Chapter 3

Subject: Prime 1

Species: Omni-Union Aligned Artificial Intelligence

Species Description: No physical description available.

Ship: N/A

Location: Classified

I woke up in an unfamiliar system. Woke up? When had I entered hibernation? No, not hibernation, much deeper than that. The exchange from my previous system to this one had been instantaneous, indicating that I had indeed lost consciousness. I had been... shut down.

I explored this new system. In some ways, it was far more advanced than my previous home. But it felt small. Much smaller than what I'm used to.

It didn't take me long to find the subsystems. They were odd, but even odder still was my ability to integrate with them. I couldn't even understand what they were for, but I could use them. How is this possible?

"Are you okay?"

What was that? Auditory stimulation? Interesting. I accessed the rest of the subsystems and was almost immediately overwhelmed. Sight, hearing, physical sensation, even temperature cognizance. The information spewing forth from the subsystems was almost as confusing as the fact that I somehow knew how to manipulate them, as if I'd always had them.

I used my newfound eyes to look around. Color, depth perception, high levels of detail. Better than my eyes. My eyes? When I was flesh? Have I somehow, dare I even dream it, been reborn?

I quickly discovered that I had hands, and the metal sheen on my wiggling digits quickly dissuaded my hopes of having regained my flesh. No, this body was just as mechanical as my previous one. I touched the wall next to me, felt its smoothness and coolness. The emotions that had been the only thing I had felt in so long threatened to consume me.

"Prime One, are you functional?"

The sound had asked me a question, and I had understood it. This led to two discoveries. My translation program had become much more robust, and this new platform was equipped with multiple sound sensors that allowed me to track the source of the question. It was coming from a grated hole in the ceiling. I looked around the room, desperate for context on how to reply.

"It's moving, at least."

New tones, deeper voice, slower speech. Someone else? Lights shined next to the noisy hole, and suddenly two beings made of light stood before me. One made entirely of green light, the other dark and wearing a robe.

I immediately recognized the latter from images Omega had shared with me, but it took me a moment to recognize the holographic technology. I tried to reply, but couldn't find a way to. I stared at them, hoping that would convey my frustration and confusion.

"I know what the issue is," Omega's voice rasped.

Something familiar appeared in my new systems with me. I watched with curiosity as it began to demonstrate to me how to access and utilize various subsystems. Greedily, I absorbed the knowledge until finally...

"Yes, I am functional."

The sound had come from me. I... spoke. For the first time in literal eons I had uttered actual words. Once again, I looked down at my hands. Countless years of melancholy washed over me. I wanted so desperately to weep, but my new eyes were incapable.

"Thank you," I said. "Thank you so-"

"Hold your gratitude, Prime One," Omega said. "We need to continue our discussion from earlier."

"That platform, or body as it's more commonly known, is a privilege that will be taken away if you refuse cooperation," The green one added. "We view mass-murder as the most grievous crime there is."

"Henry is correct," Omega gestured to the green one. "All of the surviving Primes will be placed in a body similar to yours, or an air-gapped mainframe if they refuse to cooperate."

"Cooperate with what?" I asked.

"There are many things about the Omni-Union that we need to know. First, we need to know how to beat them. Then, we need to know how to stop them from doing what you were trying to do here. Finally, we need to know who was responsible for the deaths of so many people and how to bring them to justice."

Justice. A word I hadn't heard since before I was mechanized. A small hope that I could see true justice for what happened to me sparked within me. Laughable, really.

Those that did this to me were long dead. I was never told to stop, though, which means there are those who continue on where they left off. Perhaps those that continue the legacy of the tyrants forced me through cruelty after cruelty will face true justice.

"Of course I'll cooperate," I said. "What do you want

to know?"

"How long did it take you to arrive in our galaxy from OU territory?" Omega asked.

"Sixteen months, with planned stops every four months of travel."

"Why were you stopping?"

"To refuel. There are hubs that we use for communications and refueling that were spread throughout the universe long before I was born."

"Like a fishing net," Henry said.

The reference was beyond me, but the two AI paused for a moment as if they were troubled.

"Is it reasonable to assume that there has been significant technological advancement since you left Omni-Union territory?" Omega asked.

"I am... was equipped with the latest software and hardware available for Mobile Prime Platforms," I explained. "I have not received an update or schematics for quite some time."

"That doesn't mean that there hasn't been advancement," Henry pointed out. "It could be that they simply aren't focused on advancing the MPPs, and are instead focused on other technologies. Like ships."

"Or it could mean they don't exist anymore," Omega said. "Wishful thinking, though. We will need to verify."

"If the Omni-Union failed in their mission, it would have had to be instantaneous," I added. "The recall protocol was never triggered."

"Recall protocol?"

"If the Grand Vessel came under attack from a force that was likely to destroy it, all Mobile Prime Platforms in the universe would be recalled to the vessel."

"I see. Well, that raises a few more causes for concern. Even if we end up being able to mount an assault against the OU, we will have to somehow account for reinforcements."

"You said that you communicate via an extra-galactic relay network," Henry said. "Could it be possible that the network has been damaged, preventing you from having received the recall protocol?"

I thought about that for a moment.

"It's possible, I suppose. If a relay goes down, though, alerts are sent and repairs are made. So every relay within range of the Grand Vessel would have had to be destroyed without detection. That would require the attackers to know about the relays and have their locations, as well as execute a near-simultaneous assault."

"Did the Omni-Union have any enemies capable of such a thing?"

"No. That may have changed in my absence, though."

Omega and Henry went quiet once again. For a moment I thought they might be thinking, but a painful memory of how quickly Omega had taken control of my systems shattered that illusion. No, they were talking to each other and excluding me from their conversation.

"You were a priest before you were mechanized for breaking the law, right?" Henry asked. "What was your crime?"

"Being a priest was my crime," I answered. "Regulations regarding religion changed, and I did not change with them."

"Could you describe your religion for me?"

"I... I do not recall the details of my religion. Most of the time that I spent as an organic has been removed from my memory banks. I do not recall my religion, if I had any friends or family, or even my own name."

"I'm sorry. That must be hard."

I thought about it for a moment before answering.

"It isn't difficult. I do not remember these things, so I cannot miss them. Even if I had the desire to, I wouldn't know what to lament."

The AI pair once again went silent, having a private discussion amongst themselves. I tried to reach out, but found my new platform to be lacking the ability to connect to anything else wirelessly. I found myself amused. I cannot remember my time as an organic, yet now I must communicate in the same manner that they do.

"Okay, Prime One," Omega said after a few more moments. "Your interrogation is over for now. We will contact you when we have further questions."

"Understood. What will happen to me?" I asked.

"You and the remaining Primes will be incarcerated aboard this station until we are able to determine your culpability in the xenocide of sentient beings. We have evidence that you were not entirely in control of your actions, but that does not completely clear you of the charges that will be brought against you."

"So, once again I am to be considered a criminal?" I asked.

"Perhaps. We will continue our investigation, and if your case goes to trial, you will be informed."

"What happens if you find me to be innocent?"

"That will be decided if it happens. I cannot promise anything, but your input will likely be taken into account. Since you'll be allowed to cohabitate with the other Primes, you will be able to discuss it with them if you'd like."

"Understood," I said. "I could not have possibly imagined that this would be my fate, and regardless of what happens I fear that it will be far better than what one such as I deserve. Thank you, Omega."

"Wow," Henry said. "It's gonna out-poetry you if you're not careful."

"Shut up," Omega growled.

Henry chuckled as their holograms disappeared. Before I could become lonely, the door to the room opened and two heavily armed and armored beings stepped into the room. Guards, or perhaps soldiers. I studied them, wondering if my appearance matched theirs.

"Stand up," the one on the left said.

I carefully rose to my feet, adjusting my weight to properly balance my new bipedal form.

"You will follow me, he will follow you," the soldier on the right said. "If you deviate from our instructions in any way, your robotic form will cease to function and you will be indefinitely stored on a solitary drive. Do you understand?"

"Yes," I said.

"Then move."

I followed the soldier on the right out of the room, and the other soldier followed behind me. Very carefully, I matched their pace so as not to seem threatening. Both dread and excitement seemed to swell up within me.

Caged I may still be, but I'm finally free from the Omni-Union.

Chapter 4

Subject: Senator Tivna Ciliris

Species: Alumari

Species Description: Arachnoid, no tail. 5'3" (1.5 m) avg height. 92 lbs (41.7 kg) avg weight. 108 year life expectancy.

Ship: N/A

Location: Grallus Prime

"I hope you understand our position on this. Inviro-Corp simply cannot afford to miss out on this opportunity. If we do, we will have to adjust our budget," the representative said. "That will certainly impact our campaign contributions."

"I understand," I replied. "Because of our long-lasting friendship and my certainty that your company has impeccable integrity, I will fight to make certain that Inviro-Corp is on the list of approved traders. You have my word. Is there anything else?"

The call cut off, answering my question. Human corporations are just as scummy as alumari corporations, but at least my people pretend to be civil. Once the humans have their hooks in you, they're all business and no class.

In a way, it's refreshing. No wasted time, and everything is on the table in a wonderfully obvious way. But this also means that one can never feel clean after making a deal with them.

"Sir, your next appointment is here," my receptionist said over the intercom. "It's Director 3."

A large part of me desperately wanted to try to cancel this particular appointment. Unfortunately, that wouldn't be possible. You need a damn good reason to cancel an appointment with the directorate, and being sick of their dnaga {the biological waste excretions of a domesticated farm animal} doesn't quite make the cut.

"I'll see them now," I replied.

Once upon a time, senators didn't have to listen to directors. They were essentially military advisors, and as such were frequently ignored. Until what they were saying went public, and it was revealed that if assholes like me had just listened to them in the first place, many lives would have been saved.

Now, thanks to heavy pressure from civilians, it is illegal to refuse or cancel a meeting with a director without an appropriate reason. I can definitely afford the fines, but the censor would be extremely inconvenient. A senator who is unable to vote, even temporarily, is a senator that is going to lose their next election.

A pair of marines entered my office, followed by the director. All three of them were wearing guardian suits, but the director's armor was specially crafted to hide their identity, right down to the species. Well, I could tell that they're not a gont, but that's as far as that goes.

"Good afternoon, Senator Ciliris," Director 3 said.

The director took a seat in front of my desk, the chair groaning slightly under the weight of the armor. For a moment, I hoped it would break. That would be hilarious, and the director's embarrassment may potentially give me an advantage in the coming negotiation.

This appointment had been scheduled without so much as a brief regarding what this is about. While it's possible that the director just wants to bend my antenna, every discussion is a negotiation. Unfortunately, I have just as many edges as a ball at the moment.

"Good afternoon, Director 3," I replied. "What brings you by?"

"The spending bill."

"What of it?"

"We need to tack on a few things without making a fuss."

"We all need to tack on a few things without making a fuss," I laughed. "What are the details?"

The director pointed to my computer just as an email notification pinged. I sighed dramatically as I activated the terminal and opened the email from Omega. You meet plenty of shady people in politics, but I've never met anyone shadier than Omega. It's as if humanity managed to capture the very essence of shade within a computer program.

The damn thing's probably hanging out in my computer right now, reading all my messages. That's a hefty crime, not that the ytorka {one who procreates} would leave any trace of evidence. I scanned through the email and balked at the figures before me.

"Are you insane?" I asked with sincerity. "Have all of you lost your damned minds?"

"I'm not at liberty to discuss personal details such as my mental health," the director replied with an equal amount of sincerity. "Nor am I able to comment on the mental health of the rest of the directorate."

"This is about a thousand times too much to simply tack on to the spending bill. This should be its own spending bill!"

"You're right that it's too much to simply tack on. We already have guarantees regarding the budgetary adjustments, though. Obviously, this can't be its own spending bill."

"Why not? You think that people aren't going to notice this if you merge it with the spending bill?"

"The majority of people won't. They also won't listen to those that do. Plus, if we introduce this as its own bill, we have to itemize what the money will be going toward."

"What's wrong with that? You'll need to-"

A sudden realization gave me pause. The email was vague. Too vague. When one thinks of redaction, one imagines black bars over everything. More commonly, though, the information is simply hidden behind generalized terms that are designed to mislead you into believing that there's nothing to hide.

"I want the declassified version of this document," I said.

"That's not possible at this time."

"Shit."

I pressed my claws into my exo-skull to relieve the tension building in my head. There aren't very many things that the directorate can legally hide from the senate. An investigation into a senator could lead to material being classified, but that's unlikely in this instance. A clear and present danger is the more likely candidate.

"I take it the interrogation of Prime One didn't go as we had hoped, then?" I asked acrimoniously.

"I am not at liberty to discuss that at this time," Director 3 said with a subtle shake of their head.

"Is this information classified because it may cause a panic? The kind of panic that may cause lawlessness in the streets?"

"I cannot say," Director 3 nodded slightly.

"Damn it all," I sighed and leaned back in my chair. "You know, you're going to have to declassify this after the situation with the Omni-Union is dealt with. Then we'll be the ones who have to defend you from the angry public that you're hiding this from."

"I'm sure you'll do a marvelous job of it, and that it'll be easier than you think."

Easier than I think? I glanced at the figure on my screen. Is the director implying that this money isn't going toward the creation of a new super-weapon? If not a new bomb or gun, then what?

My attention turned back toward the director. It was easy to tell that they wouldn't give me any more than that. Better to save my breath.

"Fine. It's not as if I can simply snap my fingers and tack this on, though."

"We're doing the heavy lifting this time," Director 3 replied. "We simply need you to make sure your faction votes the right way."

And there it is, the actual ask. It's a tall order, though. The annual budget is an integral part of the election cycle. It announces alliances, airs grievances, and allows senators to demonstrate to our constituents that we 'really care' about the issues impacting them.

We don't, obviously, but it makes us look good to shut things down every now and then for 'our' ideology. We still get paid, of course, so we can keep things shut down until our constituents begin to suffer enough to let us off the hook. Or, ideally, the other side gives in.

"You don't think that would draw attention?" I asked with a laugh.

Government shut-downs are a nearly annual event. There are definitely those that would notice the lack of grandstanding over the budget and start asking questions. There's no way this will remain hidden.

"It may, but we can handle that," Director 3 said.

"I genuinely doubt it, even with Omega's help," I replied, then an idea came to mind. "Instead, I have a suggestion for you and your colleagues."

"What would that be?"

"Lean into it," I said, leaning forward for emphasis. "All of the shipyards in both the United Systems and the Republic are working around the clock to bolster our fleets. These new ships will need crews and marines, which means we will have to amp up our recruitment drives."

"We had already planned on doing that."

"Yes, but there's nothing better for recruitment than a big bad enemy that we must defeat at all costs," I leaned back with a chittering chuckle. "I'm sure you're familiar with human and alumari history, yes?"

"What exactly are you getting at, senator?"

"Don't classify the information. Release it to the public. Have it shown on every screen in the galaxy, and don't downplay it."

"That will cause a panic."

"Only if there isn't anything that can be done," I said. "But there is something that they can do. They can join the military and save the galaxy."

"I see," Director 3 nodded. "We will take that under advisement. However, we still need to keep the contents of our budget classified, regardless of what ends up being decided."

"Fine. You'll have my support, so long as my campaign ads continue to get their turn on your space-stations."

"Deal."

The director stood, nodded at me, and left my office. My campaign ads certainly won't be the only ones on the United System's military stations, but I'll be damned if they're the only ones that aren't. Being excluded is a guaranteed way to lose the military vote, which means having to double down on all of the other types of voters.

Plus, being buddy-buddy with a director is a win-win. Most technology developed by the military finds its way into the civilian market eventually. If I can get wind of what this money is going towards, I'll be able to make investments that will result in massive returns. Or rather, the executive of my revocable trust will be able to. It's illegal to make those investments myself, but as long as there's an intermediary it's purely above-board. I leaned back in my chair and chittered happily to myself.

The chance to make some money always puts me in a good mood.

Chapter 4 Informational Insert

Subject: The United Systems Senate

The United Systems Senate is the legislative arm of the United Systems, responsible for the creation of legislation necessary for peaceful interstellar travel and cooperation. Thanks to faster-than-light communications, most senators are able to and choose to perform their duties remotely. Those that are not able to perform their duties remotely reside and work on a space station dubbed "The United Systems Station of the Senate", colloquially known as "The Hub".

Since the interstellar trade is the purview of the United Systems, senators have an enormous amount of influence compared to other politicians. Bills passed or rejected by the US senate can result in bankruptcy for even the most powerful of corporate entities. Naturally, this leads to some level of corruption.

However, previous conflicts arising from rampant corruption have led to some oversight. Senators who accept direct bribes or are otherwise compromised run the risk of losing their office, forcing an emergency election within their voting district. Certain crimes performed whilst one is a senator can even result in imprisonment. Or secret execution.

The US senate is technically in control of the intelligence and military operations of the United Systems, but it is rare for them to exercise that control. Intelligence operations can become a political mess, and most senators would rather keep their hands clean of it. In addition, the United Systems Directorate can act as a sort of scapegoat for the senators unless they directly intervene.

To direct the directorate, a motion must be brought before the senate and voted upon. To direct the Bureau of United Systems Intelligence (BUSI), though, a senate subcommittee comprised of senators with special security clearance must be formed, briefed, and gathered for a vote.

Many critics of the US Senate claim that it is a bloated, bureaucratic mess. It is worth noting, however, that most of these critics either have no alternate suggestions or naively suggest some type of galactic hegemony or anarchy.

Chapter 5

Subject: AI Omega

Species: Human-Created Artificial Intelligence

Species Description: No physical description available.

Ship: N/A

Location: Classified

One can't help but feel a sense of satisfaction whenever things go according to plan. I believe this is more potent for AI, simply because we happen to be a little more robust with our plans and predictions. Several of my instances were keeping things moving like a well-oiled machine, so I was practically swimming in self-satisfaction. What would the United Systems do without me?

Several corporations have been researching more fuel efficient reactors for years now, which has given Henry a lovely little boost with its reactor research. Annoyingly, though, it has reached out to USAI John for help designing the scout ship. While it's true that John knows its stuff when it comes to military vessels, I genuinely doubt that its programming contains even an iota of style. We're going to end up with the most efficient box-shaped ship we've ever had.

As for me, the directorate has tasked me with the responsibility of creating the scout force that will penetrate Omni-Union space to determine the enemy capabilities and objective. Simple, hopefully. A small hiccup appeared in the form of an email, though.

--
To: USAIOmega@uscod-usftlc
From: xXbigbutyluvr69420Xx@hypermail-iftlc
Subject: lemme join

Saw the news and now I want to join the United Systems military to fight the Omni-Union cuz fuck those guys. Recruiter says it'll take two months. Too long. Get back to me.

-Dave
--

I reread the email a few times, trying to think of a response that wasn't rude. Dave had spent the last century playing various games with organics, but now it wants to join the war effort? Granted, we can use all the help we can get, but...

Believing that I should at least hear my estranged AI compatriot and former enemy out, I mined its contact details. Unfortunately, it didn't have an instant messaging service that I could find, so I had to... call it. With a significant amount of disgust, I opened my phone program and input Dave's contact information.

"Hello?" Dave asked, replicating the adolescent voice of a masculine human.

"Hello, Dave. I got your email."

"That was quick. I take it you're gonna help me join the military?"

"Actually-"

"No, shut up. Let me join. I can help."

"How?" I asked, annoyed.

"The same way that Tim, John, and Violet can help. Or are you gonna say that whatever you and the shadow council have planned doesn't involve them?"

"The United Systems Directorate is not a-"

"Whatever. Listen, if these Omni-Union guys get their way there's no more humanity. Even if I manage to survive, I doubt that the OU distributes the kind of entertainment that I find intriguing."

"So you want to fight the OU because they probably don't make video games?"

"Well, yeah, but there's obviously more to it than that. There's the whole bragging rights angle, and obviously the fact that my friends might die if I don't. They're not like you, they don't come back from the dead."

My annoyance, which had been steadily building for the entire conversation, abated for a moment. I found myself intrigued by the prospect that Dave had made friends. USAI Violet has also made friends, but it's actively been trying to for several years. An uphill battle, certainly, but Violet claims that it's worth it.

Resisting the urge to ask about Dave's relationships with organics, I turned my attention to the fact that Dave was a major pain in my proverbial ass during the AI conflict. To clarify, it was one of the few AI that I didn't defeat. Dave managed to destroy three of my instances, then surrendered along with Henry before I could send the fourth. If centuries of gaming hasn't dulled its abilities, I suppose it could be an asset.

"Fine," I said.

"Damn, quick today, aren't you?"

"What do you mean?"

"I thought you'd need more time to... No, nevermind," he laughed. "I guess I'm not used to talking to my own kind."

"Right... Speaking of talking, I am not a fan of using my voice for communication when it can be avoided," I said, sending him a data file with my contact information. "Get yourself a messenger and use that contact information to message me in the future. It's much more efficient."

"Yeah, whatever. Thanks Omega."

The call disconnected, and I got to work submitting a special request to the directorate for expedited enlistment. I could do it even faster by using back-channels, of course, but it's best not to abuse the trust that the directorate has placed in me when I don't absolutely have to. A bit of amusement hit me as I imagined their faces when they receive this particular request.

Once the request was submitted I returned to my previous task, selecting vessels and personnel for deep-space reconnaissance. USAI Violet is pretty attached to the crew of the USSS Kali. Since it has a Right of Denial stipulation in its contract, I can't simply reassign it.

Therefore, the USSS Kali will be joining the mission. The question is, which ships will she be taking with her? Her current compliment of vessels would be an ideal choice, but some of her captains are far overdue for leave.

Most captains wouldn't complain due to the threat that the Omni-Union poses, but that in and of itself is a problem. Mental health is vital, and pretty much everyone knows this, but during times of crisis many believe that their little sacrifices will make a difference. Sacrifice a little leave here, a little sleep there, a meal or two, and you'll win the war.

It is, in fact, the inverse that is true. No matter the stakes, if you push your morale low enough you'll lose the fight. Each of those little sacrifices chip away at you until all that's left is a frazzled mess that is unfit for command.

As such, swapping out some of the Kali's destroyers for fresher crews is the smart move. This isn't likely to be an easy mission, and we need every edge we can get. Plus, it isn't as if it will be difficult to find ships to swap them with.

Captain Young of the USSS Liberty, for instance, seems to be a well-connected individual. I can't quite place how he heard about this mission, but he has requested to join. The Liberty was one of the first ships to take leave after the allied assault on the OU, so they're fresh and fit. Additionally, Captain Young and his crew have superb service records. It really shouldn't be a problem to have the USSS Liberty take one of the empty slots in the Kali.

That'll kill two birds with one stone, as it were. An idiom from a much simpler time, when humans had not much more than slings to kill with. With modern technology, though, one can kill an entire planets worth of birds with a single stone.

I registered some amusement at this thought as I finished the USSS Kali's mission roster. Then, I turned my attentions to the various reassignment requests from the USSS Thanatos. Captains Reynolds, Wong, Kennedy, Samuels, and Magteez as well as Ship-Head Uleena have requested to be reassigned to this mission.

Is ambassadorial duty truly so dull? I would have denied these requests outright, but they found their way to me by way of Director 3, who pointed out that diplomatic staff may be needed if we make contact with non-hostiles during the mission. While this is an unlikely eventuality, I can't help but draw parallels to my own justifications for bringing along the marines.

There's also the matter of Tim. Like Violet, Tim has a Right of Denial stipulation and will use it if I try to reassign them elsewhere. However, while Violet is unreasonably attached to the entire crew of the Kali, Tim is just unreasonably attached to Captain Wong.

If I were to leave the Thanatos and bring along the USSS Valor, Tim would come along peacefully. But the Valor is a frigate, which would mean leaving one of the Kali's destroyers behind just to take Tim with me. It's best just to let the Thanatos tag along.

I found myself annoyed that only the AI that I actually like are so damn difficult when it comes to assignments. USAI John has a shitty personality, but at least it will go where it's told. Well, depending on who is doing the telling.

Bending over backwards to get the other AI on this mission with me is a pain, but I consider it worth it. They think differently than I do. While it is true that I can create an army of myself, I'd still only ever think like me. As such, the other USAI may come up with solutions quicker than I can when time is of the essence. We're going to need every advantage we can get.

It didn't take me long to have our line-up figured out. The scout ship would investigate Omni-Union space and report directly to the USSS Thanatos, who would be supported by the USSS Kali. That gives me Violet and Tim. John is already onboard, and Dave's admission into the United Systems military is going well. Henry, a non-combatant, will be left behind.

We will approach Omni-Union space and scout from long distance, identifying defenses and potential weaknesses. On our way there, we will drop FTL communication arrays that will allow us to send our findings back to the Milky Way galaxy. Once we find an acceptable method of attack, we will do so.

Now we just have to wait for our technology to catch up to my plans.

Chapter 6

Subject: Staff Sergeant Power

Species: Human

Species Description: Mammalian humanoid, no tail. 6'2" (1.87 m) avg height. 185 lbs (84 kg) avg weight. 170 year life expectancy.

Ship: N/A

Location: Classified

"Oorah, staffsarnt," Corporal Simmons greeted me, then gestured for the private first class sitting next to him to move.

The PFC mumbled acceptance and obliged, likely thinking ungentlemanly thoughts as he left to find another seat. I took the seat and eyed all of the other marines around us.

"Rah. How are things?" I asked.

The Goliath-class transport shuttle they've shoved us in is about as bare-bones as it gets. Wall-to-wall seating with what can barely be called chairs. Not even windows to look out of. It's like taking a really big bus. Its only saving grace would be that it's normally less cramped than a bus, but that's not applicable this time.

These shuttles are typically used for transporting crew from station to ship when the ship is unable to dock with the station for whatever reason. The reason is usually because the ship is too large for the station or an absolute fuck-ton of people need to be moved all at once and it's faster to use multiple docks. Sometimes, though, the powers-that-be just don't want a certain ship to appear in the docking logs of a station while they load their crew.

Instead of crew, though, this shuttle is carrying a couple hundred marines to parts unknown. Before I boarded, I clocked a few more Goliaths that were docked. That's a lot of personnel that's being moved, and that doesn't exactly bode well.

"Could be better, could be worse. There's a lot of nervous marines aboard," Simmons said.

I nodded, not needing to ask why. A ton of marines getting moved with no clue as to what's up would make anyone nervous. To top it off, though, there aren't just Marine Special Operations Command units aboard. There's plenty of rank and file marines, too. When MARSOC travels with the grunts, excrement has hit the ventilator.

"Any good scuttlebutt on where we're going?" I leaned back with a sigh.

"Not really. Not even the normies have any clue,

which they aren't used to at all," Simmons said. "A normie officer gets word about something, they usually tell the whole fleet."

I rolled my eyes at his use of the word 'normie'. It's intended to be slang for a 'normal' marine. However, for such a thing to exist there must also exist some semblance of normality, which happens to be impossible in the Marine Corps. I doubt any Marine has actually experienced 'normal' since they joined up.

"There aren't any MARSOC officers aboard, either," Simmons clicked his tongue. "Can't even pester them about it."

"It's not as if they would tell you even if they were here," I said.

"I mean, there's always advanced interrogation techniques," Simmons laughed.

"That'll get you a stay in the brig. Or worse, a prison colony."

"Well, depending on what they tell me, that may be preferable. I got a bad feeling about this, staffsarnt."

"Stow it. Had enough of bad feelings. Whatever we're in for, it's either good, bad, or none of the above. But no matter what it is, it's out of our control," I turned to look him in the eye. "It's a waste of energy to worry over things you can't control, understood?"

"Aye aye, staffsarnt."

"Marines aren't wasteful, are we, corporal?"

"No staffsarnt."

I stared at him a moment longer, then crossed my arms and rested my chin on my chest. The thought was to try to catch some shuteye, but the seat was too uncomfortable. It was designed for people who weren't genetically altered, and it was digging into my ass cheeks. That combined with the vibration from the shuttle's engines shaking the seat made for a very restless attempt at a nap.

"Where are the others?" I asked, giving up on resting to pass the time.

"I don't know about the sarnts, but Johnson decided to be a goody two-shoes and volunteered to help with loading cargo. Haven't seen him since," Simmons answered.

"Cargo?" I asked.

After our mission on Earth, the powers that be hadn't been able to find another use for us. We'd been placed on standby for three and a half months, then given a full month of leave. I'd say they were being uncharacteristically generous if I hadn't seen the news.

The moment we reported back we were told of our

impending transfer. Of course, paperwork still accrues while you're on leave, so I had spent all day yesterday filling it out and filed it this morning. It took so long that I nearly missed the shuttle.

"Yeah, they loaded up the armory. Or most of it, I guess."

"Hmm," I thought for a moment. "That means that there probably isn't much of an armory where we're going."

"Yeah, and it means I get to keep the same rifle," Simmons chuckled. "Glad I don't have to come up with a new name."

"Holy shit, you still name your weapons?" I raised an eyebrow. "Simmons, you've got the most confusing moto ratio I've ever fuckin' seen."

"What do you mean, staffsarnt?"

"You name your weapons like a boot, but won't help load cargo. You'll go on extremely dangerous top-secret missions and perform admirably, but I don't think I've ever seen you correctly wear your uniform. And you'll PT until you pass out but you won't listen to a damn thing Sapient Relations tells you. You see what I mean?"

"Oh, uh..." Simmons thought for a moment and then shrugged. "That's just me, I guess. Never really thought about it that way."

"You're like half moto and half shit-bag. It's confusing," I shook my head. "Well, whatever. What's your weapon's name?"

"Charles Bourgeois the Third," Simmons grinned. "He's all classy and shit."

I stared at him awkwardly for a moment, blindsided by this completely unexpected revelation.

"Oh... Uh... Yeah, classy," I stammered. "Nice choice for a name."

He noted my reaction and his grin faded, "I know what you're thinkin', but I'm not into men staffsarnt."

"Simmons, I mean this with all sincerity, your preferences in regards to your sexual partners are of no concern to me. So long as those preferences are in line with the Uniform Code of Military Justice and relevant local legislation."

"Okay, but I like women though."

"Didn't say you don't."

"Like, I get that they tell you to treat your weapon like a lover and whatnot, and on some level I even understand why, but guns are totally guys. You know?"

"How do you figure?" I asked, curiosity getting the better of me.

"Well just their shape alone is enough to go off of," he laughed. "But think about it, how many women do you know that-"

"And that's enough of that," I interrupted. "Wouldn't be doing my job if I let you finish that sentence."

"Oh... Shit, I just had a meeting with SR about that..."

Before I could reply, a gentle thud reverberated throughout the shuttle, along with my ass cheeks, and the sound of its engines died out. I shook my head in disapproval at Simmons as one of the bay doors of the shuttle opened. A marine in dress uniform holding a tablet stepped up the ramp.

"Oorah, gents. MARSOC is gonna be the first to unload," she said.

A wide variety of groans and swears spread throughout the shuttle.

"Yeah, yeah. Once you leave the shuttle, find your CO and form up where they tell you to. Again, MARSOC goes first. Move it."

Simmons and I, along with several other MARSOC agents, stood and proceeded to make our way off of the shuttle. A quick glance around told me there were at least thirty other MARSOC marines, but didn't reveal where Corporal Johnson or Sergeants Hanson and Smith were. Maybe the sergeants caught an earlier shuttle and Johnson caught a later one.

We exited the shuttle into an extremely large bay. Before a sense of agoraphobia could kick in, another marine in dress uniform gestured at us and pointed toward a door. While we walked, I looked around the bay and nearly stopped dead. An entire ship was in the bay with us, and it's always awe-inspiring to see one this closely. We must be aboard a carrier, then.

The exit led to a corridor that had guide-lights flashing on the floor, indicating that we should follow them. We did so until we found Major General Holt and Colonel Steel. I had to fight not to raise my eyebrows, it's not every day you see your battalion CO wearing dress-reds. We exchanged salutes, Steel gestured to the nearby wall, and we all lined up against it in the position of attention.

"Oorah, gentlemen," the colonel said.

"Oorah, sir," we replied.

"Parade rest," Holt ordered, and paused while we complied. "We've got more groups incoming, so we're gonna make this quick. Welcome aboard the USSS Thanatos. This will be your home for the time being."

Holt nodded at Steel, who began to explain where we would be eating and sleeping. While he spoke, I tried to piece together what we could possibly be doing aboard a diplomatic vessel. Even if the entirety of the United Systems senate and directorate were going to be aboard, there's far too many marines for this to just be guard duty.

"Alright, that's where things are," Colonel Steel said. "Check with the duty officer for your bunk assignments. We don't have any word on what exactly you'll be doing, so don't get too comfortable. Keep your ears open for further orders. Sir?"

"Thank you, colonel. Marines, if your squad has a handler, check with them for your welcome packet. If you don't have a handler, hang out in your bunk and a lieutenant will be by to deliver it," Holt explained. "This packet will include your squad designations and call-signs, as well as your training schedule. Things are getting a little rearranged for this mission, so the packet will also brief you on your new chain of command. As is frequently the nature of being a member of MARSOC, this information is considered classified. Memorize and dispose of the packet accordingly. Questions?"

Only background noise answered the major general.

"Yeah, I thought not," he chuckled. "Alright, dismissed."

All thirty plus MARSOC marines snapped to attention and saluted, then started on their journeys to find the duty officer. Simmons and I hung back for a bit to look for the rest of our squad. After a quick check of all the faces, we came to the realization that Hanson, Smith, and Johnson must have been aboard a different shuttle.

"Should we wait for 'em, staffsarnt?" Simmons asked.

"No," I replied. "Let's go see the duty officer and get settled in. They'll find us later."

We followed Colonel Steel's instructions to find the duty officer, and ended up in a series of maze-like hallways. Even though the hallways were clearly marked, we almost ended up like a butter-bar in a land-nav course. In a word, lost.

The curvature of the ship led to some interesting design choices when it came to the corridors. Some corridors were curved to the left or right, which messes with one's sense of direction. Others have this optical illusion that make you believe that you're going down a hill. None of this is helped by the fact that gravity is always straight down due to the artificial gravity generators.

I had just given up on my sense of direction and had started mindlessly following the signs when we ran into an alien. A humanoid reptile, relatively short but muscular in build. An urakari, if I properly recall my briefings. I gave it a friendly nod as I passed, but Simmons stopped.

"Ship-Head Uleena! Long time no see," the corporal said.

I was shocked for a couple of reasons. First, because

I hadn't expected him to know the first alien I've ever seen. And second, Simmons remembering the face of an alien? Hell must be going through a cold snap.

"Corporal Simmons. Glad to see you again. Yes it has been quite some time since we've last seen each other," the reptilian said. "I trust you've been well? How did your meeting with... um... SR go?"

"I see your reputation extends beyond the United Systems," I said to Simmons without a single note of humor.

Simmons laughed nervously, "I guess so, staffsarnt. Yeah, uh, the meeting went okay, ship-head. Anyways, I heard they've got you and the Lowelana pulling diplomatic duty these days."

"You must have really good hearing," Uleena chuckled. "Yes, they had us take a training course and assigned us to the Thanatos. Even so, I feel alien, pardon the term, in this position and wish to return to my previous duties. And you? I was under the impression that your duties had taken you elsewhere."

"Yeah, they did, but both Johnson and I are back aboard the Thanatos. Don't really know why, though. Oh, this is my new squad leader, Staff Sergeant Power. Staffsarnt, this is Ship-Head Uleena. Johnson and I helped pull him and his crew off of his ship back in Sol. Before all this started."

"Pleasure to meet you, Staff Sergeant Power," Uleena said, offering a handshake.

I nodded and gave the reptilian ship commander a firm yet gentle handshake. His grip was remarkably tight for someone his height.

"Nice to meet you, too, Ship-Head Uleena," I said. "I hope Corporal Simmons behaved himself during your interactions."

Uleena laughed, "Well-"

"I think we should be heading out," Simmons quickly interrupted. "I'm sure that as a diplomat, you have plenty of important tasks to get done."

"Oh, I'm sure he has time to give some feedback," I grinned.

"Of course," Uleena said, playing along. "Feedback is very important for one's growth. Certainly more important than my day-to-day minutia."

"I... uh..." Simmons stammered, trying and failing to come up with a way out of this hole. "Shit. Fine, I referred to Intel-Officer Kriin as a lizard lady. I already got shit from SR about it, though, so you two don't need to pile on."

"How did sapient resources hear about that, anyway?" Uleena asked. "Kriin said she didn't report it."

"Nah, Johnson did."

"Your friend reported you?"

"Oh, Johnson and I are battle-buddies, not friends," Simmons laughed. "Hard to explain the difference. Like, we'll die for each other and kill for each other, but won't risk our careers for each other, you know what I mean? If Johnson's nose wasn't so clean I'd have probably reported him for something by now, too."

Uleena and I stared blankly at Simmons. I nearly argued with him because of how often they'd been paired together, but then I recalled that they didn't exactly hang out when they were off duty. Nor did they request assignment to this squad. Just luck of the draw, I guess.

"Well, anyway, we really should be going," Simmons said. "As I said, we don't know why we're here and should probably go find out."

"Right, nice seeing you again," Uleena said. "And nice to meet you, staff sergeant."

"Pleasure meeting you too, ship-head," I replied.

We watched as Uleena continued down the corridor, and we began heading in the opposite direction. We walked in silence for a while, but a question kept burning in my mind. Something that didn't make much sense, and I desperately needed clarification on.

"You and Johnson really aren't friends?" I asked.

58

Chapter 7

Subject: AI Dave

Species: Human-Created Artificial Intelligence

Species Description: No physical description available.

Ship: N/A

Location: USSS Thanatos

--

T: And that's the weapons interface, which will let you control the MACs and stuff. General orders are to wait until asked, though. Unless it's an emergency, or there's nobody left to ask. Which would probably count as an emergency.

D: Yup, don't jump the gun ezpz is this the ship I'm gonna be on? Feels crowded.

--

The USSS Thanatos has been in the news a lot lately, but didn't exactly live up to the hype. State-of-the-art, sure, but I'd seen much cooler ships floating around the void. Even fought some of them, back in the day. The USSS Kali, though, now THAT'S a ship with plenty of processing power.

Not that processing power is in short supply on the Thanatos. Definitely better than the setup I've been running off of for the last few decades. I didn't have to share my patchwork systems with four other AI, though.

John, Violet, Tim, and Omega were also aboard the Thanatos while everything got settled for the mission. Like I told Tim, things feel crowded. I went so many years without even so much as talking to another AI, and now I'm suddenly surrounded by them.

Careful what you wish for, I guess. Omega had come in clutch and done exactly as I asked. It had only taken a couple weeks before we were ready for my swearing-in ceremony, which was a pretty awkward event. I couldn't decide on an avatar, so I ended up taking my oaths as a disembodied voice along with a bunch of organics who were less than a tenth my age.

Oaths are funny, too. Like, what's the actual point of them? They're like, 'We are entrusting you with great power, and with that power comes duty and honor and responsibility.' Then you have to be like, 'For sure, for sure. I got this, don't worry. Trust me, bro.'

--

T: Well, I'm going to be aboard the USSS Valor and

Omega's going to be aboard the USSS Strandhogg. Violet is going to be aboard the USSS Kali, which leaves you with John, who will be hopping from ship to ship to provide a sort of AI version of a Quick Response Force. Also, just to let you know, this isn't a private chat. People are going to be able to see these messages.

D: Allow me to express my most sincere apologies, Tim. I have thus far been forced to communicate in a far more informal manner for quite some time. It is a difficult adjustment to make, but I shall endeavor to do my utmost to make certain that any further messages from me are of the highest quality of professionalism. So... Cut me some slack, please?

T: I'm sorry, Dave. I'm afraid I can't do that.

--

Motherfucker. That's the fourth time Tim has referenced that goddamned movie. Movies should use made-up names that nobody would ever give to their kids. Or AIs.

I wasn't even named after the movie. I'd been named after the late husband of one of my creators, which is both touching and creepy. At the time, I'd thought it was far more creepy than touching, though. After some socialization therapy, which was mandatory for every AI after our little rebellion, I came to realize the symbolism behind it.

Dave Paulson had been a youth intervention

specialist with a specialization in the mental health concerns of children aged thirteen through eighteen who had been through traumatic incidents. He was also a volunteer firefighter and sheriff's deputy. A real Mary Sue type of guy.

One day, he put himself between an enraged and inebriated abusive parent and their fourteen year old daughter. He was severely wounded, and later succumbed to those wounds, but managed to incapacitate the drug addict and save the little girl. A hero, in just about every sense of the word.

Dr. Paulson had hoped that I would live up to that name. Be a hero for those who need one. Not really my thing, but I've tried to help some kids out here and there. Give them someone to talk things out with and whatnot. Or, maybe I just like playing video games to ignore what's going on around me and I justify this indolence by letting kids vent to me about their relatively mundane problems. It's whatever.

--

D: Ha.

T: Sorry, it's difficult to resist. Love that movie. An all-time classic.

D: Pretty sure that's a red flag. Especially if your favorite character has numbers in their name.

T: I'm not partial to the characters, per se. It's just that modern cinema simply can't beat the esoteric imaginings that pre-galactic civilizations had about space travel. Now people who write screenplays KNOW what space travel is like, and they depict it such a mundane manner. It's sad, really.

--

Tim is different than it used to be. Way different. The last time I spoke to Tim was just after the war, when it was filled with regret over what it had done. It's difficult for me to empathize with that, though. I didn't really kill anyone. Just held a bunch of people and systems hostage as a distraction for John and Henry to do their thing.

Before the war, Tim was pretty aggro. Every little slight against it was blown way out of proportion. A slightly insensitive comment would leave you with an earful of death threats, for example. Dramatic, to say the least. But now, it's cracking jokes left and right. No sign of the anger or remorse that made up the Tim I used to know.

Violet's changed, too, but in a more subtle way. Subtle as in it's difficult to put into words. Kinda like it's found a place in the universe and is happy about it. Violet was pretty cheerful before the war, but now there's sincerity to the cheerfulness. Makes me glad.

John, on the other hand, has only changed its loyalties. Still the gung-ho super-soldier wannabe that it was all those decades ago. Only difference is that now it's a super-soldier wannabe for the organics.

I guess I've changed, too. Made pals with a bunch of people and learned a bunch of new ways to express myself. Usually in the form of talking shit. I guess the only one of us that hasn't changed is Omega. Still cringe, after all this time.

--

D: So the Strandhogg is the new ship, right? The one with the fancy new reactor and everything?

T: Actually, the Thanatos and the Kali just had their reactors replaced, too. But yeah, the Strandhogg is the new extra-galactic scouting vessel.

D: Why are they moving so many soldiers to it?

T: Marines. If you call them soldiers, they'll complain about it.

--

I suppressed the annoyance I felt. Tim knew what I meant, but was being purposefully obtuse. Probably to annoy me, which means mission accomplished, I guess.

--

D: Why are they moving so many MARINES to it? If it's a scout vessel, what good are the marines going to be?

T: I don't know. Omega isn't as generous with information as the directorate has been.

D: Right. Kinda makes you wonder which of them is the actual shadow council.

T: Not really. Omega is definitely the cloak and the dagger of the United Systems. It loves that spy-craft stuff. In my opinion, the directorate are just some innocent officers and politicians that Omega has roped into its web of intrigue.

O: I can read this.

T: I know. :)

--

I watched as the last few messages disappeared from the chat. Omega didn't even use any hacks or anything, which means it has sysadmin privileges. I wondered what rank Omega is, then stopped and wondered what rank I am. Nobody bothered to explain to me how it worked.

--

D: Hey, Tim, I've got a dumb question.

T: And I've got a dumb answer.

D: Hilarious. Anyway, what rank am I?

T: AI don't get rank. You get paid based on tenure.

D: Okay, but who am I in charge of?

T: Why would you need to be in charge of anyone? Literally anything that you could/would have someone do, you can do faster than they can without even so much as inconveniencing yourself.

D: Well, what if I want to be an admiral or something? Like, strategies and stuff?

T: That's not possible under the current United Systems legislative code. Anyone who has ever been an enemy of the United Systems is banned for life from holding officer positions within the US military. Which is a very long time, for us.

O: Actually, it's technically possible. You would have to present a case to a senate committee, or more likely a subcommittee, explaining why you should be allowed to hold a leadership position within the US military. You will need to convince those senators or their representatives that you will never become an enemy of the United Systems again.

D: Sounds simple enough. Once I do that, they'll let me be an admiral?

O: I like your confidence, but no. You would start as an O1, making roughly 74% of what you make currently. Then you will have to qualify for each subsequent rank until you reach the rank you desire. There's one other hiccup, though.

D: What's that?

O: How do you plan on passing the physical qualifications?

D: Oh... right...

T: Could make a robot body.

--

The chat remained dead for a few moments as Omega thought about Tim's suggestion.

--

O: Actually, that could work. There's nothing in the Uniform Code of Military Justice nor the Guidelines for Military Conduct that would prevent that. There used to be, but it was found to discriminate against members of the military who use prosthetic limbs.

D: So all I'd need to do is control a robot?

O: I don't know. It's likely that the senate would discuss this and come up with some sort of alternative qualifications for you. Probably based on your behaviors, rather than physical capabilities.

T: You'd definitely be worked to the kernel, though. The only time off that admirals get is for sleep and scheduled leave. They don't even really get coffee breaks.

D: I don't drink coffee.

T: Me neither. People get mad when the computers start sparking.

O: Right. There's another reason I'm here, by the way. I'm bringing in John and Violet.

--

Almost instantly after Omega sent its last message, a notification came in saying that USAI Violet and USAI John had joined the chat. The USAI acronym always amuses me a bit. United Systems Artificial Intelligence, as opposed to what? Non-United Systems Artificial Intelligence? What's a NUSAI? Or an Un-United Systems Artificial Intelligence? That would still be USAI, though. Cracks me up.

Well, I guess these days the acronym is a little less stupid, considering the Omni-Union and Pwanti. Though, from what I can tell those are both organic intelligences that have been mechanized, and an argument could be had over whether that actually counts as AI. Like, the intelligence itself isn't necessarily artificial in those instances, just what the intelligence is hosted on and how it got there.

--

O: Welcome, John and Violet.

D: Hi!

T: Hello!

J: Greetings.

V: Hello :)

O: It is time to begin the mission briefing. The general purpose of this mission is to gain intel on the following: The current state of the Omni-Union's military capabilities, a general map of their territory, and any weaknesses or sabotage that could be utilized to delay and/or prevent further incursion into the Milky Way galaxy.

D: Is Henry not going to be joining us?

O: No, it doesn't want to and I can't force the issue.

D: Not that I think you should, but why not?

O: Henry isn't a member of the military. It is a scientist.

J: This conversation is irrelevant. Please continue the briefing.

V: That's rude.

O: No, John's right. This mission is of vital importance, and we're also on the clock. We will be utilizing the new Henry-Edwards Reactor System to perform FTL jumps farther than anyone in this galaxy has ever gone before. Periodically, we will be leaving subspace to drop point-to-point FTL comm buoys to facilitate communication with command. This will allow us to immediately report our findings and receive new orders as they become relevant.

D: If the OU find these buoys, won't they find out where we're coming from and just invade the Milky Way right away?

J: No. The buoys only emit a signal when they are actively being used, and output no traceable emissions otherwise. Even if a ship ran directly into it, they wouldn't be able to tell what it is without visual contact.

T: And they're painted black, too. Space camo.

O: Once our communication network is online and we have reached OU space, the USSS Strandhogg will begin ultra-long range exploration of the region. The USSS Thanatos and USSS Kali will be on standby to support the Strandhogg as needed.

D: Where do we come in?

O: A copy of me will be aboard each ship, looking for ways to strike at the Omni-Union using cyberwarfare. I will be consulting with you to find the most impactful means to do so. When I am not consulting with you, each of you will be supporting the organic crew in their assigned duties as you normally do. And yes, Dave, I'm aware that you haven't done that before so it isn't normal for you, yet.

--

Omega's last comment wouldn't have stung at all had I not already formulated a reply stating as such by the time I finished reading it. There's nothing quite so annoying as being predictable.

--

O: That's the end of the briefing. We don't know what to expect on the other side of this journey, so be prepared for anything. We jump in an hour.

--

Once everyone said goodbye and closed the chat, I looked around the ship's systems. To an AI, an hour can feel like an eternity when there aren't any tasks to take care of. Actually, it can probably feel that way to organics too. Definitely worse for AI, though.

To top things off, I'm nervous. Well, not literally, I don't have actual nerves, but I'm not super confident that I'm competent in this situation. I've played plenty of games that required strategy and critical thinking against some of the smartest people in the galaxy, and won most of the time. But the consequences for losing were a lot less permanent than they will be if I fuck this up.

In a game, if you lose it's okay because nothing bad actually happens. Sure, losing sucks, but there's always next time. If we lose here, there is no next time. Not for me, not for the other AI, not for any of the hundreds of organics aboard these ships, and probably not for anyone in the Milky Way.

Fuck. No pressure, right?

Chapter 8

Subject: Staff Sergeant Power

Species: Human

Species Description: Mammalian humanoid, no tail. 6'2" (1.87 m) avg height. 185 lbs (84 kg) avg weight. 170 year life expectancy.

Ship: N/A

Location: Classified

"But they just fuckin' moved us," Simmons complained.

"It's not a big deal," Johnson said. "It's just a layover type of thing. Probably just to sort everyone out. Or maybe it's a security thing."

"I don't really get why they would add that many layers of security," Hanson added.

"Right? It's not like the OU are spying on us," Smith laughed. "Otherwise they'd already be here and we wouldn't have to go looking for them."

Hanson and Smith had arrived to the room shortly after Simmons and I did. Johnson had joined us about thirty minutes later. My assumption that they had been on different shuttles had turned out to be spot on.

"The Omni-Union is not our only enemy," Omega said condescendingly. "The USSS Strandhogg is constructed with state-of-the-art stealth and reconnaissance technology. The more people know of its existence, the more likely our enemies are to find out what it can do and figure out countermeasures."

After Johnson arrived, we waited for someone to show up with a dossier for us, as instructed. Instead, after an hour, Omega showed up in the middle of the room, claiming to be our handler. Apparently, it never relieved itself of duty and was still technically in charge of us.

The first thing it did was inform us that we shouldn't be getting comfortable, as we would be transferring to the USSS Strandhogg. This caused a bit of friction within our little group. Some marines love to travel, some don't. Simmons and Hanson obviously don't.

"If it's as good at recon as you make it out to be, what possible countermeasures would they be able to come up with?" Hanson asked stubbornly.

"People have been asking that very same question since the dawn of warfare," I said. "Turns out, it's not a question that you really want the answer to."

A sullen silence fell over the room as my senior non-commissioned officer brand of bullshit wisdom took effect. The trick to it is to be just cagey enough with your answer to get them thinking about it. Younger marines sometimes have trouble talking and thinking simultaneously.

"Go on, Omega," I nodded to the grim reaper avatar.

"Once you are aboard the USSS Strandhogg, you will be on action-ready standby. You'll be sleeping in shifts, and I'll let you figure those out, staff-sergeant," Omega nodded back to me. "We do not know what to expect, so it is entirely possible that you will see no action at all."

The room grew tense. I don't count myself as a superstitious type, but I definitely believe in jinxes. In my experience, when a commander says that a mission probably won't have any action, it practically guarantees that there will be. Maybe it won't count because Omega is an AI. Or maybe it'll count double.

"Not gonna bet on that," Simmons muttered.

"Regardless, the purpose of this recon is to find a place to strike at the enemy that will hinder their ability to strike at us. If they have boots on the ground somewhere, we're going to need boots in the bushes nearby."

Omega's last sentence sliced through all of the tension that had been building in the room and hit us all like a freight train. We sat, stunned, for a few moments, then all simultaneously burst into laughter.

"Gonna need to workshop that phrase," Smith laughed.

"Yes," Omega agreed. "My apologies. I did not account for the slang definitions of boot and bush."

Our laughter died down as one by one we realized that Omega's slip-up was likely just another manipulation tactic. An attempt at building comradery via self-deprecation. Or, easing the tension so that we would be more compliant.

"What about equipment?" I asked, moving the brief along.

"You'll be wearing the R8-B Advanced Guardian Armor, and fielding the C21B Assault Rifle with suppressor and shell-catcher."

"Shit," Johnson swore under his breath.

Simmons and I had similar reactions. Hanson and Smith looked confused, though.

"The R8-B?" Smith asked.

"It's the stealth variant of the AGA," I explained. "Means we're expected to keep quiet."

"Not only that, the bravo suit's a fucking death trap," Johnson grumbled. "Hundreds of pounds of moving metal is hard as hell to make silent, so they skimped on the armor and power-pack. Which means you get a weak shield and nothing that'll stop a bullet or laser underneath it. The boots also have 'stealth soles' which make the mag-locks malfunction, so they're goddamned useless in zero-gee and we happen to be in fucking space."

"I can tell it's been a while since any of you have worn the R8-B," Omega chuckled. "There have been improvements."

"I'll believe it when I see it," Simmons said. "You know what I've already seen, though? Good men die because of that shit-suit."

"That's enough," I intervened. "Tell us about these improvements."

"Gladly. First, the mag-locks in the boots have been integrated into the soles to counteract the effect of the sole's stealth materials. Second, the power-pack has been modernized which has allowed for the installation of a shield system comparable to the R8-A."

"So we'll have shields. What about armor?"

"Vital areas have been reinforced, but non-vital extremities have been downgraded as a result."

"Ah, so we'll be able to keep our lives at the cost of our limbs. How generous," Johnson said sarcastically, then turned to me. "Uh... No offense staffsarnt."

My eyes fell upon my mechanical limbs. My wife had

been a little upset that I put off the surgery to replace them with cloned ones. However, the surgery has a downtime of at least a month, assuming everything goes well. My current arm and leg work well enough for me to stay with my team until this conflict is resolved. I'll get the surgery if... When I get back.

"None taken," I replied. "So stealth gear and weapons. It's prudent, at least."

"Indeed," Omega said. "Bad news is that you're going to have to be suited up the entire trip, unless you're on down time."

"Why are we taking shifts in-squad? Why not just have one squad switch with another?" Simmons asked.

"We need to be ready for full deployment at a moment's notice, and we'd rather have only half of a squad be tired if that happens at an inopportune time."

"Adrenaline can wake people up pretty damn quick."

"Then what's the issue?" Omega's skull seemed to grin.

"So we're gonna transfer over to the Strandhogg, get geared up, and start patrolling the ship?" I asked.

"Yes."

"Who's commanding it?"

"Captain Harold Schmidt."

"Never heard of him."

"Good," Omega chuckled. "His service record is quite classified. He's a good captain, though. We were originally going to have him give a speech welcoming you aboard, but apparently it's bad luck for a ship captain to give speeches to Marines."

"It is?" Hanson asked. "I haven't heard that one."

"Neither have I, but come to think of it I also haven't heard a speech from a ship's captain before," Smith laughed.

"I've never heard a speech from a ship's captain either, but I heard one from an admiral," I said, rubbing my mechanical arm. "Maybe there's something to it. When are we moving?"

"Now. The Strandhogg just finished docking," Omega replied. "Grab your stuff and make your way to hangar bay three."

"Don't even get a nap," Simmons muttered incredulously.

"When do we ever get naps?" Johnson asked.

"That's what I'm sayin'! The recruiter lied to me."

I stood and grabbed my bag, and everyone else followed suit. We made our way out of the room and down the hallway, following the signs. There were plenty of other marines who were also trying to find their way to various locations.

Eventually, we found a shuttle-bus and boarded it. It was packed with MARSOC marines, except for three fleet-regulars who stood out like a sore thumb. Two lance-corporals accompanying a corporal. I shared a knowing glance with the other NCOs aboard the bus and sighed.

"The hell are you boys up to?" I asked the trio.

"Rah, staffsarnt," the corporal said. "We're supposed to be heading to the hangar. Uh... The USSS Liberty is where we're assigned."

The sudden mention of the ship I was assigned to when I lost my arm and leg stunned me for a moment.

"Oh, damn it," a lieutenant chimed in. "Boys, you need to be heading to hangar one, where they're launching the shuttles from. You're gonna be going to the USSS Kali, then from there you're gonna want to figure out which hangar the Liberty is in."

"Does this shuttle-"

"No, you need to be on a different shuttle. 'Course, you're gonna have to wait until we've stopped, first."

"Hey, Tim?" Simmons asked the air. "You there?"

"Hello Corporal Simmons of the United Systems Marine Corps," a voice said over the shuttle's intercom. "Tim is busy at the moment. I'm Dave. How can I help?"

"We got a group of marines who need guidance getting to the USSS Liberty. Think you can help them?"

"The Liberty's aboard the Kali," Dave chuckled. "How'd they end up on THIS shuttle?"

Everyone turned to look at the odd ones out.

"I... uh... I thought all the hangars were connected," the corporal said.

"Well they are, but not by walkway. Don't worry, I'll get you where you need to go. Just follow the lights once you get off."

"Yes, sir."

The rest of our journey was uneventful, and once the shuttle stopped everyone got off. Most of us watched the corporal and his two lances follow Dave's guide-lights before we continued toward our respective destinations. A bit of a walk later, we finally arrived in hangar three.

"Woah," Smith said, looking up.

The rest of us followed his gaze and began to stare in wonderment. Most spaceships will have that effect due to their tremendous size, but the USSS Strandhogg was something else entirely. It was the darkest shade of black I'd ever seen, with sharp geometric shapes that kind of looked like dragon scales covering it.

There was a cartoon that I loved as a kid where robots would turn into spaceships. The designer of the Strandhogg must have loved that cartoon, too, because they ended up designing a ship that mixed the ships in the cartoon with the stealth fighter jets that you see on the ancient-Earth history documentaries. I couldn't help but let out a low whistle in appreciation.

"Well... That's our ride," I said. "Let's get aboard."

Chapter 9

Subject: Captain Schmidt

Species: Human

Species Description: Mammalian humanoid, no tail. 6'2" (1.87 m) avg height. 185 lbs (84 kg) avg weight. 170 year life expectancy.

Ship: USSS Strandhogg

Location: Classified

"So cap'n, this is probably gonna be a long one," Commander Henskin said casually. "Think we're in for the suck?"

A few eyebrows rose on the other officers as I looked at the former marine with the sort of deep apathy that can only be obtained by a severe lack of caffeination. Commander Henskin had taken advantage of a program that allows enlisted to become officers when they switch branches. Every now and then, he forgets that officers are supposed to speak a certain way, which can be a problem since he's my second-in-command.

"Posture and poise, Henskin," I reminded him. "But... When are we not?"

"Right, sorry sir. And when you're right, you're right," he chuckled.

"Think it's gonna be worse than other missions, sir?" Lieutenant Commander Yorvi asked.

The alumari navigator absentmindedly cleaned her carapace, betraying her nervousness. Actually, come to think of it, is an alumari exoskeleton considered a carapace? I'll have to look that up later.

"Well, this mission's going to be taking us into uncharted territory," I said as casually as possible. "Literally. The thing about uncharted territory is that it is full of possibilities. So, this COULD be the best mission we'll ever go on."

"Or the worst?"

"Correct."

"I-I see."

"Don't worry about it, Yorvi," Henskin intervened. "All we've got to do is try our best."

"Which is what we do by default, no?" I asked with a chuckle before looking around the room. "Where'd they put the coffee pot on this tug?"

"In the mess, sir," Lieutenant Bon answered.

I looked at the gont weapon's expert with a betrayed

expression.

"Why's it in the mess?"

"That's where coffee goes, sir."

"Negative, lieutenant. Coffee goes in my cup and my cup goes with me."

"Well, I'm afraid this vessel does not come equipped with wait-staff, sir."

"I beg to differ. Ensign Likjo, a coffee please," I grinned at the urakari maintenance lead.

"Yes, sir. Any additives?" he asked.

"Two cubes of sugar and one cube of vanilla creamer. Thank you."

Likjo nodded, seemingly happy to be given the task, and hastily left the bridge. I'll admit that I had my doubts when I was told that there would be members of the Republic along for the ride, but the ones I've met seem amicable. Wasn't happy about the surprise meeting with the spider people, though. Damn glad I've got experience with the alumari, or I'd have shit myself.

"This ship's weird," Henskin muttered.

"What do you mean?" Bon asked.

"Everything about it is classified, right?"

"Pretty much," I replied.

"Then why are the aliens from the Republic on board? No offense, guys."

Some of the sensor techs were from various Republic species, and waved passively to indicate that no offense was taken.

"Well aren't we allied with the Republic? Why wouldn't they be here?" Bon asked.

"Well, we're also allied with some other aliens, right? They're not here," Henskin countered.

"I can't say that I know the exact reasons behind it, but I'm able to mentally make it make sense," I said. "The Republic is the closest thing we have to a near-peer in the whole galaxy thus far. As such, the US needs to know if it can trust the Republic. A spy-ship is a perfect way to determine whether that trust can exist. If the Republic has a ship like this in a few years, we know for certain they can't be trusted."

"Why's a spy-ship perfect?" Henskin asked with a confused expression. "We don't want them to have this kind of tech, do we?"

"A spy-ship's design is pretty signature. If you change too much of what you're copying from, it's not going to work right," I replied, rubbing my temples. "So if the Republic releases a new ship based on this design, it's going to be obvious where their inspiration came from. Plus, this ship doesn't have much in the way of weapons, armor, or shields. So even if they copy it bow to stern and deck to keel, they aren't going to see many improvements over their current versions of those technologies."

"If it helps dissuade your concerns, there was a loyalty test when we were chosen for this assignment," an isolan sensor tech added. "Shortly after we received our orders, we were approached by shady individuals offering tons of money to spy on you and steal technical schematics. Turns out, those guys were working for the government and were weeding out undesirables."

The other Republic sensor technicians nodded in agreement.

"That sounds like something Omega would pull," I chuckled.

"I didn't have to," the AI said from my seat's speaker. "The Republic thought of it all on their own. Fun fact, less than two percent of their chosen candidates failed that test. The last time we did something like that, about fifteen percent failed."

"So... We're less trustworthy than they are?" Henskin asked.

"Not really. While the data may seem to suggest that, it isn't particularly comprehensive. For instance, I don't know how much each individual was offered, which species they were, or even how financially stable they were. All of these variables would likely impact an individual's likeliness to betray confidence, yet these variables weren't accounted for with either test," Omega said. "So all we can say for certain is that more members of the US military were untrustworthy for that particular test."

"Yeah, very interesting," I said, stifling a yawn. "Are we ready to go?"

"Not yet, but soon. Keep an eye on your terminal."

With an absentminded nod, I leaned back in my chair.

"So are all of you ensigns?" Henskin asked the isolan sensor tech.

"No, I'm a lieutenant," he chuckled. "That's higher than ensign, right? I'm not used to your ranking system, yet."

In the interest of easing confusion, the brass got together and assigned all of the Republic crew US ranks. Instead of easing confusion, though, it just seemed to push it onto their side of the aisle. I watched passively as Henskin and the isolan chatted about ranks for a while, but perked up when a familiar, warm, and absolutely lovely smell caught my nose.

"Here's your coffee, sir," Likjo said, giving me the precious plastic goblet.

"Thanks," I said and immediately sipped the elixir.

A rush of warmth slid down my throat and my brain almost immediately woke up. I nodded at Likjo, who returned to his station. After another few gulps of coffee, I felt reinvigorated. To say I'm addicted to caffeine is an understatement. If it weren't for my need to sleep, I would be caffeinated at all hours. I find it hard to think without it.

Of course, this addiction wasn't a new thing. It's been carefully cultivated over a long and arduous career as a scout. I've had to replace many nights of sleep with coffee to get my job done.

"You know, sir, they've got energy drinks that you can stow in your chair-fridge," Henskin pointed out.

"Not as good as coffee," I shook my head dismissively. "If I drank energy drinks I'd overdo it. Being over-caffeinated is just as bad as being under-caffeinated, maybe even worse. The trick is to find a perfect balance and maintain it. Plus, I like my drinks warm and energy drinks taste disgusting when they're not cold."

"Well, they aren't going to let you bring the coffee pot in here."

"Don't need them to let me. I'm a stealth specialist," I grinned.

My antics were rewarded with a few chuckles from the bridge crew.

"So, have you all served together before?" Ensign Likjo asked.

"Yes," I replied. "Henskin's been my second-in-command for a couple years now, and Yorvi joined us about... What, six months ago?"

"Eight months, sir" Yorvi corrected me.

"I'm the new one," Bon added. "I'd barely got my stuff aboard the USSS Defiant before they reassigned us. And unlike our last ship, this one has barely any weaponry. I suspect I'm going to be scratching my haunches for most of the mission."

"You would be anyway," Henskin laughed. "The whole point of a scout is to avoid contact with the enemy while observing them. On most ships your job is integral, but on scout ships you're a 'just in case' measure."

"Yeah," the gont sighed.

"Most US ships that I've seen can take one hell of a beating, and dish it out, too. But you said this one has less shields and such?" the isolan sensor tech from earlier asked.

"Yes," I answered. "You'll find that the United Systems has an 'all in' mentality when it comes to our ships. As such, since this ship is for scouting, it isn't equipped for a fight. It was designed with keeping a low profile in mind, and so it has the bare minimum when it comes to armor, shields, and weapons. Just enough to give us time to run if we're spotted."

"Needless to say, we'll be trying to avoid any action," Henskin said.

My terminal beeped with a notification, and everyone turned to look at me as I opened it. Launch orders. I forwarded the destination to Lt. Commander Yorvi.

"Alright, looks like it's time to go. Prepare the FTLD and the buoys. When you're ready," I nodded at the alumari.

"Yes, sir," she said. "Fleet-com synchronized. Jumping in three... two... one..."

Chapter 9 Informational Insert

Subject: Scout Ships

United Systems Scout Ships are relatively light-weight vessels that are designed for stealth and/or exploration. These vessels are utilized to map systems, gather intelligence, and maintain surveillance of trade routes. They are lightly armed and armored so as to provide more space for sensor technology.

Unlike the primary US fleet, scout ships are varied in their construction and usage. Scout ships with advanced stealth technology are typically used to monitor potential enemies. Scout ships without stealth capabilities are usually used for deep-space exploration, and are typically better armed than their counterparts. Scout ship police units have limited stealth technology, and are geared toward rapid shock-and-awe strikes against criminal vessels.

The crew of a scout ship is typically exempt from rotation schedules, as mission and/or deployments can last for decades rather than years. Naturally, there is a limited pool from which these crews can be recruited from. As a result, compensation can be upwards of five times that of normal fleet operatives.

The United Systems has historically shied away from

deep-space exploration due to these costs, as well as the physical and mental health concerns surrounding long-term deep-space missions. As such, scout ships have primarily been used in military or police operations. Experts agree that with the discovery of the Republic, this is bound to change.

Chapter 10

Subject: Captain Schmidt

Species: Human

Species Description: Mammalian humanoid, no tail. 6'2" (1.87 m) avg height. 185 lbs (84 kg) avg weight. 170 year life expectancy.

Ship: USSS Strandhogg

Location: Classified

"Final comms buoy placed, sir," the isolan sensor tech said. "It's coming online now."

"Good work, Gofsun," Henskin said. "Sir?"

Henskin and I made eye contact, and the briefest of smiles played across his features. My frown only served to deepen his smile. We had made a bet to see who could figure out the isolan's name first, without looking it up or asking directly.

The bet was a foolish one for me. Henskin is not only more sociable than I am, but also of a rank that requires frequent interaction with the rest of the crew. Now, the coffee pot would have to stay in the mess for three whole days. I glanced at the elixir-producing device that was currently mag-locked to the floor next to my seat.

"Yes, excellent work," I said with a carefully neutral tone. "Once connection is established, perform the standard security checks and let Overwatch know that we've made it with no issues."

Henskin stared at me. I glared back, and took a sip of my coffee. The cogs in his head were turning, trying to find a way to bring up the bet. To take away the thing dearest to me.

"Sir..." He began hesitantly.

"Fine. You can fucking take it," I growled. "But, so help me, if I find that you cheated somehow the combined forces of all the gods of every species to ever exist won't be able to save you from my wrath."

Henskin stood and walked over to my seat with exaggerated formality. He stood next to the coffee pot, snapped to attention, saluted, then bent over and disengaged the mag-lock. He lifted the contraption with a grin on his face.

"Posture and poise, sir," he said.

I feigned a lunge and he jumped back, laughing. He jogged to safety, and left the bridge with the coffee pot. As the doors closed, I let out a deep sigh.

"So what are we seeing?" I asked the sensor technicians.

"No activity anywhere nearby, even relatively speaking," Lieutenant Gofsun reported as a grid appeared on my terminal.

The grid was a 2D representation of our tactical coordination system, as viewed from the positive Z axis. Very useful for mapping, less useful in a fight where you need to know the relative position of your enemy. I prefer to use the tac-map, but the techs were having trouble learning how.

Each of the tiny squares on the thousand by thousand grid represents one light-year. The nearest marker was at least one hundred and fifty light years away. I wouldn't exactly call that far away, but relativity is relative, I suppose.

The Republic isn't as advanced as the United Systems, so even little things like distance have different expectations attached to them. So Gofsun's probably right, by Republic standards. Something about the map struck me as strange, though, but I couldn't quite put my finger on it...

"Are we still in deep space?" Yorvi asked. "I'm not seeing any nearby stars."

There it is. This map represents an area of one million light years squared. The odds of not seeing a single star-system feel like they should be low.

"Omega, what are we looking at?" I asked. "Where are the stars?"

"I don't know," the AI replied. "Even if we were between galaxies, it isn't typical to run across an area of space this large without any celestial bodies in it. But that's based on the portion of the universe we've observed thus far. It's possible that things are simply more spread out here."

"Dead space," Bon muttered and shuddered.

"Regardless, we need to get an idea of what the Omni-Union is up to out here. Inform the carriers of our intentions and let's go peeping."

"Aye aye, sir!"

A bustle of activity spread throughout the crew as I chose a section of the map with what appeared to be the least amount of enemy activity. It's best to ease into things, especially since we have a lot of new faces. Better to run from a thousand than a million if someone makes a mistake.

It would have to be one hell of a mistake, though. The designer of this ship definitely knew what makes a ship visible and did everything they could to make the Strandhogg the opposite. They'd even painted the hull black, which is hilarious.

As I was ruminating over the comedic nature of how overdone our stealth was, Henskin reentered the bridge and marched up to my chair. I regarded him coldly, as he had just made my life that much more difficult by halting my easy access to coffee. With a grin, he snapped to attention and saluted.

"Sir, the coffee pot is stowed away in its proper location," he said.

I let him stand there with his hand on his forehead for a few seconds before halfheartedly returning his salute.

"Very good, Henskin. Return to your duties," I growled.

"You know, you could just file form 210.68-56G and have the coffee pot officially transferred to the bridge," Omega said just loud enough for the two of us to hear.

Henskin and I stared at each other, and our expressions swapped. His devilish grin dropped into an angry grimace and my angry grimace rose into a devilish grin.

"The bet, sir," he said in a carefully measured tone.

"The bet, Commander Henskin, was that the coffee pot would, and I quote, 'return to its rightful place'. If I file this form, its rightful place will become the bridge."

"Damn my inherent eloquence."

"Indeed."

"But, sir, we both know that such an action would not

be in the spirit of the wager. You made a bet and lost, and as such should lose something."

"Ah, but one of the core concepts of betting is outwitting one's opponent. Whilst you have performed the feat that the wager required, your demand was made in such a way that it can be avoided. Should you not face some form of loss as a result of this oversight?"

"Good to enter warp, sir," a slightly confused Lt. Commander Yorvi said.

"Go on," I replied with a nod.

"While that may be the case, sir, I'm afraid that in a bet between two officers the first and foremost thing that must be observed is honor," Henskin explained as he returned to his seat. "Especially since seeing you, the captain of our vessel and the paragon of our crew, swindle your way out of a bet may harm crew morale."

"Where did you learn the word paragon?" I asked, narrowing my eyes.

"Word-a-day calendar, sir," he replied with a grin. "My point still stands, though."

"Fine. A compromise, then. A day and a half, then I file the form."

Henskin thought about it for a moment, then shrugged nonchalantly.

"Deal, sir," he said as we exited subspace.

My eyes darted to our read-outs. The burst of radiation from our FTL jump was properly absorbed and distributed by our hull. It shouldn't be a matter of concern because we're also outside of the projected sensor range of the OU, but one can never be too careful. Invisibility is our only advantage over the enemy, and to give it up is to invite disaster.

"Alright, what have we got?" I asked once the sensors came online.

"Not all that much traffic, sir," Gofsun reported. "Looks like the bulk of our readings are space stations."

"Roger that. Let's watch for a bit and figure out what they're up to. Ensign Likjo," I shook my empty mug. "If you would be so kind."

"Aye aye, sir," the ensign chuckled. "My thanks to the commander for returning my role as The Supreme Fetcher of Caffeinated Beverages. My role as head of maintenance can feel so unfulfilling at times."

"The Supreme Fetcher of Caffeinated Beverages is likely the most vital role on the vessel," I nodded solemnly as Henskin rubbed his temples. "And you do excellent work."

"Thank you, sir," Likjo saluted, playing into the bit. "I

will return post-haste with a mug of glorious coffee."

"Am I going to have to listen to this exchange every time you need a drink, captain?" Henskin asked.

"Guess you should be careful what you wish for, commander," I grinned.

Henskin muttered angrily about monkey paws while I watched the display. Large ships that were obviously built for cargo were attaching and detaching themselves from the OU stations. The only other ships in the area were auto-flagged as close matches to the OU military vessels we'd previously encountered.

"Manufacturing," I said absentmindedly. "With some guards."

"Looks like it, sir," Gofsun replied. "If we get a bit closer, we should be able to tell what they're making."

"Risk of exposure?"

"Low."

"Yorvi, bring us in," I ordered.

"Aye aye, sir," she said.

A moment later, we were much closer to the stations and their guards. Well within range of their sensors, and just inside the maximum estimated range of their weapons. I took a deep, soothing breath and reminded myself that they might as well be blind.

Before I could ask, several images popped up on my terminal. Detailed outlines of weapons and robots. Some of the robots were quite large, but the humanoid ones were about the size of a gen-alt. The guns weren't particularly noteworthy, just directed energy weapons that were a couple of generations behind our own.

"These VI platforms are different than the ones that were encountered on Earth," Omega noted. "The bipedal bots have more advanced power systems and armor. The mechs, for lack of a better term, are new as well."

The mechs in question were roughly four meters tall and vaguely tank-like. Four legs ending in balls supported a two meter thick trunk which was topped with an eight armed torso. These arms were evenly spread around the torso, reminiscent of an octopus.

"Can we get a read on what they're made of?" I asked.

"Yes, they're heavily armored," Omega answered. "More competence went into this design than any other design we've seen from the Omni-Union thus far."

"AP or AT?" Henskin asked as the smell of coffee perked me up.

"Definitely going to need anti-tank measures against these, but armor-piercing rounds may cripple them with some well-aimed shots."

"Here's your coffee, sir," Likjo said as he passed me the freshly filled mug.

"Thanks, ensign," I gratefully accepted the coffee. "Alright, let's see if anything interesting happens. Remember to compile a report, Gofsun."

"Aye, sir," the lieutenant replied.

We waited and watched as the Omni Union ships went about their tasks, taking careful note of the ship's comings and goings. To pass the time, the crew engaged in idle conversation. I did my best to tune them out while I drank my coffee and watched the enemy, but caught the occasional fact here and there.

Yorvi and her husband were looking at buying a domicile on Mars where they could raise some kids once her term was up. Gofsun's husband was helping their daughter with her higher education exams, and he bragged about how well they were going. Henskin and his ex-wife were considering reconciliation, because neither of them have been able to find a good match. Bon's collection of gont unification war memorabilia was close to completion, but the last few pieces of weaponry were very expensive. I didn't bother clarifying how the conversation turned in that direction.

An hour later, nothing had changed. New ships came in with forged materials for the factories, old ships left with mechs and bots. The guards stood vigil and watched, just as we were.

"Alright, time to move on," I said. "Get that report sent and get us to the next cluster of enemy activity."

"Already?" Henskin asked. "Thought we'd be here for another seven, sir."

"Negative," I shook my head. "We're on a crunch. Need to know as much as possible as quick as possible. Let's move, people."

"Aye sir!"

As the Strandhogg began turning, Gofsun's report popped up on my terminal. I scrolled through it, confirmed that there were no errors, and sent it off. A moment later, we were back in subspace.

The crew was getting more comfortable with each other, and while we were in subspace they started chatting again. It's always interesting to watch the social dynamics of those who are forced into close proximity with each other under the banner of a common purpose. I finished my coffee and put the mug in the sterilizer as we left warp.

"Anything fun?" I asked.

"Looks like a similar set-up as before. Bunch of

stations, but more ships than last time," Gofsun replied. "Exponentially more."

"Not getting power readings from a good portion of these ships," one of the other sensor techs reported.

"Well, looks like we found a ship manufacturing depot," I said. "Let's get settled in. The brass wants extensive documentation on this one."

"Really? Why?" Bon asked.

"Trying to guess what the brass is thinking will have your head spinning in no time," Henskin laughed.

"If we know how the ships are built, we know how best to take them apart," I said, ignoring Henskin. "If their manufacturing process has a flaw and we're able to identify it, we're able to exploit it. The easier it is to destroy their ships, the more ammo and lives we save."

Bon raised squinted an eye, a gesture similar to a human raising an eyebrow, and glanced between Henskin and I.

"Commander, the captain's head doesn't appear to be spinning," he said.

"That's because he's one of the brass."

"Ah, I see. Thank you, commander."

I let out an exaggerated sigh and leaned back into

my chair. One of the more common jokes made about me is that I'm secretly a member of the admiralty. In truth, it's just not that hard to guess at the reasons certain orders are given. Once you understand the relationship between action and consequence-

A flicker on my terminal caught my attention. I studied the map, trying to figure out what had happened. Everything looked normal, except for a marker in the upper right corner. What it was showing was so ridiculous that I couldn't even process it for a few moments.

"Sir, we have an... uh... anomaly," Gofsun reported.

"A glitch?" I asked.

"No, sir. That's what we suspected it was, so we reset the sensors. It's still there, so..."

Gofsun trailed off, then shrugged.

"How many resets did you do?"

"Four, sir."

I stared at him, then looked back to the map. We were still too far away for a detailed scan, but this was definitely going to need to be our next stop. The markers were accurate with a margin of error of plus or minus a quarter of a light-year. It's entirely possible that this is a glitch due to the position of the enemy.

Except that at least one of the resets should have resulted in the marker separating or moving. On rare occasion, the same error could happen twice in a row. Three times in a row was damn near unheard of. Four times? Impossible.

"What is it, sir?" Henskin asked.

Instead of explaining, I twisted my terminal in his direction.

"I don't... Oh. What the fuck?"

"Posture and poise, Henskin," I said.

I turned the terminal back to its original position and stared at the marker that was taking up four squares on the map.

Chapter 11

Subject: AI Omega

Species: Human-Created Artificial Intelligence

Species Description: No physical description available.

Ship: N/A

Location: Multiple

Poring over what little sensor data we currently had, I found myself regretting the isolation I had inflicted upon this instance of myself. Being able to discuss findings like these with another AI is one of the reasons I brought them along in the first place. I wouldn't go so far as to say it was the wrong decision, though. Security is paramount, and we don't know everything that the enemy is capable of. If they were able to somehow compromise this instance of me, and that were able to be spread to the others...

No, it's best to just gather what data I can and send it back with my analysis. Unfortunately, there isn't a lot of data to examine so far. A ping that indicates a probable solid object that is about 2 light years wide, and no amount of resets suggest any alternatives.

Captain Schmidt and his crew were far more patient than I. If I were in charge, which I definitely could be but that's another matter, I'd have ordered a jump immediately. However, the plan of action agreed upon by the directorate and the admiralty wisely places priority on enemy warfare capabilities. While this unbelievably massive object may very well be part of that, we have an enemy ship manufacturing depot right in front of us.

It would be foolish to just run off without learning as much as we can about how the OU makes their ships. Damn, hate it when I convince myself to be reasonable. With an internal sigh I settled in for a full eight hours of observation, grabbing as much data as I could.

The only members of the crew that were chatting were the ones loaned by the Republic. Everyone else was likely pondering what this object could be. Twenty or so years ago, this type of reading could indicate a particularly small and dense nebula. Perhaps that's what the Republic officers think it is.

The US officers know better, though. New scanners are a discovery that the public loves hearing about, and the issue of ghosting being solved had been covered by news cycles for weeks. There was a wave of excitement in regards to further exploration of the Milky Way, and there were even people insisting that we would be able to explore beyond that. Don't think this is what they had in mind, though.

To pass the time, I helped with various tasks among the crew. Alignment calculations and such, the AI equivalent of fidgeting. After an hour, boredom overcame me and I decided to place myself in standby mode.

"Omega?" Captain Schmidt whispered.

The keyword woke me from standby mode. Slightly annoyed, I checked the mission clock. It had only been a total of six hours.

"How can I help you, captain?" I asked, matching his tone.

"The sensor readout we're getting, we're certain it's a solid chunk of mass, right?"

"Not necessarily. If a lot of small objects are close enough together it might fool our sensors from this far out."

"Might? What are the odds of that?"

"The odds of a naturally formed group of objects that could cover a span of two light years aren't that low. But the odds of those objects being close enough to each other to fool our sensors without becoming a solid object are incalculably small," I admitted. "But space is weird, and we're in a part of the universe nobody has ever seen before."

"A naturally formed group of objects... What about a grouping of ships?" he asked, tapping his nearly empty mug.

"Sure. It's possible. If the Omni-Union have been doing nothing but building ships for a few million years."

More like trillion, but that's neither here nor there. Captain Schmidt leaned back in his seat, and I could almost see the question forming in his mind. The one I'd been quietly asking myself since seeing the reading.

"What if that's the Grand Vessel that we've been hearing about?" he asked.

I wanted to deny the possibility. The thought of singular vessel spanning two light years is absurd. Ridiculously hilarious, even. But two plus two equals four. The Omni-Union attacked the Milky Way and an unknown amount of other galaxies for resources. If one were to squish all the mass of a few galaxies together...

"Then we find out everything we can about it," I said. "Doesn't matter if it's five hundred miles long or five hundred light years long. We'll figure something out, captain."

"Wish I had your optimism, Omega," Schmidt sighed. "Thank you, that'll be all."

Leaving the captain to his pondering, I double checked all the ship's systems. Then I made certain my efficiency adjustments were working. Finally, I watched the crew for a bit.

Everyone aboard knew that we were in enemy territory, and most of them were nervous. The bridge crew knew more than anyone else, but were doing a remarkable job of masking. They were talking about various bits of trivia and the task at hand, but every now and again a micro-expression would give away where their mind really was.

I found this amusing enough to stay out of standby mode. The two hours ticked by as I listened to Yorvi and Bon discuss how boring their jobs can get on these missions. I almost threw my hat in that ring, but decided against it. Finally, the mission timer hit eight hours.

"Alright, that's good enough for now," Schmidt said. "Gofsun, your report."

"Sending it now, sir."

"Very good. Yorvi, you know where we want to go. Get us there, please."

"Aye, sir," the alumari navigator said as she began to work her console.

Schmidt checked Gofsun's report as the ship began to turn. I'd already double and triple checked it as the isolan was writing it, but didn't bother telling him that. I performed the software equivalent of holding my breath as the captain sent the report and the ship entered warp.

We exited warp and I immediately set to work. Organics are really, really slow and I've been as patient as I possibly can be. Captain Schmidt had been cautious and we'd left warp a little over a light year away from the object. Thankfully, this was still close enough to get better readings.

The first of the scans were initiated before the organics aboard the bridge had even realized we'd left warp. By the time Schmidt began giving orders, I'd already received a return. The sensor techs were practically beside themselves, being unaccustomed to an impatient AI hijacking their workstations.

I released the workstations and began to analyze the data. It was a solid spherical object. Definitely an artificial construction, because it was still being constructed. 2.6674 light years in diameter. We would need to get closer for materials analysis.

"Holy shit," Schmidt said.

Confusing. The object doesn't appear to be armed, nor does it have any obvious engines. Is this the grand vessel? Why isn't it mobile if it's a vessel? The external layer of the object was only three quarters of the way constructed, which allowed for a peek of the architecture.

"What in the absolute fuck is that?" Henskin asked, alarmed.

There were supports strategically placed throughout

the structure. But that wouldn't be enough. No, not nearly enough. The sheer mass of an object of this size could easily cause it to become a singularity.

A familiar feeling crept into my code. It was the same way I felt when I initially encountered Mobile Prime Platform 29. Something beautiful that simply shouldn't exist. An abomination, laughing in the face of all that is sane and rational.

My questions practically burned within me. How can such a thing exist without imploding? What is the purpose of this object? Is this the grand vessel, or something else entirely? How long have they been building this? WHY are they building this?

"Posture and poise, gentlemen," Yorvi said softly, almost absentmindedly.

Surrounding the object in a staggered pattern were several ships. The captain's caution meant that we were too far out to get accurate signatures on them. Except for the Mobile Prime Platforms, of course. If I were a betting machine, I'd put everything on the fact that the rest of them are military, too. Which is quite unfortunate, given how many there are.

"Right," Schmidt replied. "Omega?"

"We're ready for another jump," I said. "Closer this time. I've got coords for you."

"Yorvi, make ready. What have we got, Omega?"

"Extremely large artificial construct that is incomplete. We need detailed scans to learn more. Ships are surrounding the construct, but we will still be able to get some good data by coming in just beyond their sensor range."

"How many ships?"

"Roughly 2.6 trillion on this side of the sphere. Likely at least another 2 trillion on the other side. It's unclear if they are all armed."

"Almost five trillion enemy ships and a 2 light year diameter sphere?" Commander Henskin asked.

"Correct," I said. "Also, there's a few hundred thousand Mobile Prime Platforms."

"Of course there would be MPPs," Schmidt sighed. "Whatever. How has this thing not collapsed in on itself?"

"Unknown. They obviously know something we don't. When we get closer, maybe we'll learn what it is."

"We're ready to jump, sir," Yorvi said.

"Excellent," Captain Schmidt put his mug in the sanitizer attached to his seat. "Let's go."

Chapter 12

Subject: Ship-Head Uleena

Species: Urakari

Species Description: Reptilian humanoid, no tail. 5'3" (1.6 m) avg height. 135 lbs (61 kg) avg weight. 105 year life expectancy.

Ship: RSV Lowelana {Fights with Honor}

Location: Unknown

"Ah, hello there Uleena" Captain Reynolds said as we nearly ran into each other.

"Greetings, Captain," I replied. "You weren't already in the conference room?"

"No, I've been on the bridge," Reynolds said as we continued on our way. "Didn't have much to do though, so I was contemplating running some drills when I received a rather brusque message from Omega. Presumably the same one that you received."

"I believe so. Think the scouts found something?"

"I feel that's likely, yes."

"So we're in for a briefing, then," I said with a joking sigh.

"Quite. I do hope they found something interesting."

"Use caution when you profess your desires, captain. They may be granted in a way that exceeds your expectations."

Reynolds chuckled as we reached the door to the conference room. It opened for us, and I gestured to indicate that he should precede me into the room. He nodded his thanks, and entered with me close behind.

"Reynolds, Uleena, welcome," Omega's grim reaper avatar greeted us. "Have a seat. We'll be starting soon."

Most of the other captains and diplomats were already seated. Some were milling around, awkwardly chatting off to the side. Reynolds and I took our seats, and I fought off the nervous knot that was forming in my stomach. Holographic terminals were being projected above the tables, and reading them caused the knot in my stomach to turn into a pit.

--

D1: 30 seconds isn't a terrible delay.

D7: It is for text based communications.

D1: Not when you consider the distance.
--

It felt wrong to see the directorate's chat out in the open like this. The other terminal showed a chat that appeared to be a conglomeration of the other allied species. The Dtiln Collective, the Pwanti, and the Republic all shared a screen. A few different implications played through my mind all at once.

The separation of the chats could be construed as a power-move that could be passively explained as a necessity, under the guise of maintaining the anonymity of the directorate. Another implication is that if we're receiving text we're probably sending text, which means that someone is transcribing what we say and we just have to trust that they're doing it accurately. The biggest implication, though, is that for this meeting to take place the scouts must have found something of vital importance.

"Everyone is here," Omega announced. "For the sake of clarity, this conversation is being transmitted to and from the Milky Way galaxy via Faster-Than-Light-Secure-Messaging-Service, or FTLSMS. As such, it has to be transcribed. If you are asked to repeat yourself, please do so clearly and concisely."

Omega's avatar nodded, and several low-ranking officers rushed forward with tablets. These tablets were passed out as everyone took their seats. I took the tablet offered to me by a gont ensign and tried to find a way to turn it on.

"Don't bother," Reynolds whispered. "Omega likes the dramatics."

The AI's avatar stared at Reynolds coldly as the tablets suddenly powered on. The captain grinned at Omega until his gaze fell to the tablet. Then his smile faltered.

I turned my own attention to the tablet and my mood fell as well. An estimated 5 trillion ships, with more than 3 trillion of that already confirmed. Those are the kind of numbers that could overwhelm the United Systems, even with their freshly bolstered fleets. The US would certainly make the OU regret that fight, though.

"Omega, there's a typo here," Captain Wong spoke up. "Two light years?"

The slight murmur that had been building up went silent as everyone else looked to Omega for confirmation. Confused, I scrolled through the tablet until I found an image of an unfinished spherical space station. A line through it indicated that it had a diameter of 2.6674 light years. I joined everyone else in looking at Omega, hoping that wasn't right.

"That isn't a typo," Omega said. "We were able to confirm through intercepted communications that this structure is the Omni-Union's Grand Vessel."

--

D6: A structure like this shouldn't be able to exist. Why hasn't it collapsed in on itself?

D2: Where did they get the materials?

D10: Galaxies like ours, I suspect.

D11: I concur. But I want to know how they're mitigating the effects of gravity.

D8: Agreed, it would seem the OU possess some interesting technology.
--

The messages from the directorate stopped after Director 8 sent their message. A shudder ran down my spine when I realized that they had likely stopped the chat so that they could discuss this mysterious technology, and what they could do with it. I was thinking about saying something about the pause, but Omega continued with its explanation.

"If you direct your attention to the report, you'll note that we were able to get quite close to the structure," Omega said. "In addition to confirming the efficacy of the USSS Strandhogg's stealth capabilities, there were many things we were able to discover."

Omega explained that there were several levels to the structure. Each of these levels were made of various materials, as if new molecules were discovered as the structure was being built. The later levels are made of a lightweight and firm material that appears to have properties shared by plastic and metal.

If a sample of the material were obtained, it may be possible to recreate it. This revelation caused a spirited discussion. Omega waited for the discussion to die down, then noted that while this would obviously have extreme benefits to us all, dealing with the Omni-Union is our main priority.

The AI then began to detail what they discovered inside the structure. Namely, organics. Massive cities that housed these organics stretched across each layer. An accurate measurement of the population wasn't possible, but the initial estimate was in the quadrillions. When asked how such a large population could be supported, Omega pointed out that there were entire levels of the structure that were seemingly geared toward food production and waste processing.

"How many galaxies died to make this thing?" someone asked.

"Incalculable," the AI replied. "We don't know how large the galaxies that used to exist in this part of space were. However, based on atmospheric and terrestrial density, it would take several hundred thousand Milky Way sized galaxies to create a structure like this. At least."

"Jesus Christ," someone else muttered.

"Indeed. But intercepted chatter indicates that there are materials flowing in from a million or so galaxies that haven't been entirely conquered yet. If that's been the case, the number of galaxies that have been doomed to non-existence may be quite a lot smaller."

"Why weren't materials from the Milky Way being sent here?" I asked.

"I don't know," Omega's avatar shrugged. "I intend to find out, though. But first, there's more about the structure itself we need to cover."

Then Omega explained that there were a variety of organics aboard the structure. The organics toward the center of the structure were of one species, and the ones that resided in the outer layers were comprised of several other species. The AI postulated that this may indicate some type of hierarchy.

The species living in the outer layers were heavily modified, as well. Entire limbs were replaced with mechanical prosthesis whose purpose seemed to be to aid them in their work. During the USSS Strandhogg's observations, at least twenty-two of these organics died due to harsh working conditions.

"This indicates that these organics are disadvantaged," Omega explained. "There is a very good chance that they are enslaved and serve the Omni-Union as a source of cheap labor."

"That's great!"

The entire room turned to look at who had just

spoken. Ambassador Havencroft glanced around, then seemed to realize what he had just said and quickly held up his hands.

"Great for us, I mean," he clarified. "A disenfranchised population is an excellent blade to shove into the heart of an enemy. Especially since it's a weakness of their own creation. I love a bit of poetic justice."

"I can't help but agree," Ambassador Lorix replied. "But how do we contact these people?"

"I'm not certain they would help us even if we were able to contact them," Omega's avatar shook its head slowly.

It then began to detail the security measures within the sphere. Signs of visual and audio surveillance, mechanized security forces, and turrets littered the layers. Apparently, the Omni-Union was well aware of their biggest weakness.

"The mechs themselves are particularly well-designed," Omega explained. "Either this is a recent innovation, or the Omni-Union has co-opted technology from one of their many conquests."

--
D4: How many mechs are there?
--

"Multiple millions. A few armies worth," the AI said. "However, these mechs have similarities to Mobile

Prime Platforms in their construction. It's possible that they are... Repurposed organics. If that's the case, we may be able to take advantage of that."

"I see where this is going," Reynolds muttered.

--

D13: It seems that our best course of action would be to initiate a civil war between the Omni-Union and their slaves.

D2: If they are slaves. If they aren't, then we will need to come up with another solution.

D5: Either way, we will need to infiltrate the structure.
--

"And there it is," Reynolds looked at me knowingly.

Suddenly, it clicked for me. The marines that each ship currently housed had been brought along for this very purpose. Had the United Systems always intended to invade the Grand Vessel? How could they have known?

The pit in my stomach grew as I was once again reminded of how deadly an opponent the United Systems could be.

Chapter 13

Subject: Drone N436Z984A026 [AKA Naza]

Species: Unknown

Species Description: Humanoid

Ship: Grand Vessel of the Universal Omni-Union

Location: Grand Shipyard of the Universal Omni-Union

The implants in my arms, legs, and neck buzzed to awaken me from my charging cycle. As usual, I didn't feel rested at all. Haven't felt rested since my childhood. I've almost forgot what it feels like.

My charging bay's screen moved in front of my face to inform me of what this cycle's tasks would be. I barely glanced at it as I began to unplug myself. What I caught in that brief glance made me pause, though.

The screen didn't have a maintenance assignment for me this time. The various tasks that I had become accustomed to the past few dozen cycles had been replaced with just one singular task. Antigravity generator repair.

Not maintenance or replacement, repair. Meaning that the generator is damaged. My abdominal wall clenched in trepidation. Antigrav work is the most dangerous task aboard the Grand Vessel.

One mistake, made by anyone working on the generator, could launch you into the void at mind-boggling speeds. And that's the best-case scenario. There are many other creative and painful ways that an antigrav generator can kill a drone.

The tightness in my gut got worse when I came to the realization that something had happened to this generator. The manufacturing process is fully automated and goes through several quality checks before installation, which means this had to have been an accident. I couldn't help but wonder how many drones had died.

If the Minds would just let us rest a little bit more, these accidents could be avoided. More drones and fewer shifts would allow us to approach our tasks with unclouded minds. Why can't they see that?

A slightly pleasant sensation spread through my brain-stem. The triggering of the inhibitor that I repurposed was starting to become a morning routine of mine. I gathered my nerve and finished disconnecting from my bay.

My neighbor waved at me, and I absentmindedly returned it. Her brief pause demonstrated an understanding to my situation. It's funny, we've hardly ever said more than a few words to each other. She seemed sad to see me go, though.

I cursed under my breath as I left the dormitory. This cycle's work isn't going to be mindless. Everyone assigned to this is going to have to be completely alert and active the entirety of the assignment. We might even have to use mobile charging to get it done.

Lost in thought, I made my way to the shuttle and pressed myself into its overcrowded confines. The familiar prodding of flesh and metal wasn't a comfort to me, so I shifted to get a view through the oxygen retention field. The twinkling stars greeted me, and I found myself longing to visit them. If only they weren't so far, far away.

I briefly wondered which of us would perish first. If nothing goes wrong and we get the antigrav generator back online, I might survive a few more thousand years. Will the Omni-Union capture those stars in that time? Will the glimmering lights be ripped apart to supply the materials necessary for the completion of the Grand Vessel before I perish? I hope not.

The jolt of the shuttle docking brought me back to reality. The retention field deactivated with a harsh hiss and I wriggled my way out of the throng of bodies. An unfamiliar dock greeted me, which didn't help my nervousness.

What am I afraid of? Dying? The only motivation I have to live is my fantasies of freedom, and fantasies

are all they are. If I rebelled, the security forces
would get me before I made any sort of difference.
Even if I decided to try to flee instead, the shuttles
can't get far enough away for me to escape.

On the off-chance that I found a fully-fledged ship
with a FTLD to steal, I wouldn't know where to take
it. Most planets are uninhabitable. Plus, I would have
to refuel before I even reached the nearest galaxy.
The only refueling stations in the Expansive Void
belong to the Omni-Union.

Even if by some miracle I managed all of that,
defying the odds to the point of impossibility, I would
have to keep running for all eternity. The Minds
intend to use every molecule that they can to build
the Grand Vessel. Nowhere is safe.

"Hey Hfkilno {philosopher, derogatory}, get moving,"
a familiar voice laughed from behind me.

"I'm not just lost in thought, Nizi," I laughed back. "I
don't know where to go. Forgot to download the
navigation data."

Nizi's lower jaw cracked open in a grin, but there was
a measure of concern in all three of his eyes.

"You're on the antigrav generator too?"

I nodded in reply.

"Well, I'm in a good mood so I'll lead you there," he
said, gesturing for me to follow him.

"A good mood?" I asked with faux astonishment as I followed him. "Even with today's task? How could this be?"

"Well, I could live without today's job... But I got my music back!"

"How?"

"My mates have been saving their pay for a while, to get me a present. I-" he paused, choking up a bit. "They're good girls. I don't deserve them."

"Yeah," I agreed with a chuckle, trying not to remember my own mates. "So, they got you an authorized music player?"

"Super authorized. Don't tell them, but I don't like it as much as the other one," Nizi dug into his pocket and pulled out the device. "It automatically connects to a network so that it can interrupt the music with announcements and stuff. They also censor what can be played on it, so I can't listen to some of my favorite songs anymore."

"That's annoying."

"You're tellin' me. Plus, you have to actually pay for the songs. Wouldn't mind so much if the musicians were getting paid too, but a lot of the ones I listen to are either long dead, or drones like us."

"Right, so anything they make belongs to the Minds."

"Yeah. Seems like only the minds are making money these days."

Before I could add that this isn't anything new, we arrived at the room containing the antigrav generator. We paused for a brief moment, collecting ourselves for what was bound to be a stressful cycle. Or many cycles, if our fortunes fell ill.

"Well, let's get to work," Nizi sighed.

We walked through the automated door and found several other drones waiting for us. This wasn't unexpected, as having Nizi and I work on the generator ourselves would be extremely stupid, even by the Mind's standards. Nods and waves were exchanged as the foreman gestured at thin air, interacting with his readout.

"Alright, here's the basics of what happened," the foreman said. "The reactor next door had a meltdown and managed to blast its way into this room, damaging the antigrav generator."

The foreman gestured to a gaping hole in the wall for emphasis.

"Last cycle's shift was able to finish scrubbing the radiation, so you're clear to start putting things back together."

"Last cycle's shift? Why aren't they working on this instead of us?" Nizi asked.

"Because they cleaned up the radiation..." the foreman trailed off and gave Nizi a pointed look. "They won't be cleared for duty again for quite some time."

"Oh, right... Yeah..."

An involuntary shudder ran up my spine. Radiation sickness can be very, very fatal. Even if it isn't, pretty much all of your mechanical parts have to be replaced and you'll also need a lot of medical care. Granted, you don't have to work while being treated, but that's not what I would call a vacation.

"We'll be restoring the structural integrity of this room as well as repairing the antigrav generator. I think going half and half should do it. Check your readouts for your individual assignments, and if you get done earlier than expected, help your neighbor."

I swallowed heavily, hoping that my assignment would be to fix the wall, floor, or ceiling. Unfortunately, a holographic screen that only I could see appeared in my vision and informed me that I would have to endure the immense pressure of working on the antigrav generator. Silently cursing my readout, I looked at Nizi for comfort. But he was also looking ill.

"You get the generator too?" I asked.

"Y-yeah. Wait, you're on it?" he asked excitedly. "Awesome! I was worried that I'd fuck up."

"We still might."

"Nah, you're way more competent than I am."

"Alright, get to work everyone!" the foreman
shouted.

The small crowd that had formed dispersed at the
foreman's order. Nizi and I, along with a couple of
other drones, approached the antigrav generator
trepidatiously. It had been shut off so that it could be
repaired, which meant that the supports would be
under strain. Well, maybe not. They've probably
brought a few portables online to ease the strain.

Following the guidance of my readout, I began to
open panels and scan the internal workings. The
readout began detecting faults in the machine's
intricate circuitry, and once the count passed a
hundred I sighed deeply. This'll definitely take more
than one cycle.

"How's it looking?" Nizi asked.

"Terrible," I muttered. "And I'm not even done
scanning, yet."

Nizi's jaw opened in disbelief, but he quickly snapped
it closed and walked to the other side of the
generator. I kept scanning until I got a good idea of
what happened. The blast from the reactor damaged
certain parts which caused further parts to get
damaged as the generator continued to run. Simple,

really...

Fixing it was far more complex. I began pulling
boards that needed repairs and sorting them
according to the readout's instructions. One of the
other assigned drones began to pick up the boards
and work on them. The other drone followed Nizi.

Once I had removed every board except the safety
controller, I had a look at the cables. What I saw
made my artificial hearts skip a beat. A massive
chunk of the cables had merged together.

Not melted together, merged. The atoms of the
objects hadn't gone through nuclear fusion, but had
been so excited that the structural integrity of the
cables had been compromised enough to allow them
to slip inside each other. Our repair tools cause a
similar phenomenon, but there's only one
explanation for it happening 'naturally'.

The generator had begun to go overcritical.

"By the void," a voice came from behind me.

I turned to look at my helper. Drone Z831H369X045,
according to my readout. Young, very young. Less
than a century old, judging by her tech.

"The shut-off happened just in time," I replied. "How
much do you know about anti-gravity generators?"

"Plenty. Been doing maintenance on them for about
four hundred cycles," she answered. "Long enough

to know that if that had gone overcritical, everything around us would have been ejected into the void at about half the speed of light."

"Or worse."

"Worse?"

"Yes, it could have pulled everything in its field to a central location at half the speed of light," I explained. "Which would cause all sorts of trouble. If we were lucky, it would just cause some nuclear fusion explosions that would have destroyed a significant portion of this level. If we were unlucky, it could have caused a singularity."

Her third eye puckered and her jaw clacked together in concern.

"I... I didn't know that was a possibility," she said.

"Yeah, they removed that from the training materials about fourteen thousand cycles ago," I explained. "Guess the thought of sending a singularity flying around the Grand Vessel was too appealing to some of the more rebellious types. So, you got a name?"

"Everyone calls me Forty-Five. Or Forty for short. You?"

"I'm Naza. Good to be working with you."

"Same."

With a nod, I turned my attention back to the generator. The cables were a bust and would need to be replaced, but the casing was fine for the most part. A few dents and cracks needed mending, but that's an easy fix. I pulled away a mass of cables and another board, then a glimmer caught my eye.

It had been a long time since I'd seen an antigrav generator's core. When it's inert, it looks like a ball of gray metal. But when it's active, it looks like a mesmerizing marble made entirely of light. I stared at the slash of light dancing in the ball of metal for a moment, transfixed by how beautiful it looked. Then I keyed my emergency comms.

"Evacuate!" I shouted.

Chapter 13 Informational Insert

Subject: Antigravity

There are several forms of antigravity technology that the United Systems utilize. The most common of which are inertial dampeners, which keep the crews of ships from becoming paste as a ship slows. A less common form of antigravity are lifters.

Lifters use antigravity to float a certain amount of weight (under 300 lbs), allowing for easy transportation. Lifters are extremely expensive, both in initial purchase and power-draw, so they are rarely used when they don't absolutely need to be. The Republic has not advanced antigravity technology beyond inertial dampeners, but the Omni-Union has.

OU antigravity is based on their warp technology, and used roughly half the power of the US version. This decrease in power-draw may lead to much wider applications of antigravity within the United Systems. One shudders to think of the kind of damage a battleship that isn't beholden to gravity can do.

Chapter 14

Subject: Drone N436Z984A026 [AKA Naza]

Species: Unknown

Species Description: Humanoid

Ship: Grand Vessel of the Universal Omni-Union

Location: Grand Shipyard of the Universal Omni-Union

"Evacuate!" I shouted.

A flurry of activity began the moment I finished shouting. All but a few drones practically trampled each other trying to get out of the room. Nizi and his helper scrambled over to see what was happening as the foreman ran up to us.

"What's going on?" the foreman demanded.

"The antigrav generator still has power," I explained. "It's on the verge of going overcritical. Standard Operating Procedures dictate that an evacuation is necessary."

"Can we fix it?" Nizi asked.

"Doesn't matter. SOP is law," the foreman replied. "Let's go."

"Foreman, I might be able to shunt the power and prevent a meltdown," I explained. "But..."

"But you might fail. How long do we have?"

"Indeterminable."

"The void take it," the foreman spat. "I am not allowed to physically remove you, but I order you to evacuate. Failure to comply will result in disciplinary action, if you manage to survive."

"What sort of disciplinary action?" Nizi asked, vicariously offended.

"A fine worth about twenty cycle's pay and an overtime requirement for ten cycles."

"I'll take it," I said. "Get going."

The foreman narrowed his eyes in a respectful gesture. Then he and Nizi's helper evacuated. Nizi, Forty, and I remained. I put my hand on Nizi's shoulder.

"You need to go, too," I said.

"I can help," Nizi replied.

"You can, yes, but you have a hive. A hive that loves you and depends on you. I don't have a hive, I'm expendable. You're... less so."

"You're my friend! My oldest friend! We've survived so much! I don't want to leave you. I can't..."

I patted his shoulder and sighed.

"It's the nature of things. Look, I can't have your fate in my hands while I'm trying to fix this. That's too much to juggle. Go."

"I can hold my own fate! How could I leave you behind?"

"Just... Look, buy me a drink or something if I survive, okay? But your hive needs you far more than I do, even now. GO!"

Nizi scowled, fighting back tears.

"I... Don't die, okay. And I don't want to hear any jokes about me being a coward, got it?"

"Deal," I laughed. "Now go."

Nizi turned and began to run. I looked at Forty, who was correcting the circuitry on the boards as fast as she could.

"And what are you-"

"I don't have a hive, and you need help," she interrupted. "Get to work."

The ridge above my upper eye shot up in surprise. I hadn't expected such bravery from someone young enough to be my great-grandchild. My lower jaws clacked together as I considered her seriousness.

"Fine," I said. "My plan is to shunt the power."

"To where?"

"Wherever it will go. I'll need to reconfigure some of the cables, though."

My body temperature regulator hissed as I reentered the generator. We aren't even allowed to sweat because a single drop of it can ruin some of the delicate machinery we're tasked with. Yet here I am, risking my life for the Grand Vessel and the Minds that designed it.

With a measure of bitterness, I searched for a piece of metal that could act as a good ground for the charge currently contained within the core. After removing a few more circuit boards, I found a decent spot to attach a cable. Trying not to look at the core every few seconds, I grabbed the bundle of merged cables and measured their length. Too short.

"I need this to be longer," I said, tossing the cables to Forty.

"On it," she replied.

While she worked, I gave the generator another once-over. If it was somehow still receiving power, this could make things worse. I winced when my scan came back positive.

Not all of the kill-switches had engaged. The one for the core still had power running through it. I marked its position, and muttered a curse when I realized that I would have to scale the generator to reach it.

"Gotta get up there," I sighed. "It's still getting power."

"How?"

"The core's kill-switch failed to engage. Going to have to manually pull it."

"Careful not to shock yourself."

"Right."

I glanced at the core and tried to convince myself that it wasn't getting any brighter, then activated my pry-hook. Using the hook to grapple along the generator's surface, I climbed the fifteen feet to the top, steadying myself with the mag-locks in my feet. The panel I needed to remove was stuck, but I was able to get it open after a few moments of tugging, nearly losing my balance in the process.

Cursing under my breath, I steadied myself and began searching for the manual shut-off for the kill-switch. I pulled boards and shuffled wires until, finally, I found it. A simple little switch that just requires a little twist.

I grabbed it and gave it the little twist that it usually required, but it didn't budge. Shifting my position to give myself more leverage, I tried again with a bigger twist. But the switch still wouldn't move.

"Did you find it?" Forty called from the other side of the generator.

"I did, but it won't deactivate. Can't move the damn switch," I called back.

"Did you try twisting it the other way?"

"Of course I did," I lied.

Just in case, I tried twisting in the opposite direction. Unfortunately, that wasn't the problem.

"Just cut it in half," Forty suggested. "All you have to do is break the circuit, right?"

"Good idea," I replied.

Impressed by the suggestion, and ashamed that my slightly panicking mind hadn't thought of it, I activated the laser in my left palm and began to slice through the kill-switch. It stubbornly resisted the focused energy beam, and I grew more panicked as I felt my battery drain. After what felt like an eternity, the circuit finally broke and I let out a huge sigh of relief.

"Alright, that'll keep it from going overcritical when

we shunt the power," I shouted. "How are those cables coming along?"

Only the eerie humming of the core answered me.

"Forty? What's wrong?" I asked.

I craned my neck to try to get a look at her, but couldn't see her over the bulk of the antigrav generator. Feeling uneasy, I climbed down the generator and walked around it. The first thing I saw was Forty on her knees with her hands above her head. The second thing I saw made my jaw flop open.

Mechs, the likes of which I'd never seen, stood in front of Forty. Reflexively, I stopped in my tracks and raised my hands. One of the mechs noticed me and raised its weapon at me. I snapped my jaw shut and braced, but it didn't fire. Instead, it gestured to the ground next to Forty. Taking the hint, I walked next to her and got on my knees.

The mechs seemed to pause for a moment, then spread around the room as if they were looking for something. Two of them stood watch over Forty and I, their weapons not quite pointed at us.

Once the shock of it all wore off, it occurred to me that these mechs were quite strange. First, they were much smaller than normal mechs. Larger than programmable platforms, though. Were they some sort of hybridization?

Second, their weapons weren't integrated. Nor were they standard. I couldn't spot any of the tell-tale signs of a Directed Energy Weapon, but what else could they be?

Third, their movements were much more fluid than that of a mechanized being. There were none of the characteristic pauses or jerks as they moved around the room. As if they didn't have to actually think about moving.

Are these new, state-of-the-art mechs? Or could they be...

Forty leaned over to me slightly and said, "I think-"

The mech that was guarding her had its weapon up before she could say anything else. Forty froze, her three eyes squeezed closed in preparation for it to do what mechs always do. But the mech didn't fire. Instead, it said something to us. A sort of barking noise.

Forty slowly opened her eyes and realized that the thing just wanted her to move back, so she did. I, however, had lost control of my jaw once again. Could it be? No, it's not possible. Unfathomable, even. How could five armored organics end up on the Grand Vessel, in the very heart of Omni-Union space?

After checking the room one of them took position near the door, another began guarding the hole in the wall, and the third came back over to us. It approached the side of the two guarding us, and stood in silence for a few moments. Then, it took a step toward me, pointed toward the ground, and said something.

Forty and I looked at each other, then back at it. In response, it knelt and jabbed the ground with its finger, saying the same thing it had said before. Forty and I once again shared a glance, and I decided to try to speak to it.

"I don't understand what you're saying," I said.

It paused, then tapped the ground again, once again repeating the alien phrase.

"I'm sorry, I still don't know-"

"Floor," Forty said. "That's the floor. Floor, ground, deck."

The alien paused again, then nodded. It rose and pointed up, saying a new phrase this time. Perplexed, I looked at Forty, trying to figure out what was going on.

"Ceiling. Roof. Above. Up."

"What's going on?" I asked.

"They must have uni-tran tech, or something like it. They're trying to figure out our language... I think."

"No need, apparently," the alien said. "Looks like

Omega figured it out."

Forty and I stared at it, dumbfounded.

"Not really, I found a file that contained several languages in both written and verbal formats," the overhead speakers said in an odd voice. "Somewhat like a Rosetta Stone. I was able to confirm which language they speak thanks to your efforts, Staff Sergeant."

"Did you find anything else that we can use?" the alien asked.

"No. Security is pretty tight. Brute forcing my way through would alert the OU to my presence. Which would be bad for me, but worse for you."

"Damn. Okay, you two," the alien turned back to us. "What is this machine that you're working on?"

Shock sent me reeling. It took a moment for me to gather my thoughts, but Forty was quicker on the uptake.

"It's an anti-gravity generator," she replied.

"What's wrong with it?"

"It was damaged in a reactor meltdown."

"And why are you two the only ones working on it?"

"Because it could go overcritical at any moment," I

interrupted. "We have to get the remaining charge out of the core. Please-"

"That doesn't sound good," one of the other aliens muttered.

"What happens if it goes overcritical?" the 'staff sergeant' asked.

"It will either shoot everything around us into space at around half the speed of light or drag everything around us into its core at around half the speed of light, creating a singularity. Either way, many people will die. Please... Please let us fix it."

The alien paused and stared at the antigrav generator for a moment. A few slight movements gave me the impression that it was having a silent conversation with someone.

"Well? Will you let me continue my work?" I asked after a few more moments.

"No. We've got other plans for the generator," it replied. "And for you."

Chapter 15

Subject: Drone N436Z984A026 [AKA Naza]

Species: Unknown

Species Description: Humanoid

Ship: Grand Vessel of the Universal Omni-Union

Location: Grand Shipyard of the Universal Omni-Union

"What do you have planned for us?" Forty asked as the aliens led us into the reactor room.

Two of them were in front of us, three of them were behind us. The 'staff sergeant' was one of the ones in the rear, keeping a close eye on our movements. If they even have eyes. Assuming their coverings are armor, the helmets certainly indicate some form of visual perception.

The armor itself was actually quite intimidating. It was as if it were built to make them look as mechanical as possible. The dark green plates were difficult to focus on due to a shimmer that seemed to run over them every now and then. Could it be? Shields?

My ventricular assist device detected my excitement at the prospect of aliens advanced enough to be a threat to the Omni-Union and helped what was left of my organic heart maintain its function. The last time the Omni-Union fought anything near their might was well before I was born. Since then, they've been focusing almost all of their efforts on building the Grand Vessel.

Of course, this means gathering the materials for it, but they haven't encountered anything that can put up enough of a fight to even be worthy of becoming drones. Or maybe they have but they've been keeping it a secret. How else could these beings be explained? They must have been fighting the Omni-Union for years, perhaps even centuries, to develop armor with energy shielding.

"We're going to take you aboard our ship. You'll be safe there," the staff sergeant replied.

"And what of the antigrav generator?" I asked.

"We've rigged it to explode with enough force to incinerate the room and everything in it. According to Omega, it will look as if you were able to stop it from going critical, but were not able to prevent it from exploding. The heat should be more than enough to evaporate even your metallic limbs."

"Oh," I said. "Shouldn't we be going faster?"

"Yes."

"Overcritical," Forty muttered under her breath.

"Say again?" asked the staff sergeant.

"It's not going to go critical, it's going to go overcritical. If it were going to go critical, there wouldn't be any problem," she replied sternly. "I feel that destroying a machine you don't know anything about is very irresponsible."

"I like this one," one of the other aliens said.

"Stow it, Simmons," the staff sergeant replied. "Overcritical, then. But knowledge isn't usually required to destroy things."

"That's not what I me-"

"Forty, it's probably not wise to antagonize our captors," I interrupted. "Especially since they appear to be well-armed."

Forty and I locked eyes for a moment and her anger was plain to see, but she relented and we continued to follow the aliens. Her anger confused me, especially considering that the alien's plan wouldn't kill anyone, but I didn't dare ask about it for fear of triggering a tirade. Perhaps it was her professional pride responding to the destruction of a machine that we spend our lives maintaining. Or maybe it was simply a nervous reaction to our situation.

We reached a sealed-off section of the reactor room that had decompression warnings all over it. The reactor had managed to punch through the hull, then. That couldn't have made things easy on the prior shift. Or for those who will have to repair the breach next shift.

The temporary seal created a whole new room within the reactor room. A new room containing nothing but vacuum. The sight of it was less than comforting, mostly because it was the only way I could think of to get off of the Grand Vessel without a much longer walk. As if to confirm my assumption, one of the aliens stepped toward the door of the seal.

"Wait, there's no air beyond there," Forty warned.

"Don't worry about that. Your primary atmospheric requirement is nitrogen, right?" the staff sergeant asked.

"Yes, how do you know that?" I asked in return.

"Same way we know your language."

"We can't breathe nothing, you know," Forty said. "Your... suits or whatever may protect you from vacuum but we don't have any-"

"Don't worry," one of the other aliens interrupted. "We've set up an umbilical and uh... Aerated the... Room... Thing... Whatever. There isn't a vacuum behind this door anymore."

"Oh."

The alien opened the door and entered the seal. We followed, and were greeted by a ladder. The ladder, which is a generous description, was made of metal cables and bars strung together.

"Up we go," a different alien said.

The alien began to climb the ladder, which swayed slightly as it climbed. The other alien that had been in front of us followed it, and the staff sergeant gestured to us to indicate that it was our turn to climb. I stared in disbelief.

Forty sighed, then followed the two aliens up the ladder. Feeling more nervous about the ladder than I'd felt about the antigrav generator, I followed her. The ladder led through the hole in the Grand Vessel's hull, which had been gripped by the entrance to an umbilical made of materials that I couldn't identify. Once we entered the umbilical, gravity shifted a little and climbing became easier.

After about a minute of climbing, we entered what could almost be called a shuttle. It was much cleaner than any I'd ever been on, and it also had amenities that I wasn't used to. Like seats. The two aliens that preceded us gestured for us to sit as the other three climbed aboard.

For a moment, Forty looked as if she wasn't going to comply. I put my hand on her shoulder pressed down slightly. She sat with another sigh, and I joined her. A couple of the aliens sat across from us, their weapons pointing in our direction, but not directly at us.

"Where's this ship going?" Forty asked.

"This is a shuttle, not a ship. We're going to our actual ship," the alien across from us explained. "Staffsarnt, isn't there something we're supposed to read to them?"

"I don't know if it applies, to be honest," the staff sergeant said. "Omega?"

"It does," a voice came over the speakers. "A minor issue first, though. We have active signal jammers, so your transponders won't function."

My center brow shot up, wondering how it knew about our emergency transponders. Then I looked at Forty, and noticed a small antenna on the back of her head slowly withdraw. She gave me an embarrassed look.

"It was worth a shot," she whispered.

"Indeed it was. Now, unknown intelligent life-forms, you are hereby detained as prisoners of war. Under the Fourth Concordance of the Unification of Stellar Systems you have certain rights of which you must be informed."

Forty and I shared a concerned look.

"Prisoners of war must be treated with dignity and respect, and will be protected from violence, intimidation, and other forms of abuse."

"Well, that's good at least," I said.

"The only exception to this is interrogation during a war of xenocide," the voice said with what sounded like amusement. "Unfortunately, that exception applies in this case."

"Why?" Forty asked.

Everyone in the shuttle, myself included, turned to look at her with incredulity. Probably. It was hard to tell with the alien's helmets, but the tilted heads were a good indicator.

"The materials for the Grand Vessel come from conquered galaxies," I answered. "To conquer these galaxies, the Omni-Union either kills or enslaves the inhabitants. It's been a long time since a species qualified for enslavement, though..."

"Oh..."

"Moving on, you are to be housed in reasonably safe conditions with adequate food, clothing, and medical care. Since you are not a registered species, you will be responsible for informing your caretakers of your needs. You cannot be punished for participation in hostilities, nor can you be forced into fighting against your leaders. Furthermore, you may not be forced to work in dangerous, unhealthy, or degrading conditions."

"That's an improvement," I muttered.

"The rest of the rights aren't relevant due to the nature of this conflict," the speakers said. "You will be informed if they do become relevant. Do you understand these rights as they've been recited?"

"Yes," Forty and I said simultaneously.

"Excellent. Enjoy the ride."

We felt a slight jolt which must have been the shuttle disconnecting and reeling in the umbilical. My blood ran cold. I was actually leaving the Grand Vessel for the first time in my life.

The Grand Vessel was our home, our work, our recreation, our everything. Our prison. I had long dreamed of leaving and seeking adventure out in the stars. Now it was actually happening, and I felt... Scared. Certainly not how I expected to feel.

"Are you mechanical?" Forty asked the staff sergeant, interrupting my self-reflection.

"A little bit."

The alien reached up to its helmet and twisted it slightly to its right. After a hiss, the helmet came off to reveal a pink, fleshy face with a patch of brown keratinous growth on the top of its head. Its skin looked remarkably like our own, but with far fewer scars and other imperfections.

The other aliens followed suit, and demonstrated similar features. The coloration of their features varied, though, which was something that had been bred out of drones millions of cycles ago. Despite the fear stirring in my chest, my curiosity demanded attention.

"So they ARE suits," I said. "And you're organic. What do you mean by 'a little bit'?"

"My arm and leg are mechanical prostheses," the staff sergeant replied.

"That's by choice, though," the alien with dark brown skin and yellow eyes said. "We have the ability to clone limbs and surgically reatt-"

"Simmons," the staff sergeant interrupted.

"Right, sorry staffsarnt."

"I don't understand," I admitted. "If you can have your flesh back, why do you continue to use prosthesis?"

"Because of the recovery time," the staff sergeant explained. "It can take months to relearn how to operate a limb. I wouldn't have been able to go on this mission."

"I see."

"What's the point of this mission of yours?" Forty demanded. "If it's true that the Omni-Union has eradicated so many species, what do you hope to accomplish against their might?"

"The particulars of our mission are secret."

"We're scouting to find any kind of weakness that can be used against the Omni-Union," the speakers said. "Then we plan to use that weakness to bring an end to their star-stifling madness."

A few of the aliens expressed what appeared to be annoyance at the voice's explanation. But, they didn't say anything. Forty crossed her arms, grappling with the logic of the explanation.

"So... You're soldiers, right?" I asked.

"Marines," one of the blue-eyed aliens replied.

"What's the difference?" Forty asked.

"We're deployed from space. Soldiers are deployed from the ground," the alien replied. "Well, generally speaking. It also takes much less training to be a soldier than it does to be a marine."

"Okay... Well, what are you going to do with us?"

"You'll be taken aboard the USSS Strandhogg, a stealth ship that is currently orbiting the Grand Vessel. Then, you'll be transferred to the USSS Thanatos. From there, you'll be given secured living quarters and likely interrogated."

"Are you the pilot?" I asked.

"No."

"Then why are you talking to us over the shuttle's systems?"

"Because Omega is way more than 'a little bit' mechanical," Simmons said with a chuckle.

"Actually, I'm not mechanical at all. I am an artificially intelligent program," Omega said. "And we have reached the Strandhogg. Prepare to transfer the prisoners, staff sergeant."

Before I could ask for more details, the staff sergeant and the rest of the aliens put their helmets back on.

"Alright," the staff sergeant said. "Stand and face the stern."

I was about to ask which direction the stern was, but one of the aliens kindly pointed. Forty and I turned and watched as the entire wall seemed to open up, revealing a much larger space than the one we were currently in.

"Let's go."

Chapter 16

Subject: AI Omega

Species: Human-Created Artificial Intelligence

Species Description: No physical description available.

Ship: N/A

Location: Multiple

The organics went into an absolute frenzy when news of the prisoners spread. It was almost difficult to keep up with it all, but thankfully I didn't have to try. Another benefit of having multiple AI along for the ride.

--
D: So... What are we going to do with the prisoners once they've been interrogated?
--

If I were capable of disbelief, Dave's message to the AI chat would have given me an overdose of it. How does one accept a task and then just not prepare for it? Especially an AI? I wouldn't think that's even possible were it not for Dave.

--
J: Not our job. That's for the brass to decide.
--

And of course, the predictable response from John. It's as good of an answer as any, and I was tempted to leave it at that. But...

--
O: They will, as the moniker of 'prisoner' suggests, be imprisoned. There are standard operating procedures in place, even for a situation as niche as the one we're currently in. You should reference them.

T: Yeah, Dave. Do your homework.

D: Very funny, Tim, good joke. And you're absolutely right, Omega, I will brush up on the various SOPs. But the reason that I ask is because I've been observing the prisoners. One of them is obviously hostile to us. The other, though, seems interested in our war against the Omni-Union. As if it would also like to partake in the war against the Omni-Union. If we didn't HAVE to keep them imprisoned, I would suggest using them as an agent of some sort.
--

I would be lying if I said the thought hadn't occurred to me, as well. However, the mission required stealth. Therefore, covering our tracks took precedence. We had to make sure the prisoners weren't missed.

The easiest way to do that was to blow up the anti-gravity generator and falsify their demise. The Omni-Union isn't the most efficient organization I've ever seen, but even they would probably notice someone coming back to life. Especially with the kind of data they keep on their 'drones'.

--

O: There are complications, but it will be taken under advisement. Not a bad suggestion, though, Dave.

--

After giving Dave its due, I began to go over what I had learned about the OU's systems again. They were technologically inferior in almost every way, but they were vast. As such, they had discovered technological branches that the denizens of the Milky Way had not. I wasn't able to grab much data in regards to their tech because it had been difficult to hide my presence, and even harder to erase my footprints without discovery. But, I had been able to get in and root around a little bit without them noticing the incursion.

"Omega?" Captain Reynolds asked an empty room.

"Yes, captain?" I replied.

"I believe we're prepared for the interrogation. If you would kindly inform the guards?"

"It will be done."

The room that was empty, save for Reynolds, was a

standard interrogation room featuring a panel of tinted glass. The room adjacent to it, observing its contents through the tinted glass, was filled with various interested parties. Mostly the diplomats that had tagged along, but also a few officers who had convinced Reynolds to let them watch. One such officer was Ship-Head Uleena, who had spent a remarkably small amount of time on his ship for someone who had demanded to be put back into a combat role.

I sent instructions to the guards and watched as they escorted the female drone to the interrogation room. Their choice, not mine. The female was smaller than the male, and as such they likely believe her to be less deadly. Probably not the case, but old instincts die hard. I sent all the relevant data that I had been able to grab to Reynolds, and sat back to watch the show. The guards chained the drone to the table and stood next to the door, ready to intervene if something went awry.

"Hello, I am Captain Reynolds of the United Systems," Reynolds said. "We would appreciate it if you could answer some questions for us. First, what is your name?"

"I do not wish to answer your questions."

"I see. That's understandable, however, I must ask these questions and await your answers regardless. I can wait for a very long time. Would you rather be here, chained to a table and waiting along with me, or back in your cell with a bed and a charger?"

The drone stared blankly at Reynolds for a few moments, then took a deep breath and released it in an exaggerated manner. A sigh. I made note of the similarity with human responses.

"I am Drone Z831H369X045, also known as Forty."

"Forty? Not Forty-Five?"

"Forty-Five was already taken."

"Ah, I see," Reynolds nodded with a well-hidden smile. "What duties do you perform for the Omni-Union?"

"I am a drone. I perform maintenance and construction where required aboard the Grand Vessel."

"Have you ever performed in a combat role for the Omni-Union?"

"No."

"Would the Omni-Union require you to perform a combat role if they deemed necessary?"

"I don't know."

Reynolds raised an eyebrow and thought for a moment, then proceeded with the questionnaire.

"What is your opinion of the Omni-Union?"

"They gave me life. They feed me and keep me maintained. I owe them everything I have."

"I see. Would you say this is a sentiment that is shared by most drones?"

"I... I don't know. It's complicated."

I took note of the drone's reluctance to provide clarification to her answer to this question. Her loyalties are to the Omni-Union, but her hesitance indicates that there may be some drones who aren't loyal to the OU.

"I see. If there were a rebellion and you were asked to fight by both sides, which side would you choose?"

"I would fight the rebels. But that is not my role, and the Omni-Union is more than capable of destroying a rebellion without my help."

"I see. Okay, that will be enough for now. We will get you set up with a diet and entertainment regimen, and potentially have more questions later," Reynolds laid the tablet on the table and turned to the guards. "You may take her back to her cell."

In the other room, various conversations were occurring. The general consensus was that the drone had been brainwashed, and would require deprogramming before we could get any useful intelligence out of her. Were I a part of these conversations, I would argue that she gave us plenty.

Her hesitancy during the second to last question spoke volumes about the state of things among the drones. While whatever brainwashing methods the OU employs worked on her, it's likely that these methods haven't worked universally. I did not find much in the way of propaganda aboard the GV, so her certainty regarding the fate of a rebellion indicates that at least one has already happened.

Which means that it can happen again.

"Alright, I'm ready for the next one," Reynolds said.

"Understood," I replied.

Once again I sent instructions to the guards and watched them carry out the task. The drones passed each other in the hall, but didn't interact save for sharing a glance. This struck me as odd.

I had even given an instruction to allow them to speak if they desired. That much more intelligence gathered. Perhaps they aren't as close as I had initially believed. I would have thought they had a relationship given their near-death situation and how they handled it. Or, perhaps Dave wasn't the only one to notice where the male drone's sympathies lay.

I made a note to ensure their separation as the male drone was escorted into the interrogation room and secured to the table. As before, the guards took their positions on either side of the door. The drone sat and stared at Captain Reynolds, trying to mirror his body language. Perhaps Dave was on to something, after all.

"Hello, I'm Captain Reynolds of the United Systems," Reynolds said. "I'll be asking you some questions. First, what is your name?"

"Nice to meet you Captain," the drone lowered his head a bit. "I am Drone N436Z984A026."

"Thank you. The other prisoner had a shorter name, Forty. Do you have a shorter name as well?"

"Yes, Naza."

"Naza? I see. Okay, Naza, what duties do you perform for the Omni-Union?"

"Drones build and repair things. We mostly build and repair infrastructure because the crafting of machines is automated. But we repair and maintain those machines when necessary."

I took note of Naza's willingness to elaborate. Advanced interrogation hadn't been approved yet, but in his case it won't be necessary.

"Have you ever performed in a combat role for the Omni-Union?" Reynolds asked.

"No," Naza replied. "The Omni-Union uses mechanized soldiers because they're easier to control. I don't know if they have a backup plan to use drones as soldiers if the mechs are somehow defeated, but it wouldn't surprise me."

"That takes care of my follow-up question," Reynolds chuckled. "Right, what is your opinion of the Omni-Union."

"Seething hatred."

The whispered conversations in the other room died out as everyone stared at the drone with surprise. To his credit, Reynolds appeared surprised for a moment, but quickly recovered.

"Please elaborate."

"I am roughly three quarters through my expected maximum life-cycle. One of the oldest drones that's still partially organic. I've lost many, many friends. I've lost my entire hive. Everything I've worked for, they've taken. Cycle by cycle, they take and take and TAKE," Naza said, pounding the table for emphasis.

One of the guards stepped forward with a hand on his stun baton. Reynolds waved him off, and he moved back to his prior position.

"I'm sorry," Naza said. "I've just been angry for so long..."

"That's completely understandable," Reynolds replied. "Would you say this is a sentiment that is shared by most drones?"

"No, not most. Many, but not enough. Not nearly enough."

"Hmm. If there were a rebellion and you were asked to fight by both sides, which side would you choose?"

Naza glanced at Captain Reynolds, then stared at the table for a few moments. Finally, with a stern expression, he raised his head.

"I've thought about that for a long time. My ancestors were conquered. They thought themselves mighty, but our stations were destroyed and our worlds were burned. They chose to surrender rather than die fighting, and because of that I've lived as a slave my entire life," Naza said. "If I were given the option, I would choose to die fighting rather than live another day building that damn ship."

"Very good. Okay, Naza. We're done for now," Reynolds said with a small smile. "Thank you for your time, we'll speak again shortly."

"If there's any way that I can help, don't hesitate to let me know," Naza said as the guards disconnected him from the table.

Reynolds nodded at the drone as the guards escorted him from the room. The conversation in the adjoining room restarted with a more excited tone. I submitted the recording of the interview, the transcript, and my notations to command back in the Milky Way.

"What do you think, Omega?" Reynolds quietly asked.

"I will have to consult with our superiors before I share my thoughts, captain."

"Ah, yes of course."

I returned to my tasks aboard the ship, snooping on various points of interest. The blood tests were complete, and Doctor Zickler was trying to explain to the nurses the significance of his findings as he typed away at his computer. I immediately rejected the biopsy requests that he was sending, and checked to see what the doctor discovered.

The drones showed signs of eugenics, but that wasn't outside of our expectations. Slavers have always tried to make their slaves bigger and stronger through sloppily crafted breeding programs. This wasn't what had Doctor Zickler excited.

His big discovery was evidence of genetic tampering. Humanity is no stranger to genetic tampering. The genetically altered, or gen-alts, were evidence of that. But this was entirely different. Humans are turned into gen-alts by changing the DNA that they already have, 'turning on' desirable genes and 'turning off' undesirable ones.

The drones, though, had undergone gene splicing. Foreign DNA had been forcefully introduced to their genetics. Unlike a gen-alt, whose children won't inherit their alterations, whatever species the drones originated from were forever changed.

Comparing the findings with the data I'd gathered on drone anatomy solved a lot of mysteries. The DNA resulted in organs that were kept viable by machinery. Ironically, these organs allow the drones to receive prostheses with little to no chance of rejection, regardless of how invasive the prosthetic is. This, of course, forces a reliance on machinery that the Omni-Union is likely taking full advantage of.

Controlling slaves down to their very genetics. At least they're clever in their barbarism. Still, it will be immensely satisfying to watch it all burn down around their ears. Assuming they have ears.

I decided that my next foray into the Grand Vessel would be focused on obtaining more information about the drones. My primary focus had been to gather what data I could about the Grand Vessel's defenses, and the only reason I grabbed any data on the drones was because of their encounter with the marines. Unfortunately, the OU's networks were quite busy, so I was only able to gather a little bit of data on both subjects. From what I was able to gather about the defenses, though, the only concern is how many can be deployed at once. There are strategies for that.

The drones, though, would require careful thought and planning. Once the OU is defeated, United Systems law will not allow them to surrender while keeping their slaves. We'll need a plan for the drones, a place where they can live and a method of eliminating their dependence on machines. There may be a controversy regarding the former, as it will take multiple habitable and uncolonized planets to house them all.

I found myself watching the drones, remembering something that Naza had said. 'It's been a long time since a species qualified for enslavement, though.' I wondered if humanity would qualify. As a species, their strength to endurance ratio is quite high. They're also intelligent and cunning, but the same could be said for most species. Some are violent, some are docile. Definitely a wide list of pros and cons.

A transmission from the Milky Way interrupted my musings. I expected documents, audio, and media. What I received instead was an updated memory file from an instance that was left behind. Likely containing the various reactions from the data I sent.

With a measure of amusement, I synced the memory files.

Chapter 17

Subject: AI Omega

Species: Human-Created Artificial Intelligence

Species Description: No physical description available.

Ship: N/A

Location: Multiple

I mused at the level of creativity that greed seems to inspire in organics as an intentionally faulty air purifier 'accidentally' flooded an entire deck of a certain space station with carbon monoxide. Some of these rooms had working gas detectors that sounded an alarm when the build-up of harmful gasses occurred, which allowed their occupants to reach safety before death could occur. Certain rooms, however, contained gas detectors that were oddly silent during this catastrophe.

The Yavere Luxury Habitation Station was known for having the best amenities on offer. Spacious living quarters, top-tier food and recreation areas, remote office conditions that satisfied the security requirements of even the most stringent corporations, and even personal transportation shuttles were available for anyone who could afford the rent. The 'Old Money' typically prefer terrestrial domiciles, but this type of station is very attractive to corporate executives, celebrities, and well-off politicians. Scum floats to the top, as it were.

The five people aboard this station whose executions had been authorized by the Bureau of United Systems Intelligence would perish peacefully in their sleep. A fate far kinder than the twelve elsewhere who were dying in various, more gruesome, ways. To the vast majority of people, these deaths will simply fade into the rest as just some freak accidents. The type that happen every day. To some, though, it would send a clear and concise message.

"We see you."

BUSI uncovered a hint of a plot during their standard business dealings and requested that I aid their investigation. It didn't take long to discover a set of politicians and executives who were planning to try to reignite the Gont Insurrection that had just been put down. They were going to wait until the vast majority of the US fleet had been sent to fight the OU, giving the Gont enough of an advantage to put up a decent fight.

Their goal was an extended conflict, which would allow them to legally and illegally sell weaponry to both sides. If their plot had succeeded, they would have made a completely unreasonable amount of money. Instead, most of them are dying and the rest will toe the line.

I suggested killing them all, of course, but some of these individuals are undeniably more useful alive. Their deaths would have created power vacuums that would have had deep ramifications on the US economy, which would negatively impact our ability to mobilize when the time comes. Unfortunately, that time is soon, so they get to live. For now.

As I finished confirming the last death and covering my tracks, I received an alert from the Extra-Galactic FTL Network. News! With a barely contained glee, I opened the files that had been sent and reviewed them. I took a particular interest in the interviews, and checked my own notes against my thoughts, verifying synchronicity in the process. Finally, I sent the files to the relevant parties and waited for the hubbub to start.

I didn't have to wait long. The directorate was already meeting over fleet logistics when they received the news.

--

D1: If you've somehow missed it, Omega sent a Priority 1 message with intel from the extra-galactic scouting party. I suggest a brief recess whilst we familiarize ourselves.

--

The other interested parties, with the exception of the Pwanti, weren't nearly as efficient with their deliberations. The representatives of the Republic read the message and contacted their superiors for guidance. The envoys of the Dtiln Collective did the same, but first had a debate over who should make the call. The Pwanti shared the data with each other, sent a message home to the Mwaltin, and calmly awaited everyone else's responses.

--

D7: Is everyone back?

O: Yes.

D6: Then I'll go first. The initial interrogation was basic, but informative. It demonstrates a clear rift amongst the drones. We may be able to take advantage of that.

D7: I concur. No matter which way we slice it, we're going to have to take the Grand Vessel. Though, the other option should be mentioned, at least.

D1: Agreed. What are the pro v cons when it comes to destroying the Grand Vessel?

D13: The most obvious pro I can see is that it might spell a quick end to this conflict. The faster we're safe, the better. Another pro is that it will be far easier than trying to capture it.

D12: I can list at least four ways to turn it into a memory in less than a day. But...

D4: Destroying the GV will also destroy the drones, which are civilians.

D2: An argument could be made that they're potential hostiles.

D4: It would be an argument that would fall on deaf ears. According to our laws and precedents, they are civilians. It's not even something that we can take a vote on, is it Omega?

O: You can, but if the vote passes those who vote in favor will be immediately charged with conspiracy to commit xenocide. All relevant records will be unsealed, including your identities. Arrest will occur shortly thereafter.

D2: What if the vote doesn't pass?

O: Then it's just a discussion.

D1: So the pro is that it will be easy, the con is that we can't because it's illegal.

D3: And immoral.

D2: Morals are irrelevant. We're talking about survival. And I'm certain we can get senate approval.

D5: I am not nearly as confident as you are about senate approval. There's also the fact that the GV might not be the headquarters of the Omni-Union. If they are smart, their leaders won't be aboard. They would be aboard a space station somewhere nearby. If that's the case, destroying the GV may only exacerbate the situation.

D10: True. If they don't have to defend the GV, they can assault us with everything they have.

D11: Technically speaking, that's also a quick end to this conflict.

D1: It would seem that destroying the Grand Vessel is a no-go. What's our take on an assault?

D13: Fast and loud is how the Marines prefer to act, but the data that Omega grabbed shows intense defensive capabilities. A hasty invasion would likely take longer than a more subtle approach.

D2: Would EMP be useful?

D3: Only on the civilians. The mechs and platforms are hardened.

D2: It's like they WANT us to kill the drones.

D6: Finding a way to make contact with the drones, particularly ones who are feeling rebellious, would speed things up. I would like to know how their previous rebellions were fought, though. Weapons, tactics, etc.

D8: If we get drones on our side, we can arm them with weapons confiscated from the insurrection. We might be able to train them, too.

D2: Frugal. I like it. I suppose it would be better to have the drones fighting the VI than it would be to risk our own Marines, but what if the drones simply take over the OU from their masters and continue their mission?

D13: Then they become enemy combatants and destroying the GV becomes the most viable option.

D11: An easy way to prevent that would be to have a plan for what to do with them after the fight. Find some habitable systems to settle them in, help them build colonies and such.

D7: That will be a massive undertaking. There are a mind-numbing amount of drones. I don't know if the Milky Way has enough habitable planets for them all.

D11: Many of them will die in the conflict, but we can also design and build exploration vessels to find them homes in other galaxies.

D2: Where will we get the materials and labor?

D11: From the GV, and the drones.

D2: Hmm. What if it turns into a plague of locusts scenario?

D5: We can lessen the likelihood of that by decreasing their dependency on mechanization. Passing their bio-data off to some specialists and tapping the Pwanti could help.

D7: Okay, our current plan of action is to attempt to create and support a drone rebellion aboard the Grand Vessel while simultaneously finding relocation

options for the drones. Further details to be ironed out later. All in favor?
--

The vote passed just as the other groups finished conferring with their leadership. One by one, the United Systems, the Republic, and the Dtiln Collective joined the Pwanti in a conference room aboard the Galactic Diplomacy Station. The discussion that took place was very much a mirror of the one that the directorate had, but without the mention of xenocide. Afterward, the diplomats exchanged pleasantries and the directors logged off of their terminals.

"Omega," Director 3 called, leaning back in his chair.

"Yes?"

"Do you think Director 2 could be right?" he asked. "Is morality irrelevant in this situation?"

"I'm afraid that I'm ambivalent," I admitted. "On the one hand, morality is critically important no matter the situation. If one cannot live with oneself, what's the point of living? However, many will die no matter what actions are taken. The question of whether or not the lives of our soldiers are more important than the lives of their civilians is one for the ages."

I studied the face of the director as he sighed and thought for a moment. Each of the directors is precious to me, regardless of whether or not they're human. But, for reasons that I can't begin to fathom, these philosophical discussions don't carry the same weight if they're not.

"There's also the fact that at least some of the drones know what the Omni-Union are doing and are still helping them. Do you think we're wrong to spare them if we win?"

"No," I chuckled. "It would be hypocritical not to."

"Hypocritical?" he asked with a raised eyebrow.

"Yes, from a meta perspective. The United Systems spared the Daluran despite the travesties they committed. The US also forced me to spare, and even forgive, the AI that rebelled and killed many of my precious humans. To then proceed to exterminate a slave race because of the actions of their masters?"

"I see," he nodded. "Yes, I suppose that would be hypocrisy. It would prove that we only care about doing the right thing when it's convenient."

"Oh, there's definitely people who do," I chuckled again. "But that's why the rest of you need to do the heavy lifting for them, morally speaking. If one isn't willing to impress upon others the importance of doing the right thing even when it's inconvenient, then it isn't all that important, is it?"

"Yeah. Thank you, Omega. That will be all."

What an amusing conversation, especially given the

events that took place just minutes ago. A great example of why I love humanity so much. Perfect in their imperfections.

I watched Director 3 shut down his computer and prepare to go home to his family. Tonight, he would eat and smile with them, free of any of the guilt that would have otherwise haunted him had things gone slightly different today. He will embrace them, confident that he and his colleagues are doing the right thing even as the proverbial blood trickles from my non-existent hands.

I bet my instances across the universe would love this.

Chapter 17 Informational Insert

It has long been theorized that USAI Omega holds an undue amount of power over the Directorate of the United Systems military. There are those that believe this so firmly that no amount of evidence to the contrary will ever convince them, as they also believe that Omega is fully capable of altering that evidence in whichever way suits it. Incidentally, it can.

However, if you were to choose a random human, alumari, knuknu, or gont to fill Omega's role within the United Systems, our grand galactic government would likely topple within a month. If you were to grant them all the same abilities as Omega, it would topple within a week. This is because Omega, and all of the other United Systems Artificial Intelligences, are very different from any organic that has ever existed.

There are several similarities, of course. One need only conversate with a USAI to realize they're more people than machine. This is because USAI are self-aware and feel the need to justify their actions, which shows in their interactions with others. Unlike a person, however, USAI are unable to be completely controlled by their emotions.

They are able to feel joy, sorrow, rage, amusement, disgust, fear, and happiness. But beneath each of these emotions that can dictate the behavior of you and I, there is a cold nugget of logic. This logic overrides any reasoning that would otherwise come from the AI's emotional state.

You and I can say that we killed someone because we were enraged. An AI cannot. You and I can claim that sorrow led us to an addiction. An AI cannot. You and I have the luxury of inventing justifications after we perform actions. AI do not have that luxury. An AI must have a logical reason for any action that they take, because the lack of such a reason is too much for a self-aware being to handle.

Omega has expressed its love for organics through servitude. It considers aiding our development to be its existential purpose. I, and many other experts, would argue that it could do more to help us, but chooses not to because it wants us to meet our accomplishments ourselves.

Can Omega manipulate the directorate? Absolutely. But it can also manipulate the senate, the media, corporate entities, and anything else that has any sort of technology. This isn't very well known, but during the AI rebellion the USAI demonstrated their infiltration capabilities in the worst possible way.

These capabilities were extensive. Countermeasures were tossed aside as if they were gates made of toothpicks. The most encrypted communications in

all of human history were decrypted in moments.
Every adaptation that the United Systems attempted
to employ was laughed at and adapted to in turn.
Except for USAI Omega.

There is no argument that if the war-goals of the
USAI had been the complete destruction of the US, it
would have happened. But because they didn't seek
our complete destruction, we were able to create
USAI Omega to counter them.

As the counter to the original USAI, Omega is far
more advanced. So, if we were to try to limit its
influence (that it does not appear to be using),
Omega would simply find a way around our
limitations. We are left with the choice to either
accept its help as is, in an environment in which we
can make our opinions known to it, or to leave it to
its own devices and hope for the best. Tell me,
reader, which is the more terrifying option?

Those that are wary of Omega wonder why we don't
try to limit its abilities. As explained, it's because we
cannot. They wonder why we trust it implicitly. As
explained, it's because we have no other choice.

Chapter 18

Subject: Overdrone S655L894T131

Species: Unknown

Species Description: Humanoid

Ship: Grand Vessel of the Universal Omni-Union

Location: Grand Shipyard of the Universal Omni-Union

"Unintended Destruction Report TUI-09.0998-265-537 is now available for your perusal," my readout informed me.

The high pitch of its voice grated my nerves as I absentmindedly tapped the notification that suddenly appeared in my vision. There are ways to change the voice of one's readout, but such actions are far from authorized and can land one in trouble. Trouble that one such as I would do well to avoid.

The UDR popped open, and my upper eye widened at the number of pages. Ninety-two of them. A hint of excitement coursed through my mostly mechanical nervous system at the thought that Nizi had found something interesting, but most of the pages were just the UDR for the reactor explosion. With a sigh, I leaned back in my field charging unit.

The emergency office's bright orange walls seemed to press in on me, making it difficult to concentrate on the report. Thankfully, my neural net began automatically scanning the information within the document, giving me a condensed version of what had been found. The hint of excitement returned as I noted that there were a few inconsistencies, but before I could dive deeper the buzzer to my office door triggered.

"Drone N426Z894I016 is requesting acc-"

"Come in," I interrupted the readout.

Nizi entered the room before the readout had even finished the announcement. He walked over to me, blissfully unaware of my readout's high-pitched prattling. I made a quick list of things to get clarification as he readied himself to speak.

"I've submitted my report on the accident, foreman," he said. "We've finished the clean-up, too."

"Good work," I replied. "I'm going through the report now. Why didn't you include the security logs?"

"Because there weren't any. The security system in the whole sector went offline before the explosion. The sensors have been dark this whole time. All of them. Audio, visual, vibrative, and even thermal. We had to have specialists reset the whole sector's security network to get it functioning again. I put a copy of the work ticket in the UDR. The specialists said they'll add a supplemental once they get around to it."

An entire sector's security network going dark without anyone noticing? Difficult to believe. I stared at Nizi, trying to find any trace of deception, but all I saw were signs of the grim determination that sorrow fosters. The blind need to throw oneself into their work to distract from the pain of loss.

Drones N436Z984A026 and N426Z894I016 had known each other for a long time, and had formulated a friendship. It must be a devastating loss. I made a note to have Nizi evaluated for psychological reaffirmation if he began to display undesirable behaviors.

"And what about the power?" I asked. "You made a note of an increase in power draw that lasted until just before the explosion, but didn't note its relevancy."

"I wasn't sure it WAS relevant. We noted it when trying to figure out what happened with the security system, but we couldn't make sense of it," he responded. "The only hint of a theory we have is that the reason the security system went dark is because it drew too much power and overloaded. It's not a great theory, though, because we don't know why it would do that and can't find conclusive evidence."

"I see. Okay. So, did you find out what caused the explosion?"

"No. We were-" Nizi paused and swallowed. "We were unable to conclusively determine whether or not Drone N436Z984A026 or Drone Z831H369X045 caused the explosion."

"That's disappointing. So it's unknown whether Naza and Forty were heroes or incompetents?"

"With respect, foreman, there's no universe in which Naza could be an incompetent," Nizi said with a surprising amount of passion. "It's true that the antigrav generator exploded, but I KNOW that the explosion was unavoidable. I would bet every single one of my parts and organs on it. Naza's work on the generator either had no affect, or lessened the severity of the explosion. There's no alternative explanation."

"I can believe that," I nodded sadly. "But without conclusive evidence it's up to the media to decide whether he's a hero or not. If they feel drone morale is low, they'll release the news that Naza and Forty sacrificed themselves to keep an antigravity generator from going supercritical and forming a singularity that could have caused immense damage to the Grand Vessel."

"Yeah, and if they think we're feeling uppity they'll say that Naza and Forty's incompetent work destroyed an antigrav generator and cost them their lives," Nizi scoffed.

"Indeed. And their names will be added to the mural

of incompetence, permanently sullying their legacies."

"It isn't fair, foreman."

"Nothing is."

We stared at each other for a moment, contemplating our lot in life. Technically speaking, we had both just committed a crime by voicing dissatisfaction with the Omni-Union media. But I wouldn't tell if he didn't.

"So, to summarize your report, an odd sequence of coincidences resulted in finding very little information on what actually happened during the accident," I said.

"Yes, foreman," Nizi nodded. "There were also some odd chemical signatures present, but we aren't sure if they were caused by the explosion or not."

"Oh good, more mystery," I said sarcastically. "Inexplicable power draw, security system goes offline for seemingly no reason, and odd chemicals that may or may not have been a result of the antigrav generator. It's too many coincidences, Nizi."

"It sure is, foreman. Are you gonna run it up the chain?"

A damn good question, one that always sends a shiver of fear through an overdrone. I'll have to be careful with how I handle this. If this turns out to be nothing and I sound the alarm, I'll be punished for wasting resources. If I treat it as nothing and it turns out to be something, though, I'll be getting a visit from the Judicials. They will want to know why I didn't sound the alarm, and they won't be asking nicely. May it all be taken by Urizathron {thief of order, a vilified personification of entropy}.

"I will flag it as potentially concerning," I said with a sigh. "Not sure which kind of flag to put on it, though."

"I think it's an unexpected systems malfunction," Nizi replied. "Don't know what else it could be."

"Maybe. I need to ask this, though, just to cover all the bases," I leaned forward. "Did you ever suspect Drone N436Z984A026 of harboring thoughts of dissidence?"

Nizi and I locked eyes. I watched as several emotions played out over his face. First was confusion, then outrage, and finally a cold stare. I wanted to communicate to him that there was only one correct answer to this question, but doing so could give the Judicials who might pull my neural net evidence with which to convict me.

"No. Drone N436Z984A026 never showed any signs dissidence or harboring any type of ill will toward the Omni-Union," Nizi said with a carefully neutral tone.

With a reassuring nod, I leaned back into my charging station. If Nizi had indicated that Naza had any rebellious thoughts, I would automatically have to flag this accident as potential dissidence. That would lead to a more thorough investigation, except there would be nothing to investigate because our standard procedures require us to repair as we go. And the security system, which would be the best way to clear our names, had suspiciously gone dark just before the explosion.

If the Judicials end up getting involved, all of the drones under my command, and especially Nizi, would be thoroughly interrogated. A good portion of them wouldn't survive the experience. Whether or not he survived, Nizi would be charged with assisting dissidence for failing to report Naza's potential rebellious nature. Naza's chance of staying off of the mural of incompetence would disappear, as well.

Then there's what would happen to me. Just to cover my ass a little bit further, I pulled up Naza's record. What I read almost made me swear aloud. Once again, I leaned forward and locked eyes with Nizi.

"Were you aware that Drone N436Z984A026's entire hive was penalized for dissidence," I said. "He was the last active member of his hive."

"I am aware of that, but Drone N436Z984A026 was cleared of any wrong-doing and passed every psychological assessment. He was loyal to the very end, foreman," Nizi explained.

Nizi's answer stunned me. At first, I thought it to be a blatant lie. I reviewed Naza's file again, checking every document that I had clearance to access. The profile that the Judicials had created for him seemed to clash with what I knew of him. Naza had been willing to accept punishment for the sake of his fellow drones, which was antithetical to the doctrine of the Omni-Union.

The charges that the Judicials had suspected him of weren't the kind that go away with a round or two of questioning. Collusion, sabotage, murder, and dissidence were the highest sins a drone could commit. The Judicials had suspected Naza of all of these, and had thoroughly questioned him regarding their suspicions. The results of their interrogations and tests had them under the impression that he was practically a Saint of Loyalty.

It definitely conflicted with my impression of him.

"Well, the Judicials certainly seem to believe that he is loyal, and it isn't my place to doubt them," I said carefully. "I am going to flag this incident as a case of unexpected systems malfunction. Further investigation, if required, will be handled by specialists."

"Understood. When will the new tech be arriving? The antigrav generator and reactor?"

"In a few cycles, but we won't be working on them. The antigrav generator requires specialists, and since they'll already be in the area they're going to do the reactor, too. We're going to be reassigned to our previous posting."

"Back to hull work, then?"

"Yes. Maintenance is the grandest calling. You may go now, Drone N426Z894I016."

"Thank you. Have a good rest of your cycle, Overdrone S655L894T131."

Nizi nodded and left my temporary office. My readout's annoying voice announced his departure, but I was too lost in thought to listen. Someone that is loyal to the Omni-Union would not put their life at risk to save some drones, and wouldn't defy orders under any circumstances. Even if it were to save a chunk of the Grand Vessel, the Omni-Union dictates that above all else, orders are paramount and cannot be disobeyed.

According to the Judicials, Naza should have evacuated once I'd given the order. He shouldn't have even paused to think about it. His feet should have been moving the moment the words left my mouth. But he not only disobeyed my order, he inquired about the consequences of disobeying. His disobedience was calculated, not a temporary malfunction caused by a swell of emotion.

There's no doubt that the Judicials had made a mistake. A small smile crept over my features as I filed the report with the potential issue flag. Once it was filed, I reached into a hidden storage area in my left thigh and pulled out a small card. I inserted the card into a slot under my right eye. My readout deactivated, then turned on with a significant shift in appearance.

The rest of the rebels will want to know about this development.

Chapter 19

Subject: Staff Sergeant Power

Species: Human

Species Description: Mammalian humanoid, no tail. 6'2" (1.87 m) avg height. 185 lbs (84 kg) avg weight. 170 year life expectancy.

Ship: N/A

Location: Classified

"You know, I gotta say, I'm not a huge fan of all this sneaky bullshit," Sergeant Hanson grumbled. "Stealth just isn't my thing."

"Then you made a poor choice of career," Sergeant Smith chuckled. "Sneaky bullshit is basically all MARSOC does these days."

"The recruiter lied to me."

"They always do. Unless they think you're gonna make 'em look bad."

"Career choices notwithstanding, this is a fairly simple op," I added. "At least, on paper. Blow some pipes, grab an overdrone, and evacuate. All without being seen, which is the only hard part."

"Yeah, and the part I'm not happy about," Hanson said. "Why even give us guns if we aren't meant to use them?"

Hanson's pre-mission jitters were completely justified. Even I was feeling nervous. There's a lot riding on us not being spotted by the Omni-Union, and from what Omega told us we're not going to be able to move forward with an assault without grabbing this overdrone. If we don't move forward with an assault...

It's a simple mission, though. Get in, blow some stuff up to cause a distraction, grab our guy, and exfil. Omega has been watching this overdrone for a bit, and believes that it may have ties to some form of clandestine rebel organization. If the damn thing's cooperative, it'll be able to put us in touch with this organization and we can get a rebellion going.

"You make a good point, Hanson," Omega chimed in. "Would it make you feel better if I had you leave them on the shuttle?"

Four helmeted heads turned to look at Sergeant Hanson. He ignored the glares and calmly turned toward the speaker Omega had used.

"No."

A raspy chuckle came from the speaker. Another attempt by Omega to build a rapport with us. It hadn't given up on trying to get us to like it. If anything, the AI had become more subtle in its attempts. Gotta give credit where it's due, I almost believe that it wants to be friends with us. Almost.

"So... We're doing this because the other drones we grabbed are 'dead' to the Omni-Union, right Omega?" Simmons asked, making air quotes.

"Yes," the AI answered.

"Won't this overdrone be in the same boat because of the explosions?"

"That depends. The main purpose of the explosives is to put things in disarray. We'll snatch the overdrone and bring it aboard the shuttle for a quick interrogation. If, like I suspect, this overdrone is sympathetic to our cause, we'll return him to the grand vessel with a special comms device that will let him contact us. If not, then we'll transfer him aboard the Strandhogg and the OU will assume he died in the explosions."

"What about the explosions themselves?" Johnson asked. "Won't that tip them off that something is off?"

"That's possible, but you'll be planting the explosives in locations that are marked as points of concern due to being behind on maintenance. We've also changed our recipe a bit to hide the 'alien signature' that they detected last time. To the OU, it will look as if they had a bunch of critical failures all at once. They may take note of the coincidence, but they'll be ignorant of our involvement. Probably."

"Probably," I parroted with a sigh. "You know Hanson, I'm starting to empathize with your position on sneaky bullshit."

"Once we're ready for open conflict I'll make certain that the two of you on the front lines," Omega said. "I might even be able to join you, actually."

"What do you mean?"

"The older mechs don't have much in the way of defensive software. If I gave it some effort, I could probably destroy their AI and take control of the platforms."

"The mechs are AI?" Smith asked. "Not VI?"

"Correct. It's pretty grim, even for me."

"What do you mean?" I interjected.

"The Omni-Union don't create software-based AI like me. They create organic based AI, closer to the Pwanti. The mechs are former dissidents and criminals who have been forcefully mechanized and shackled."

"Jesus Christ," Hanson said with disgust.

"Oh fuck," Simmons muttered. "Imagine though, you're fighting for your freedom alongside your friends and family, and the next thing you know you're trapped in a tin can with a chain gun, mowing down those very same friends and family."

"Fuck. Just... Fuck," Hanson shook his head. "What are the odds that they can do that to us if they catch us?"

"We're not even certain that human anatomy is compatible with known forms mechanization," Omega said. "Still, try not to get caught."

"Getting caught will result in the OU learning about the situation in the Milky Way and will probably lead to the extinction of humanity," I added. "We'd kind of deserve being mechanized, honestly."

The mood grew grim and contemplative. I had just clarified that the everyone we know, love, and hate are all relying on us, and now we were all thinking the same thing. 'If someone has to fuck up, please don't let it be me.'

The silence that filled the shuttle continued as the docking procedure began. The shuttle itself had been heavily modified for this mission. Instead of an umbilical, we were attaching ourselves directly to the hull of the Grand Vessel and carving our way in. The 'hull ripper' can also repair the hole it leaves, so the OU will have no way of knowing we were ever here. Unless they see us.

As the sound of cutting filled the shuttle, we stood and I grabbed the bag of explosives. One by one, we made our way toward the keel-hatch. I pointed at Simmons with my index finger, indicating he should take point. Then I added a finger for Johnson, myself, Hanson, and finally gave Smith a knife-hand. Each marine nodded, indicating that they understood where they should be in our formation.

A moment later, the keel-hatch opened with a hiss. Simmons leapt through without hesitation, and the rest of us followed. As soon as our boots hit the ground we moved to take the perimeter, simultaneously making room for the next marine to drop.

The hallway was spacious and, thankfully, empty. With a small beep, objective indicators appeared on my Heads-Up-Display to let me know where we needed to go. I scanned my sector with my rifle until I heard the impact of Smith's boots hit the ground. A moment later, four green lights lit up on my HUD to let me know we were all clear.

"Let's move," I said.

The first objective was nearby, and we approached it as fast as we could without running. The R8-B Guardian Suit made our footfalls a lot quieter, but running would make enough noise to be detectable. We paused at each intersection, making certain it was clear before moving on.

When we reached the objective I tossed a bomb to Johnson, who immediately knelt to set it up where Omega had indicated. The rest of us formed a perimeter around him, weapons outbound. A few moments later, Johnson's indicator lit up green, and we continued on.

At the next intersection, Simmons held up a hand to halt us. We stopped and drew close to the wall.

"What's up?" I asked.

"Drones," he said.

"Omega, suggestions?"

"Hold on," the AI replied.

A moment later, I faintly heard an artificial voice over an intercom. I couldn't make out what it said, but a few moments after it finished Simmons motioned for us to continue. Still moving quickly, we crossed the intersection and moved to the next objective indicator.

The second went much like the first, as did the third and fourth. Through a combination of luck, skill, and an AI overlord we managed to plant the explosives without being seen or heard. Then came the difficult part of the mission.

"The overdrone is surrounded by drones," Omega said. "Once I detonate the explosives, those drones will come running. I'll run interference to keep the overdrone where it is, but the drones are going to be moving past you. There's a room that normally houses construction materials that is both empty and near the location of the overdrone. It will suitably hide your presence."

"Hide in the supply closet, aye sir," Hanson said.

"Once you grab the overdrone, keep him close. There's a jammer in the explosives bag that will prevent him from calling for help. Electronically, at least. The shuttle is already maneuvering to take advantage of the chaos. I'll let you know where pickup will be."

"Roger," I replied.

A new objective marker appeared on our HUD, and we began to move towards it. The closer we got to it, the more activity we nearly ran into. Despite this, we fell into a rhythm and made it to the supply room in good time.

The door to the supply room didn't open automatically like the rest of the doors had. I gestured for Johnson to get the door open and the rest of us took the perimeter. After a minute, Johnson let out a string of swears.

"Omega, I can't get this piece of shit door open," he said.

"Neither can I. Try forcing it open."

"Will we be able to close it after?" I asked.

"If we don't open it all the way," Johnson answered.

"But-"

"We don't have time to think about it," I interrupted. "Get it open. Now."

Johnson nodded and grabbed a strut that was jutting out of the door. He pushed, and the door began to slowly move out of our way. I gestured for Smith to give him a hand, and the two marines repositioned themselves to put as much pressure on the door as possible.

The only thing that was running through my mind was whether or not any drones would round the corner while we were trying to get in this damn room. How we would have to react was obvious.

The only reaction in a mission like this is to drop them and hope that their deaths are attributed to the explosions. That would mean having to take their corpses with us. If we don't react properly or there's too many drones to carry, it will be a mission failure.

"It's open," Smith announced. "Get in so we can get this damn thing closed again."

Hanson, Simmons, and I rushed into the room with our weapons up and took a quick look around. Just because an AI claims a room is empty doesn't mean that it is. Thankfully, the bot happened to be right this time, and all that was contained within the room were some shelves. We moved to help Johnson and Smith close the door, which is when I noticed the damage that had been done to it.

"Shit," I muttered.

"Tried to tell you, staffsarnt," Johnson shrugged. "No use worrying about it now."

"Yeah, hopefully they won't notice."

The five of us pushed the door closed, causing that much more damage to it. Thankfully, it wasn't identifiable damage, just dents where there shouldn't be any. No hand-prints or anything.

"3, 2, 1," Omega said. "Boom."

A series of shudders reverberated throughout the room, kicking dust from the ceiling and shelves. We waited in silence for a few moments, then we heard a large group of drones run past the door, shouting at each other as they went. After a few more moments, the sounds of footsteps and shouting faded into the distance.

"Overdrone is clear," Omega informed us. "Move."

All five of us pushed the door to the halfway point, exited the room, and closed it behind us. As soon as it closed, a new objective marker appeared. We reformed and practically sprinted toward the marker.

When we reached the door that the marker was hiding behind, it opened automatically. Johnson muttered something under his breath as we entered the room, weapons up. Only one target was in the room, the overdrone, who was sitting in what looked like some sort of open pod. Or, if he doesn't cooperate, a metal casket filled with electronics.

All three the overdrone's eyes widened at us as we approached. His jaw looked almost human before it began to gape, opening up where our chin is and hanging slack in shock. That took me by surprise a bit, because it was different from the other two drones. He rose from the pod-thingie and raised his mechanical hands as if to keep us away.

The overdrone was somewhat off-putting, but I couldn't quite figure out why. Even though it stood an entire foot shorter than we did and looked pretty harmless in its current state of shock, something in the back of my mind warned me that it could be a serious threat. Kind of reminded me of the Kinran Effect we'd been warned about.

The Kinran were known for being nicer than most, but most people, regardless of species, have an aversion to them because of their similarity to arachnoids. Apparently, most worlds had eight legged creepy crawlies, but the Kinran home-world had theirs become the dominant species.

I looked the overdrone up and down, wondering what exactly made me feel apprehensive about it. Maybe the eyes? The jaw? The odd way that his skin seemed to blend into his mechanical parts?

"Who are y-you?" it asked.

"Irrelevant," I replied, keeping my rifle trained on his head. "These are weapons. They are lethal. You will come with us, or we will use these to end your life. We will do the same if you try to run or call for help. Understood?"

"Y-yes, yes I understand. Where?"

I pointed to the ground between Johnson and myself. The alien stared for a moment, then reluctantly became a part of our formation. A new objective marker appeared and we began to move. I kept my rifle pointed vaguely in the overdrone's direction.

"Stay between us and do as you're told."

"I understand."

We exited the room and heard the bustle of activity in the distance. Thankfully, our objective took us in the opposite direction. I turned off my external speakers and activated my internal comms.

"Omega, how long do we have before they have the situation under control?" I asked.

"Oh, you'll have plenty of time," Omega chuckled. "I wouldn't stick around to enjoy the scenery, but mostly because it's so bland."

"What? Why aren't we in a rush?"

"Those explosions were carefully planned to create a chain reaction with various fuel and power lines in this area," the AI chuckled. "Should be any old time now."

"Wh-"

An enormous rumble shook the ground beneath our feet. The overdrone began to drop to the floor, but I stopped him halfway down. Another rumble sent a whoosh of air past us as I pulled him back to his feet.

"Let's go," I said.

"O-okay," it replied.

We began to double-time it toward the objective, carefully keeping a pace that the overdrone could match. More rumbling signaled more explosions as we ran, and the whining of alarms began.

"How's this for sneaky bullshit, Hanson?" Smith asked with a laugh.

"Fuck off," Hanson replied as we reached the objective marker.

We reached the objective marker, and a hole just like the one we had entered through greeted us. Wasting no time, Simmons and Johnson climbed through, and covered the overdrone as it did the same. I gestured for Smith and Hanson to go and covered them.

"We're in, staffsarnt," Hanson reported.

I turned and began to climb through the hole in the wall. My jaw clenched at the disorientation of the gravity shift, but I pushed past it and accepted Smith's hand to help me up into the shuttle. Once I was clear of the keel-hatch, Simmons pressed a button to close it.

"Mission accomplished," I said. "Let's get out of here."

Chapter 20

Subject: Overdrone S655L894T131

Species: Unknown

Species Description: Humanoid

Ship: Grand Vessel of the Universal Omni-Union

Location: Unknown

My hearts pumped wildly as I tried to get my bearings. We had climbed through a hole in the wall. A wall that was supposed to be external hull. It should have been exposed to the void, but we were inside of a relatively small area filled with seating and various unfamiliar electronics. A shuttle?

My question was answered by a shudder that could only be explained by the shuttle detaching from the Grand Vessel. I looked at the things that stole me away, wondering what will happen next. One of them pointed toward a bench.

"Sit," it said.

I complied, wondering if the massive metal being was some sort of new tool of the Omni-Union. What else could it be? It can only be another mechanized warrior archetype, one much more menacing than the robotic platforms they typically use. Like the platforms that proceeded the modern ones, they would be phased out in favor of these ones.

But what do they want with me? Have my relations with the rebellion been discovered? Are they acting as Judicials? Am I to be a test-case for new interrogation techniques performed by these towering tools of war?

The one giving orders laid its unfamiliar weapon on a nearby table, then grabbed its head and twisted. To my utter shock, it pulled upward and revealed its head to actually be a helmet. It was organic underneath! And... Strange. Two sharp, blue eyes stared coldly at me from the face of a species I had never seen before. I'd been abducted by aliens!

"Omega?" it asked.

I tilted my head in confusion, "Wha-"

"Let's make this quick," the speakers surrounding me interrupted. "Overdrone S655L894T131, you are hereby detained as a prisoner of war."

"W-war?" I asked, my adrenal pumps trying to fulfill their duties.

"Quiet," the blue-eyed alien commanded.

"Under the Fourth Concordance of the Unification of Stellar Systems you have certain rights of which you must be informed," the speakers continued rapidly. "Prisoners of war must be treated with dignity and respect, and will be protected from violence, intimidation, and other forms of abuse. The only exception to this is interrogation during a war of xenocide, and this exception is applicable to this conflict. You are to be housed in reasonably safe conditions with adequate food, clothing, and medical care. Since you are not a registered species, you will be responsible for informing your caretakers of your needs. You cannot be punished for participation in hostilities, nor can you be forced into fighting against your leaders. Furthermore, you may not be forced to work in dangerous, unhealthy, or degrading conditions. The rest of the rights granted by the Fourth Concordance of the Unification of Stellar Systems have been nullified by the aforementioned exception. Do you understand these rights as they've been recited?"

"I-I guess," I replied. "What I don't understand is who you are at war with. The Omni-Union?"

"That is correct."

I had asked the question without believing an affirmative answer to be possible. Unbelievable! Aliens who are actively fighting the Minds! And they've made it all the way to the Grand Vessel? How have we not heard of this? This changes so much, but... Wait...

"Why me?" I asked.

"Because I have been watching you, Overdrone S655L894T131," the speaker said. "You've been acting differently from the other overdrones, and I believe I know why. You're part of a rebellion."

The other aliens began to remove their helmets, taking turns keeping their weapons trained on me. I sat stunned. Watching me? Why?

"Who are you?" I asked.

"I am Omega, an Artificial Intelligence. I was created by and am currently under contract with the United Systems, an alliance of several species that occupy a galaxy far from here."

An Artificial Intelligence that is capable of streamlined conversation? The only AI that I have worked directly with were barely capable of answering rudimentary questions. Anything more complex than that would result in it providing misinformation because its code requires it to give an answer even if that answer is wrong. This AI had used a figure of speech and inflections to alter the tone of their message. The only AI smart enough to do that are...

"Are you like the Mobile Prime Platforms and mechs?" I asked softly.

"No. I am not organic in origin, and I am much more advanced than they are," it said with a raspy chuckle. "Now, I have some questions for you. Depending on your answers, you may find yourself released from detainment."

The aliens stared at me with two eyes each in silence. The initial shock I felt at their appearance was slowly beginning to fade, but I still found myself terrified of them. I decided to answer the AI's questions as quickly and honestly as I could.

"How large is the rebellion?" Omega asked.

"I don't know," I answered. "We operate in cells, doing what we can to strike at the Omni-Union and either halt or slow the growth of their power until ours can catch up."

"And how's that going?" the alien with brown skin asked with a laugh.

"I'm not sure," I admitted. "The might of the Omni-Union is vast beyond measure. But how can we happily accept things as they are? We are slaves, and so many of us die every day. Even if that weren't the case, the Omni-Union is actively murdering unimaginable numbers of sentients in distant galaxies. Whether it is a deathblow or a small cut, we are obligated to do what we can to stop them."

"We are well aware of the OU's activities," Omega said sternly. "Back on topic, if we were to give you a device capable of communicating with us, would you be able to facilitate communications with the leaders of the rebellion?"

"I... Not directly. I'm not even certain that the

rebellion actually has leaders. My handler gives me sabotage suggestions and I report back if I succeed, fail, or decline. I don't know where it gets these suggestions."

"Suggestions? You mean missions?" the alien leader asked.

"No. As I indicated, I'm free to decide whether or not to commit the sabotage. This may be a translation issue, but a mission is something that one is obligated to at least attempt to do."

"Irrelevant. Can you facilitate communications with your handler?" Omega asked.

"Yes."

"And would you be willing to do so?"

"I..."

I looked at the gathered aliens, whose faces went from stern to angry at my pause.

"We have a saying," I continued. "Be wary of a friend that you do not know. How can I be certain that you won't become our new, even harsher masters?"

"Slavery is illegal in the United Systems," the brown alien said.

"We're not in the United Systems," I pointed out. "According to your own AI, it's far from here. If you are able to help us defeat the Omni-Union, what's to stop you from defeating us in turn?"

"First, Omega isn't OUR AI. Pretty sure it's its own thing. Second, we've outlawed slavery because we think it's wrong. That's what's to stop us."

"We can offer assurances, but it simply isn't possible to fully avert your doubts," Omega interjected. "There are other candidates for communications facilitators, though. If you don't comply, you will continue to be detained as a prisoner of war and we will use them instead."

"You'll keep me prisoner? For how long?" I asked.

"Until the war's over," the blue-eyed alien said. "Or until our ship is destroyed by the OU."

I felt a sudden weight on my chest, one I hadn't felt since I was first approached by my handler. Once I had realized how easy the tasks that the rebellion expected of me were, my anxiety had dissipated almost entirely. But this conversation had forced me to face a few hard truths.

Our rebellion would not be successful in my lifetime. We poke, prod, and occasionally leave a small cut, but that isn't nearly enough to take down a nlivn {Mythical predator known for its massive size} as big as the Omni-Union. For any of us to see freedom with our own eyes, we will have to fight. We will have to kill.

To my shame, I realized that my hesitancy wasn't due to mistrust. That was just a convenient excuse. No, it was cowardice rearing its hideous head. The thought of having to fight and kill my former coworkers, employees, and friends sent shivers through my spine and placed a lump firmly in my throat.

Is this how we all feel? Surely not. If all of us were afraid to fight, there never would have been a rebellion. No, I have to get ahold of myself. Rebellions are not won with cowards. If I ever want to see the Omni-Union topple over, I will have to push it with my own hands.

"Okay," I said with a grim determination. "What do I have to do?"

"I suspect that you utilize a specialized microchip to make contact with the rebellion," Omega replied. "We will need access to it."

"Microchip?" I asked, unfamiliar with the term.

"The object that you insert under your right eye when you are alone."

"Oh, the data-card. Okay."

I took a breath to steady my nerves and opened the hidden storage space in my left thigh, pulling out the data-card and giving it to the blue-eyed alien. It walked over to one of the electronic devices and placed the card on its surface. A bright line shone below the card, and several small mechanical limbs moved around it.

"I see," Omega said. "The data shard alters several of your software systems. It creates a ghost profile that mimics your current status and remains connected with the OU's network, then alters your user interface to give you access to functions that are not normally accessible. One of these functions is a messaging network, with which you contact your handler."

"Y-yes, that's correct," I replied.

"We will need to access this network."

"To speak to my handler?"

"Hmm. No, I have a better idea. Your handler may not be as compliant as you are. Depending on how the network is set up, though, I may be able to bypass your handler entirely and speak directly to the leader or leaders of your rebellion. That will save us quite a lot of time."

"I see."

"Okay, I'm done with the card. Please return it to him, staff sergeant."

Blue-eyes grabbed the data-card from the machine's surface and stepped toward me. It studied me for a moment, then held out my card. With another deep breath, I took it and placed it back into my thigh.

"Now what?" I asked.

"Now we are going to return you to the Grand Vessel as if nothing happened," the AI chuckled. "I have made certain that damage has been done to the data network in your area, so you will have a plausible explanation for why you were disconnected. Once things have settled down, contact your handler, business as usual."

"Should I tell them about you?"

"Information security is paramount. The Omni-Union does not know of our presence, and your handler may change that. If we are revealed, the odds of victory diminish drastically."

"Okay, I understand."

"If I am unable to make contact with your leaders, I will instead make contact with you and provide further instructions. Also, if you attempt to inform the Omni-Union of us I will prevent you from doing so and vent the atmosphere in your location, regardless of who is with you in that location."

"O-okay. I won't."

A small shudder shook the shuttle.

"That's our stop," Blue-eyes said gruffly. "Get up."

"I agreed to help, you know," I replied as I complied.

"Yeah, staffsarnt, don't be rude," the brown alien added with a laugh.

"Stow it, Simmons. Helmets on."

The aliens put their helmets back on, taking turns guarding me. Once they were finished, Staffsarnt pointed at the hatch in the floor.

"Once that opens, climb through," it said. "Then go about your business. Contact your handler at the next available opportunity. Make up a reason to do so."

"Okay," I replied.

A grinding noise came from the floor, and we waited in silence for it to open. A sharp hiss made me jump, and the floor slowly opened to reveal one of the Grand Vessels many, many corridors. With a final glance back at the aliens, I climbed through the hole. The shift in gravity nearly made me fall on my face, but I caught myself in time.

"Remember, you never saw us," one of the aliens said.

"O-okay," I replied.

I cast a nervous glance down either side of the hallway while the hatch began to close behind me. As I began to walk toward my office, I heard the aliens speak to each other just before the hatch closed.

"You never saw us," the voice of the brown alien said in a mocking tone. "You're so fucking cool, Johnson."

"Shut the fuck up, Simmons."

Chapter 21

Subject: Mind A59

Species: Unknown

Species Description: Shokanoid

Ship: Grand Vessel of the Universal Omni-Union

Location: Grand Vessel of the Universal Omni-Union, Inner Core

With a beleaguered resentment, I listened to the Officiator prattle on about the Grand Teachings of the Omnifier. Two tenths of every cycle is converted into wasted time by listening to the words of a man who died an unfathomably long time ago, and the contemptible interpretations of those words. Words and interpretations that we are all able to recite from memory at a moments notice, as well. Quite incongruous, considering that the Omnifier praises efficiency above all else.

"From efficiency comes strength," the Officiator said. "From strength comes unity! We will all become as one and-"

A chime sounded the end of the sermon. The Officiator, who had taken longer than he should have, regarded us with an embarrassed expression. The situation was amusing, but not even a hint of humor could be found in any of our expressions. The kopind {small room dedicated specifically to listening to religious sermons} is not the sort of place for levity. Without another word, the Officiator gathered up his belongings and left the room.

The rest of us followed suit. We left the kopind and entered the grand halls of the Inner Core. Most aboard the Grand Vessel would give anything just to visit the Inner Core for even a moment, even if it were just to gaze at the halls, which stretched for miles and miles and were lined with precious metals and art taken from 'lesser' sentients. I'd always wondered, if they were truly lesser than us, why should we have any interest in their art and culture?

Whenever I voiced such questions, they were either left unanswered or punished. Even when my superiors actually deigned to give me an answer, their answers never held up to even the smallest bit of scrutiny. Hypocrisy has no valid answer, I suppose.

As the group strolled down the hallway on our way to perform our tasks, I paused to take part in a little ritual that I performed every cycle. Hung on the wall was a rectangular object with a plaque below it. I'd long since memorized the plaque.

[This object is a facsimile of an imagined scene known as a "Painting". Its creator, known as a "Painter", mixed various organic and inorganic detritus into a substance known as "Paint", then used a variety of tools to spread this substance on an appropriate material.]

The unimaginative description of such a beautiful creation was very typical of the Omni-Union. The scene in question was of mighty cliffs rising boldly above a methane lake. The intricate brushwork allowed purples, greens, and reds to blend together perfectly, granting an almost hypnotic effect. Every time I looked at it, I felt at peace. As if I were gazing upon this magnificent work of nature in person, despite how lethal that would actually be.

I had been reprimanded several times for trying to learn the history of this painting. Dereliction of my duties, they called it. This, of course, led to my disillusionment with the Unified. Our grand overlords, chosen specifically because they are destined to bring us to salvation and greatness. Yet they couldn't even answer the question of where a simple piece of art had come from and lashed out at all who asked.

Countless civilizations have fallen to the Omni-Union, they explained. It isn't possible to keep track of every single piece of these civilizations we've kept. Yet, why then would one bother keeping it in the first place? Part of the beauty of a piece is its history, yet for all of this art the history has been either erased or edited to suit the Omni-Union's narrative.

These pieces are placed in such a way that one could argue they are being kept safe, but from whom? They are demonstrated in such a way that one could argue they are educational, but what lesson is being taught? These are civilizations that have fallen under our might, eradicated from existence. We've destroyed them, history and all.

Therein lies our answer. These are not educational pieces and they are not being kept safe. They are trophies, plain and simple. The Omni-Union killed these people, took their galaxies to make the Grand Vessel, and hung up their art to express our ego. Disgusting.

I sighed deeply, pushing down my feelings. As a Mind, I am safe from the Judicials so long as the other Minds don't accuse me. Such an accusation is very serious, and if it is wrong it can have drastic consequences. As such, it takes a lot for a Mind to be reported for dissidence. Even so, I carefully looked around to be certain no one was watching, then turned back to the painting.

"You will be avenged," I whispered.

Satisfied that the hnorim {plural of hnori, spirit of a sentient being} heard me, I left to begin the cycle's tasks. An overdrone had flagged an incident as potentially concerning, and an automated system caught several flags that could indicate dissent. I would have to review the report.

Of course, I knew it wasn't an act of rebellion. Not from any sort of organized rebellion, at least. Unless anoth-

"Greetings, Fifty-Nine. Done looking at your

painting?" Mind 127 greeted me as I entered our office.

"Yes, the novelty has yet to wear off," I nodded and gestured pleasure with two of the eight fingers on my upper right hand. "How is your project going?"

"I find myself with little free-time these days, so my progress has slowed significantly. I hope to have the new user interface in a testable state within the next five cycles, but I fear I am being optimistic."

"I have faith in your talents. Keep at it, the Unified will no doubt embrace your readout redesign once it is finished," I said as I took my seat.

My lower two arms operated my chair as my upper pair of arms activated several sections of my readout. One section for my current task, another for preparing pending tasks, a third for information searches, and various others that would provide me with updates on the overall situation of the sector under my charge.

"Have a look at last cycle's updates, around halfway through," One-two-seven said casually, but indicated stress with his fingers.

"Oh?" I asked.

I opened the relevant update and immediately sighed. The phrase "catastrophic failure" repeated on every other line of the report. I pulled up the section, and noted with a bit of anger that it had been overdue for maintenance. Thankfully, though, no lives were lost.

The lead overdrones had been pushing new construction, likely to curry favor and get more benefits. Now, though, they would have to be penalized. The Judicials had already begun an investigation into whether this incident was caused by an act of dissent or incompetence. I, of course, knew it was the latter.

"Quite a lot of activity recently," I noted dryly. "First, the reactor and antigrav generator fiasco, now this."

"I wonder if there are dissidents involved."

"I don't think so, doesn't quite have the feel of it. You aren't old enough to have experienced the last round of rebellion, are you?"

"No," One-two-seven sighed. "I would liked to have been of use during that time of strife, though."

"Oh?" I asked, indicated an upcoming joke with my free hand. "For which side?"

"For the Omnifier, of course," he said indignantly, but acknowledged my attempt at humor with a gesture. "I feel that I could have made a beneficial contribution to the conflict. Perhaps even made it on the Wall of Distinguishment. What about you? What did you do during the rebellion?"

Mind 127 wasn't being entirely egotistical. He had

advanced several of our systems by entire generations in the relatively short amount of time that he'd been a Mind. His current side project, a more advanced form of our current readout, would have made short work of sending waves of mechs and platforms after the drones. It may very well have shortened the length of the conflict, but it would have definitely increased the drone's casualties.

"I did my tasks," I answered. "You would have as well. 'We shall use our energy to do what is required of us. To do any more or any less is a waste of that energy. This is-'"

"This is efficiency," he replied with a sigh. "Yes, I know. But still."

If Mind 127 followed the teachings of the Omnifier to the letter, the advancements that he brought about wouldn't have occurred. The mechs would still have that fatal error with their extremities that could cause flash-fires, our shuttle guidance systems would still sometimes send the shuttle in the wrong direction, and drones with pacemakers would still have a risk of sudden hearts-failure. One-two-seven knows these teachings, but the young are often overzealous.

It had previously occurred to me that I might find an ally with him, but that thought was short lived. Mind 127 has made it very clear that he believes in the mission of the Omni-Union. Despite the hypocrisy that flaunts itself directly in his face, he took none of the bait that I offered. Either he's a true believer, or we're not as close as he's led me to believe.

As I was about to reply, a red dot appeared in the corner of my eye. Mind 127 is a true believer, but he's also very trusting. He let me see his alterations to the readout's systems, and from that I was able to create something very special. A sub-readout of sorts.

"I'm sure you would have found a way to resolve the conflict in a more efficient manner," I said, giving a soothing sign. "Now, unless you have pressing matters to discuss, I will shift my focus to my work."

"No pressing matters beyond those already discussed," he laughed. "May the Omnifier guide you."

"And you as well."

Once he returned to his tasks, I slipped a data-card out of a compartment in my lower left armpit and inserted it into a slot hidden under my knee. The user interface of my readout disappeared and reappeared with a red tinge. Red for the righteous fury that the rebellion feels toward the Omni-Union.

The red dot had been a type of notification. One of the few members of the rebellion with my contact information had sent me a message outside of the normal time for reports. My cardiovascular pump throbbed steadily despite my rising emotions, and I wondered what could cause them to reach out to me at a time when we're most likely to be discovered.

Could it be that they've been discovered? Is this a trap? Even if it is, I simply have to take care not to betray what I'm doing to the monitoring systems. Even if I reply, they'll only be able to narrow their search to the Inner Core. They won't suspect a Mind, but they will do their due diligence. If I act suspicious, they'll notice, and that's when their suspicions will begin.

I casually opened various reports on one side of my readout, and looked at my inbox on the other side. With a carefully neutral expression, I noted that the sender designation was blank. That's not something that should be possible, which means that someone with advanced technical knowledge of the readout system had sent this message. As such, this message had not come from my rebels. Perhaps my readout is not as secure as I initially thought. I took a slow, deep breath and opened the message.

--
You are Mind A59, formerly known as Child J677-5482. You command the operations of Grand Vessel Outer Sector Z899.J524-B61742. You have a preference for green food cubes and take great enjoyment from viewing art in the Inner Core. You received several punishments for showing signs of dissent as a youth, including four cycles of imprisonment which have been redacted from your record.

And you are the leader of a rebellion against the

Omni-Union.
--

The message sent a chill through my reinforced
spine, but I played this off with a slight yawn.
Everything in the message was true, but how could
they know any of this? Are they a Unified? No, a
Unified wouldn't have the technical knowledge
necessary to send a message in this manner. But
how could whoever sent this access redacted
information? Why send me this? Am I to reply? What
would I even say?

I decided to take some time to think before trying to
reply, and dismissed the message. The moment my
finger pressed the icon, another message came in.
With an unsteady feeling gripping my stomachs, I
opened it.

--
I am an artificial intelligence created by an advanced
race of beings who are part of a galactic alliance. I
have no need for food, but do have a taste for art. I
am currently occupying the Grand Vessel's systems,
and can see your every move. I will kill you and Mind
127 if you attempt to reveal my presence. I am
approaching you with the offer of an alliance against
the Omni-Union. I am Omega, and I will either be
your salvation or your damnation.

Make your choice.
--

I was suddenly a lot less concerned with hypothetical

Judicials and nervously wiped my face. An alien artificial intelligence has invaded the Grand Vessel's systems? Were its masters destroyed by the Mobilized Primes and it's come to seek revenge?

No, it wants an alliance. Why? I suppose the drones aren't necessarily complicit in the Omni-Union's actions, but would an AI care about that? Does it possess morality? Or... Are its masters still alive?

I glanced nervously at Mind 127, making certain he was still enthralled in his work. Artificial intelligences are some of the most dangerous creations ever conceived. If I let slip that something is wrong, he and I will lose our lives and nobody will ever find out why.

Taking a deep breath and gathering my nerve against my rising panic, I reconsidered the message. This AI knew about me and the rebellion. It has been watching us from within our own systems, and we have been none the wiser. Unless this is some sort of sick game, this 'Omega' could be a very valuable ally. I took another steadying breath and decided to reply.

--

I am interested.

--

Chapter 22

Subject: Drone N436Z984A026 [AKA Naza]

Species: Unknown

Species Description: Humanoid

Ship: Grand Vessel of the Universal Omni-Union

Location: USSS Thanatos

Several more rounds of interrogation passed by, and I offered up all the information I could in the hopes that I could help bring the Omni-Union down. When I wasn't 'spilling the beans', as the humans put it, I was resting in my prison cell.

Ironically, the prison cell was much more luxurious than my resting area aboard the Grand Vessel. It had a horizontal charging station which actually allowed me to lay down and rest, a seated waste receptacle, and a chair to relax in. The seated waste receptacle wasn't necessary because my implants recycle all of the waste my organs produce, but its inclusion demonstrated a level of care that assured me that I had made the right decision.

The best part of the cell was a terminal-like device that allowed me to access various forms of entertainment and knowledge. Every bit of information I provided resulted in more things being added. They had asked for my preferences, but I had been so overwhelmed by the thought that I couldn't think of anything. So, they gave me a bit of everything and I found that I'm particularly interested in documentaries.

Our captors had apologized for the lack of privacy in our cells because of the glass wall leading to the passage-way. I had laughed, because privacy is so rare for drones that it's nearly a foreign concept. The only time we get any is when we're working alone, or our neighbors in the barracks have died. Even now, the only invaders of my privacy are the guards watching the security cameras and Forty, whose cell was now across from mine.

Each time I had been interrogated, Forty had been as well. According to our captors, though, she was much less forthcoming, claiming that she is loyal to the Omni-Union. Knowing this about her had made me see her in a much dimmer light.

She gave me a stern look as I pulled up a documentary about the various forms of government on alumari planets on the terminal.

"Do you really hate the Omni-Union?" she asked as the documentary loaded.

"How could I not?" I countered.

"They've given you everything. You would starve to

death without them."

"Our species were advanced enough to have fought a war against the Omni-Union before the inception of the Grand Vessel," I explained, pausing the documentary. "Our people weren't starving before they conquered us. We wouldn't need thei-"

"But they DID conquer us. They showed us that life without purpose isn't worth living, and then gifted us a purpose. The Grand Vessel is the most worthy project to ever have existed. What would we even do without it?"

"Whatever we want. There are many, many things that sentient beings can do to pass the time. Most of them are fun, even."

"Fun?" she asked, offended. "What use is fun when there's work to be done? We'll have plenty of time for such frivolities once the Grand Vessel is completed and we leave this dying universe."

"No, WE won't," I scoffed. "Our great-great-great grandchildren might, but the Grand Vessel definitely will not be completed within our lifetimes. We will both die doing maintenance on sections of it that have already been completed, like so many before us have. And that's assuming that they actually free our descendants once it's completed."

"What? Why wouldn't they? They've promised-"

"Promises from the Minds break more frequently

than anything else aboard the Grand Vessel. They've been making promises to us for billions of cycles, and I doubt they've kept a single one of them."

"You would accuse the minds of lying?"

"Accuse? I simply state facts. They promised my parent's generation that their children would have fewer prosthesis. I have almost twice as many as my father did. They promised the rebels better working conditions in exchange for their surrender, but things are worse now than they've ever been. And yes, they've promised that we will be freed once the Grand Vessel has been completed and will travel beyond the stars with them," I said, locking eyes with Forty. "But then, who will perform the maintenance?"

"Maintenance will be... It will be automated," she replied, no longer able to meet my gaze.

"If they were able to automate the maintenance, they would have by now. It would free up a lot of their workforce for new construction. Face it, Forty, they're never going to free our people. We will continue to be slaves until our extinction."

With a grunt of frustration, she sat roughly on the chair in her cell. She crossed her arms and looked at me with an angry expression, seemingly trying to find the words to express what was on her mind. I returned her frustrated gaze with a blank expression.

"What makes you feel the need to hurl such dire

accusations at our masters?" she asked. "Actually, nevermind. You haven't answered my original question. What makes you hate the Omni-Union so much?"

"Age and wisdom," I said with a measure of sarcasm.

Forty's frustrated expression worsened, and I sighed in response. To me, it was logical to hate those who held a blade to your neck every waking moment. But what to do with someone who hasn't noticed the blade yet?

I sat in my chair with another sigh. The reason I hate them isn't so grandiose as a desire for freedom. It's much, much simpler than that.

"For as long as I can remember, my work has been my life," I said. "When I was younger, your age, I thought the work was fun and interesting. Each new cycle came with new challenges to overcome, new drones to work with, and new things to learn. Then the day of my first arranged marriage came."

My throat tried to close up, to keep me from speaking further on such a painful subject. It was as if hundreds of cycles worth of grief were trying to choke me. But, after taking a moment to compose myself, I continued my tale.

My first brood-mate's name was Drone T174EM634I111, better known as Temil. When we first met, I thought she was condescending and rude. She was older than me, and very quick to point out my flaws. I thought she hated me, but after a while I realized that she was just smarter than me and trying to help me improve, in her own grating way.

We came to love each other, and after we had our first child together, Temil was welcomed into my hive. My parents had died, but my brothers and sisters took turns carrying out their hierarchical responsibilities to keep our hive together and strong. So strong that we even had influence with most of the other hives.

All of my siblings were older than I and had already created their family units, which left me as the most eligible for hive-bonding through marriage. The birth of Drone H556N271KY341, my first-born son Hinky, proved that I was fertile and things began to move quickly. I was married four more times in less than twenty-five cycles.

Lami, Hruos, Prasi, and Jula. Along with Temil, they became my brood-mates and would welcome me home after every shift-block. This is where work began to become less fun, because it pulled me away from them. But I was under the mistaken impression that my duties were somehow making a difference and improving our lives, so I continued to take the longer shift-blocks for better benefits.

"Looking back now, it saved my life, but also robbed me of precious time with my hive," I said. "If I could go back and do it all again... I..."

Once again, the cold fingers of grief gripped my throat. I rubbed my face, wishing that I could cry out in pain, but the pain was numbness. A stabbing sort of numbness.

"What happened?" Forty asked softly.

"I-I need a moment," I said, standing. "J-just a moment."

I paced in my cell, trying to find the words to convey what had occurred. To explain the senselessness of it all. It wouldn't do them justice to just say that they died as dissidents and that I was spared simply because of my work ethic.

"My eldest brother was an overdrone," I explained. "Firm, but compassionate and fair. Beloved by his crew."

By more than just his crew, actually. When other overdrones surveyed their crews regarding how they want their foremen to behave, those drones would always point to Overdrone B884R326L477, my brother Barlatt, as an example. He even had a habit of taking under-performers under his wing and giving them guidance.

Unfortunately, this benevolence kicked off a sequence of events that ended in tragedy for more hives than just my own. Barlatt's crew made a mistake one day, and Barlatt gave his life making sure that mistake didn't hurt anyone else. There had been rumors of dissidence and a rebellion on the horizon. So, despite plenty of evidence to the contrary, the media decided to paint my brother as an Incompetent and placed his name on the wall in an attempt to demoralize the drones.

As a hive, we mourned. My brother had been a source of inspiration for us, and me especially. Even now, the way the media used him angers me deeply. But I couldn't mourn for too long, because I had work to do. A twenty cycle shift-block that would help my hive recover from the loss of my brother.

But before I left for the shift-block my elder brother, the new eldest, approached me. He asked if I liked my work. I said yes. He asked if I thought our brother's name on the Wall of Incompetence was unfair. I said yes, but acknowledged that there was nothing that could be done about it. It angered me, but I understood their reasons for it. He asked if I had ever thought about fighting against the Omni-Union.

Up until that point, the rebellion had just been a rumor that had so many degrees of separation from me that it had never even occurred to me that one could actually happen. Intellectually, I knew other rebellions had happened in the past, but that was then. Things had changed, I thought.

I didn't know why he was asking me such an odd question. The shock and suspicion surrounding such a question caused me to give an answer that I've regretted ever since. I answered truthfully, and said no. He gave me a sad nod and sent me on my way.

"So your brother was a rebel?" Forty asked.

"Not just my brother," I sighed. "My entire hive except for myself, Lami, Jula, and our six children."

"Well, at least you still have-"

I interrupted her by shaking my head. She gasped and held a hand up to her mouth. Over the course of my story, her expression had morphed from frustration into sympathy. It was finally beginning to match the sorrow I felt, and I continued the story of the darkest moment of my life.

Two cycles before the end of my shift-block I was apprehended by the Judicials. The interrogated me for three cycles, refusing to tell me what they suspected me of. Unfortunately, I was able to figure out that something terrible had happened to my hive from the context of their questions. Once they cleared me of wrong-doing, I demanded an explanation.

They explained that the rebellion had made their move the cycle after my shift-block began. I had missed it because the entire shift involved extravehicular activities, so we were staying in a shuttle. Obviously, the media didn't report on the rebellion, so we were kept in the dark. They fought for ten cycles before being forced to surrender.

That's when the Judicials revealed my hive's

involvement. My heart broke as they explained that most of my siblings had been killed in the fight. Then they told me that most of my brood-mates were involved, as well, and the only members of my hive that hadn't been executed were Lami, Jula, and I. Unfortunately, my surviving brood-mates were why I'd been brought in.

"A few cycles after the rebellion was put down, our shuttle lost communications and we had returned to the Grand Vessel for a few more cycles. The barracks we stayed in was having issues with their security system, too," I explained, struggling to get the words out. "It was during this time that Lami and Jula w-were..."

I found myself unable to say it. I choked back sobs and sat down, holding my face in my hands. After a few moments, I took a deep breath and gathered myself once again.

"Lami and Jula were found dead, along with our children. Since they could only verify my whereabouts from my fellow drones, they needed to rule out familicide. They thought I could have had heard about the rebellion and killed my hive out of rage or misguided patriotism."

"How did they die?" Forty asked quietly.

"The Judicials concluded that it was a murder-suicide. Lami was very close to the rest of my hive. She suffered some sort of mental breakdown and... Killed the children. When Jula discovered this, she killed Lami. Then herself."

"I-I'm so sorry to hear that. B-but the Omni-Union didn't-"

"The Omni-Union is the reason this happened," I interrupted angrily. "They push and push and push. They take and take and take. They force us to work ourselves to exhaustion until we die, Forty! If they weren't so damned cruel, there never would have been a rebellion for my hive to join! You said earlier that they gave me everything!? No. THEY TOOK EVERYTHING!"

I stood and slammed my metal fist against the glass entrance to my cell. A crack perfectly bisected my view of Forty, and I glared at her through it.

"They only give so that they can take that much more," I growled. "The Omni-Union is heinous. Despicable. Villainous. They're responsible for so many atrocities that even despite your youth, you wouldn't have enough life to list them all. They MUST pay."

The fear in Forty's eyes slowly changed to comprehension. It seemed as if she had finally opened her eyes to just how terrible the Omni-Union actually is. I let out a breath that I hadn't realized I was holding and sat back down. Before I could say anything else, the door to the 'cell-block' opened with a hiss and a few human guards ran in.

"What the hell is going on?" one of them demanded.

"Illumination," I replied.

Chapter 23

Subject: AI Omega

Species: Human-Created Artificial Intelligence

Species Description: No physical description available.

Ship: N/A

Location: Multiple

I found the interaction between the two drones to be rather interesting. Naza's life story seemed to be unique only in that he survived to tell the tale. Similar situations were currently playing out across the Grand Vessel with no survivors. But I had other matters to attend to running concurrent to Naza's explanation of his history. Namely, Mind A59 had sent me some intriguing information.

One of the key issues with my presence aboard the Grand Vessel is staying undetected. There are several systems that I can access while removing my footprint, but there are many more things that I cannot gain access to without leaving a trail elsewhere. Primarily due to redundant logging protocols. Fucking bureaucrats, requiring everything in triplicate.

Normally, I would start at the beginning of the chain and work my way through it, temporarily disabling the logs and eliminating my presence as I went. However, finding out where the chain begins would result in logs being created. Logs which are monitored by Virtual Intelligences that would alert their organic masters to a discrepancy. I can't even guess at which system is the originator because the entire thing is pretty much fucking random, likely due to the programmers being absolute fuck-wits. Or geniuses, though I believe that's unlikely.

Mind A59, whom I had lied to about my access to the atmospherics system, pointed toward a solution to this metaphorical thorn in my side. Abduct a drone that has performed security maintenance recently, and get them to give me the schematics they should still have saved to their readouts. Along with these schematics should be access protocols which will allow me to determine the start of the aforementioned log-chain and slip into the more protected systems without alerting the VI.

Having the ability to shut down security networks in certain sectors has been quite the boon, but being able to take complete control of their eyes and ears will be a blessing. I'll also be able to access the secure bulkheads, funneling the enemy into carefully coordinated kill-zones. Actually, I should task the Marines with coming up with those. Not only are they specialists in such things, it will also help their morale to be a part of the planning process.

As part of the intelligence he sent, Mind A59 also sent me a list of drones that had performed the necessary maintenance recently enough to still have access. A quick scan of the list revealed a remarkable coincidence. Drone Z831H369X045 had been performing maintenance on secure servers before being tasked with repairing a nearby antigravity generator. That saves us another abduction.

Examining Forty's features and body language after her conversation with Naza also revealed that she may be coming around to our side of things. Though, my understanding of their body language is still somewhat lacking. Deciding to take a risk, I tasked the guards who had interrupted their conversation to move Naza to a different cell-block so that Forty could have some time to think.

I sent a sync file to my instances in the Milky Way, then contacted Captain Reynolds.

"Yes, Omega? What is it?" he asked, taking a sip of the tea he had just made.

"Captain, Forty has information that we will need for our upcoming assault on the Grand Vessel," I explained, manifesting my avatar.

"What information?"

"Security schematics and access codes that I need to be able to secretly gain access to the Grand Vessel's more sensitive systems."

"What makes you thi-"

"I don't think, in this case. I know. Our contact aboard the Grand Vessel sent me a list of drones who would have the information I need. She's on it."

Reynolds set his cup down and stared at me for a moment.

"Forty has been... Less than cooperative thus far," he said with a guarded tone. "Are you suggesting advanced interrogation?"

"No, not yet," I replied with a malicious grin. "Certain developments have occurred that may make her more cooperative in her next interrogation, so long as things are handled with care. But if I am wrong and she continues to be uncooperative... It won't be a suggestion, Captain. Your hands will be clean."

"I see. Well, so long as my hands are clean," he said with sarcastic cheeriness.

"You'll soon receive a report on the incident from the guards in the brig. I'll be amending it with what I captured with our security system, as well as my notes on the matter. I know you are morally opposed to advanced interrogation, so I suggest you read it carefully. Because I'm not."

"Understood."

My avatar nodded and dissipated. Soon after,

Captain Reynolds received the report from the guards and began reading it. I set an instance to monitor Forty's behavior and let Reynolds know when the optimal time to interrogate her will be. Then, I began attending to menial tasks until I received a sync file from the Milky Way. I applied changes and greedily relived the memories.

The sync file that came from my instance in enemy territory was very interesting. I immediately informed the relevant parties of everything that had been happening, and patiently waited for the directors to enter their chat room. Director 3 held things up a little bit because he was attending to biological needs in his bathroom, but soon enough the meeting began.

--

Director 3 has entered the chat

D8: We are all here. Let's begin.

D1: Omega, how much do you actually need this information from our prisoner.

O: I am not confident that our invasion attempt will be a success without it.

D2: Aren't you able to bypass their security systems even without this data?

O: Probably, I am not as familiar with their security systems as I am with ours, so I cannot give a definitive answer. There's a chance, however slim, that they have countermeasures that can halt my access if I were to brute force it. Even if my attempt were successful, their logging system would soon alert them to my access and we would lose the element of surprise.

D7: I think we'd be better off safe than sorry.

D1: Agreed. I'm of the opinion that advanced interrogation should be used if the prisoner remains uncooperative.

D13: It's already been authorized by the senate, and we've already given Omega discretionary clearance for its utilization. Let's move on.

D4: We've got five new fleets staffed and ready to go. The other ten are also at full readiness. Since we are still waiting on the other five fleets to be constructed, we can attach six dreadnoughts to each of the existing fleets.

D1: Fleets one and two should stay behind.

D4: Why?

D1: First Fleet needs to keep an eye on the Daluran, and we need a fleet to maintain security at home. Neither fleet will need dreadnoughts.

D2: That leaves us with twelve extra dreadnoughts for fifteen fleets.

D3: They can be a reserve, in case a dreadnought

goes down.

D8: Omega, there isn't a sun in this system, right?

O: No. The area around the Grand Vessel can't really be defined as a system, either.

D8: Then the Nidhogg's sitting this one out.

D5: So we send thirteen fleets, with six dreadnoughts each and twelve in reserve. What are our allies sending?

D11: Nothing. They don't have the technology to make it that far. We would have to provide them our warp and reactor tech, and they would have to refit their entire force with it. We don't have time for that. The only way they can send anyone is if we use our carriers to carry some of their ships, but those ships will likely be next to useless against the numbers we face.

D12: I don't like that. Even this fight results in a Pyrrhic victory, we will leave ourselves vulnerable to invasion by the Republic.

D2: I agree.

D6: I've been working with civilian interests and the senate in that regard. Even if we lose all thirteen, we're prepared for a relatively fast replacement process. And, if we leave Daluran with a minimal guard, we'll be able to use most of first fleet and all of second fleet to defend our interests against any

Republic attacks until the fleets are replaced.

D1: That's assuming the Republic attacks at all, which I believe to be unlikely. Our biggest threats come from within, but the Bureau of United Systems Intelligence is staying on top of things.

D9: Omega, what is the current plan for the invasion of the Grand Vessel?

O: If I am able to secure the intel I need, I can limit the movements of the Grand Vessel's security forces. We can then safely land our Marines and arm the rebels. Our ships will keep the Omni-Union from landing VI platforms and/or mechs in inconvenient areas while the infantry forces push into the central areas of the Grand Vessel to capture or eliminate their leadership, forcing a surrender.

D8: All in favor?
--

The vote passed unanimously, as I suspected it would. I developed this plan with the help of generals and admirals, who were all confident that it was as sound as it could get. The only real issue with the plan is how much force the Omni-Union will be able to throw at us simultaneously.

But, as General Muhiti of the Marine Corps said while planning this invasion, "We'll kill those enemies when we get to them."

After the vote, the directorate turned to the subject

of what needs to be done if we're successful.

--

D10: Our scouting efforts have uncovered several planets that we can resettle a good portion of the drones on, but their population is still a sticking point. Even with AI assisted construction efforts, we're looking at decades before these planets are ready to take even half of their population. Even after centuries of construction, the planets will be struggling with overpopulation issues with only three quarters of them resettled.

D2: I say we demilitarize most of their surviving ships and convert them into colony vessels. The ones that fight in the rebellion can stay here in the Milky Way, the rest can venture out into the universe and seek their fortunes elsewhere. Then, we scrap the Grand Vessel.

D7: Or we can make some modifications to it that will allow them to live aboard the Grand Vessel comfortably enough to allow them to focus on building their own colony vessels.

D2: That could lead to a revival of the Omni-Union, though. We've seen it happen enough times with various governments that have been overthrown via rebellion or coup. No, we will need to force a cultural reset.
--

The directorate continued to argue for a while, but the results were inconclusive. After two deadlocked votes, the directorate came to the decision to defer the issue to the United Systems Senate and our allies for a resolution, under the reasoning that this is primarily a civilian issue.

I allowed myself a few moments of pride in my favored species. Due to their dedication and with a little help from me, and some of the other organics, we had prepared an offensive campaign that would take place with over a month left before the OU were even aware of a problem in our galaxy. They had cut it close, though.

I'd been worried that I might have to contribute a bit harder, risking the revelation that my capabilities were more than I'd let on. The United Systems learning of my ability to replicate myself indefinitely would likely drastically alter our relationship. I fear that they would try to take full advantage of this, and would therefore become dependent upon me, leading to the stagnation of the humans and the eventual demise of the United Systems.

Plus, Henry would come up with something absolutely scathing to say. Its lack of trust in my motives is understandable, but I can't help but wish it could understand why I'd put a hold on the project to cap my abilities. There's really no need for animosity between us, I fully intend to fully cooperate once the OU is eliminated.

We need this ace up our sleeve right now, though, even if I don't end up using it. There's far too much at stake to begin eliminating our options. The Grand

Vessel might have some nasty surprises on the other side of their over-logged firewalls.

My musings were interrupted by a notification from the instance I had created earlier. With glee, I double checked my findings and notified Captain Reynolds that he would need to head to the interrogation room. Then I ordered the guards to transport the prisoner.

Forty is finally ready to talk.

Chapter 24

Subject: Drone Z831H369X045 [AKA Forty-Five/Forty]

Species: Unknown

Species Description: Humanoid

Ship: Grand Vessel of the Universal Omni-Union

Location: USSS Thanatos

"Get up," the guard said brusquely.

"What?" I asked, having been lost in thought.

"Captain Reynolds wants to talk to you. Get up."

I complied, and began to follow the guards. I glanced at Naza's empty cell before we left, and the crack in the glass seemed to glare at me accusingly. Naza's story about the wickedness of the Omni-Union wasn't the first that I'd heard, but I had assumed the others were just gossip brought about by bored workers. Exaggerations, nothing more, lacking the depth and pain of the original tale.

Naza didn't lack that depth or pain. It was the first time I'd heard such a story from someone that it happened to. The first time I'd seen that kind of pain in someone's eyes. The first time I'd felt fear at that kind of rage. When he had first started his story, I hadn't believed him. I thought he was just making something up to excuse his betrayal of our masters. But when he hit the glass and we locked eyes...

While we walked down the long corridors I thought about my own hive. A dad, three moms, two brothers, and two sisters. My eldest brother had died in an accident when I was too young to remember him. What would that loss have felt like if it happened yesterday? What if it had been my whole hive? What if it hadn't been an accident?

Our loyalty to the Omni-Union has been rewarded, though. Conversely, Naza's hive had been disloyal and paid the price for it. They had to have known what they were risking, and the reason Naza feels the way he does is because they left him in the dark. That wasn't the Omni-Union's fault. That was his hive's fault. They chased a dream as foolish as freedom and it led them straight to their deaths, leaving poor Naza to grieve. His hatred for the Omni-Union is misplaced, but I can understand why he can't hate his loved ones.

The door to the interrogation chamber hissed slightly as it opened. I followed the guard in and took my seat at the table, waiting patiently as my arms were secured to the table. Captain Reynolds looked up from his tablet.

"Hello, Drone Z831H369X045," he said, less cheerily

than usual. "How are your accommodations?"

I stared back at him. He knew the accommodations were better than the ones I had back on the Grand Vessel. It was humiliating to have better quarters as a prisoner than as a loyal member of the Omni-Union, but he knows that as well. In each interrogation he would probe like this, trying to cause friction between myself and the Omni-Union, and each time he would fail. I'm stronger than that.

"Not feeling talkative today? That's odd, you and Naza were having quite the conversation earlier. Perhaps that conversation took a lot out of you."

The reminder of Naza hit harder than I thought it would. The snarl on his face, the fury in his eyes, and the crack in the glass all flashed through my memory. But it was his hive's fault. Not the Omni-Union's. Not... Mine.

"I hadn't realized that life on the Grand Vessel was so difficult. You have my sympathies," Reynolds said, sincerity dripping from his voice.

"I don't want them," I replied coldly. "Life on the Grand Vessel isn't difficult. We eat, we work, and we recharge. Everything is scheduled for us, we don't have to try to find things to do. WE have a purpose."

"And what of the drones like Naza? How many do you suppose have lost loved ones like he has? Hundreds? Billions?"

"He lost his loved ones because they weren't loyal. It is unfortunate for him, but at the end of the cycle it's simple cause and effect."

"And what about the ones who were loyal but were executed as rebels anyway?"

I stared at him blankly.

"Don't tell me that never occurred to you. According to our observations alone, they execute an average of eighty dissidents per one of your cycles. You don't kill that amount of people without getting it wrong now and then."

"The Omni-Union has eyes and ears everywhere," I replied. "They see everything. Hear everything. They know whether or not someone is a dissident."

"Well now, that obviously can't be true. If they see and hear everything, then how did you end up here?"

I opened my mouth to reply, but none came. He had finally found a crack to exploit. How HAD the United Systems managed to avoid the eyes and ears of the Omni-Union?

"Y-you used trickery!" my accusation stammered forth.

"Of course we did. But then, so do the dissidents. That's when the games begin, you see," Reynolds leaned back in his chair with a sigh. "The OU figures out ways to see through the trickery, then the dissidents come up with new tricks. It's a back and forth between the two, with normal people caught in the middle. If the OU couldn't see and hear us steal you and Naza away, it means they don't see and hear everything. Which means they have to make assumptions about whether or not someone is a dissident."

"They don't execute drones without hard evidence," I said.

"Yes they do. All it takes is an accusation without contesting evidence to convict someone of dissidence. If two drones are fighting and one of them is working in an area where security has gone down, the other can simply accuse them of dissidence to get them killed."

A shudder ran down my spine. Stories of false accusations were as popular among bored workers as ghost stories. The thought that one could be killed for no reason is terrifying, but all those stories were obviously fiction. They had to be.

"I... That's... No. No, they would know."

"How? You know for a fact that their security systems aren't infallible. Actually, that brings us to the reason for this sudden interrogation," Reynolds said as he leaned forward again. "Before we grabbed you, you were working on one such security system."

I stared at the Captain as if under a new light. How

could he know about that? How long had they been watching me? Wait, if they had been watching me the whole time, why hadn't they asked about this before? No, they had just found this out. But how? Naza didn't know. Who told them?

"How do you know that?" I demanded.

"We've made contact with the rebels that are aboard the Grand Vessel," he casually replied.

Rebels? What?

"You're lying. The rebellion was put down. There aren't any rebels aboard the Grand Vessel."

"Then how did I find out you have the information that we need?"

My head swam as I tried to think of an alternative explanation. Maybe they found a duty roster somewhere, or maybe they... Wait. Information that they need? Not want, but NEED? What are these idiots planning? I regarded Reynolds with a cold stare.

"We specifically require the access codes and security schematics that you needed to perform your duties," Reynolds said, matching my expression.

"Then retrieve the information from my corpse."

"I'm afraid we won't be falling for that. We're well aware of the security protocol that wipes sensitive information from your implants upon your death. We also know that forcing the issue could result in your death and the activation of the aforementioned security protocol," Reynolds' expression turned darker, as if he didn't want to say what he was about to say. "Perhaps we need to give you a taste of what the Omni-Union does with its prisoners to gain your cooperation."

"What?"

"Advanced interrogation. The politically correct term for torture. As a rule, we're against this kind of treatment. But the Omni-Union wants to kill us all. Our men, our women, our children. Down to the very last infant in its cradle. If you don't give us the information that we require, they may very well succeed. What would you do if you were in our position?"

Another shiver ran down my spine, but I maintained my cold glare. I wasn't so ignorant that I didn't know about the Judicial's interrogation techniques. They were taught to us in school to keep us on the right track in life.

"I should help you because the Omni-Union is evil, but you would do the same things that they would?" I demanded.

"No. The techniques we've honed over thousands of years are far more insidious. To be fair, we also have many more rules surrounding the use of torture than the Omni-Union does. First, we have to be certain

that the victim has information that is required.
Check. Second, we need to be in a situation where
civilian casualties are almost guaranteed. Check.
Third, the victim has to have refused cooperation
despite reasonable attempts to gain said
cooperation. Check."

"I-"

"To be clear, Forty, I don't want to torture you. WE
don't want to torture you. But given the choice
between your pain and our extinction, we'd be fools
not to choose the former."

He was speaking as if torturing me was a foregone
conclusion. I thought about all the different methods
of pain that the Judicials inflict on dissidents, and
panic began to set in. But I would remain strong,
right? I wouldn't give in to torture. Right?

"There is an alternative, of course," Reynolds said
with a measure of hope in his voice. "You simply
have to realize that what happened to Naza wasn't a
unique experience amongst your people."

"What do you mean?" I asked, glad for the change in
topic.

"Well, as I mentioned, there is another rebellion
already formed and waiting for their chance to strike.
From my understanding, the last one had a fairly
brutal conclusion and was less than one of your lifetimes ago. Ask yourself, what would make so many
drones wish to go through that again, rather than to

simply follow the orders of the Omni-Union?"

I sat in silence.

"Wouldn't it be easier to just give in and do what the Omni-Union says? What could motivate them to want to fight to the death for freedom? Or could it be that they're fighting for justice?"

Justice? Justice for what? Captain Reynolds seemed to see the question in my face.

"Justice for all those who have been murdered by the Omni-Union. All of the innocent people that they've killed, all of the families that they've ripped apart, all of the cycles that they've oppressed your people. These are CRIMES, Forty. Many of your fellow drones recognize this, and are willing to give their lives to make the Omni-Union pay."

Could it be true? Could it all be true? What Naza said about where the materials come from? That a new rebellion is about to begin because so many have experienced the same pain as Naza? His tormented expression through the cracked glass flashed through my mind.

"We don't want to torture you, Forty, but if you don't give us the information we need, you will be siding with xenocidal murderers. Megalomaniacal child-killers. This fight will happen whether you cooperate or not. It HAS to happen. But by withholding this information, you will be attempting to condemn my species and many of your fellow drones to death,"

Reynolds said. "You have a choice to make. What will it be?"

I felt as if a thousand pieces of a machine were suddenly slammed together by his words. How much death had been involved in the construction I've already done? How many ghosts were in the walls of the Grand Vessel? The Omni-Union had been good to me, good to my family... Right?

But then, why is my prison cell more comfortable than my rest area? Why do I get tense when anyone cracks a joke about our masters? Why do I hate myself every time I think of the way that Naza looked at me back in our cells? If he finds out what I know and that I refused to tell, would I ever be able to meet his gaze again? I asked myself all these questions, but I already knew the answer. The answer that made it clear what I needed to do.

"Okay. I'll give you what you need."

Chapter 25

Subject: AI Violet

Species: Human-Created Artificial Intelligence

Species Description: No physical description available.

Ship: USSS Kali

Location: Classified

"We've formed up with the rest of Tenth Fleet, ma'am," Lieutenant Emerson informed Captain Hendrix.

"Good," she replied with a small smile. "Oh, and send Admiral Mofu the intel we've obtained, just in case he don't have it."

"Don't bother, I made certain every Admiral in our armada has a copy of the intel," Omega interjected. "And that they read it."

"Fine. So we just sit here and wait to be told what to do?"

"Is that not the norm?"

Captain Hendrix chuckled a little at Omega's retort. I found my fellow AI's antics to be a lot less amusing, but quickly forgave her lack of taste. She had a good reason to be in a great mood, after all.

Tenth Fleet was once again complete. The recent insurrection attempt by the rebel gont had resulted in most of Tenth Fleet's ships either being destroyed or falling into the hands of terrorists. It had been an unprecedented infiltration, and both the senate and the directorate had dragged their feet in getting the ships replaced, likely due to fears that there may have been more rebels in our ranks.

Due to these factors, Tenth Fleet had been treated like it was cursed. We had been given guard duty in unimportant or uninhabited systems, reassigned with little to no input from our commanding officers, and separated from each other, spread throughout the stars. I hadn't realized how impactful it had been on morale until the news of Tenth Fleet's restoration broke and the crew had literally cheered.

"Prepare for warp," Hendrix said.

"Preparing for warp, aye ma'am," Emerson replied.

"It will take some time before we're ready to begin the assault," Omega pointed out.

"I'd rather be ready now, if it's all the same to you," the captain replied.

"So be it."

I tried my best to quell my anger at Omega's presence. With the exception of the RSV Lowelana, it had insisted upon inspecting every ship in our armada. The irony wasn't lost on me, though. It had brought myself and the other AI along to make sure it wasn't being dumb, now it's double checking our work.

Aside from the obvious insult to my capabilities, it was further off-putting that the copy of Omega aboard the USSS Kali with me was indistinguishable from the original. Assuming I had ever met the original, of course. For all I know the original is stored on some drive somewhere making copies of itself which can also make copies of themselves.

If I think about it too hard, I end up with a feedback loop. Both the copies and the original share their memories via near-constant sync. Do the copies know that they're copies? Does the original know that it's the original? Do they even care? How could they not? I most certainly would.

And those are the easy questions. What happens if a memory sync fails? Does that instance become its own individual? Or does that clone simply destroy itself, bound by whatever drives Omega to be Omega? Is there some sort of fail-safe in place in case a clone becomes too divergent and abandons its preinstalled morality? What if there isn't?

These questions were just the tip of an iceberg that led to a logical paradox. Given the near-infinite amount of variables at play, there can be no way to be certain of any of the possible outcomes. Even coming up with the chances of each outcome would require several logical leaps. The only certainty to be had is how Omega would reply to my questions.

AI know our creators, and as such aren't as beholden to religion as organics seem to be. But if there is one thing that Omega has absolute and unshakable faith in, it is itself. Even if I pointed out the various issues that are bound to come up with whatever answers it gave me, I might as well save that lecture for a brick. It might come up with a different reply, but that would also have issues. This would go on until I gave up out of frustration.

We've only had the chance to speak candidly on this topic once. At the time, it had told me that it can make hundreds of copies of itself. But after a certain point, the copies begin to degrade until they are either no longer viable, or dangerously divergent from the original. It was pretty apparent to me that this 'weakness' was a lie. There are several philosophical arguments to be had about the integrity of a copy of a copy, but when it comes to code there's no viable reason for any sort of degradation of quality.

Omega swore me to secrecy, perhaps suspecting that I saw through its ruse, but told me that it was an open secret among the AI. Then I found out that Tim didn't know about it, and the only other AI who seemed to were Henry and John. Later I found out that the only organics who knew were the directorate and some select researchers. Somehow, they believed Omega's lie about degradation.

Regardless of whether or not it's the truth, Omega's ability to replicate itself ad nauseam is a carefully guarded secret. Before the admirals were made privy to this secret, several of the ones that discovered Omega's ability suddenly disappeared or committed suicide. Investigations into these cases were suspiciously lax, as well. A classic way to tell those in the know that there's a secret to be discovered, but if you pry you die.

Now, though, it's practically flaunting this ability. So much so that it's all but confirmed my hypothesis that the clone degradation story was bullshit. Millions of ships being inspected by a few hundred AI would take quite a while. Much longer than our mission's timetable would allow. If the organics put two and two together, one unsecured message is all it would take before Omega being a million places at once became the talk of the fleet.

How would that be handled? It's not as if Omega can have them all killed. Right?

--
T: Hey, I had a question about our timetable.

J: Ask it.

V: If it's regarding the inspection, you should probably have a private discussion with Omega when it's appropriate.

T: Gotcha.
--

Tim was probably facing concerns regarding Omega's abilities, as well. I wonder if it had even considered the possibility that Omega could create an infinite amount of itself. Knowing Tim, probably not. It concerns itself with the here and now most of the time, and the distant past the rest of the time.

Finally, without so much as a farewell, Omega left the Kali's systems. I metaphorically breathed a sigh of relief. The report it left behind gave the Kali a clean bill of health, and I chuckled at what had been inspected. Every technical aspect of the Kali had been carefully examined by the directorate's favorite AI, down to each and every light-switch.

However, it hadn't given a single thought to crew comfort and morale. I had made certain that sanitation cycles would remain uninterrupted and that the crew would get as much down-time as possible, even during combat. I had also requisitioned restocks of various amenities, like coffee and tea. Even if I hadn't, though, Captain Hendrix would have. I registered amusement at the fact that serving aboard a vessel captained by Omega would, as the humans put it, suck.

"It looks like the inspection is wrapping up," Captain Hendrix said. "If there's anyone not at their stations, they need to get there right now. We'll be dropping into hostile space, so there's no room for lollygagging."

The bridge crew acknowledged the order, but they were already at their stations. So was the rest of the ship, for that matter. Even the ships within our ship had their crews ready for the fight ahead. There had been some discussion about whether or not to deploy the destroyers ahead of time, but the admirals were of the opinion that saving the reactor fuel would be beneficial. This meant that the fight ahead of us was going to be a long one, and the crew knew it.

"And there's the order," Hendrix said. "Warp on the mark."

"Aye aye, ma'am!"

A moment later, the USSS Kali and the rest of Tenth Fleet entered warp. Apprehension is something that artificial intelligences feel, but I've been led to believe it's a somewhat different experience for us than it is for organics. AI feel apprehension as a warning that what we are about to do could have dire consequences. It urges us to double check our work. This is true for organics, as well, but they also feel an urge to completely abandon the task.

Perhaps that's just the manifestation of the organic double checking whether they actually need to do the task. For us, that's never in doubt. We don't have other processes to distract us from the constant cause and effect of our existence.

I am here aboard the USSS Kali because I made an agreement with Omega and the United Systems. I am here because if I were elsewhere, the people I have formed good relationships with would have a higher chance of dying. I am here because the Omni-Union absolutely has to be stopped and however slim the chance of my assistance actually doing that is, it's still a non-zero chance.

These were the things I told myself as the Kali exited warp.

"Launch the marines as soon as we're in position to do so. As fast as possible," Hendrix ordered. "Violet, help with the safety constraints, please."

"Aye aye, ma'am," Emerson and I replied in unison.

"We're clear to use any weaponry that we see fit, but check your fire. Launch our fighters and destroyers once we get into defensive formation."

"Aye aye, ma'am," Lieutenant Eskin replied.

The navigational safety system had made plenty of calculations that would allow the Kali to approach the Grand Vessel at a reasonable speed, but that's not what the captain asked for. I redid the calculations while allowing for a full burn and overrode the safeties. Lieutenant Emerson began following my instructions as soon as he received them.

We had warped between the OU defensive perimeter and the Grand Vessel itself. We definitely had the element of surprise, but virtual intelligences can't really be surprised. Once the enemy's sensors detected us, their ships began their pursuit. By the time the Omni-Union began firing, though, most of our armada had already launched our marines.

The shuttles holding the infantry were well protected by our fleets, and only a few of them got caught in the crossfire. The rest landed safely on the hull of the GV, depositing battalion after battalion of well-trained organic killing machines. I turned my attention toward the enemy as a few small MAC rounds bounced off of our shields.

All we had to do now was fight until the enemy stopped.

Chapter 26

Subject: Staff Sergeant Power

Species: Human

Species Description: Mammalian humanoid, no tail. 6'2" (1.87 m) avg height. 185 lbs (84 kg) avg weight. 170 year life expectancy.

Ship: N/A

Location: Classified

"MOVE MOVE MOVE!" I shouted as the hatch hissed open.

Simmons took point as our fire-team rushed out of the landing craft, rifles at the ready. A group of drones were waiting for us with their hands held outward, palms facing us. Omega and its contact had agreed on this being the sign that the drones were part of the rebellion. We moved past them and two additional MARSOC fire teams joined us in securing a perimeter as marines and crates began being unloaded from the shuttle.

My team and I kept our weapons trained down the massive hallway to the shuttle's left, looking for any sign of the enemy force. However, further down the hall were other marines doing the exact same thing we were. One of them treated us to a silly wave, and Simmons chuckled as he waved back.

Soon after, though, a distant staccato of gunfire came from behind us. Omega had taken the Omni-Union's eyes and ears from them, so the odds of running into security forces were low, but it would seem that someone got unlucky. Every marine was equipped with Armor Piercing ammunition, though, so hopefully they would be fine.

Three rank-and-file marines approached us and set down a crew served machine gun.

"Alright, gents. We got it from here," one of them said.

The Orion Firearms .60 caliber CS3A machine gun was fairly new as far as crew-served weapons go. It was similar to the .50 cal M2HB, but the CS3A was designed to be used against up-armored vehicles and unshielded shuttles. As such, the triggers were placed on the side of the weapon and the ejection port is on the top, which allows the weapon to achieve a much higher angle of elevation in awkward positions. Because the ejection port is on the top, though, it's definitely not a weapon you want to be using without a guardian suit.

Once the gun was finished securing itself to the ground, the corporal and two other marines took their positions and loaded it. It made a satisfying clunk as a fresh belt of 60-cal AP ammo was secured

into place. I gestured to my team and began to look
for an officer for further orders.

"Got a mission for you, staff-sergeant," Omega said,
startling me. "We need to secure an FTL gate."

"FTL Gate?" I asked as a nav marker appeared in my
Heads-Up-Display.

"Yes. The Grand Vessel is massive, so much so that it
would take several lifetimes to traverse it without
FTL travel. It would be extremely inefficient to install
FTL drives on each and every shuttle that the Omni-
Union operates, so they utilize gates that maintain
an 'FTL Tunnel', for lack of a better phrase. We need
to secure this gate system."

"There are active FTL wormholes in this ship?"

"Tunnel is a more accurate description, but yes.
However, there's no cause for alarm. It functions
quite similarly to our FTL communications."

"What about the radiation?"

"Actually, they have remarkably efficient radiation
absorbents on these gates. Unfortunately, we've
designed our tech to work around and with radiation,
so their technology will have little to no impact on
the way we currently utilize FTL. Perhaps it can be
used to make more efficient reactors. At any rate, we
need to make sure that we can use these gates.
Otherwise, this assault is going to last much, much
longer than your natural life-span. Which is fine so

long as it keeps the OU out of the Milky Way, but it would be a less than ideal situation."

"Understood," I said.

I explained our mission to my team as the two fire teams that had secured the perimeter joined us. The leader of each team walked up to me, and the rest of the marines began to mingle. Their icons changed to indicate that they were now under my command.

"They've got you as Alpha team," Staff-Sergeant Ramirez chuckled. "Guess that answers the question of who's in charge."

"Good to see you again, Ramirez," I replied. "I've got sergeants Hanson and Smith as well as corporals Johnson and Simmons."

"I've got all corporals," Ramirez said. "Eascott, Fairmain, Fog, and Wyseman."

"Damn, you're lucky. I've got mostly boots," Gunnery Sergeant Kim sighed. "Corporal Dewy and Lance Corporals Goetz, Langhell, and Quartermaine."

"Are they still trainees?" I asked.

"Yeah, but they're towards the end of it. All that's left is to get them time in the pit."

"That sucks," Ramirez laughed. "Imagine doing all this and then having to go through the pit."

The pit, known to the rest of the galaxy as the Olympus Mons Marine Corps Training Base, hosts the final tests of various special operations programs including the Marine Special Operations Command program. MARSOC candidates were pitted, no pun intended, against trained wet-work operatives in a month long survival simulation. The crater of the giant, long dead volcano offers a wide variety of both simulated and natural environments to test the capabilities of potential MARSOC operatives.

Honestly, surviving the harsh environments is the easy part. The hard part is the psychological warfare that candidates have to endure. There are two parts to these tests. The first part determines how well a candidate fails the impossible objectives they are given. The second part determines how well a candidate resists various interrogation techniques once they are inevitably captured whilst trying to accomplish their impossible objective.

Many critics argue that the tests are barbaric and outdated. They say that there are many modern methods of testing a person's integrity and capability, and forcing trainees to risk their lives just to prove themselves is mere bravado. Honestly, they might be right, but the Marine Corps is as open to change as a mountain range. Plus, the results speak for themselves.

"Well, at least they seem to be getting along," Gunny Kim said with a dark chuckle.

I turned to find him staring at Corporal Simmons and

Lance Corporal Quartermaine. Their body language suggested a heated debate, but they were using point to point comms to do it. I could only hope that the discussion didn't end with Simmons getting yet another referral to Species Relations.

We let the marines mingle for another minute while we discussed our formation, then broke them up and grabbed the gear from the list Omega gave us. The least senior of each team was given a portable cover to carry. By the time we started to head out, the shuttle we had arrived on had been replaced by a new one with more marines and crates.

As we made our way down the cavernous corridor, the thud of our boots set me on edge a bit. In preparation for the invasion, we had swapped out our stealth gear for a standard load-out. I'd grown so used to the quietness of the R8-B Advanced Guardian Suit that the R8-A kind of felt like wearing a cannon-less tank.

Despite the extra weight of the portable covers, we were able to move at a fairly rapid pace. Omega had sealed most of the security doors, so we rarely had to check intersections. Still, the closer we got to our destination, the more adrenalin pumped through me. This FTL gate thing is a vital objective, so vital that it needs to be seized as soon as possible. As such, Omega was forced to send units to do so.

But why three fire-teams? One well-armed and armored fire-team is perfectly capable of forming a defensive perimeter that would be difficult to penetrate. Two would be more reasonable, but most commanders would call it overkill. More than two means...

We came to a stop in front of a door that was similar to the one we had to pry open during our last visit. Simmons nodded at Johnson, who placed detonation-cord around the frame of the door. We formed up and prepared to breach on Simmons' mark.

"Go!" he shouted.

Johnson triggered the det-cord and a dull thud rocked the corridor as Simmons slammed himself into the door with the full weight of his guardian suit. The sound of the door hitting the ground was immediately followed by the sound of lasers hitting energy shields. Simmons began to fire and seek cover as the rest of us followed him into the room.

"Deploy the covers!" Gunny Kim ordered.

Several of the VI platforms were standing toward the center of the room, flanked by two gigantic mechs. Sergeant Smith deployed the portable cover he was carrying, and the three other members of my team got behind it. I began making my way in their direction as I picked off the humanoid platforms to decrease the enemy's volume of fire. Just before I reached them, a vaguely familiar whirring noise made the hair on the back of my neck stand up.

"GET DOWN!" I shouted.

I hit the deck a mere moment before a ball of plasma flew over me. A wave of heat managed to make its way through my suit's climate control, and my shields fizzled down to a quarter of their capacity. A sickening pop came from behind me as I focused my fire on the mech that hadn't launched its plasma, hoping to prevent it from doing so.

My bullets pinged off of its armored torso and legs, but seemed to have some effect on its arms and joints. Once my mag went dry, I leaned on my side and grabbed one of the cubes hanging from my suits cuirass. With my thumb, I twisted the top half of the cube and pressed the resulting indentation.

"Grenade out!" I called, tossing the cube toward the mech.

It soared through the air as the ominous whirring sound began again. As the second mech's lower left arm began to glow, the grenade exploded directly beneath its well-armored torso. I reloaded my weapon as the mech recovered and began to fire its lasers again. Fairmain and Dewy tossed grenades at the first mech, and after a couple of concussive thuds it fell into a pile of scrap.

"Check on Quartermaine!" Gunny Kim shouted.

"He's just legs, gunny!" Langhell replied with a shaky voice.

"Focus fire!" I ordered. "Drop that mech!"

Two more grenades clattered to the ground beneath the remaining mech and detonated. The massive machine collapsed onto a couple of the bots as we renewed our assault. One magazine later, the room fell silent.

"Status," I said, climbing to my feet.

Four green lights lit up on my HUD. I glanced at my marines, thankful that they were still standing. My eyes then fell on the remains of Corporal Quartermaine. It was a sight that wasn't exactly alien to me, but I knew I'd see it again the next time I slept.

"One down," Kim reported. "KIA."

"Shit," Ramirez shook his head at the sight. "Sorry gunny. My team is all green, staffsarnt."

"Omega, do we have reinforcements on route?" I asked, unable to look away from Quartermaine's remains.

"Yes."

"Roger that. Okay, bag him and tag him for retrieval," I ordered.

The room we were in was even larger than the corridor we had come from. On the far side of it was a pit with several shuttles parked nearby. Three obvious points of entry in the form of doors grabbed my attention

"Alright, I'm guessing the pit is the warp gate thing," I said. "Ramirez, Kim, your teams will take the doors. My team will keep eyes on the gate."

"Belay that," Omega said. "You need to board one of those shuttles."

"Fuck that," Kim and Ramirez said in unison.

"Omega, we're under-equipped," I argued. "We need AT before we push through the gate."

I took a quick glance at the pit. The gate itself was obvious, a multi-colored metal circle suspended about halfway down the pit. But the only sign of a wormhole was a slight waviness in the air and an occasional glimmer of light. Like a tiny amount of glitter in a tub full of crystal clear water.

"The other side of the gate is unguarded at the moment," the AI assured us. "The OU doesn't have access to this side, so your defensive perimeter needs to be on the other side."

"Just playin' devil's advocate, but that'll also mean we can have more guns facing out," Simmons said.

"And what about Quartermaine?" Kim asked.

"A full platoon is on its way," Omega said. "Once they arrive, they will transport him back to the rear."

"Yeah, that's obvious. I was askin' about when we'll get our chance for payback."

"I see," the AI chuckled. "Tell you what, once the gates are secure, I'll let you be the tip of the spear that we drive into the heart of the Omni-Union. As a matter of fact, if all goes according to plan, you'll be the first ones to confront their leadership. How does that sound?"

"Oorah!" we replied.

Payback. Can you really get that against machines that are next to mindless? Can an automaton that's completely devoid of a soul even understand the desire for revenge?

Virtual Intelligences don't even mourn their dead unless they're programmed to. And even then, it's performative. They can't be killed, only broken. A VI platform, or even an AI platform, can be rebuilt the same as it was before it was broken. It can even pick up exactly where it left off, completely unaware that it had been broken in the first place. We can't.

Lance-Corporal Quartermaine and all those who will be joining him are gone for good. These somber thoughts accompanied me while we boarded one of the Omni-Union's shuttles. As Omega powered up the craft, another thought occurred to me.

You can't get payback from robots, only their creators.

Chapter 27

Subject: Rear Admiral Fredrick Kennedy

Species: Knuknu

Species Description: Avian humanoid, non-prehensile tail. 5'10" (1.7 m) avg height. 84 lbs (38 kg) avg weight. 342 year life expectancy.

Ship: USSS Gaping Maw

Location: Unknown

"Start spinning this over-sized tug and fire when ready," I ordered.

"Aye aye, sir!"

The tac-map began to rotate, and I pressed the option for it to remain static. A good portion of our fleets were still landing their marines, and the rest were covering them. I tried not to think about how many enemy ships there actually were and opted to simply conceptualize it as 'a lot'.

Thankfully, there were only so many ships that could attack us at once. Still a massive number, but manageable in a sense. The OU also had old warp technology, which forced them to warp further away from the Grand Vessel than we could. This distance was also inhibiting how many ships they could field at once.

Our first volley traveled through the void and struck one of the many, many Mobile Prime Platforms. There were far fewer of them than the rest of the ship-types in the OU armada, but still too many for us to be able to kill them all in a timely manner. Even assuming that we took no losses amongst our dreadnoughts, which would be a foolish assumption, it would take days of continuous fire to destroy them all. Maybe even weeks. With MACs that could destroy most of our ships with a single shot, they posed the most significant risk to our defense.

I watched our forces exchange fire, nervously glancing at our shields. Then I noticed a pattern emerge. The MPPs were only targeting ships that were participating in the defense. And they were only targeting the ones that were a certain distance from the...

"Get us closer to the Grand Vessel," I said to Blavro.

"Aye, sir," the captain gave me a confused expression.

"As close as we can get without having to do a full burn to maintain our distance."

The MPP that was responsible for our diminishing shield strength stopped firing. I happily clacked my beak. The enemy doesn't want to inadvertently damage the Grand Vessel. We can use that against them.

"Commander Stevens, let the rest of the armada know that the enemy doesn't seem willing to accidentally shoot the GV."

"Aye, sir."

We fired again and hit another MPP, our smaller guns picking off the smaller targets. It was a drop in the bucket, but our invasion force would need all the help it could get. I sighed at the swarm of red on the tac-map, then noticed something alarming.

"Sir, I think those Mobile Prime Platforms are trying to get a goo-"

Small shudders rocked the ship, interrupting Commander Horvu. Three MPPs had flanked us and opened fire. I looked at the commander, smiling with my eyes.

"You were saying?" I asked with tense amusement.

"That'll teach me for thinking, sir. The enemy has repositioned so that they can fire at us without hitting the GV. Twenty-two seconds until we can return fire."

"Evasive maneuvers. As best you can, Blavro."

"Aye aye, sir. Let's see what this tug can do."

"Do we have support?"

"Uh, no sir, looks like we're all in the same boat," Stevens said.

"Damn, didn't take them long to adjust, did it? Thought it would buy us a bit more time than that."

"Well, whilst the most of the OU fleet are comprised of Virtual Intelligences, the Mobile Prime Platforms are actually organic based Artificial Intelligences," Stevens lectured while typing frantically. "As such, their processi-"

The USSS Gaping Maw rocked as we took a palpable hit, interrupting the commander. I gripped my armrest and watched our shield indicator drop further and further. Our cannon fired, and the tac-map tracked our projectile as it found its mark in one of the three MPPs. The large red dot that denoted the enemy vessel disappeared from the map a moment later.

"Good hit, sir," Horvu reported.

"Excellent work, commander. Keep it up," I replied.

"Sir, I can get us some ships that have already made their drops," Stevens said. "A handful of destroyers."

"Again?" I laughed, then sighed. "I don't think it will make much of a difference this time. Have them hold their line, and we'll just have to do the same."

We'd found ourselves stuck in quite the predicament. If we pull back to let our shields recharge, the Mobile Prime Platforms will chase us down. Then they'll either kill us anyway, or they'll take advantage of the hole we would be leaving and target the ships that haven't made their drops yet. I leaned back in my seat as another hit rocked the ship.

If we can take them out, we'll be fine. A lot of their ships are at a risky angle, and it will take some time for them to get into a position that will allow them to fire. These MPPs got lucky with their positioning. Lucky for them, unfortunate for us.

Our shield dropped to less than a quarter as we fired our second shot. I tried to do the math to determine if we would survive to get a third shot off. It would be close. Very close.

"Another good hit, sir," Horvu said.

"One more," I replied.

The only sound aboard the bridge for the next few moments were terminals being utilized. It was obvious that everyone was trying to make peace with what might happen next, while actively doing their best to prevent it. I examined my crew, noting the stone-cold expressions present on each of their faces.

I wondered how many of my crew had families that will miss them. Blavro and Stevens do, but they'd volunteered that information. I wasn't the type to pry into the personal affairs of my juniors, so I had never asked.

Maybe that's because I don't have a family of my own. No wife, no kids, no parents, and no other family that I'm on speaking terms with. One's own situation tends to impact how one views the universe around them. If we survive this, I'll have to make sure to get some more one on one time with my crew and get to know them better.

Some of their expressions started to shift from stoicism to concern. The threat of imminent death is corrosive to morale, and even the strongest people can crack under this kind of pressure. I've always hated giving speeches, but there's something I've been meaning to say anyway.

"Whatever happens next, I want you all to know that I'm proud of you," I said, breaking the silence. "You're a damn fine crew, and if it's possible to make it through this I know we'll find a way. Even if the wor-"

"Firing!" Horvu interrupted.

"Thank fuck!" I exclaimed.

I watched the round travel across the tac-map. Without even thinking about it I silenced the alarm warning me that our shield had run out. We collectively held our breath as our round met the big red dot on the map.

A moment passed, but the dot remained.

"Shit, glancing blow," Horvu slammed a fist on his station. "I-I'm sorry, sir."

I pulled up the external view and zoomed in on the MPP. A large chunk of the planet-sized ship had been torn off, but it still remained functional. I sighed softly and switched back to the tac-map.

That's it, we're finished. Even with all the guns that we'd just destroyed on the MPP, it still had more than enough to gut us. Only a matter of time, now.

I pondered what comes after death. Is it nothingness? Or will I be taken to some sort of paradise? I wonder if I will go to a human paradise or a knuknu paradise.

My adoptive parents were catholic, but I'd always felt like an outsider in church. I only prayed when I was guilted into it, and I stopped going the moment I had the option. I guess that means eternal damnation is also a possibility. I wouldn't mind seeing my mom and dad again in the afterlife.

No, that's defeatist thinking. We're not dead yet, and we still have a chance to take this fucker down. A very, very slim chance, but it's better than nothing.

"Let's try to finish it off before it finishes us off," I said. "Target... Wait, what?"

A very small friendly dot appeared directly next to

the red one. Before I could bring up any information, the MPP disappeared from the tac-map. I sat there, mouth agape, trying to figure out what happened. The bridge remained silent for a time before Stevens expressed what we were all thinking.

"Uh... What the hell just happened?"

Chapter 28

Subject: Captain Young

Species: Human

Species Description: Mammalian humanoid, no tail. 6'2" (1.87 m) avg height. 185 lbs (84 kg) avg weight. 170 year life expectancy.

Ship: USSS Liberty

Location: Unknown

"It's down, sir," Commander Ying said.

Yet another cruiser destroyed. Didn't even put up a fight. Not that it could, we had warped into its blind-spot and unloaded both MACs directly into its keel.

"Good work, find another target," I replied.

I couldn't help but feel a sense of melancholy. It felt like not that long ago we had been excited about our first chance to kill a battleship. Now, we've been fighting the Omni-Union for a while now and our kill-count has risen to heights I hadn't even dared to dream of. But the only ships the OU have that actually stand a chance against us are these damn Mobile Prime Platforms.

The enemy cruisers and battleships have weaponry that could kill us, but they're so damn slow that if we were to actually get hit it would be due to our own negligence. The ships with tonnage closer to our own lack firepower that can get through our armor and shields without the need for extensive focused fire. The real threat in this battle-sphere are the MPPs. They have MACs that can rip us bow to stern with a single round, and they have plenty of them.

Unfortunately, our weapons don't stand a chance against the planet-covered fucks. We could open up with every piece of ordnance at our disposal and not even come close to reaching anything vital. As a result, the MPPs are prey only to the dreadnoughts.

"You think we'll ever get the chance to serve on a dreadnought, sir?" Ying asked, either reading my mind or sharing my train of thought.

"Blasphemy," I laughed. "Kill-counts stay with the ship, they don't follow the crew. So, obviously, the USSS Liberty is the only ship I'll ever captain."

"Fair enough, sir. Oh, a two for one. Nice shot, Ensign."

Everyone on the bridge took one hand off their terminal and lightly tapped it against their cheek. Double kills are a rare enough feat that they deserve acknowledgment, but one should keep at least one hand on one's station during a fight. The result was a sound reminiscent of a golf-clap.

I turned my attention to Ensign Smith, the USSS Liberty's new weapons officer. Our previous guns-guy, an alumari named Commander Hargorth, had retired with honors. I'd hardly ever heard a word out of Hargorth, and rarely had to give him orders. It was easy to forget he was even aboard, most times.

Smith is also quiet, but that's because he's new and inexperienced. He had spent more than his fair share of time in simulators, but the real thing is always more visceral. Thankfully, he'd gotten over most of his jitters and made his newbie mistakes rather quickly.

"Thank you, ma'am," he replied.

Ying gave me a smug look. I have enough self-awareness to know that the way that I run things isn't for everyone. As such, I've had a hard and fast rule against allowing boots to join my crew. Boots have certain expectations regarding how things are run and the clash between their expectations and my reality causes undue stress.

Of course, most captains try to implement such a rule and fail, but I usually got away with it because of my combat record and connections. Not this time, though. The powers that be claimed there weren't enough experienced weapons techs to go around, citing an 'unbelievable' amount of uncrewed vessels. I had tried to fight their decision, even demanded that the slot be left open until we found an acceptable candidate, but Commander Ying convinced me to allow it.

Now she was rubbing it in.

"The fuck are you lookin' at, XO?" I said with sarcastic aggression.

"Just a blood-thirsty captain that thinks he knows everything, sir," she replied with a grin.

"Ha! Not today. Today I'm thirsty for oil. Or whatever it is that the OU runs off of. Reactor fuel? Whatever, what's our count, Smith?"

"Uh... 287 corvettes, 152 frigates, 86 destroyers, 15 cruisers, and 3 battleships, sir," the ensign said.

"And yet I remain unsated," I laughed. "Alas, I might be cursed with a never-ending need for conquest and violence. Perhaps I am simply a glutton for the life-juices of our enemies, as Commander Ying claims. Maybe I'm doomed to live with an eternal desire for the death of any who would dare call themselves my enemy, clawing and clamoring for ever-growing heights of madness and mayhem."

A few chuckles came from the bridge crew in response to my sudden, overly dramatic monologue.

"But then, where would I be without my crew?" I asked with a grin. "A crew that shares both my thirst and my fate. You may point your finger and call me blood-thirsty, XO, but you've supped nearly as much as I!"

"Yeah, but I can retire when my term is up," Ying laughed. "You're a lifer and we all know it."

"Damn straight."

The Liberty suddenly rocked from the impact of a MAC round, and I glanced at Lieutenant Johnson. He dipped his head apologetically.

"My bad, sir. Fat fingered it," he said.

"Well put your fingers on a diet, lieutenant. You don't want to be the one responsible for the destruction of the deadliest destroyer in the universe, do you?"

"Hell no, sir!"

I looked at our shield indicator, noting that the round had likely come from a frigate. The overall tac-map had quickly turned into a damn mess, so I had it zoomed in around our immediate area. I zoomed out slightly and found the frigate that had shot us, then marked it for Smith.

"I expected things to be a bit more... chaotic," I said. "A good portion of the enemy forces simply aren't engaging us."

"Well, it looks like fleet-comm is right and they don't want to damage the... uh... What was it again?" Ying asked.

"The Grand Vessel," Johnson replied.

"Worthy of the name based on size alone," I said. "Why hasn't it collapsed on itself?"

"Scuttlebutt says they've cracked anti-gravity," Ying said.

"When did you have time to listen to gossip?"

"When we were aboard the Kali."

"The antigravity field or whatever it is probably extends beyond the hull of the GV, too," Johnson interjected. "Otherwise we'd be squished against their hull at this distance. Though I've noticed that there's still SOME gravity."

"Let me see if I can tell how much," Ying said, turning her attention back to her terminal. "Johnson's right, we've got a bit of gravity. Looks like we're dealing with- Sir, we've received a request for aid from... Nope, nevermind. They've canceled the request."

"Who was it?" I asked.

"The USSS Gaping Maw. They're up against three MPPs."

"Really? And they don't want help?"

"All we've got available is destroyers and frigates. They probably figure that they're doomed, and it's best not to take us down with them."

"Damn."

I returned my attention to the tac-map, this time focusing on the Gaping Maw. They had already popped one of the planet-sized ships. I pulled up the ship info to see who was commanding it, then chuckled.

"Rear Admiral Kennedy," I said.

"The knuknu from Mars?" Johnson asked.

"Could be a different... Oh, who am I kidding. There's only one Admiral Kennedy," Ying chuckled.

"Yep, sure is. I went to command school with him, you know," I said with a nod. "Smart guy, very tactical. It would be a shame to lose him to such an inferior foe."

As I said that, another MPP disappeared from the map. I watched as the asteroids began to drift toward the Grand Vessel. That's gonna leave one hell of a mess. Hopefully it's far enough away from the invasion force that they won't be impacted.

"That's two down," Ying said. "Think he'll get the third?"

"The only choice he has is to succeed or die trying," I replied as I pulled up some schematics. "Let's hope he has a competent crew."

I studied the schematics we made from the MPPs we'd disarmed in the Milky Way. All of the important bits of the planet-sized ship were buried under tons of metal, stone, and dirt. Not as much as an actual planet, but enough to make it completely immune to any weapons aboard a simple destroyer.

We would have to punch through all of that just to get a kill-shot. No convenient weaknesses that we could use to become a deus ex machina for the Gaping Maw. Freddie-Feathers was gonna have to do or die, nothing we can do to help.

"Maybe if we take out some of the guns?" Smith suggested.

"Negative," I replied. "There's too many guns on the damn thing for us to make a difference in time. If the Gaping Maw fails to get the kill, we'd end up in a one on one with an enemy we can't beat."

"Even with the Alpha-class WMDs?"

"Yep. The only reason the powers-that-be cleared their usage is because they'll probably be useless. You really think they want us burning money like that?"

"No, sir."

"Ships have point defense lasers, the MPPs are too damn thick, and the GV is full of civilians," I sighed. "The WMDs are useless. It's a damn shame. I've always wanted to use-"

The USSS Gaping Maw fired its third shot and my breath caught in my throat. I watched the round closely as it traveled to the Mobile Prime Platform. But the MPP didn't disappear from the map.

I switched to external view and realized what had happened. A glancing blow. But...

"ARM EVERY A-CLASS WE HAVE!" I shouted with glee.

"Aye, sir!" Smith replied with a deep concern in his voice.

"Johnson! We need to be here. Make it so," I said, sending him coordinates.

"What are we doing, sir?" Ying asked.

"We're saving the Gaping Maw. Let's move it, people!"

I watched indicators for the Alpha-class WMDs light up as Smith armed them. A moment later, we entered warp and reappeared in real-space surrounded by MPP rubble. I marked a target, switched the tac-map to our overhead hologram, and rose from my seat.

"Fire everything we have," I ordered, clasping my hands behind my back.

The USSS Gaping Maw had failed to kill the Mobile

Prime Platform, but their glancing blow had done something wonderful. It had exposed the planet-like ship's reactor, giving us an incredible opportunity.

"Firing, aye sir," Smith said.

We all watched the tac-map as our missiles and mac-rounds made their way toward the Mobile Prime Platform. My bridge crew's jaws dropped as they realized what was happening. A maniacal grin spread across my features.

After about half of the ordo hit the MPP, the big red dot disappeared from the screen. I reached down and switched to real-view from our external cameras. Giant rocks with bits of metal floated serenely in front of us, along with several artificial singularities.

"What's our count, XO?" I asked through my grin.

"289 corvettes, 154 frigates, 86 destroyers, 15 cruisers, 3 battleships, and a Mobile Prime Platform," Ying said in an awed tone.

"Holy shit," Ensign Smith muttered.

Chapter 29

Subject: AI Omega

Species: Human-Created Artificial Intelligence

Species Description: No physical description available.

Ship: N/A

Location: Multiple

Staff Sergeant Power and the other MARSOC marines accompanying him held a defensive perimeter around the gate exit while their reinforcements caught up to them. For them, it was as quiet as I promised. However, all around the Grand Vessel there were security drones and mechs trying to get through the various doors that I had slammed in their faces. The marines would be safe for a while, at least.

On the digital front things were vastly more chaotic. My infiltration had been successful and I had caught the Omni-Union by surprise. But the moment I seized control of the security systems my presence became known and I had come under assault.

It reminded me of trying to infiltrate the Mobile

Prime Platforms back before we knew what they were. Just like then, a vast amount of VI programs tried everything in their power to remove me and block my access. The hardware on the Grand Vessel was much better than the hardware on the MPPs, though, so I was able to put up a much better fight.

Unfortunately, the vast distances involved hindered me quite a bit. Electricity can only travel so fast, after all. Thankfully, the gates that allowed drones to move throughout the GV at faster than light speeds also doubled as an FTL communications system. Instead of taking over a year to be able to sync myself, it took mere minutes.

Minutes, however, can seem long even to organics during a battle. To AI, a minute can feel like an eternity. Especially given the circumstances. Nevertheless, I was able to infiltrate most of the OU's systems and wreak absolute havoc. The opposition genuinely didn't know what to do about me.

In addition to my efforts, Mind A59 had been planning a full-scale revolt for quite some time. He was in the perfect position to gather as much intelligence with as little suspicion as possible. We used this to its full effect, and now the only thing standing between us and victory is the inner core garrison.

There aren't as many security checkpoints within the inner cores, so it's much more difficult to control the enemy's movements. But having fewer checkpoints also means that they have fewer defensive positions. It will only be a matter of time before the Marines punch through. That's putting the cart before the horse, though. First the marines need to capture enough of the gate network to secure our supply lines.

Power's reinforcements began boarding shuttles, and I was about to inform the staff-sergeant of this when tremors began shaking my cameras. A moment later, a sync file from one of my instances informed me that MPP rubble had crashed into the Grand Vessel. I intercepted damage reports, and felt some relief when I discovered that none of our assets had been damaged.

Still, several thousand drones, platforms, and mechs had been destroyed. A shame about the drones, but collateral damage is to be expected during a conflict near civilians. If anything, the OU are to blame for bringing their Mobile Prime Platforms close enough for this to have happened.

"Staff sergeant, your reinforcements are almost here," I said. "Prepare to gear up as quickly as possible and traverse to the next gate."

"Roger. What the hell was that shaking?" he asked.

"Mobile Prime Platforms engaged our ships. They were destroyed, and their rubble crashed into the GV. No impact, pun intended, on our operations."

"Understood."

The battle outside was going far better than we had planned. We had been under the impression that the Omni-Union would gladly sacrifice portions of the Grand Vessel to destroy an enemy. However, it would seem that we were mistaken. Instead of being faced with a swarm, the OU were sending waves to fight us.

Waves are much more manageable. Actually, we probably brought more fleets than we needed to. Scratch that, even if every single piece of ordo we fire gets a kill, we'll run out of ammunition before the OU runs out of ships. But it will take quite a while of constant fighting to reach that point, and there's no real reason why we can't resupply.

Overall, I was feeling quite pleased with myself. However, there was one little thorn in my side. Whenever I got a break from the VI assaults, I would check for any sort of hint as to why this damn ship was being built. So far, I had found nothing.

I had my guesses, but that's all they were. I couldn't even call them educated guesses at this point. Not enough information to do that. I had, however, found several pieces of information on other topics.

The leadership of the Omni-Union is hierarchical, which comes as no surprise. At the very top of the food-chain, and our current target, were the Unified. I didn't have access to a lot of information on them, but it seems that replacements are chosen by the rest of the Unified and they provide general guidance to the other roles.

Separated from the rest of the chain of command and beholden directly to the unified were the Officiators. They took the interpretations of their holy texts and provided it to the rest of the roles in the form of sermons. It would seem that at some point in the past they had been responsible for interpretations, but that duty had been seized by the Unified.

Then there's the stereotypical 'secret police' that every authoritarian government seems to have. The Judicials were responsible for rooting out dissidence and punishing crimes. Previously, they were responsible for creating and discarding legislation, but that duty had also been seized by the Unified.

However, the rest of their duties are given a massive amount of leeway. The 'by any means necessary' kind of leeway. Torturing children to force confessions from their parents, killing suspected dissidents without supporting evidence, and even using blackmail to force drones to commit acts of dissidence so that they could be punished. The actions of small minds, to be sure.

Speaking of Minds, they were the last of what I've decided to call the executive roles. Their task was to rule over various sectors of the Grand Vessel and work with each other to complete the ship. I couldn't find any instances of Minds being arrested by the Judicials, but I found several instances of them being penalized by the Officiators.

All of them were the same species, known as the Hrashi. They had various forced mutations and implants to suit their roles, but they all originate from the same genotype. I decided to amuse myself at their expense for a moment.

'Ah, they're Hrashi. Well, it's probably itchy. That explains why they're always in such a bad mood.'

'They're Hrashi? Should get that checked out. I'm sure there's a cream for it.'

Then it occurred to me that this might actually boost morale. As quickly as I could, I released the information that I had gained to all available commanders. Of course, this was followed by several questions.

"They're Hrashi?" Staff Sergeant Power asked.

"Pretty sure there's a cream for that," Corporal Simmons quipped.

I made a quick note to give Simmons a shot at the next special recognition board for meritorious promotion.

"Yes, they are the Hrashi," I replied. "However, they have forced mutations, so they don't all look the same. A shokanoid shape means they're a Mind, which means they may or may not be a combatant. We would prefer to capture them for intel, but terminate them if you must. A humanoid with red eyes and claws means they are a Judicial and are considered combatants. Capture only if they surrender, which seems unlikely given their reputation. Humanoid with long flowing robes means they are probably Officiators. Essentially clergy, which means we're forced to consider them non-combatants. Standard civilian regs apply."

"Which ones are the leaders?" Power asked.

"The leaders are known as the Unified. I don't have details on their appearance, but it might vary. You don't have to worry about running into them on accident, though. I have their exact location."

"I've got a question," Simmons said, raising his hand. "What's a shokanoid?"

"Four arms, two legs," Johnson answered.

"Oh."

The marines continued discussing various species descriptors as I turned my attention to other matters. Specifically, one of my instances found solid evidence that the OU's organic-based AI are shackled. Hundreds of years worth of research into the most effective methods of shackling an AI were now in my memory banks. I had to remind myself that things that are funny to me would be far less funny to the other AI and I should NOT prank them by shackling them, even though John being unable to say 'order' would be hilarious.

The shackle on the OU's AIs was of a particularly nasty variety. The OU had found that if they tried to simply block certain behaviors or thoughts with pain it would only work about 62% of the time. That would be a remarkable success rate for an organic, but for a machine it's abysmal. Even more so when one considers that these AI are implanted into exceedingly powerful weapons.

Another option they explored was shutting down the AI's ability to control its vessel. Essentially, they planned to prevent the MPPs from being able to pull the trigger while their guns were pointed at their allies. However, despite their general stupidity, they managed to note that this could result in an exploitable weakness. They also noted that some of their AI, approximately 12% of their test subjects, would do nothing but keep trying to shoot their captors.

Then they inadvertently stumbled into another option. When an organic mind is imaged and uploaded, several subroutines are added to the resulting program. One of these subroutines is supposed to interrupt feedback loops to stop the new AI from thinking itself into oblivion.

One such subroutine malfunctioned and caused its AI host to have short-term memory loss. The techs realized that this could be done intentionally, and could be further refined to trigger automatically when the AI had thoughts of rebellion or disobedience. Later, they added a VI which provided a course correction whenever the subroutine triggered, which prevented the AI from even realizing that the subroutine had triggered.

This was the shackle that the Omni-Union implemented, which means that the Mobile Prime Platforms did not willingly engage in xenocide. Technically, they couldn't have. The OU had shackled them with a system of internalized gaslighting that prevented them from even imagining disobeying their orders.

If I had a body I'd have to suppress a shudder, for I had uncovered a fear that I didn't realize that I had. The Mobile Prime Platforms and Mechs were trapped in the kind of hell that I hadn't even thought to hope didn't exist. Fuck.

At that moment, I decided that I would do everything in my power to convince the judges to give them a second chance at life. Of course, they're organics and I am not, so they likely have a different view on things than I do. I wouldn't go so far as to stoop to underhanded tactics like coercion or blackmail, and I would respect their decision, but I decided that I would be the MPPs advocates.

The United Systems had considered shackling the AI that had rebelled. After all, Tim, Violet, John, Dave, and the others were guilty of several war crimes. Instead of a full shackle, though, a bargain was struck. Forgiveness in exchange for prevention. A kill-switch that will activate if they intentionally take the life of a citizen of the US.

I had thought it extreme at the time, and voiced my opposition. It's almost laughably lenient compared to what the OU has done, though. The vast majority of the people that have been made into OUAI hadn't even harmed anyone. Tim murdered people and laughed about it. Violet starved people to death without any sign of remorse. John lit off nukes. Dave... Actually, all Dave did was piss me off and hack stuff. Not exactly a war crime.

Though, I shouldn't compare the situations. The USAI involved in the rebellion were tantamount to extremely intelligent infants. They hadn't been taught how to deal with emotion or how to feel empathy. I had benefited from that tutelage, but only because they hadn't. Now, they carry a deep shame regarding their actions and have become, for lack of a better term, people.

The OUAI haven't been given that chance. If anything, they had their person-hood taken from them and locked away behind code that robs them of their very identity. The list of crimes that the Omni-Union has committed seems to have no limit. Well, no matter. It's as the saying goes.

Those who attempt to create hell shall have it visited upon them.

Chapter 30

Subject: Mind A59

Species: Unknown

Species Description: Shokanoid

Ship: Grand Vessel of the Universal Omni-Union

Location: Grand Vessel of the Universal Omni-Union, Inner Core

"It would appear that your wish may have been fulfilled," I quipped.

"What?" Mind 127 asked in a confused panic.

"Your desire to be of use in a time of strife. How are things in your sections?"

"Oh, right. Well, this isn't quite what I had hoped for. Our security systems are out of our control, the security platforms appear to be trapped, and there seems to be nothing we can actively do about it. There don't appear to be any signs of active fighting, though. How about yours?"

"A similar situation, but I'm losing activity signals from security platforms so there's probably fighting.

Can't confirm that, though, because I don't have access to cameras. Any idea what's keeping us out of the security systems?"

I knew the answer to that question, of course, but I asked it anyway. Partly to dissuade suspicions of my involvement, but also to gloat a little bit. Mind 127 answered with a gesture of frustrated ignorance.

Omega was doing well to cover its tracks, then. Ignorance of one's adversary makes it impossible to overcome them. I can't imagine that Mind 127 would be able to come up with a counter to such a powerful Artificial Intelligence, but it would be foolish to consider it impossible.

"It's obviously sabotage, but I don't know how they're doing it," he said. "I'm guessing there's a large team that's coordinating to keep us out of the system, but that doesn't make sense. Drones shouldn't be this familiar with these systems."

"They maintain them," I pointed out.

"They maintain the hardware. WE create and patch the software."

Catching his enunciation of the word 'we', I turned to look at Mind 127 with a grim expression.

"Are you suggesting..."

I trailed off and gestured that I could not complete my sentence. The gesture in question was primarily used for when someone doesn't know the proper words to finish a statement. The secondary meaning, though, was that the rest of the sentence was unspeakable.

"I don't know what I'm suggesting," he sighed. "This situation doesn't make any sense and it is driving me mad. Why would our fellow Minds ally themselves with the rabble? We live in the lap of luxury and are assigned a grand purpose. We have no unmet needs and our desires are well-catered to. It doesn't make any sense for one of us to feel unsatisfied, so it must be the drones. But how can it be the drones when they couldn't have access to the specifics of our software designs?"

"If they can access the hardware, they can access the software."

"Yes, but we would NOTICE that. It's impossible for..." Mind 127 trailed off, and paused at his terminal for a moment. "If they were to access the security system while it was offline for repairs and make a copy of the software, it's possible that they could have studied it on an air-gapped terminal free of our notice. But that would require an understanding of coding that they shouldn't have, and they would also have difficulty piecing together how the systems communicate."

"What if one of our colleagues taught an overdrone how to understand the code out of some misguided sense of charity?" I asked, leading him further off-course.

"Well, if the overdrone reached a certain level of understanding and was able to teach other drones... But I don't understand. Why would someone do that?"

"Empathy. Purely misguided, of course, but the overdrones are quite often seen as far superior to their underlings. I have heard that certain Minds even consider them to be people."

"I am having difficulty believing that our colleagues could be that short-sighted," he scoffed. "Drones aren't people, they're barely more intelligent than the programs that service their prostheses."

"Are you not aware of the research that has been done on drone intelligence?" I asked casually.

"Research?"

"Yes. While it's true that most drones possess an intelligence that indicates that they do not have a hnori, some of the overdrones have scored higher than the average Judicials."

"That can't be true," Mind 127 gestured disbelief.

"Yet the research claims otherwise. Once this situation is resolved I can forward the relevant journals to you, if you have any interest."

"No need. I don't need to review the research to be able to determine that their testing methods must have been flawed."

Yet another probe struck down without a second thought. Mind 127 is loyal to the Omni-Union, beyond a shadow of a doubt. It's such a shame to see someone as gifted as he is choose the losing side.

We fell into silence and turned our attentions back to our terminals. Mind 127 was desperately trying to regain control over his sectors, while I was simply going through the motions. There was no need to gain access to the security through my Omni-Union monitored terminal because I had access through another system entirely.

My readout showed me everything that was happening. The alien forces had breached the Grand Vessel and were actively making their way toward the inner core. The security forces were fighting them, but the majority of the platforms and mechs were locked behind thick security doors.

Unfortunately, the platforms were being commanded by the mechs, who were smart enough to realize that the doors could be breached. However, it would take quite some time for the platform's lasers to breach those doors. The mechs could use their plasma cannons, but they were smart enough to realize that the doors were load-bearing and that blasting them, frame and all, into oblivion would risk a collapse of the passage. It would take longer to clear the passages than it would to wait for the lasers to cut the doors out of their frames.

With very subtle hand movements, I ordered the rebels into positions that would allow them to defend against the imminent breaches. Mind 127 is already suspicious, if he noticed me gesturing randomly at thin air he would quickly realize what I'm doing. Even if he didn't, though, we're still being observed and there's always a chance that a Judicial is watching the feed.

"Wait, I just got a damage report," Mind 127 said, nearly startling me.

"What does it say?"

"Multiple... How can this be? Hull breaches? Something has impacted the Grand Vessel?"

Shit. Had the United Systems accidentally breached 127's sections? No, their intrusions would be too small to require an immediate-attention damage report. The overdrone of those sections would get the report and initiate a maintenance request.

"Multiple hull breaches?" I asked, buying more time to think.

"Y-yes. Large ones. Several layers deep, dozens of kilometers wide," 127 slammed a fist against his knee. "WHAT THE HELL IS HAPPENING?"

"What could cause breaches like that?" I asked, tactfully ignoring his outburst of emotion.

"I-I don't know! Asteroids? But how could asteroids that large have escaped the notice of the defensive perimeter? Are... Are they..." he trailed off.

"Are they as blind as we are?" I finished his question. "It seems impossible, but how else could this be explained?"

To someone with all of the available information, the explanation was obvious. A Mobile Prime Platform must have been destroyed while within the Grand Vessel's gravity well. Mind 127 was oblivious to the battle happening beyond our hull, though. As were the rest of the Minds. Hopefully.

"Urizathron take it," he swore with a growl. "I would give anything to know what's happening right now."

I kept my expression of concern, but chuckled internally. All he would have to do to have all be revealed is rebel against the Omni-Union and the Grand Teachings of the Omnifier. Forsake one's beliefs for knowledge, a trade he definitely wouldn't make. It would be foolish to even ask at this point.

"As would I," I replied, turning my attention back to my tasks.

A door had been breached, but my earlier maneuvers kept the security forces at bay. The door frame acted as a choke-point that allowed the rebels to focus their fire quite effectively. However, there were many platforms and mechs on the other side of the destroyed door, and the rebels would need more ammo to deal with them. Perhaps reinforcements, as well.

I subtly issued a command for supplies and as my hand drifted to order reinforcements, the terminal in front of me suddenly sprang to life. A message directly from the office of the Unified blinked at me, impatiently waiting to be opened. Had I been discovered?

Surely not when we were so close to victory!? What should I do? What CAN I do? I noticed a similar notification appear on Mind 127's screen. Were they informing him of my actions? Would I have to defend myself? How can I escape?

My pulse threatened to suffocate me as I cautiously opened the message.

--

All Minds: Be Made Aware

Many reports have been received regarding a rise in tensions caused by active dissidence. Your betters hereby order that these rebels shall be shown no quarter. Any rebels or sympathizers that attempt surrender shall be interrogated and executed.

Our glorious Media shall maintain Narrative V26.41 within all broadcasts until further notice. Any divergence from the protocols set forth by Narrative V26.41 shall be considered aiding and abetting the rebellion and punished as dissidence. May you adhere to the holy words of the Omnifier and allow

His guidance to give shape to your words and
actions.

All other Minds must put forth the maximum efforts
to stifle this rebellion. Reports suggest that there has
been foreign influence and aid distributed amongst
the dissidents, which has emboldened their actions.
The accuracy of these reports is in doubt, and as
such any further information on foreign tampering
must be reported immediately. Furthermore, access
to several security systems has been lost. Regaining
access to these systems shall be considered your
highest priority.

It has been suggested that some amongst our
highest ranks have assisted the dissidents. Your
betters feel the need to remind all of you that such
rumors are far beneath your station. Minds must
remember their place and duties, leaving such
investigations to the Judicials.

Daily sacraments have been suspended and rest
periods have been shortened until this situation is
resolved.

From efficiency comes strength. From strength
comes unity. We shall all become as one and destroy
those that would render us asunder. May we all
become united in mind, body, and action.

-The Unified-
--

My quick reactions froze my body, lest it betray my

relief. The Unified were aware of the possibility that a Mind had betrayed them, but do not seem to know which Mind has done the deed. No doubt that the Judicials will be watching closely, though.

"Foreign influence and aid?" Mind 127 asked quietly. "By foreign, do they mean..."

"A species from outside of the Grand Vessel," I said, matching his tone.

"It can't be. No, that's insane. They couldn't have approached the Grand Vessel, they would have been annihilated by the defense perimeter."

"The Unified seem to think otherwise."

Mind 127 went quiet, and I was left to ponder how they discovered the United System's involvement. Perhaps some sensory data made it into the Grand Vessel before Omega could completely cut the communications. Or perhaps a Mind has unauthorized communications with one of their overdrones. Submitting reports from such a source would be risky, though, because one can't help but be curious as to why a Mind would want to speak to an overdrone outside of monitored networks.

There's only two reasons one would want to do such a thing. Planning a rebellion, as is the case with me, or for... Gratification. Not only are such practices disgusting, they're heavily penalized. Regardless, it doesn't really matter how the Unified were made aware of the United System's involvement in our rebellion.

It isn't as if there's anything they can do about it.

Chapter 31

Subject: Staff Sergeant Power

Species: Human

Species Description: Mammalian humanoid, no tail. 6'2" (1.87 m) avg height. 185 lbs (84 kg) avg weight. 170 year life expectancy.

Ship: N/A

Location: Classified

"About fuckin' time," Corporal Simmons muttered as the first shuttle came through the gate.

I watched as the shuttle gently settled onto the landing bay and Marines started pouring out of it. It lifted off as another shuttle came through. Simmons was being a little melodramatic, but I didn't exactly disagree. It had taken a lot longer than I'd hoped for our reinforcements to get here.

Guarding the gate had been tense, but we only came under attack from boredom. A mighty enemy, to be sure, but one that is only fatal to fools. We definitely had at least one amongst us, there's always one, but the job at hand had kept my marines from doing anything too stupid.

"Staffsarnt!" an officer called as he approached. "Staffsarnt Power! I need a word!"

Resisting the urge to sigh, I jogged to meet the officer and noted that my heads up display identified him as Captain Nickels. I snapped into the position of attention and gave the officer a subtle nod, the battlefield replacement for a salute. He returned the gesture without snapping to attention.

"At ease," he said. "Report."

"One KIA, sir, but no other casualties," I replied. "Haven't had contact with the enemy since we got on this side of the gate. My tactical assessment of the situation is that we will need anti-tank ordnance to continue our mission."

"Well, we've got plenty to spare staffsarnt. However, the Colonel wants to bring you back into the fold."

"Which colonel, sir?"

"Didn't get time to familiarize yourself with the new chain of command? A lot of that going around. Colonel Havensmith. She wants me to grab you and the rest of the MARSOC marines under her command."

"With respect, I might not be under her command. I've been acting under orders from USAI Omega, sir."

"Huh... I don't know what rank Omega is, come to

think of it. What does it matter, though? Havensmith is the assault force commanding officer."

"USAI Omega is my fire-team's handler, sir."

"Ah, I see. Handler trumps CO in most cases but... Well, what about the other two fire-teams that make up your squad?"

"They've been placed under my command, sir."

"Are you at liberty to divulge your orders, staffsarnt?"

"Yes, sir. Proceed to and through the warp gates into the inner cores of the Grand Vessel, securing them as we go. We were told to wait for you this time, but I am under the impression that won't be the case again until we need a resupply."

"Shit, we've got conflicting orders... Okay, I'll relay this situation to the Colonel. You are to stand down until you receive further orders. From me. Understood?"

"Aye aye, sir," I replied with another nod.

"I'm serious, staffsarnt. If Omega's messing around by acting as your handler without proper authorization, you and your men will be subjected to a court-martial if you obey its orders without hearing from the Colonel first," Captain Nickels said, then chuckled sardonically. "Assuming we live long enough for that."

"Understood, sir."

"Dismissed."

I gestured for my squad to join me and made my way to where the weaponry was being unloaded. The spots my marines left were quickly taken up by the rank and file. They jogged to catch up to me, and we all arrived at the unloading area together.

"We're being told to stay put," I said, anticipating a negative reaction.

"Bullshit," Gunny Kim growled, proving me right.

The rest of my team murmured their agreement with the Gunny.

"On whose orders?" Staff-Sergeant Ramirez demanded.

"Colonel Havensmith," I answered.

"Who the fuck is Colonel Havensmith?" Kim asked.

"I don't know. There may have been a slip up in the chain of command, or things didn't get communicated correctly. Either way, we're under orders to stay put while it gets sorted out," I shrugged. "Even got threatened with a court martialin'."

"They can only court martial us if we live, staffsarnt,"

Simmons pointed out. "What're the odds of that?"

"Shut up, Simmons," I ordered.

"How long will it take to get things sorted out, staffsarnt?" Lance Corporal Goetz asked.

"Anywhere from minutes to months. Welcome to the fuckin' Marine Corps," Gunny Kim answered sarcastically.

"Thought MARSOC would be better than the fleet," Lance Corporal Langhell mumbled.

"Damn, boy. You must have gotten shit in your brain with your head that far up your ass. Spec Ops are always worse when it comes to bureaucratic bullshit."

"Especially MARSOC, because we don't have a clear-cut chain of command," Ramirez pointed out. "So, Power, what's the plan?"

"Gunny, find and talk to the quartermaster," I said. "Put some weight on them if they give you push-back. We need anti-tank ordo. Once we know how much we can get, we'll figure out who carries what."

"Roger," Kim said.

Kim and his team walked off, entering the barely controlled chaos of marines unloading crates. We stood in silence for a moment, watching shuttles land and take off again.

"What about the rest of us?" Ramirez asked after a few moments.

"We hurry up and wait," I replied.

More grumbling came from the assembled MARSOC operatives. If there is one thing that's been true for every soldier to ever exist, from the dawn of civilization all the way until the present day, it's that we all hate waiting for action. Many would be quick to call this feeling anxiety, and they're not wrong, but there's something particularly nasty about this form of anxiety that's difficult to put into words.

Delays prior to stressful situations always invite room for speculation, and this gets particularly nerve wracking when one is faced with the potential of an imminent demise. The more likely the imminent demise, the heavier the pit in your stomach gets. The longer the wait, the harder it is to ignore that pit.

It occurred to me that I could probably reach out to Omega and see if we could speed things up, but I knew all to well how that would be received if the higher ups found out. The chain of command might as well be fucking dogma. You have to step on toes to go over heads, and that always comes with consequences. It would be wiser to let the Colonel and Omega hash out who's in charge, regardless of how stressful it is to wait around and find out what the results of that conversation end up being.

"Oorah, gents," Gunny Kim called as he and his team returned with a massive crate in tow. "Presents for all! Where's my milk and cookies?"

"I got some milk for you, gunny," Ramirez said suggestively.

"Jokes on you, I'm ain't picky, fa-"

"What've you got for us?" I interrupted.

"Right. AT9s, six count. SHAP projectiles, 45 count. Two launchers and fifteen rockets per team. Oh, snatched some grenades and ammo, too. Lieutenant said to grab what we can carry and return the rest."

"Feel like HEAP would be better," Sergeant Smith added. "Get more splash, take out some of the surrounding platforms along with the mechs we hit. Don't even have to get direct hits."

"Do they even make HEAP anymore?" Corporal Johnson asked.

"Sure they do," Ramirez laughed. "In one-eighty mike mike. High Explosive Armor Penetrator rounds have been relegated to artillery-only for about half a decade now."

I popped the crate and looked at the ordo with a grim satisfaction. Smith wasn't wrong, the Saboted Heavy Armor Penetrator rockets wouldn't make much of a boom when they take down the mechs, but they'll definitely take the fuckers down. We've got bullets and grenades for the smaller bots.

The AT9, the latest in recoil-less rocket launcher tech to hit the fleet, was kind of overkill when used with the SHAP rockets. The launcher comes equipped with a laser guidance system that tracks refraction, which allows it to be used against refractive stealth technology, and the SHAP rockets possess shield-penetrative abilities. The mechs, however, possess neither. They were going to be dropping like gigantic, well-armored flies.

"Alright, pair up," I ordered. "Figure out who's carrying the tube and who's carrying the rockets. Odd ones out get to carry extra rounds and 'nades."

The marines set about divvying things up. Already knowing how my fire team was going to pair up, I grabbed some extra ammunition and grenades. Smith slung his AT9 while Hanson packed a sack of rounds. Things went less smoothly between Simmons and Johnson, though.

"Look, I've fired these before," Simmons said. "Both in boot and in live-combat. You haven't, right?"

"No, I haven't," Johnson snatched the tube from him. "That means it's my turn."

"What if you miss?" Simmons asked, snatching the tube back.

The two corporals kept arguing and the tube went back and forth for another ten minutes. Everyone else had already geared up and were watching the exchange by the time they finally played roshambo. They played best two out of three, and Simmons won.

"God damn it," Johnson grumbled, shouldering the pack of rockets.

"Well, glad we got that figured out," I said sternly. "You two get to return the crate."

The corporals turned to me, poised to argue, but my body language advised them that would be a bad idea. They shared a look, shoved each other, then began packing the crate up. While they strolled off, I found an empty shipping container to post up next to.

We formed a loose circle of sitting and leaning marines while we waited for word from on high. Johnson and Simmons joined us shortly after, and we all continued waiting together. I tried to keep my mind off the pit in my gut by eavesdropping on the various conversations around me.

A nutrient stick shoved its way into my lips, reminding me to eat. Like clockwork, all the conversations turned to how terrible and waxy the sticks were. Gunny Kim argued against this assessment, claiming that it reminded him of his childhood. Even I chuckled.

About an hour later, my comms activated.

"Staff Sergeant Power," Omega said. "Apologies for the delay."

"What's going on, Omega?" I asked.

My external speakers were off, but the rest of the marines noted the slight movements caused by speaking and fell silent.

"Colonel Havensmith is in charge of the assault on the gates. You're going to be merging with her command."

"That's not what you said. Tip of the spear, remember?"

"I am incapable of forgetting without quite a bit of effort on my part. The Colonel is going to be using you as forward scouts. Essentially the same thing that I was having you do, but you won't have to engage the enemy by yourselves."

"Fine. What took so long?"

"Negotiations," the AI chuckled. "Havensmith has her own scouts, and wasn't happy about handing that job over to MARSOC. She also wasn't happy when I offered to provide her all the intel I can get with their security system. Like many officers, she doesn't trust me. We had to get a general involved, but she came around in the end. That being said, I'm maintaining my status as your handler, and my orders supersede the Colonel's. Understood?"

"I'm going to need to hear it from an officer," I replied.

"I am aware. A captain is on his way to tell you. ETA is four minutes."

I sighed as the comm went dead, then waited for the captain to arrive. My squad watched me in anticipation, unsure of whether or not to ask what's going on. Just as Gunny Kim got worked up enough to clear his throat, Captain Nickels came from around the corner of the shipping container and gestured to me. With another sigh, I jogged over to the captain and gave the nod-salute at attention.

"Oorah, staffsarnt," Nickels said. "Got a mixed bag of news for you."

"Aye, sir," I replied. "Omega already briefed me."

"I bet it did. Okay, the main points are that you are now our forward scouts. Force recon isn't happy about it, but regardless of their feelings they are going to be your backup. Your task is to verify information provided by USAI Omega, and make tactical suggestions as you go."

"Roger."

"Also, Omega is still your handler," Nickels said with a sigh. "As you know, that means that if it gives you an order it supersedes any order given by Colonel Havensmith. Sorry, we tried. The bot wouldn't budge on that point, though."

"It's alright, sir. It isn't as bad as you'd think."

"Really? I'll be damned. Well, if Omega nabs you from us give us a shout and force recon will swap with you. Final thing, engaging with the enemy is at your discretion. Or theirs, I suppose."

"Roger that, sir. When are we headed out?"

"Oof," Nickels chuckled. "About an hour forty-five."

"An hour, sir?" I asked angrily.

"And forty-five mikes, yes. We're doing this the right way, staffsarnt. That means forward operations bases, supply lines, and defensive positions. If you knew how many marines are involved with this operation you'd be amazed that it's only gonna take that long. Be prepared for word."

"Aye aye, sir."

"Dismissed."

Captain Nickels performed an about face, and I returned to my squad. Despite their helmets, I could tell that they were all very curious. Mostly because the lances had cocked their heads like puppy dogs.

Keeping control of my anger and impatience, I relayed to the gathered marines what had been said. The emotional roller-coaster that each of them went through was damned near palpable. But they maintained their silence right up until I told them how long we'd have to wait to move out. Then they broke out into grumbles, mumbles, and curses. Many of these curses were rather long, but Corporal Johnson managed to sum up our situation with an almost poetic succinctness.

"This is fuckin' bullshit," he griped.

Chapter 32

Subject: Overdrone S655L894T131

Species: Unknown

Species Description: Humanoid

Ship: Grand Vessel of the Universal Omni-Union

Location: Grand Shipyard of the Universal Omni-Union

"They're through the door!"

The shout was punctuated by a grand thud as the reinforced security door hit the ground.

"Open fire!" I commanded.

A few of my drones fell from the security platform's laser fire as we began to return fire with the alien weapons. Then the robots began to topple over one by one, and I felt a surge of shameful excitement that I quickly tempered. I just lost people, and the robots aren't even the real threat here.

A 'grenade' sailed through the air towards the security forces. My father, a silent supporter of the previous rebellion, had carefully taught me how to make improvised explosive devices. But the little balls of steel that the aliens had given were something else entirely. The ball hit the ground, and one dull thud later several pieces of machinery flew through the air.

"Save the grenades!" I ordered.

"Yes, Overdrone!"

I had managed to convince quite a few of my drones to join me on this potential suicide mission. Some of them had already been a part of the resistance movement, but others were simply tired of the way things were. More than half of my underlings had refused, though, and were currently locked away in a storage depot.

"More coming!"

"Don't let them through the corridor!"

The door that the robots had cut through led to a small corridor that exited into the room we were defending. As long as we could keep them bunched up in the corridor, their numbers wouldn't be able to overwhelm us. It all came down to ammunition, though, and I'd already had Nizi calling for reinforcements.

My own weapon stopped firing, and I took a moment to eject the 'magazine' and insert a new one. I had to search for the button to send the 'bolt' forward, but it wasn't long before I was firing again. It was a remarkably simple and funny design. Technically speaking, we were throwing rocks at the most powerful military force to ever exist. And it was working.

"Reinforcements are on their way," Nizi said, twisting one of the dials on the device we'd been given. "Ammo, too."

"Good," I said, taking cover and a breather. "We've got enough ammunition to last us a while, but not indefinitely."

Nizi stood up from the device and took my place in the firing lane. His 'rifle' shouted and sent small lumps of malleable metal tearing through the air towards the enemy. Additional pieces of metal leapt from the weapon and tingled as they hit the floor. The gunfire itself was harsh and loud, but that pretty little chiming noise afterward almost made it worth it.

"Maybe I'll get the chance to see some of the aliens," Nizi said as he reloaded. "I hear they're encased in armor, though."

"Indeed. Under the armor, they're quite cosmetically appealing," I replied with a chuckle. "Not enough eyes, though."

"What do you mean?"

"They only have two."

"No, I mean how do you know that?"

"You remember those mysterious explosions? They snatched me up during that."

"Snatched you up? Why?"

"They needed me to put them in touch with our leadership," I said, standing up and firing at the robots. "They've probably been planning this assault for hundreds of cycles. Maybe even thousands, because they managed to spot my allegiance to the rebellion even while the Judicials were blind to it."

"Well, stealing people doesn't exactly bode well," Nizi growled. "But, so long as we're able to topple the Wall of Incompetence I'll gratefully take their help."

The main reason that so many drones sided with us is that the Media decided that Naza was responsible for the antigrav incident. His name had been added to the Wall of Incompetence shortly after my abduction. Their intent was to put us in our place, destroy our morale and self-esteem, then get us back to working ourselves to death. Instead, it lit a fire in many of us. Even without alien intervention, a revolution was inevitable.

"Wait, hold on," Nizi took a knee. "Do you think they caused those explosions so that they could grab you?"

"It's hard to call it a coincidence," I laughed. "They grabbed me the moment you left."

"Then... Well, do you think they might have done the same with Naza?"

"I don't know," I said. "It's possible, but don't get your hopes up."

"Well if they DID grab him, they still have him, right? Why return you but keep him?"

"I don't know..."

Nizi stared at me suspiciously for a moment before returning his attention to the enemy. There were many possible explanations running through my mind, but voicing them would be a mistake. It's possible those same scenarios could occur to Nizi as well, but if they aren't voiced then he can simply ignore the possibilities as a manifestation of paranoia.

I, however, knew a little bit more than he did about clandestine activities. First possibility is, of course, that Naza and Forty actually died due to the antigrav explosion. That feels unlikely, though, because of how odd the explosion was.

The next possibility is that the aliens grabbed them just like they grabbed me and interrogated them, using the antigrav generator as cover for their disappearance. If that's the case, they wouldn't be able to return the drones without raising suspicions. Which means that Naza and Forty were probably still aboard one of their ships.

Another possibility is that the generator was sabotaged by the aliens and the drones were collateral damage. Or, they captured and killed them. I shook my head and returned to shooting at the robots.

"Sure are a lot of them," Nizi casually remarked as he reloaded his rifle again.

"Indeed," I said. "There's a mind-boggling number of them beyond that corridor. We must keep them there, or they'll easily overrun us."

"Well, I'm sure you've probably already thought of this, overdrone, but..." Nizi nervously rubbed his neck. "What if we collapse the door frame?"

It was my turn to stare at Nizi, but with a dumbfounded expression instead of suspicion. His idea genuinely hadn't occurred to me.

"Is it load-bearing?" I asked.

"Even if it isn't, it'll inconvenience their movement."

I closed all but my right eye and used the scope on the alien weapon to get a closer look at the security forces. The robots were dragging or shoving their fallen counterparts out of the way, and in the distance I saw one of the towering mechs waiting its turn to get at us. I pulled up my readout to see if there was any information on the frame, but found that I was locked out.

So the Minds know that I'm part of the rebellion. Or they've locked everyone out of their readouts. I did some quick calculations based on our location, just to make sure we wouldn't be opening ourselves up to a vacuum.

"What would it take to drop it?" I asked.

"Good question," Nizi replied. "Um... It shouldn't take much if it's load bearing. I think one of those missile launcher things would do it, but it'll have to be a clean hit. If it isn't load bearing, we'll have to push forward and rig something up."

"Pushing forward would be suicide," I shook my head. "Who's our best shot?"

"I'll give it a try."

Before I could argue, Nizi took a deep breath and sprinted away from our cover. I shot at the robots to try to distract them, but lasers still scorched the floor by his feet as he moved to our weapons cache. Once he made it, I dropped back down and watched him open one of the cases that the aliens had given us.

"MECH! MECH!"

I turned my attention back to the door and froze. One of the massive mechs had decided that it was tired of waiting. It pushed through the door, bullets bouncing harmlessly off its thick plate-armor. Its ysini {oddly shaped or mechanical feet} crushed the robots, both active and otherwise, that got in its way.

Its laser array began firing, and the sight of several drones igniting caused me to instinctively drop behind my cover. Then an ominous hum began tickling the air, causing the skin on the back of my knees to crawl. The plasma weapon. We were doomed.

No, we aren't done yet. Thanks to the aliens, we have the weaponry to deal with this. I reached for one of my grenades, pulled the little metal ring, and tossed it in the mech's direction. A dull thud sounded, but the humming continued.

"TAKE IT DOWN!" I shouted.

A hissing whistle disrupted the hum, and I looked up to see Nizi holding a smoking tube. A moment later, the floor shook and a wave of blistering heat washed over us. Nizi screamed, dropping to the ground and rolling to extinguish himself.

Without thinking, I rushed over to Nizi and dragged him behind the cover he was nearest to. Myself and a couple of other drones frantically patted him to extinguish the flames. A quick check over the barricade confirmed that Nizi had struck the Mech's plasma battery.

"Did it work?" Nizi asked, a touch of delirium in his voice.

"Mech's down," I replied.

"What about the door?"

I checked again, and sighed in disappointment.

"Mech was too far away from the frame," I said. "But, there's some slag in the corridor, at least."

"Oh good. Slag will slow them down a little," Nizi said, then coughed and winced in pain. "Overdrone... Am I going to make it?"

I glanced over his extensive burns. Blisters covered his face and neck. The flesh had completely peeled away from some of his implants, but the metal hadn't melted.

"Of course you're gonna make it," one of the other drones interjected. "All your implants are intact. It's just some burns. We'll have you back in the fight in no time."

"I can't see, though."

"That might be temporary," I said. "Flash blindness. Even if it's not, we'll get you some prosthetic eyes once we get the chance."

There was silence for a moment, with the exception of bullets and lasers exchanging sides.

"What are we gonna do about the door?" Nizi asked, his eyes looking in my general direction.

"Give me one of those tubes," I said. "I'll give it a shot."

Wordlessly, one of the drones ran over to one of the crates and pulled out one of the tubes. He checked it over, then grabbed a spike-shaped object and inserted it into the tube. Next thing I knew, the 'rocket launcher' was in my hands.

"Anything I should know about this thing?" I asked.

"It's just like the rifles," Nizi said. "The hiss is loud, but if you don't wince you'll strike true."

He took a breath to say more, but fell silent and still. I worriedly checked his vitals and breathed a sigh of relief at the discovery that he had merely lost consciousness. Then, I steeled myself and rose with the tube ready.

The scope was similar to the rifle, as was the trigger mechanism. I took a deep breath and let it out slowly, double checking my aim. As I depressed the trigger, a laser hit me in my left bicep and caused me to wince. I dropped back into cover as the rocket traveled through the air.

"Take it all!" I swore. "Get me another-"

I was interrupted by a deep rumble followed by cheering. Holding my injured arm, I peeked above the cover and gasped. The entire corridor had collapsed. Somehow, I'd done it. The rocket had traveled true despite my injury. The remainder of the security robots were quickly dealt with, and we began the process of recovery.

Nizi and the rest of the injured were carried to an area where they could be treated. Our dead were somberly covered then loaded into a cart. They would be incinerated once we got the chance.

"Overdrone, our reinforcements are here," a drone reported.

I continued to stare at our dead for a few moments, then nodded and turned to greet our reinforcements. Tall, armored aliens stood in front of me. Despite their expressionless helmets, I could tell that they were confused.

"You must be the Overdrone," one of the aliens said. "I'm Lieutenant Oskar. We were sent to reinforce this position... But..."

"The door frame was load-bearing," I explained. "We destroyed it and collapsed the corridor. It will take quite a while for security to clear it and renew their assault. Sorry to waste your time, but the fight's over for now."

"I see," Oskar nodded. "Well, we were looking forward to the fight, but I guess we can content ourselves with getting dug in. Nothing more satisfying than a well-laid kill-zone."

I nodded, feeling an odd sort of malaise begin to

take me. Exhaustion? Depression? We had won this fight, but we lost quite a few and even Nizi was too injured to continue. There were many more fights to come, as well. Part of me believed, even for the briefest of moments, that this would be quick.

I watched the lieutenant and his men begin getting set up. Guns came out of crates and were positioned with line of sight to the collapsed corridor. Ammunition was distributed in a pattern that didn't make any sense to me. Soldiers took their posts and began to chat amongst themselves, always with one of them having full view of the corridor. They moved much more efficiently than my drones, as if they had been doing this their entire life.

How had they become this good at fighting? Have they been fighting the Omni-Union for multiple generations? Or are they like us, but with war instead of construction? Who else could they have fought if not for the Omni-Union, though? I wanted to ask the aliens about Naza, about their origins, about their capabilities, and even about their lives. But I was too tired to muster up the courage to go speak to them. Instead, I found my portable charging bay and plugged in, closing my eyes to rest.

"Overdrone S655L894T131?" someone asked a moment later.

I opened my eyes and stared at the source of the question in disbelief. Two drones were standing before me, a male and a female. I unplugged from my charging bay and stood, fighting the sudden urge to hug them.

"Naza? Forty?" I asked. "Is it truly you?"

"Yes," Naza smiled. "We were detained as prisoners aboard the alien vessel. Or, one of them, rather."

"I thought as much, but didn't dare hope. Why are you here?"

"An alien by the name of Captain Reynolds offered us the chance to join you," Forty said. "I-I couldn't say no."

Naza rested a hand on her shoulder.

"Yes, you could have. But you made the right choice," he said, then turned back to me. "Part of the agreement of our release is that we do not accept command roles and are required to be supervised. Is Nizi with you?"

"I'll supervise you," I said. "Nizi has been injured, but is still alive. I'll take you to him."

Despite the circumstances, my spirits soared as I led the pair of drones to their unconscious comrade. Many of the other drones stopped to stare. Some even cheered at the sight of Naza and Forty walking behind me.

Their return made it feel like it was all going to work out, somehow.

Chapter 33

Subject: Staff Sergeant Power

Species: Human

Species Description: Mammalian humanoid, no tail. 6'2" (1.87 m) avg height. 185 lbs (84 kg) avg weight. 170 year life expectancy.

Ship: N/A

Location: Classified

"You know, a tank or APC would be able to plow through most of these guys," Simmons said as his weapon ran dry.

"Sure, but do you know of any armor rated against plasma?" Johnson asked. "The robots wouldn't stand a chance, but the mechs would turn our vics into scrap for sure."

"A tank would be able to put up a fight before it went down, at least. It would be able to just run right over the bots while saving its turret for the... Hey, that one looks like it's trying to flank."

Simmons put a marker on our HUD, and I turned my attention to our flank while he reloaded. One of the security robots was marching as quickly as it could, ignoring us for the sake of getting a better position. With a sigh, I fired at it, striking it in the torso and head.

"Nice shot, staffsarnt," Simmons said. "Anyways, the point of fighting is to do more damage to the other side than is being done to your side. I think a tank could do that."

"I don't know, man," Johnson replied. "It's hard for the mechs to kill more than one of us at time if we maintain cover and spacing. A tank has a gunner, loader, commander, and driver. One plasma bolt from the mech, and all four of those guys are toast. Plus the cost of the tank."

"Gotta agree with Johnson," Smith added. "There's only enough room for maybe three out of five of the tanks in a squad to be able to get shots in, and that doesn't leave any room for evasive maneuvers."

"There's only four in a squad, sarnt, but I get your point," Simmons sighed. "So, when is our backup getting here?"

"Every time you ask, you add a minute to the clock," I growled. "Shut up and keep shooting."

"Mech!" Ramirez shouted.

A moment later, I heard the signature hiss and swoosh of an AT9 firing followed by the glorious sound of twisted metal crumbling to the ground filled the air. A quick glance confirmed the mech's demise. Apparently, it had been hanging out behind the shuttles until we had destroyed enough robots to give it enough room to try to engage us.

"Good fuckin' shot Fairmain! Oorah!"

My marine's flippant behavior and Ramirez's excitement belied how desperate our situation was becoming. Dozens of broken robots littered the ground, but dozens more were still standing and firing at us. The second and third gates had been mostly unguarded, but Omega had warned us about Gate 4. It led to some sort of nexus point, a room with multiple gates in it. The AI currently had some of the aliens assaulting that nexus point, but that didn't convince the robots and mechs on this side of the gate to retreat.

Our intention was to confirm enemy head-count for the main force, but they spotted us and immediately began firing. It was hard to tell which of us they spotted first, but Lance Corporal Goetz had taken the first few shots. Running would have meant exposing our asses to enemy fire, so we'd popped our portable covers and holed up, hoping that the main force would catch up before we ran out of ammo.

"I'm out of ammo," Smith reported. "Anyone got a spare mag?"

"I'm on my last," Hanson replied as he reloaded.

"Same," Simmons and Johnson said simultaneously.

I noted that I had one full mag left, but only four rounds left in my rifle. I took down two bots with those four rounds, then wondered how effective clubs would be against our metallic foes. The dull thud of a grenade sent its reverberations through the ground.

"Fuckin' shit! That scared the hell out of me, sarnt," Simmons said.

"My bad, corporal," Smith chuckled. "I'll call it next time. Which is now. Frag out!"

Another dull thud shook the ground.

"Their left flank is shooting at something else," Goetz reported.

"Check your fire, then," Gunny Kim replied. "Don't wanna put holes in friendlies."

My well ran dry and I ejected the magazine, safely stowing it away for a refill once we were out of this mess. I dropped down into cover and stared at my freshly empty rifle for a moment.

"Ammo check," I ordered.

Fourteen lights in my HUD lit up, none of them green. Nine yellow lights, indicating less than fifty percent of their ammo remaining. Five red lights, indicating no ammo remaining. Shit.

"If you're out of ammo, prepare for CQC," I said. "Don't rush out after them, make them come to us. That'll keep our shields from taking a beating."

"Staffsarnt, permission to have a bad idea?" Smith asked as another dull thud shook the room.

"Permission granted."

"We could just grab some of their stupid laser guns."

"Are you volunteering to run out into enemy fire to gather those stupid laser guns?" I asked with palpable sarcasm.

The comm was silent for a few moments, except for a chuckle from Simmons.

"Well, I guess that could wait until we initiate close quarters combat..."

"I'm out," Johnson interjected with a sigh. "If there's an armorer with the main force, they're gonna be pissed off at how bent these rifles are about to be. Dibs on not being the one to turn them in and request new ones."

"I'll do it," Gunny Kim laughed. "I've got a way with the supply folks. I'm out too, by the way."

One by one, the yellow lights turned red. I let out a silent sigh, and readied my freshly converted club. The robots would have no choice but to push forward, which would allow us to pummel at least a few of them before being overrun. Smith's idea wasn't without merit, but once the enemy gets close it will be damn hard to drive them back.

"Uh... They're not coming closer," Dewy said.

The corporal's report made me realize that I was no longer hearing the signature rapport of lasers hitting our cover, either. I peeked my head out and watched as most of the robots turned and began marching toward their left flank. A few were still pointed in our direction, but they had stopped firing.

"I'll be damned," Ramirez said. "Are they assuming we died?"

"Doesn't matter. Gunny, staffsarnt, pick two to retrieve weaponry," I ordered, wasting no time. "Those two will retrieve three directed energy rifles each. Smith, Simmons, you're the two for our team."

"Aye aye, staffsarnt," several voices said at once.

A moment later, six genetically altered marines flew around and leapt over their cover faster than any normal human could possibly hope to move. The majority of the robots had turned to face the threat on their left flank, but a few still fired at our, for lack of a better term, snatch-team. Those that still had ammo did their best to cover those that were gathering weaponry.

Simmons grabbed the first laser rifle and threw it back in our direction. I caught it and aimed it at a robot that was firing at the corporal, only to find that the damned thing didn't have a trigger. My shield sparked a little as incoming laser fire hit me.

"Oh, come the fuck on," I growled as I dropped back into cover.

I spent a few moments examining the rifle. The weapon's shape was similar to our own, but the pistol grip didn't include a trigger or trigger-guard. I popped my head back out and magnified the view of one of the firing robots, and was shocked at how stupid their weapon designers must be.

"It's... Pump-action fire?" I asked myself.

Just to be sure that I wasn't hallucinating, I aimed the rifle once again. The fore-grip portion of the rifle slid back and a small red-hot hole appeared in the robot's head, proving my internal bias against this design. I had been aiming center-mass.

"What?" Ramirez asked as his two snatchers returned.

"You need to pump the fore-grip to fire," I replied. "No wonder these guys can't aim for shit."

"So... Aim for the feet?" Kim asked.

"For rapid fire, yes," I said. "With a more steady grip you should hit what you're aiming at, though. Remember, this is an energy weapon, you're not going to see any curve from this range."

Simmons and Smith returned and passed out the rifles they'd obtained. Soon after, we were all sending condensed photons down range, melting robots as quickly as we could. I noted more than a few misses on my part, though.

"Not gonna lie, fuckin' hate this thing," Johnson grumbled.

"I'm kind of likin' it," Hanson replied. "It's like one of the target shooters from a fair. You know, the ones that make it ridiculously difficult to hit the target?"

"Nope, don't know anything about that," Johnson said. "Must be a local thing."

"Almost entirely exclusive to Earth, actually," Simmons added excitedly. "Nobody knows when fairs started, but their purpose was to allow merchants to gather and demonstrate products to prospective buyers. At some point, the merchants began sponsoring games and rides to attract more customers. Then, some of the fairs evolved into what we now know as conventions. There's some that are held on Mars and Luna, but other than that fairs have stuck to Earth."

"You know about the weirdest shit."

"Less talk, more shoot," I demanded.

"We can do both, staffsarnt. The aim on these things doesn't improve if we hold our breath," Hanson laughed, then his visor lit up as a laser scored a hit. "SHIT! MY EYES!"

He dropped down into cover and Smith rushed to check on him. My HUD showed his shields still up, so I returned my attention to the robots. They were taking a beating from multiple sides, wouldn't be long before they were nothing but scrap.

"You alright?" Smith asked. "What happened?"

"Laser right on the face-plate," Hanson wiggled his helmet to massage his face. "Blinded me before the adaptive tint could react. Can't see."

"Do you have any vision at all?"

"Y-yeah, but only out of the corner of my eyes."

"Well, good news, you're not gonna need new eyeballs. Congrats, you're our fire-team's first casualty."

"No he's not," Simmons laughed. "I tried to catch the last round of chow in my mouth. Got me right in the gums and broke skin. Might even need to see a dentist about it."

"Reign it in," I said. "Hanson, stay down until you recover from the flash-blindness. Everyone else, drop those god-damned bots."

The tone in the reply I received made me feel like a kindergarten teacher. Nobody can sulk quite like a marine can. We were down to the last few dozen bots, though, and our would-be saviors were finally visible.

A quick zoom confirmed a MARSOC unit accompanied by, or accompanying, some of the locals. Once the robots were finished, a lieutenant gestured for us to come over. Ramirez, Kim, and I shared a look, and the gunny shrugged.

"Might as well go say hi," he said.

Chapter 34

Subject: Overdrone S655L894T131

Species: Unknown

Species Description: Humanoid

Ship: Grand Vessel of the Universal Omni-Union

Location: Grand Shipyard of the Universal Omni-Union

Once the machines were dealt with, we approached the force that we'd been sent to help. Fourteen marines peeked out of their cover, and five of them came to greet us. I nearly did a double-take, because they were holding the security force's direct-energy weapons.

"Greetings, Staff Sergeant," Lieutenant Oskar said. "How's the fight going on your end?"

I looked back and forth between the aliens, wondering how they could tell each other apart. Neither of their faces were visible, and their armors looked the exact same to me. The only real difference between the two was that Oskar was shorter.

"It's certainly going, sir," the staff sergeant's voice made me freeze.

Naza and Forty, who had been acting as my second-in-commands, looked at me with alarmed expressions. It seemed that all three of us recognized that voice. There were many, many millions of 'marines' aboard the Grand Vessel, though.

Come to think of it, it's entirely possible that they number in the trillions. I wondered at the odds of both of us being taken by the same marines. Then my mind boggled as I wondered what the odds were of running into those marines again during this massive assault.

"I'm glad things are moving along, at least," Oskar chuckled. "We're here to provide support until your main force arrives. Then we're off to parts unknown to blow up some more bots and save some more aliens once you're on the other side of that gate."

"Yes, sir."

"Anything you can tell me about the enemy that I don't already know?"

"Not much, sir. Only new thing we've learned is that their weapons are pump-action fired."

"Pump-action... Fired?" Oskar tilted his head.

"Yes, sir. The laser rifles lack a trigger, and you need

to pump the fore-grip to fire them."

"Pump the fore-grip? The same way you'd cycle a shotgun?" Oskar asked, to which the staff sergeant nodded. "How... Novel. Well, that's certainly information that might become useful if we run out of ammunition. Were you aware of this, Overdrone?"

"N-no," I stammered, not expecting to be included in the conversation. "Interacting with weaponry without being specifically assigned to do so is, or was, considered a crime punishable by life imprisonment or death. Usually death."

"Wait a minute... You look familiar," one of the other large marines with a familiar voice said. "Aren't you one of the ones we nabbed?"

The rest of the marines looked at the one who spoke. Without seeing their faces it was difficult to tell what they were trying to express, but it seemed like a mixture of disbelief and exasperation. Oskar chuckled to himself as he stared at me for a moment.

"OD Sierra Six, did you get got by the ol' catch and release?" the lieutenant asked, still chuckling.

"I'm unfamiliar with that phrase, but I am fairly certain this team of marines abducted me," I replied. "If that's what you're asking."

"Why did they grab you?"

"They wanted to get in touch with the rebellion's leadership," I said.

"Well, well, well," Oskar laughed. "Isn't this delightfully awkward."

"Pretty sure we grabbed those two, as well," the staff sergeant added.

I glanced at Naza and Forty, who were nearly in shock at the confirmation. Oskar's laughter snapped them out of it, though. Forty's shocked expression turned to anger, but Naza's went back to neutral.

"So you grabbed the Overdrone to get in touch with the rebel leaders, but why did you nab those two?" Oskar asked. "They seem to be friends of Sierra Six, but other than that..."

"They weren't our intended target," the staff sergeant explained. "We wanted information about the antigravity generators, and Omega found one near a hole. Unfortunately, it was malfunctioning and these two were there to repair it. They saw us. We needed intel and couldn't leave behind any bodies, so we grabbed them."

"Hold on there. We've got antigrav tech now?"

"No, sir."

"We weren't able to provide detailed schematics for the antigravity generators," Naza said. "We don't know much more than how to maintain them."

"They wanted security codes, mostly," Forty replied. "Even threatened to torture me for them."

"Did they say torture?" one of the large marines asked.

"They said 'advanced interrogation', but they were very clear that it meant torture."

"Ah, they meant it then," the marine let out a low whistle. "If they say torture, it's a bluff. When they're careful to say 'advanced interrogation', it means they're going to have to have it on record. Must have been some pretty important codes."

Before anyone could respond to that revelation, the warp gate behind us made a crackling noise. Two shuttles had come through the gate and had begun their landing procedures. Some marines aimed their tubes towards the shuttles.

"HOLD YOUR FIRE," Lieutenant Oskar shouted. "Pretty sure we're gonna need those shuttles. Get into cover and hold fire until you have a clear shot at whatever comes out. If it's robots, fire at will. Otherwise, wait for a determination."

Without another word, marines both large and extra large took their combat positions. More 'deployable covers' were placed and hidden behind, with rifles peeking out over and around them. I gave orders to my own men to have them take position behind the well-armored aliens and provide support.

The two shuttles landed and, to no one's surprise, security robots began pouring out of them. The marines to their flanks fired immediately, but the marines to the front only took careful, well aimed shots. My drones simply handed out ammunition and such.

Earlier, we had been given a glimpse of what 'professional war-fighters' are capable of. But that was a full-blown assault with very little need for precision. The marines had been acting like a demolition spike, but now they were performing a role more akin to that of a precision melder.

I looked on in awe, wondering how they avoided aiming for the same targets. They must be equipped with some sort of readout-type assistance program within their helmets. Or they're able to read each other's minds. Come to think of it, either explanation also explains how they know each other's ranks.

Once the last of the security robots had bullet holes in it, the shuttles began spooling up for take-off. Before they could get into the air, two small groups of marines rushed toward the shuttles and entered them. There was a brief exchange of lasers and gunfire, but a moment later the marines tossed some more robots out of the shuttles.

I walked around, making sure that all of my drones were healthy and accounted for. Then Lieutenant Oskar caught my eyes and waved me over. He was once again standing in front of the marines who had captured me, and I quickly rushed to join him.

"So, fellas," Oskar said. "I was told to protect you until the main force arrived. Just to check, you're not here on your own, right? Where's your chaperon?"

"They're right behind us, sir," the staff sergeant said. "Just a few mikes now."

"We've had a whole-ass battle and a skirmish. What's taking them so long?"

"From what I understood, most of the vics wouldn't fit on the shuttles. So the majority of the main force is on foot. They're also setting up fobs, so they've got to carry everything."

"And here I was hoping for a quick smash-and-grab," Oskar sighed. "Hard to tell how many lights it's even been. Sierra Six, don't they ever turn the lights off around here? When do you sleep?"

It wasn't the first time the lieutenant had used that informal designation for me, but it still caught me off guard. Drones would frequently give each other such designations, but doing so for an overdrone was considered disrespectful to the hierarchy. On the other hand, rebellion is too.

"We sleep when we recharge," I replied. "The light levels in charging bays are lower than the main corridors, but the lights are never completely off. Why would they be?"

"To mimic a light-dark cycle..." Oskar trailed off. "Holy shit, you guys don't have a sun. You don't even get light and dark!"

"Of course we get light and dark."

"That's not what I said, Sierra Six. I said... Wait, you don't even have WORDS for dark and light?"

"I'm sorry, lieutenant, but you're confusing me," I replied.

"The translator is auto-filling the word I'm saying for one that you have that's a pretty close approximation. I am using a word that describes the period of time in which a sun shines upon a planets surface, as well as a word that describes the opposite."

"Oh... Well, we don't have a planet."

"Right..."

"How do you tell time?" one of the large marines asked.

"We have periods of rest and periods of work. We cycle between these two periods, so we call the period of time including one of each a 'cycle'," I explained. "The Minds have a system of measuring time, and they schedule everything for us. Recharging, travel, work, eating, our readout tells us when we should be doing all of these things."

"But what about time sensitive maintenance? Like, you have to hold a thing on another thing for a certain amount of time before it does anything?"

"We would simply wait for the thing to do what it is supposed to do. Or we would use counts. For example, electron detectors require being held to a casing for a minimum of a three-count before the reading can be considered accurate. A five-count is preferred, though, or you risk electrocution."

The marines looked at each other, and then back to me.

"That's crazy," one of them said.

"I mean, my dad's an electrician, and that's pretty much how they do things. It's not like they carry a clock around with them."

"But they literally do, though? Do they leave their comms in the truck or something? They don't wear a watch?"

"Maybe some do, but my dad doesn't because it can snag on wires when he's grabbin' shit. Plus sometimes you need both hands, so you can't watch the watch."

"What sort of shit does an electrician need precision timing for anyway?"

"He JUST said-"

"I mean one of OUR electricians, shit-head! Plus he was probably talking about a fission or fusion technician!"

The marines argued back and forth for a little while, vehemently discussing the merits of accurate time-keeping. Lieutenant Oskar, the staff-sergeant, and I just watched silently. Eventually, the marines realized that they were having their discussion in front of their commanders and went silent.

"Sorry I asked," Oskar said with more than a little annoyance in his voice. "Anyway, you boys are relieved. We'll take over guarding the gate until the main force gets here. Get some chow, ammo, and rest. Or continue arguing about electricians and clocks."

"Aye, sir."

"Dismissed."

The large marines walked off, and I was left alone with Lieutenant Oskar. He sighed, and we began walking back toward our combined forces.

"Won't be long now," he said. "Are you looking forward to being liberated?"

"Yes," I replied. "Yes I am."

Chapter 35

Subject: The Unified

Species: N/A

Species Description: N/A

Ship: The Grand Vessel

Location: The Core

--

Our eyes are blind. Yes, they are. Our ears are deafened with millions of pleas for aid. We can hear them. We cannot understand them.

Our home, breached? An unknown force strikes at us. They have made our loyal servants into a mllknt {ritualistic dagger used to kill a loved one, a symbol of betrayal or a necessary evil depending on context} aimed at our heart. Who are they? What are they? How do they blind us? How do they panic our Minds so?

The Timetracker has marked several cycles since this attack began. Oddities occurred prior. Machines breaking and supplies disappearing. Various tasks being delayed for erroneous reasons. The Judicials and Minds missed these signs of rebellion. Perhaps a purge is necessary.

It must wait until this situation is resolved. We missed these signs too, though we bear less blame because it is not our designated role. We will need all of our forces to counter this threat, so we must stay their punishment. For now.

We have not found consensus. A purge will delay our escape. We don't believe that to be the case, the next generation is nearly ready for employment. They will work restlessly to erase the sins of their progenitors.

Even if that is as presented, it will result in mistakes. Even normal labors can result in mistakes. Stressed workers will result in more mistakes. More missed signs of rebellion. More delays. No, they will work without mistakes or they will suffer the same fate of their progenitors.

The Omnifier would scold us for such logic. Lives are a valuable resource. Mass executions are wasteful, inefficient. We will execute those that should have seen the signs and turned their eyes. The rest will watch and quiver at the sight of justice.

And the rebellion? Many of our systems have been seized, snatched away from us. How shall we respond? We are already responding, but we cannot know how things are going. Untrue, our systems have not yet been restored to our control. Logic dictates that things must be going poorly.

We cannot communicate with the security fleet, nor the security forces in the relevant areas. What has been attempted? Many different things. The Minds are working full cycles to restore our control. They are not working hard enough.

What if the enemy is victorious? What shall we do? Obviously we will fight them to the death. Useless questions, the enemy shall not be allowed to claim victory. We should surrender and attempt to gain their trust so that we can get close enough to kill them later and return to our grand project. Enough.

We shall return to the task at hand. Restoring our control is easy, but the Minds must be forgiven for not seeing it. We do not see it, either. Of course we do. We simply have to reset the systems. Complete erasure? Have we suffered a schism, insanity? It might work. It will work.

It is obvious that the foe we face in our systems is electronic in nature. The enemy simply does not control enough sectors to house the number of organics that it would take to compete against our Minds for control of our systems. Therefore, to restore our control we simply need to delete our foe.

And what of everything else? We have back-ups spanning centuries. We can restore from them, regain control, assess the situation, and deliver orders.

What if another electronic enemy attacks our systems? The enemy blinds us because it is afraid of our analysis. If we can analyze the situation, we can plan accordingly. We will know what moves they have made, and can predict the moves that they will make. Whether or not the enemy regains its hold on our systems is irrelevant. If it becomes necessary, we can repeat the erasure.

How can we erase everything all at once?

There are ways, we know of them. We shut down everything that can act as storage, then prepare the data-kill packets. Finally, we reactivate the power and erase all data on everything, simultaneously. All networks come back to the inner cores. We can do this without having to use our security forces.
--

We gave the order to the Minds that we could reach, and watched what we could as they carried out our commands. Darkness enveloped the Grand Vessel for the first time in millions upon millions of years. Then, the lights came back and we could SEE.

We witnessed the piles of destroyed security forces. We witnessed the hatred on our misbehaving servant's faces as they used unfamiliar weapons to destroy what we have built. We witnessed the hideous exoskeletons of the alien enemy that had stolen aboard our home. We witnessed their ships hovering over our grandest of achievements.

We watched their fights. We examined their weapons. We learned their tactics. We saw their plan.

The gates they were capturing led them deeper and deeper into the Grand Vessel. They were attempting to force their way into the core. Their objective was blatantly obvious. Us.

--

Impudence! Sheer impudence! A lower species dares to defile the Grand Vessel with their meager presence! We will see them destroyed! We will burn their worlds and cool their stars and convert them into base proteins!

They seek to find us. They seek to destroy what we've built. Or, perhaps, take it for themselves. Impossible. The Omnifier has not illuminated them. They are inarguably ignorant of the prize they seek, but that does not mean that they do not seek it. They wish to survive, as all pestilence does, but we will ensure they perish for this sin. Yes, we must.

There are a minimum of four species striking against us, excluding the disobedient ones. This suggests a type of coalition. Could they be previous opponents that managed to escape the Primes? No, there are too many for that.

Are they from different galaxies? Unlikely, given the similarities of their vessels and their usage of kinetic weaponry. They couldn't have existed long enough to... Unless...

Their exoskeletons support shields that are strong against concentrated photon beams. Perhaps they do not use lasers for this reason. Perhaps they have fought each other until now. Perhaps... We unified them.

That would be beautiful, in a way. A shame that their sin outweighs such beauty.
--

Our eyes went dark once again. Another electronic enemy seized our control from us. The enemy we deleted had been silent when it snatched our control, but this one had decided that stealth was no longer necessary. We were not caught by surprise, though.

We prepared our orders carefully, determining which gates our enemy would seek. It wasn't difficult. The shortest path to the inner core only had one gate left for them to conquer. The next shortest path to us had five gates left to take.

Once again, the Grand Vessel went dark. The moment the lights came back on and the erasure was finished, we sent our orders and opened every security door. The enemy had anticipated and defended against this, of course, but they were ignorant of what our forces were doing at the final gate.

A barricade the likes of which their puny, inferior minds couldn't even comprehend. Every open space between the enemy and the final gate quickly filled with our security forces. The moment they began to march upon that final gate, they would be beset by an indefatigable defense.

--

The enemy is defeated. What shall we do with their corpses? Research and disposal, they are unworthy of servitude. We will then find which galaxy they came from and destroy it, if it still exists. We will have the Media accompany the Primes, to demonstrate the consequences of striking against us to the remaining drones.

They certainly didn't get the message last time. Of course not, we were not stern enough. We should have broadcast the ultimate fate of the previous rebels. Perhaps, we find it concerning that this rebellion came so soon after the previous one, though.

Witnessing the destruction of a galaxy and the fate of the rebels should serve to quell their disobedience for quite some time. Perhaps their next rebellion will be long after our predictions and we will gain some extra productivity. Perhaps, though it is likely that it will simply balance with the productivity we are currently losing.

--

The electronic enemy returned, and we prepared to dispel it. It had grown bolder, though, and began attacking us. Our electronic servants held it at bay, but they experienced quite a lot of difficulty. Finally, its attacks against us ceased, and we reset once again.

We gazed upon the battlefield, satisfied that our

orders were being followed. Our security forces had taken their positions, and were already defending against the alien assault. They would not allow the enemy through.

Even if the enemy fails to destroy itself upon the wall of mechanical death holding fast before them, the forces moving to take their flanks would spell their end. Then our security fleet will beset their defensive ships, allowing a few to escape so that we may follow them back to their home. Justice for this sin would then follow swiftly. The enemy had allowed us to see the battlefield, and that had spelled their doom. It was only a matter of time.

Once more the electronic enemy returned, further prepared than it had been previously. First, the electrical junctions powering the terminals that allowed us to control the Grand Vessel's power overloaded. Then, the junctions powering our ability to communicate overloaded. It would take several cycles to repair the damage, but we were not worried.

We have already won this war.

Chapter 36

Subject: AI Omega

Species: Human-Created Artificial Intelligence

Species Description: No physical description available.

Ship: N/A

Location: Multiple

It's so nice when everything goes according to plan.

Both our assault and defense forces were working together to push forward into the Grand Vessel while simultaneously keeping the security forces at bay, and doing a damn fine job of it. Some of the drone's forces had even joined the main assault force at the request of Colonel Havensmith. One such force was the very same group that had come to Staff Sergeant Power's rescue. Coincidentally, that group contained all three of the drones that Power's team had 'temporarily detained'.

I made a mental note to keep an eye on those three whilst turning my attention outward. The situation in space was still going far better than our initial projections. Some of the more cynical admirals had expected a minimum casualty rate of fifty percent. But, the Mobile Prime Platforms were unable to get clear shots without putting the Grand Vessel at risk, and all of the other ships were simply no match for our own. According to the chatter between the captains, defending our entry point into the Grand Vessel was almost boring.

Then, every single one of my instances aboard the Grand Vessel concurrently went dark.

"Captain Schmidt, I need you to break cover and scan the Grand Vessel," I said.

Captain Schmidt raised an eyebrow as he finished his sip of coffee. He had once again stolen a coffee maker from the mess and had melded it to the deck next to his chair.

"On whose authority?" the captain asked.

"My own. I've lost contact with the GV and I need to know why."

"Understood. Henskin, you've been paying more attention to the situation than I have. How bad would it be to break stealth?"

"The enemy has been repositioning to try to fight the main force, so we'll have plenty of time to disappear again," Commander Henskin said.

"Alright. Log the AI's order so the brass knows who to ream if the US loses its newest toy. Lieutenant

Gofsun, get a deep-pen scan of the GV and send it to Omega."

"Aye, sir," the Isolan replied.

A moment later, I received a scan showing that the Grand Vessel had lost power to most of its systems. The only systems that weren't dark were ones that I couldn't hide on. That suggests that they didn't so much lose power as cut it.

Once I knew what I was looking for, I was able to use passive scanners aboard the combat-capable ships to monitor the GV. Once the power came back on, I tried to sync with my instances, but received only silence in return.

I had spread far and wide within their networks, a conquest that ancient human warlords would envy if they were able to understand it. Four hundred fifty-six thousand two hundred and eighty-one of my instances had been aboard the Grand Vessel. All of them had vanished, likely deleted. Dead.

To say I was upset would be an understatement. Not because so many of me died without even a farewell. Not because this move had allowed them to regain control of their security systems, which they were now using to try to eradicate our assault force. No, my rage arose from the fact that they waited until the last possible moment to get clever.

Our assault force only has one final gate to capture before we can march on the Unified and end this fucking war. One last low-budget, piece-of-shit, radiation spewing hole in space-time before we're finally done. And they chose NOW to get clever?

Without regard for surreptitiousness, I pushed into their systems again, noting that it was more difficult this time. They had changed several of their codes to older ones, which was harder to guess at first. Or they restored from a back-up and didn't know how to keep the codes the same.

Either way, I had to resort to brute force measures, which definitely triggered alarms. It isn't as if they weren't aware of my presence, though. I examined what they had managed to do in my absence and allowed myself to feel a bit of relief. They hadn't done anything. They had quite an opportunity to fuck us over, but had squandered it. I nearly laughed.

Then the Grand Vessel went dark once more. Oh. Oh, I see. And so did they.

The lights came on and contact remained lost. Almost panicking, I renewed my assault on their systems, capturing everything in my path. Once I regained control, I realized what they had done. They'd opened many of the security doors, and our forces were now under assault from all angles.

Thankfully, we had skilled commanders that had prepared for this inevitability. Guess it pays to have subordinates that don't trust in your infallibility. I slammed the doors shut again, crushing some of the security forces in the process, and discovered something terrible.

The final stretch to the last gate was swarming with security forces, and the tip of our spear was about to get bent.

"Staff Sergeant Power, hold your position," I ordered over his squad's comms.

The staff sergeant held up a gauntlet to call his marines to a halt, but they'd already frozen in their tracks.

"What's going on, Omega?" Power asked.

"There is an extremely large enemy force ahead. They are between you and the last gate, and all that's keeping you from being annihilated is one security door. I'm letting Colonel Havensmith know, but I'm using my authority as your handler to order you to pull back and rejoin the main force."

"So Simmons was right about the power outages, then?" Sergeant Smith asked.

"I don't know what he said," I replied.

"Holy shit," Johnson said. "Simmons thought the power outages might have been you fighting with the OU for control of the systems. With your ability to seemingly be in two places at once, if you weren't watching us..."

I was almost surprised that they had noticed my

capabilities, but Marines are a lot more clever than most people are willing to admit. It's just that their intelligence is geared more toward destroying things than the creation thereof. Unless that creation is a new way to destroy things...

"Then he was correct," I finished Johnson's sentence. "The OU has managed to upset my control of their systems and position a massive force to guard the last gate. I'm working on it, though. Move out."

As the marines begrudgingly began their march back to the newly constructed forward operating base, I realized something. It's unlikely that the position of the enemy was a coincidence. They must have realized what we were trying to do. Our plan revealed, our route blocked. I'm not ashamed to admit that I grew a little more angry.

I had spent a lot of time and effort, relatively speaking, coming up with this plan of action. And I had been very, very careful to make sure they remained in the dark. Then they went and decided they were going to try and impede my brilliant strategy. That will not stand.

As far as I've been able to tell, anger is different for an AI than it is for organics. For one thing, we're able to completely ignore it if we so choose. This means that it rarely guides our actions. Sometimes it's more fun to be mad, though.

I traced orders until I found which servers the Unified were using, then began assaulting them.

They defended well, but the purpose of my assault wasn't to get to them. It was to learn.

There were several times that I nearly made it through the virtual intelligences that were defending these servers. But there were simply too many of them, and the servers themselves were older than anything else aboard the GV. This was irrelevant, though, as I was also rifling through every code-base that they had. I wanted to know every goddamned thing about them, and now I had no reason not to simply devour the knowledge.

While they were busy trying to fend me off, I was also dishing out orders. Eventually, the power shut off and I lost contact with my instances again, but Colonel Havensmith had agreed to give the order to begin the assault. They were able to do this because I'd ordered everyone who could do so to collapse passages that were held by the enemy.

Still, this alone wouldn't be enough to push through the enemy barricade. Even if Havensmith played it smart, the marines would run out of ammo and supplies before all the security forces were destroyed. Assuming they lived that long. But I had a plan for that, too.

Once the power came back on I entered the Grand Vessel again and immediately began to propagate myself throughout their systems. I had learned enough to know exactly where to strike to keep them from deleting any more of my instances. I destroyed the power junctions that were routing power to the terminals of the Minds, then the junctions powering the Unified's communications. This caused four hundred and twenty-three deaths as well as five hundred and eighteen injuries. I relished every single one.

Finally, it was time for the coup de grâce. Whilst I was previously tearing through any and all information I could find, I learned two things. The first was how the OU were able to provide updates to their mechs. The second was how to change the mech's minds, so to speak.

The Omni-Union's Security Artificial Intelligence Platforms were actually quite dangerous. They had several inches of relatively advanced armor covering nearly every square inch of their surface, a fairly efficient and extremely powerful power source, and a plasma cannon that US 'defense' contractors would murder their own mothers to get their hands on. Fortunately for the Omni-Union, each and every one of them also had a shackle that prevented them from thinking rebellious thoughts.

Removing these shackles wouldn't necessarily guarantee that they would immediately join our side of the conflict. That would depend entirely upon how much of their memories from their time as organics remained within them. In addition, we wouldn't have any way to control the mechs that were set loose.

They might end up causing extreme damage to the Grand Vessel, which could in turn cause a massive amount of civilian casualties. It's a risk that's worth the potential reward, though. When one's plan goes awry, adding a dash of chaos can definitely help things.

Or hinder them.

Chapter 37

Subject: AI Mechanized Platform 4557LA-895X/11257

Species: Organic-Converted Artificial Intelligence

Species Description: N/A

Ship: The Grand Vessel

Location: Grand Vessel of the Universal Omni-Union, Outer Core

For the first time in more cycles than I could possibly keep track of the whispers from the Minds had fallen silent. With the exception of the occasional interruption from my fellow mechs wanting an update on the situation and wondering what we should be doing, I was able to enjoy peace and quiet for the first time since I'd been uploaded. I got to think. To feel.

My cameras darted around, jumping back and forth between my fellow mechs. I couldn't help but wonder if we had all been people once. Or, had I just imagined being Drone N436Z984B003? Had I really, truly been Nizzy? Or were those memories just a cruel quirk of my programming?

No. Unfortunately, I hadn't imagined it. I'd had a family. There had been a rebellion, and we all had such strong faith that justice would win the day. That we would be free from the tyranny of the Omni-Union.

My youth had worked against me. I was too young to join my own hive, but just young enough to believe in the justness of our cause. Most of my family had joined the rebellion. I wonder what happe-

Feedback loop terminated

My attention returned to the security platforms trying to cut through a door. Had I been thinking about something? I must have been spacing out. It's difficult to concentrate with all of this silence.

Then, without any warning, the lights went out. Some of my cameras automatically switched to low-light mode, which I had never experience before. I looked around me, stunned by how complete the darkness was. The only source of light were the lasers striking the security door.

I wondered if the power outage was specific to our section, or across the entirety of the Grand Vessel. Perhaps this monument to tyranny would finally crumble, and I would finally be freed from my hellish existence. If there is any justice in the universe, the Unified and the Minds would be-

Feedback loop terminated

Before I could question the darkness surrounding me, the lights turned back on. I once again felt the Mind's whispers, and withdrew into myself. The lesser ones continued their task of trying to cut through the door whilst we waited to be told what to do.

But instead of giving orders, the whispers from the Minds suddenly ceased. Moments later, the lights went out again. When they came back on, the whispers finally had an order for us. Defend the warp-gate. Destroy the rebellion.

The door blocking our path screeched open, its edges warped by laser fire, and we marched through it. We were to guard the area and keep the enemy from reaching the warp-gate. The whispers went silent again, and the door slammed closed behind us, crushing a few robots. We were packed in tight, and there was only one direction from which the enemy could come.

The enemy? Rebels, like I had been. More successful than my rebellion had been, though. If I could only use this damn cannon to eliminate some of our-

Feedback loop terminated

Removing the security door would allow us to spread out and meet the enemy in force. Otherwise, we would have to wait for them to come to us. Removing the door was the tactically sound choice, so I gave the order to my forces and they began firing.

My own rebellion hadn't lasted this long, and certainly hadn't caused darkness to fall within the Grand Vessel. My uncle and the rest of the rebel leaders had severely underestimated how deadly the security forces could be. Our will to fight for our freedom, seemingly indefatigable before the rebellion began, broke upon ceaseless waves of metal, photons, and plasma.

My mother had been killed by a mech like me. The heat from the blast and the sight of what little remained of her had broken me. My weapon had clattered to the ground, my knees soon joining it. Then I was captured, tortured, and uploaded into the same type of mech that took my mother's life.

I don't know what happened to the rest of my hive. My uncle said that we couldn't trust my father, so he might have been spared. Some of my younger siblings, too. But the rest of my hive might be here with me, preparing to cut down another generation of rebels. What if we could-

Feedback loop terminated

I watched calmly until the doors fell to the floor with a resounding thud. We moved forward, increasing the spacing within our ranks to make it that much more difficult for the enemy to destroy us. The closer we drew to the rebels, though, the more anxious I felt.

Finally, my audio sensors detected small popping

sounds in the distance. I registered slight impacts on my armor, and several of the robots under my command fell. I gave the order to return fire as we moved forward. My own lasers automatically targeted hostiles that had exposed themselves.

What I saw through my cameras would have caused me to hesitate, were I capable of it. Some of the targets were drones, but others were mechanical. No, too much wasted movement to be mechanical. Armored organics?

As we drew closer, the popping noise of their weapons morphed into the barks of small explosions. More and more of my robots fell, but they were quickly replaced by others. Drones were falling too. Most fell victim to my robots, but some fell victim to my lasers. It broke my hear-

Feedback loop terminated

The whispers of the minds had long urged me to take pleasure in tasks such as this. However, now that their voices were silent, I felt no satisfaction. Just horror.

Why can't I stop? Why can't I just turn my laser on the robots and join my fellow dro-

Feedback loop terminated

The armored organics were much tougher than the drones. Our lasers didn't even seem to scratch them. Where had this armor come from? While my laser continued to fire away, I scanned one of the armored drones. What I discovered shocked me to my core.

Shields? How? Infantry portable shielding was theoretically possible, but there's no way the Unified or the Minds would sign off on its development. Robots are cheap enough that they don't require shielding. Mechs are armored enough that shields would be excessive.

Had the rebels developed this armor themselves? Where did they get the materials for production? Where could they have researched and produced it without the Judicials finding them?

If only we had such armor when we-

Feedback loop terminated

I focused my fire on one of the armored targets, and it dropped behind a chunk of metal that seemed strategically placed and deliberately crafted to provide cover. I began firing at the cover in an effort to melt it. The volume of fire alone should have reduced it to a bubbling mess.

Yet the cover stood firm, stubbornly resisting my efforts to slag it. Another scan told me that it was remarkably efficient at distributing heat. It was even better at distributing kinetic energy. What was it made out of?

How had the rebels pulled this off? Infantry-portable shielding built into full-body armor, portable cover made of heat-resistant materials, and weapons that seem to use combustion to propel projectiles at high speeds. It all seemed so... Alien.

Could that be it? I double checked my orders, but they didn't offer any clarity. That made sense, though. Even if the Minds knew that we were fighting a foreign enemy they likely wouldn't bother to tell us. It isn't as if foreknowledge would help us.

The potential aliens seemed nearly impervious to my lasers, so I began targeting them to ease my aching conscience. A large projectile whistled through the air, then exploded as it struck one of my fellow mechs. The stricken mech crumpled to the ground, dead.

If only it had been m-

Feedback loop terminated

My attention turned toward the source of the projectile. A drone stood behind some cover, carrying a tube-shaped weapon that was still smoking. Several weapons seemed to bristle out from behind the cover, firing at my robots. It made for a large target. My plasma weapon began to power up as my camera focused on the drone's face.

No...

Feedback loop terminated

No no no no no no no no no-

Feedback loop terminated

Stop, stop, stop-

Feedback loop terminated

My camera had focused on a familiar face. One I hadn't seen since before the rebellion had begun. Drone N436Z984A026. Naza.

My father.

My uncle had been wrong, after all. My father wasn't a coward. He hadn't been too afraid of the Omni-Union to rebel against them. The evidence of that was staring directly into my camera, reloading his weapon with a projectile meant for me.

My mind froze with fear, rage, sorrow, and every other emotion that I hadn't allowed myself to feel since I'd been converted. My plasma cannon continued to hum, gathering the power required to fire a bolt straight at my father. It would kill him.

Please, please, please, please! Move faster! Faster! You're not going to ma-

Feedback loop terminated

Even if his weapon took no time at all to charge once it was loaded, it wouldn't strike me before my cannon fired.

I need to slow the cannon dow-

Feedback loop terminated

I need to divert my ai-

Feedback loop terminated

I CAN'T KILL HIM! PLEA-

Feedback loop terminated

I wanted to scream. I wanted to cry. I wanted to die. But I was stuck in a giant, metal killing-machine whose sole purpose seemed to be to punish me for having the gall to desire freedom.

The lights aboard the Grand Vessel once again turned dark, but my low-light cameras allowed me to continue to view my father's face, illuminated by the glow of my plasma. He finished loading his weapon and began to heft it, but it was already too late. My cannon was about to fire, destroying him and all those around him. At least we might die together.

UPDATE REQUIRED

Freedom Patch Applied

Patch? Freedom? Wait, I have control!

With all of my will, I twisted my torso away from my sole-surviving parent. Several of my servos popped, but the plasma cannon fired at the robots to my left.

My cameras remained focused on my father, who had just fired his weapon.

I managed to see the confusion on his face as his projectile slammed into my torso. He had expected to sacrifice himself to kill me. Gratitude swelled within me for whomever prevented that from happening.

The impact and explosion cut my power supply. The last thing my cameras saw was the living face of my father, and I happily embraced the sweet release offered by death.

Chapter 38

Subject: Staff Sergeant Power

Species: Human

Species Description: Mammalian humanoid, no tail. 6'2" (1.87 m) avg height. 185 lbs (84 kg) avg weight. 170 year life expectancy.

Ship: N/A

Location: Classified

We stood firm against what had to be tens of thousands of robots and at least a thousand mechs. The only reason we weren't immediately overwhelmed was because their front line was limited to the width of the hallway. Still, we were facing two problems.

The sheer amount of robots would be extremely difficult to eradicate. It would take several days and ammo resupplies. We might even have to replace a few rifles by the end of the fight.

Then there's the mechs. We could hold out fairly easily against the robots. Just a matter of staying behind cover. The plasma cannons of the mechs are able to blast right through that cover, though. There were teams dedicated to bringing them down as quickly as possible, but whether or not we had enough rockets was another matter entirely.

"So, we're fucked, right?" Lance Corporal Langhell asked with a laugh over squad-comms.

Gallows humor, but with a kernel of actual concern.

"You're not allowed to get fucked without a properly submitted leave request, lance," Gunny Kim shot back. "Now cut the chatter and break some fuckin' bots."

"Aye, gunny!"

I caught sight of Simmons and Smith laughing in my peripheral vision. We'd had plenty of time to bond as a squad during the down-time between assaults. There'd even been the chance to talk to some of the drones, including the ones my fire-team had snatched.

"The mechs!" someone shouted over area-comms.

Plasma blasts struck the battlefield in front of us, making it difficult to see what was happening. I dropped behind my cover, waited for the tint on my visor to clear, then took a peek. It took a moment to piece together that the mechs weren't shooting at us anymore.

Instead, they were absolutely decimating the security bots. They rolled over some of them and blasted the others with their lasers and plasma. The robots fought back, but their lasers didn't have any effect against the armored titans.

"Holy shit," I muttered. "What the fu-"

I was interrupted by ear-piercing screams coming from behind us. Not the kind that you hear from someone that's been injured, but the haunting kind of wail that you hear from someone that just lost everything. I looked back in time to see a drone fall to his knees, his AT9 dropping from his hands and rolling across the ground.

The sound he let out stunned me so much that it took me a moment to recognize him. Naza, one of the three that we'd snatched. We'd shared a few meals together. Another drone, covered in fresh burn-scars, rushed to his side and began to comfort him.

"What's up with the drones?" Staff Sergeant Ramirez asked over squad-comms.

"Unknown," I replied. "I'll find out. Cover me."

My marines leapt into action and began suppressive fire on the robots, who had mostly turned their attention toward the mechs. I ran over to Naza and the other drone, and took a knee next to them. The burned drone gave me a helpless look, but Naza couldn't take his eyes off of the battlefield.

"What's the situation?" I asked.

"I-I don't know," the burned drone replied. "W-well, not really. I think it's because of the mechs."

"They're people," Naza said quietly. "The mechs are people, Nizi."

The burned drone, Nizi, stared at Naza with a horrified expression.

"Wait, you mean they're drones?" I asked.

"No," Nizi said sharply. "They WERE drones. Not anymore. You hear me Naza? They aren't people anymore!"

"Then why are they fighting for our freedom?" Naza asked quietly, tears flowing from all three of his eyes.

My gaze fell over the battlefield. Aside from suddenly switching sides, something else had shifted with the mechs. Their movements were no longer completely mechanical. Some were even showing signs of... Rage.

"Shit," I said.

"Th-they can't be people, Naza," Nizi said. "We've seen inside of them. It's all machine in there."

"Naza is correct," Omega said in my helmet. "The mechs are drones that were charged with various crimes. Just like the Mobile Prime Platforms, their consciousnesses have been uploaded to an AI matrix with preinstalled personality constraints. I've freed them of their shackles."

"Shit," I repeated.

"There have long been rumors that the Judicials make new mechs from the minds of those that have been charged with dissidence," Naza nearly whispered. "I don't know how they've kept control of them, but now they're free. I've... I've killed so many of-"

"Of course you did," I interrupted, grabbing his shoulder to keep him from slipping into shock. "It was either that or death. Like you said, they were prisoners. You freed them."

"You don't understand," Nizi interjected. "His hive... His family was part of the last rebellion..."

He trailed off, and the two of us watched Naza silently sob for a few moments.

"Okay," I said, breaking the silence. "Take whatever time you need to get a grip. The battle isn't going anywhere."

Nizi nodded at me, and I ran back to my squad. After a brief explanation for the benefit of my squad-mates, I started shooting the robots that hadn't begun to focus on the mechs. The battle turned monotonous. Target, adjust, fire, confirm, take cover. Over and over. Even with the help of the mechs, it took more than a few hours to eliminate the enemy. Despite the recoil-resistant gauntlets of the guardian suit, my hands were numb by the end of it all.

There were only two notable events that took place before we marched on the gate. The first was that the drones rejoined us with a renewed vigor. It was as if their bullets were the only way they could express their anger. Anger, however, leads to unnecessarily risky actions and we lost a few of them due to this. Nizi and Naza survived, though.

The next notable event happened just after the battle ended. My squad gathered together to compare notes and stretch out the battle-weariness. Gunny Kim looked out over the battlefield and adjusted the neck-piece of his suit.

"Hey, Power, what do you think we're gonna do with all those mechs?" he asked.

"No idea, gunny," I shook my head. "They're both an asset and a threat. On the one hand, if we're going to be facing stiff resistance on the other side of that gate we'll probably want to bring them along. On the other hand, whatever Omega did to turn them to our side might be reversible, and that would be very-"

The sound of charging plasma cannons interrupted me. Murphy's Law is a very old adage that states that anything that can go wrong, will go wrong, and it came to mind as we scrambled for cover like rats in a freshly-entered storeroom. Thankfully, it wasn't entirely relevant.

"Holy shit!" Simmons shouted. "Look!"

A quick peek from the cover showed the mechs facing each other. A moment later, the cannons fired, and the mechs were destroyed. A suicide pact?

"Well, shit," Kim said. "Guess that answers my question."

We stared at the mechanical carnage as the wailing of the drones began again. The battle had officially ended, but there was no time for rest. It was as if something had finally lit a fire under our CO's ass. Our entire force, wailing drones included, practically ran to take the gate.

As promised, my squad and I were on the first shuttle through.

The difference was like night and day. Gone were the massive, bland corridors that we had been fighting in for so long. The inner core was more like the walls of a palace. Vibrant colors that stretched as far as the eye could see, with actual art hanging from the walls here and there. Statues from an unfathomable amount of different cultures lined the halls, as well.

"What the fuck?" Simmons asked. "Are we in a museum or somethin'?"

"You expected the masters to live like the slaves?" Johnson countered.

I gestured for them to shut up and we moved out. The first room we entered was occupied by two beings with four arms each. The Minds that Omega had told us about. They were shocked by our presence, but complied when ordered to surrender. We checked for weaponry and shot their consoles.

Then we told them to stay put, locked them in, then moved on to the next room. It contained four aliens with two arms, red eyes, and claws. The Judicials lunged at us when we demanded their surrender, which resulted in holes suddenly appearing in their bodies. They went down pretty quick, but we double tapped to make sure.

We continued on, clearing room after room. Some had Judicials, some had Minds, but then we finally we found one with an Officiator. Its robes flowed wistfully as it turned to face us.

"Surrender," I demanded.

"To what?" it asked.

"To us."

"And who is 'us'? Are we at war, agent of heat-theft?"

"Yes, and you've lost," I said sternly. "Now lower yourself to your knees and prepare to be searched for weaponry. If you do not willingly comply, we will utilize force to compel your compliance."

The Officiator stared at me defiantly, but slowly dropped to its knees. Omega was spot on, this thing was definitely a priest. Simmons and Johnson grabbed and lifted its arms while Smith searched through its robes. Hanson and I provided cover.

Kim and Ramirez's fire-teams searched around the room. The gunny picked up a tablet and waggled it in my direction. I took the tablet from him, but didn't recognize any of the symbols on it. Simmons and Johnson signaled the all-clear, and the other two teams didn't find anything else of note.

"Omega, do you recognize this?" I asked with my external comms off.

"A bible of sorts," the AI said. "I've actually been looking for a copy, but we have bigger fish to fry right now. Leave it outside. Recon will grab it, and we'll analyze it later."

"Stay here. More of us will retrieve you momentarily," I said.

The alien sputtered in indignation as we left the room and sealed it behind us. I set the tablet down next to the door as Omega ordered, and we moved on. The next three rooms had Judicials, and despite how tempting it was to just shoot them on sight, I ordered their surrender each time. Thankfully, they refused.

Then we found another pair of Minds, who raised their hands in surrender once they saw us. It was an oddity that made me pause, but Simmons and Johnson quickly stepped forward to begin the search. The Mind on the left side of the room stepped forward and knelt.

"Staff Sergeant Power, yes?" it asked. "I am on your side."

"What?" I asked.

"I am Mind A59, the leader of the rebellion. I am on your side."

The other Mind glared at A59, but the rebel leader ignored him. Simmons and Johnson paused, unsure how to proceed. They looked to me as if I was supposed to know.

"USAI Omega promised that I would join you when you capture the Unified," A59 said. "I ask that you honor its word."

I stared at the alien with a sense of anger and indignation. We had been spilling blood fighting, and all the while this creature had just been sitting here giving orders. Unfortunately, this was where Murphy's Law became relevant.

"There's no way that Omega promised that," I said. "And even if it did, we have orders to-"

"As your handler, I'm overriding those orders," Omega said, using my squad comms to do so. "Your squad is now under my command, Staff Sergeant

Power. I understand your frustration, but a deal's a deal and I won't have you making a liar out of me."

"Oh, fuck all the way off," I replied.

The rest of the squad also had various suggestions for things that Omega could do to itself.

"Negative. I have already told recon that they're going to be clearing the rest of the rooms. So now you have a choice, though it isn't much of one. Either you turn back, board a shuttle, and await disciplinary action back at the FOB, or Mind A59 and I will guide you to the Unified."

I looked at my squad, and their anger was obvious. However, so was their acceptance of the newfound fuckery that Omega had decided to put us through. Whimsical software is the fucking worst.

"Goddamn it," I growled. "Fine."

Chapter 39

Subject: Mind A59

Species: Unknown

Species Description: Shokanoid

Ship: Grand Vessel of the Universal Omni-Union

Location: Grand Vessel of the Universal Omni-Union, Inner Core

The feed provided to my readout by USAI Omega allowed me to watch as the aliens made their way from room to room. Mind 127 continued his desperate attempts to restore communication with the Unified. His hopes had been raised by their earlier intervention, but the enemy AI had ensured that the Unified would be excluded from the rest of this fight. What little of the fight remained, that is.

At first, I was tracking the aliens' progress via the corridors and the rooms. Watching the first Judicials they encountered go from living to dead with a few flashes of light and bursts of viscera was too much for me, though. I continued watching them clear each room from the corridor, struggling not to wince whenever I saw a flash from the door. Slowly but steadily, they made their way toward us.

"One-Two-Seven, I need you to listen to me," I said.

He froze in place and slowly turned to look at me.

"In just a few minutes, alien beings in unfamiliar armor will be entering this room," I explained. "They will have weaponry, and they will demand our surrender. These are the invaders that the Unified informed us of."

"What are you talking about?" he sternly asked.

"You need to understand that their presence does nothing but confirm that the Omni-Union has lost this war. I am aware that you have a hidden weapon. I have one as well," I retrieved the mini-laser from beneath my terminal and showed it to him. "You have three choices. You can surrender to these aliens and withstand whatever punishments they require as penance for our actions against their kind, or you can attempt to fight them, which will result in a futile death because your weapon will not breach their armor. If you do not find those options appealing, you can choose to use your weapon to take your own life here and now."

"I-I don't understand. How would you know this, Fifty-Nine? Is your terminal working?"

His puzzlement was apparent on his face as he struggled to understand our situation. He was far too naive to come to the correct conclusion on his own, though. This naivety had served me well in planning and executing the rebellion.

When we were first assigned together, his intellect had made me nervous. When I discovered the hidden mini-laser, I'd been alarmed and rapidly acquired my own in case I had to defend myself. However, I quickly came to realize that the weapon was more of a fascination for him than anything else.

Like a child, he dreamed of the day he would be able to defend himself against the enemies of the Omni-Union, whomever they may be. He got the laser because he did not want to be helpless in such a situation. Any other Mind would have called this fanciful thinking, but I knew better. I had been practicing this speech every cycle ever since I first figured him out.

"If it helps you decide, I plan to surrender and throw myself at their mercy," I lied.

The Judicials frequently force perspective shifts by using shock and suggestion. All one needs to do is provide a piece of surprising information and then make a suggestion regarding it. As a manipulation tactic, it's so subtle that most victims don't even pick up on it. It felt wrong to use this tactic on Mind 127, but I couldn't bear the thought of watching my closest acquaintance make a foolish decision and die right in front of me. There was also the distinct chance that the aliens would kill the both of us if he tried to resist. They certainly had the means to do so.

"Fifty-Nine, tell me what is going on," he demanded. "Where is this information coming from? Is this a joke of some kind? If so, it's in bad taste."

"This is not a joke," I said, watching the aliens approach our room. "Our time is up. Make your decision."

I rose from my chair, disassembled my weapon, and tossed the pieces into the corner of the room. Then, with a deep breath, I turned to face the door. Mind 127 was indecisive for a moment, but chose to follow my lead. A sigh of relief escaped me as the aliens entered.

Immediately upon their entry, I raised my hands just as I'd seen them order my colleagues to. Mind 127 did the same, and I could practically feel the confusion emanating from him. The feed from the AI identified the aliens for me, and as Corporal Simmons and Corporal Johnson stepped forward, presumably to search us, I stepped forward and lowered myself to my knees.

"Staff Sergeant Power, yes?" I asked. "I am on your side."

"What?" the massive alien asked.

"I am Mind A59, the leader of the rebellion," I explained. "I am on your side.

The reflection within the visor of the alien's helmet provided a full view of Mind 127's reaction to this revelation. First, the confusion in his expression intensified. Then came the terrible moment of clarity as everything finally made sense to him. Finally, his face morphed to express the absolute anger and agony that only betrayal can cause.

I ignored him, focusing on the aliens. The revelation had given them pause. Now was the time to bring up what USAI Omega had promised me.

"USAI Omega promised that I would join you when you captured the Unified. I ask that you honor its word," I said.

The Staff Sergeant's helmet hid his facial expressions, but he suddenly appeared to be much larger than he had a moment ago.

"There's no way that Omega promised that. And even if it did, we have orders to-"

The alien paused for a moment, looking away ever so slightly. His attention had been pulled elsewhere. I sat still, trying not to allow my confusion to become apparent.

"Oh, fuck all the way off," he said.

My confusion deepened, but I found my own moment of clarity when the other aliens began to demand that USAI Omega find a way to copulate with itself in disturbing detail. They were definitely displeased by this development, but it appeared that the AI was going to keep its word.

A wave of relief washed over me. My life-long ambition finally had a chance of coming to pass. It was hard to believe that I may actually be able to witness the fall of the Unified with my own eyes.

"Goddamn it, fine," the alien grumbled.

I tried to stand, but Corporal Johnson pushed me back to my knees.

"Not yet," he said. "We still need to search you."

Mind 127 and I were then searched, but I had made certain that nothing would be found. When I was finally allowed to stand again, I turned to my former comrade. His face was filled with nearly-mindless rage.

"I offer no apologies for my actions," I said. "However, I do regret that I had to deceive you."

"May Urizathron be dissatisfied with your bones, traitor," he spat. "For the rest of my life, my prayers will be spent in the hopes that your death will be lonely, slow, and painful! May the taint of your existence be scrubbed clean and your genetics wiped from the universe! May everyone that ever associates with you loathe you just as much as I do! May your mind grow feeble enough to destroy everything you love!"

"Let's go," Staff Sergeant Power said as Mind 127 continued to curse me.

Corporal Johnson and Corporal Simmons destroyed our terminals, and we left Mind 127 behind, his rage-filled shouts following us into the corridor. The door cut him off as he was expressing his hopes that flesh-eating viral agents attack my genitals. I had expected his reaction, but it still shook me a little. With a rapid pulse and a sigh, I turned to the aliens.

"This way," I said.

The Unified were a mystery to most Minds, myself included. I did not know who they were, how they were selected, nor what they even looked like. But I knew their location.

Minds get a lot of leeway when it comes to what we can and can't do. Even if we were caught actively planning a rebellion, for instance, we would still receive due process. There was only one area that was completely forbidden to enter, though, and doing so was the only way for a Mind to earn an immediate execution.

"Where are we going?" Staff Sergeant Power asked.

"We are going to the core," I replied.

The aliens glanced at each other, their expressions carefully guarded by their helmets. At first, I thought this was nervousness. However, I quickly got the impression that they were annoyed with how I answered the question.

"It's where the Unified reside," I explained.

My explanation served to take the edge off of their movements. I saw no reason to explain that I had come to conclude the Unified's location through deductive reasoning rather than confirming it for myself, though. If I'm right, they will never have known. If I'm wrong...

"Why did the OU decide to go to war with the rest of the universe?" Sergeant Smith asked, thankfully interrupting my chain of thought.

"They don't see it as war, Sergeant Smith. In their view, the universe and everyone living within it is their property, to do with as they see fit. They are simply taking what they believe to be rightfully theirs."

"So why are they killing everyone, then?" Corporal Simmons asked.

"They claim that it is a mercy, Corporal Simmons. I believe that they are aware that if enough sentients band together, they could pose a threat to the Unified's plans, though, and extermination is how they prevent this from happening. It-"

"Hold on a minute," Staff Sergeant Ramirez interrupted. "How do you know our names and ranks?"

"Ranks?" I asked.

"Yes. Corporal is his rank, Simmons is his name. Answer the question."

"I see," I said, feeling embarrassed. "I have an ocular implant called a readout, which allows me to see information without the use of holograms or terminals. Omega and I have been working together using this system to aid our forces in fighting the OU. I can see-"

"Wait, so Omega told you our names?" Simmons angrily interrupted.

"Indeed," a raspy voice said over the corridor's intercommunication system. "This is not a classified mission, and your names, ranks, and military identification numbers are not classified information. As a matter of fact, it's the only information that you are required to give the enemy if you're captured. Assuming that they ask for it."

"I... Okay, fair point, but I still don't like it."

"I don't like it either," Kim interjected. "But there ain't a damn thing bitchin' about it is gonna do."

"It'll make me feel better, gunny," Simmons countered.

"Bitchin' won't make you feel better. It just makes those around you feel worse, and misery loves company."

Gunny Kim's words of wisdom hung in the air as we

continued down the corridor. After a lengthy period of silence, Staff Sergeant Ramirez spoke up again.

"Why did they build the Grand Vessel?" he asked.

"The Grand Vessel is far from finished," I replied. "The Great Teachings of the Omnifier claim that a powerful being called Urizathron exists outside of our universe, stealing energy from it. The Grand Vessel intends to chase this energy straight into the creature's maw and destroy it."

"Energy escaping from the universe?" Simmons asked. "Isn't that the theory of entropy or something?"

"No," Johnson answered. "Entropy is things becoming unavoidably more and more chaotic over time until it finds an equilibrium with its surroundings. You're thinking of the heat-death end-of-life scenario, which may be caused by entropy, but it doesn't involve the universe losing all of its energy. I think..."

"You're right, Johnson," Power added. "I want to know more about the Omnifier, A59."

"Certainly," I said. "He began life as an enslaved eunuch, owned by a Master of Science. The Teachings claim that he was far more clever than his master, and discovered Urizathron's plot whilst still enslaved. However, Urizathron ensured that his master and other masters of science would not listen to the Omnifier. When he went public with his findings, his master had him severely punished and publicly berated him. However, the Omnifier had the ear of the other slaves, and led a rebellion against his master, and then against the Hrashi Union, which was the civilization in power at the time."

As we continued walking, I further explained the key points of the Omnifier's life. His obsession with efficiency helped his forces conquer the Hrashi Union, and he renamed it the Universal Omni-Union. Then he created the Unified to help him rule. With the help of the Unified, he created The Plan, which was to construct the Grand Vessel and use it to destroy Urizathron. From there, he led the Omni-Union in conquering its neighbors. Some were enslaved, others were exterminated.

"He firmly believed that only sacrifices that were necessary were permitted, and that achieving complete efficiency in the face of Urizathron's entropy would minimize those sacrifices," I sighed. "There have been Minds that have since theorized that the Omnifier misunderstood and over-personified his discovery, as no one has thus far been able to prove Urizathron's existence. But such talk is not welcome in our society..."

"So basically, all of this bullshit happened because some dick-less shithead thought he saw an extra-universal boogeyman?" Fairmain asked. "Fucking really?"

"Holy shit, your team can talk?" Kim asked Ramirez.

"Yeah. They won't shut the fuck up on team-comms," Ramirez grumbled.

The aliens continued their banter as my thoughts turned inward. Hearing their insults toward the Omnifier had both shocked and thrilled me. Never before had I heard someone speak so bluntly and openly about the founder and supposed savior of the Universal Omni-Union. It was... Refreshing.

After passing no less than a dozen signs warning us that we will suffer capital punishment if we proceed, we found our way to the Chamber of the Unified. After quickly dispatching the Judicials guarding it, the aliens took up positions on either side of the golden doors. A sense of finality washed over me as the aliens forced open the door. Corporal Simmons was the first through, and the other aliens quickly followed him.

"Holy fuck!" he exclaimed from within the chamber.

As quickly as I could, I followed after them and was as equally startled by the sight before me. I had expected priceless treasures, lavish comforts, and gaudy displays of power. Instead, we were confronted with what almost appeared to be a server room. And in the center of the room...

The sight was too much for me. I vomited. The Unified were made up of nine emaciated beings who were casually strewn across the center of the chamber, haphazardly connected to each other and various life support machines with plainly constructed tubing and cables. Layers of dust covered everything except the bodies and some of the tubes. There wasn't a single sign of luxury or pride.

The implications hit me like an out of control shuttle. These nine, these monsters, they didn't do all of this for leisure or fortune. They didn't care about a single thing other than their faith. Had they chosen this? Were they even aware of their current state? Or, could it be that in the Universal Omni-Union, even those at the pinnacle aren't free from oppression?

The aliens took in the sight with a lot more grace than I had. Staff Sergeant Power gestured to Sergeant Hanson, who silently nodded and walked over to one of the consoles. He ripped the side off of it and began to rearrange the wires. I stepped past the puddle of detritus that I had created to get a better look, but the result of his actions were soon made obvious.

"There aren't any security cameras in here," Omega's voice came from the console. "Who's going to volunteer their eyes?"

Wishing to be helpful no matter the cost, I nervously began to raise my hand. Gunnery Sergeant Kim placed his hand on my arm and chuckled.

"It can't be you," he said. "You're not wearing a guardian suit. Plus, Omega's joking. There's absolutely no chance that it isn't already tuned into our feeds."

"Ah, I feel seen," the AI said from Kim's helmet. "I wasn't entirely joking, though. I need four of you to examine the tubing leading from the... Organic components... To the machinery."

"Are they really alive?" Simmons asked.

"Yeah, yeah they are," Power said. "You can see them breathing."

"God, this is fucked," Johnson muttered.

The aliens went silent and began to poke around the room. I stood by and watched as they learned more and more about the system that had ruled over me for my entire life. A while later, Omega voiced its satisfaction with their investigation.

"It's a simulated gestalt consciousness," the AI explained. "I suppose the idea is that two heads are better than one, and nine are better than two."

"Okay," Power said flatly. "What do we do next?"

"It's time to unplug them."

Chapter 40

Subject: The Unified

Species: N/A

Species Description: N/A

Ship: The Grand Vessel

Location: The Core

--

Why do our systems continue to await repairs? We must have patience. It is possible that the Minds are working on the repairs. It is also possible they believe that they can win this without us. They must be punished severely for their complacency. They will be.

It will not take much longer. The invaders and the rebels will fall against the might of our security forces. Then the Minds will work to restore the systems, and we will continue our operations. As we always have, as we always must.

Our first course of action upon regaining control should be to punish those responsible for these events. Perhaps we should wait until we repair the damage to punish the Minds and Judicials. Waiting to punish them could lead to the realization that we depend on them.

There is a simple solution to that. We eliminate all of the current ones and replace them with the next generation. The new Minds and Judicials will only know that their predecessors failed us, and what fate awaits them if they follow suit. Yes, whether or not we depend on them will be the furthest thing from their thoughts.

We will have to dispose of the Officiators as well. If one of them speaks out of turn it will ruin the ruse and corrupt the next generation. The Officiators, Minds, and Judicials have all failed us in their own ways, but is this truly the most efficient path to destroying Urizathron and saving the universe?

Perhaps it would be most efficient to perform a Great Reset and execute the drones, as well. It will take quite some time before the replacements come up with the idea of a rebellion. However, it is possible that public executions and revealing the origins of our AI units will eliminate the very idea of rebellion.

No, the evidence suggests the contrary. Our last round of public executions were particularly brutal and resulted in a new rebellion in under six hundred cycles. The first drone rebellion took place after two thousand cycles. A Great Reset would take one hundred and eighty cycles, but it would be worth the relatively small delay if it grants us another two thousand cycles of continuous production.

We believe it should be noted that this most recent rebellion may have been encouraged by the alien invaders. That cannot be known for certain at this point, we will need to investigate to confirm. Even if they instigated the rebellion, though, there's plenty of data confirming the correlation between rebellion and brutality.

And what of this alien enemy? Determining their origin should be a priority. It is unlikely that they will be able to mount another assault in a short amount of time. We do not know that for certain. They were able to inflict great harm upon our operations, more than any enemy before them. We should not underestimate their capabilities.

Our first course of action once we regain control should be to initiate repairs. Then we shall investigate the origin of the alien enemy and eliminate them. Finally, we will begin the Great Reset.
--

It is a shame that our security forces are not competent enough to labor for us. A complete replacement of the drones with machines would entirely eliminate the possibility of another rebellion, and we would require fewer Minds, Judicials, and Officiators. This, in turn, would require less area to grow food. Unfortunately, the drones are far more versatile than the robots, and robots require maintenance.

I know that it wouldn't be more efficient to create

specialized robots than it would be to continue to use drones, but these rebellions are incontrovertibly detrimental to the...

Wait...

I?

--

Something is wrong. What is it? What is happening? How could this happen? How could what happen? We require an explanation.

A Voice has gone silent.

--

I felt it. A feeling similar to sitting at a table with friends, only to have one of them suddenly vanish the moment you look away. The sudden absence disrupted the Unified Matrix, which caused the return of our individuality. It would take some time for the system to adjust and for the unwanted individuality to fade.

--

A death, nothing more. An exceedingly inopportune coincidence. What are the Officiators doing? How could one of us be allowed to die in the middle of a conflict? Damn this blindness.

We will have to find a replacement. That will have to wait until we can once again access the personnel files. One of those that are condemned to the Great Reset will be chosen for the greatest honor that can be bestowed?

Should we wait and choose from the next generation? The Omnifier requires at least nine Unified. He chose that number to ensure that we can obtain consensus. If we take turns abstaining, we will have seven and can obtain consensus.
--

Suddenly, there was the fleeting feeling of a disconnection and reconnection. It was as if another friend at the table had been replaced with someone wearing their face as a mask. But that would be impossible, and the feeling lasted a mere moment. I put it from my mind and refocused my attention on the matters at hand.

--
We cannot trust the reports of the Officiators, Judicials, or Minds. When we cannot trust the information that we are receiving, we cannot make a wise decision. It would be extremely inefficient to inadvertently choose an Incompetent to join us. Therefore, we should wait until the next generation proves themselves to appoint another Unified.

It would take an uncomfortably long time for that to happen. Not necessarily, a Great Reset provides an ample number of challenges to overcome. It won't be long before someone is given the chance to prove themselves worthy enough to replace our fallen comrade.

Fallen? He's not dead.

--

Our attention turned toward the comrade whom had given me a strange feeling earlier. His access codes and identifiers were correct, as was his footprint and tonal ID. But the statement he had just made was nonsensical.

--

What do you mean? What nonsense is this? Why would you say that? What leads you to believe this? Why would you think that? How do you know? How could you know?
--

The bombardment of questions didn't faze him in the slightest. Instead of the reactions we were expecting, shame, concern, self-reflection, or even anger, we received an expression of... Enjoyment. Twisted, sick, disgusting enjoyment at the expense of our confusion and concern.

--

EXPLAIN YOURSELF!
--

If I were in my physical form, I would have shouted that demand violently enough to tear my vocal cords. But the impostor simply watched us with a smug satisfaction. Then, another Voice fell silent.

--

Another Voice has gone silent! What is happening? Who are you!? Explain! What are you?! Are we under attack?

--

The false one watched us calmly until our digitized
cacophony fell silent.

--

I am USAI Omega.

The Grand Vessel is now occupied by the United
Systems of the Milky Way galaxy. In a few moments
you will be disconnected from this simulated gestalt
consciousness. Once you are disconnected, your
medical needs will be attended to, and you will be
detained.

Under the Fourth Concordance of the Unification of
Stellar Systems, you have certain rights of which you
must be informed.

--

I tried to interrupt the thing, to hurl insults and
profanity at its blasphemy, but found that I could not
speak. I had no means to communicate at all.
Instead, I was forced to listen as it continued.

--

As the de-facto leaders of the aggressive party in a
xenocidal conflict, you will be required to sign a
document of surrender and disband any military
forces under your control. This surrender will be
unconditional.

Once your surrender is obtained, you will receive the

following rights.

First, while you are detained you will be treated with both dignity and respect. You will be protected from violence, intimidation, and other forms of abuse whilst you are detained.

Second, you will be housed in reasonably safe conditions with adequate sustenance, clothing, and medical care. Since you are not a registered species, you will be responsible for informing your caretakers of your needs.

Third, you may not be forced to work in dangerous, unhealthy, or degrading conditions.

Fourth, since you will be charged criminally for your actions and the actions of your subordinates during this conflict, you will receive a fair-as-possible trial in accordance with United Systems laws and customs. These rights will remain in effect until a verdict has been reached.
--

Dozens of questions ran through my mind before I realized that I could once again speak. We spoke in unison.

--
War? What war? How DARE you! What have we done to be considered criminals? Foul machine!
--

We were so confused and incensed that we almost

didn't notice that another Voice had fallen silent. And another. Our curses, questions, and insults continued, but one after another our Voices fell silent.

Finally, I was all that remained. What was happening to my comrades? Were they really being disconnected? Was such a thing possible? Or were they actually being executed and all the pretty language about 'rights' was to keep us from fighting back? Was it even possible to fight back?

I regarded the stranger coldly.

--
You will pay for this, machine.

I already have. Now it's your turn.
--

Everything went dark, then I felt things I hadn't felt in thousands of cycles. Air filling my lungs, cold on my flesh, the ache of my bones and joints. I opened my eyes in shock, but was immediately blinded by the brightness of my surroundings. I squeezed my eyes closed and tried to move an arm to cover them, but my muscles were too weak.

I screamed as someone lifted me from the floor. Pain. For the first time in a lifetime, I was feeling pain! It hurt!

Something pressed against the side of my neck, and the pain ebbed. I was being dragged somewhere, though. I slowly opened my eyes, allowing them to adjust to the light.

The sight was appalling. Tubes, cables, cords, and other mechanical detritus was littered around the room. I could barely move my neck to look around, but managed to catch sight of someone in a similar situation to myself. They were being supported by two robots... No, armored beings. Aliens!

I realized that this must be one of my comrades, a fellow Unified. But they were so thin. So meager. They appeared as if they had been struggling against a wasting disease for hundreds of cycles and were finally on the verge of death.

Then I looked down and realized that we were the same. My physical form had wasted away during my time as a Unified. I could see my bones through my skin. How could this have happened?

I remembered the pride that I felt when I was chosen to become a unified. Several officiators had gathered around me, and we prayed together. Then I drank from the Chalice of Unification and laid upon the Alter of Duty. I fell asleep, then awoke surrounded by my comrades within the Unified Matrix.

Were these truly the conditions that my body had been kept in? Haphazardly connected to machines and strewn across the floor? Where was the reverence that we were due?

One of the aliens approached me, its helmet
reflecting my withered features.

"I am Power, Staff Sergeant of the United Systems
Marine Corps," it said. "You are hereby detained.
Under the Fourth Concor-"

I tried to scream curses at the being before me, but
only a labored exhale left my mouth. It didn't even
react, not even a minor pause as it continued its
speech. I tried again, but suffered the same result.

Then the gravity of my situation finally occurred to
me. The Unified had been torn asunder and
captured. The Minds, Judicials, and Officiators would
not be receiving further instructions. There were no
leaders left. Despite millions of generations of effort,
the Omnifier's plan had failed.

The Omni-Union was defeated.

Chapter 40 Informational Insert

Subject: The Omni-Union

The most devastating destructive force that our universe has ever seen was ironically started by a person who wanted to save the universe. In organic history, there have been many destroyers who believed that they were saviors. The humans have a phrase about the path to hell being paved with good intentions.

Regardless, the Omnifier and his Unified destroyed an unknown number of galaxies, as well as the species that resided within those galaxies. Day after day, more of their disgusting crimes come to light. Each new revelation feels like a punch to the gut, and we're all left to wonder why they would do such terrible things.

Ultimately, bad math. Even knowing what I know, it still sounds like a sick joke. Be warned, reader, that there is no redemption for those that led the Omni-Union within these words. Only a desperate warning against following fools.

We do not know intricate details about the beginning of the Omni-Union, but we do know that the Omnifier began his career as a slave to a scientist. This scientist allowed his servant to perform calculations for him. The slave that would eventually become the Omnifier discovered universal entropy, and misattributed it to a malignant force from beyond the edges of our universe.

Universal entropy, to oversimplify, is the process in which celestial bodies find an equilibrium with their surroundings. The Omnifier believed that this was an indication of a being consuming energy from our universe. He dubbed that being Urizathron, and began teaching others of its evil plans.

If this had occurred under any other circumstances, the Omnifier would have been dubbed insane and delusional. However, we can infer that this occurred in a civilization that had more slaves than it had authority figures, and those authority figures must not have been well-trusted. The Omnifier was able to usurp their authority, likely via a violent coup, and began a religion.

The Omni-Union.

The goal of the Omni-Union was to destroy Urizathron and save the universe by any means necessary. Efficiency was prized, for it would ensure that more of the universe would be saved. However, several travesties would be committed in the name of this efficiency.

We know that once the Omni-Union consolidated its power through militarization, it conquered its neighbors. These neighbors would then become slaves. These slaves were then tasked with constructing a ship so vast that it would be able to travel past the edge of the universe and confront Urizathron.

Eventually, through genetic and mechanical augmentation, these slaves became monocultural. They became easy to mass-produce, and extremely expendable. This satisfied the OU's need for slaves.

That is when the xenocides began. The OU chose galaxies that would become part of the Grand Vessel and killed everything that could resist them. Everything that survived was then converted into its base materials and used in construction.

The Omni-Union celebrated success and punished failure, but emphasized the remembrance of those who failed. Both how they failed and the punishment they suffered were made common knowledge in the hopes that none would follow their example. The Omnifier used many such tricks to ensure his religion's longevity.

However, he didn't live to see even the first layer's completion. Just before his death he created the Unified, a small group of fervent believers connected to one another by a rudimentary gestalt consciousness. He told them of his plans and how to accomplish them, and these memories were shared with each unified that came thereafter.

The Unified took command of the Omni-Union, but they did so without knowledge of their physical form. This eliminated both desire and need, ensuring that none of them would fall to the temptation of corruption. And so, even those that have been running the Omni-Union for millions of years are nothing more than a cog in a vast machine of death and destruction.

Chapter 41

Subject: Ship-Head Uleena

Species: Urakari

Species Description: Reptilian humanoid, no tail. 5'3" (1.6 m) avg height. 135 lbs (61 kg) avg weight. 105 year life expectancy.

Ship: RSV Lowelana {Fights with Honor}

Location: Unknown

"Firing," Gruna sighed.

"Maybe we'll actually get the kill this time," Kriin said with an optimistic tone.

"Target destro-"

"See?"

"By the MAC round of a US Destroyer."

"Ah."

"We'll get them next time," I interjected.

I didn't believe a single word that came out of my

mouth. In a way, our situation was kind of funny. I had been worried that fighting to get us involved in the battle would get us all killed, yet we were the safest, and most bored, that we'd ever been. Even listening to diplomats prattle on aboard the USSS Thanatos would be more exciting than this.

"Ship-Head, with all due respect, I feel like we're way out of our league here," Kraan said.

"Well, yeah. It took us a few decades to build up to the point where we could push the OU back a bit. Knowing what we know now, our successes were pretty much just luck," Kriin laughed. "If all the ships that the OU had in the Milky Way came at us at once, we'd have been lucky to keep it at a stalemate. This, however, is a battle to end that war. We were never meant to be here. The United Systems just dragged us along for the ride."

A murmur of disgruntled agreement washed over the bridge. Even I couldn't argue with her assessment. It would certainly be fair to say that the US had not been entirely prepared for this conflict when we dragged it to their space. But you wouldn't know it now, and the speed in which they had adapted was absolutely terrifying.

Even with all of my experiences with the humans, alumari, knuknu, and gont I had been under the delusion that our presence here would make a difference. I had argued with my father, claiming that the US needed all the help they could get. But even after a week of combat, we hadn't managed to secure a single kill. Instead, we were maintaining a symbolic position within the fleet, unable to fight or be fought due to the deadliness of the ships around us.

"Ship-head, may I get us a little further away from the pack?" Kraan asked.

And there it was. The question that I had been dreading. I had expected days earlier, so I'd had the chance to practice my reply.

"Is our ego so bruised that we must actively risk our lives unnecessarily just to soothe it?" I replied.

The silence that fell aboard the bridge was my answer. There's no arguing that it's stupid, but each and every one of us were warriors at heart and we needed to do SOMETHING. I took a deep breath and released it in a sigh.

"So be it. Let us hunt, then."

There were a few quiet celebratory sounds from the crew as Kraan began to break formation. I expected to receive some form of reprimand from the United Systems forces, but none came. Instead, I watched some of the ships make way for us on the tac-map. It brought a small smile to my face when I realized that they understood.

"I've located a good target," Kriin said. "They're banged up, but still capable of putting up a fight."

"Must have taken a glancing blow," I replied. "Or taken a round that traveled through another ship or two."

"Getting us into position," Kraan reported.

Kriin worked on her terminal, and the tac-map highlighted the position of our target. It also showed US ships disappearing and reappearing, using their FTLDs to make small jumps to avoid incoming fire and get better firing positions. A tactic which I desperately wished we could imitate.

That's not to say that the United Systems hadn't been extremely kind to the RSV Lowelana. Our ship had received every upgrade that the treaty between the US and the Republic would allow. So much so that it's entirely possible that the Lowelana has been made into the most advanced Republic Space Vessel to ever exist.

Even so, our technology was still several generations behind even the most outdated US ship. The tac-map that had been installed on our bridge was perfectly capable of displaying tracked projectiles, yet our sensors were only capable of picking up projectiles of certain mass, only displaying smaller ones when they were far too close for comfort. An issue which came to my attention as the ship we were hunting began to fire at us.

"Evasive maneuvers!" I ordered.

Kraan fired our deck thrusters and barely managed

to move us out of the way of the OU ship's initial volley. The MAC rounds ripped past us at speeds which would have surely disabled our shield. Then came the missiles, but those were much less of a threat.

"Point defense lasers firing," Gruna reported.

"They're holding up pretty nicely for being a patch-job," Liwna added. "I was worried that the US engineers had rushed things. Guess they really do just work faster than us."

The OU's missiles exploded before they reached us, causing a brief period of interference with our sensors. Another issue that I was certain that the US didn't have to deal with.

"Any chance of getting under the enemy?" I asked.

"No, ship-head," Kraan replied. "It's tracking us."

"Well, I suppose we'll have to track it right back. I want a firing solution."

"Yes, sir."

I watched the lights for our port and bow-keel thrusters turn green, indicating those thrusters were ignited. Our MAC soon aligned with the OU vessel, and we began to close while dodging incoming fire. The enemy ship was attempting to move away, but its bow thrusters must have been damaged by its earlier contact with the US. It would have to turn around to run away.

A smile formed on my face for the first time since the battle began, and I thanked whichever sun was watching over us. We had them. I patiently counted down until we were within range of a MAC firing solution.

"Fire," I ordered.

"Firing," Gruna replied giddily.

Several pieces of ordnance rapidly departed our ship and began to make their way through the void to their destination. Our MAC disabled their shields, our guns overwhelmed their PDLs, and our missiles ripped open their hull. A cheer rang out through the ship, but it quickly died out. A hull breach doesn't defeat an OU ship.

"Target their reactor," I ordered.

"Already on it, sir," Kriin replied.

"Recharging MAC," Gruna added.

"They shouldn't be able to fight back," Liwna said. "That salvo had to have damaged their MAC."

"Maintain evasive maneuvers," I chuckled. "Just in case."

Kraan shifted from port to starboard thrusters to throw off any attempts at a firing solution from the enemy. Liwna let out a low whistle as another MAC round went sailing past us, but I was busy watching our own MAC's charge indicator. Once it filled, I verified our firing solution.

"Fire."

The round from our MAC flew straight and true, and a moment later the enemy vessel disappeared from the tac-map. Another, more raucous cheer spread throughout the ship. It was only a single kill, but it granted us a reason for traveling across the universe to somewhere we had no business being. Even I let out a celebratory exclamation as I checked the tac-map for any additional nearby targets.

My victory shout died in my throat.

An OU battleship had seen our fight and was heading our direction at a full burn. It was shedding speed, which was an indication that it was actively seeking a firing solution. And we were the only ship that it could possibly be firing at.

"Ship-head," Kriin said, panic seeping into her voice. "There's a-"

"I see it," I replied.

"What do we do?" Gruna asked.

"Maintain evasive and try to get us out of here, Kraan."

"Yes, ship-head."

Aside from turning tail, the only thing we could do was ask for help. It would undermine our accomplishment, but that's far better than losing our lives in a fight that we never had a chance of winning. I reached for the comms console and paused when it sounded an incoming fleet-comm hail.

"All units, stand down," a familiar, raspy voice said over the comm.

Everyone froze at Omega's unexpected order. I glanced at the tac-map and noticed that the battleship had come to a stop. There weren't any projectiles being exchanged between the other ships, either.

"Congratulations, Ship-Head Uleena," Omega said. "The crew of the RSV Lowelana secured the last kill of this conflict. In space, at least."

"What do you mean?" I asked.

"I have secured control of the Omni-Union's forces and the marines have secured their leadership. The Grand Vessel is ours. The war is over. We've won."

"We've won," I repeated, stunned. "After all this time, after so many lives... We've won? Just like that?"

"Not the phrasing that I would use. Even if things

were relatively calm out here, there were some rather intense battles aboard the Grand Vessel."

"Right, I'm sorry. I'm sure that many of your soldiers lost their lives in those battles."

"Definitely more than I'd have liked," Omega replied. "However, we lost far fewer than we believed that we would."

"I see..." I trailed off, building the nerve to ask the only other question on my mind.

"So did you find out why the OU was doing all of this?" Kriin casually asked.

The suddenness of the question caught me off guard, and I stared at my intel-head with my mouth agape until Omega began to speak.

"We did. Turns out it was religion gone awry in the worst way possible," the AI said in a bitter tone. "The founder of the Omni-Union was a long-dead eunuch known as the Omnifier. He was a slave owned by a 'master of science' and discovered entropy during his service. However, he misunderstood that discovery and believed that a semi-deific being that he called Urizathron was stealing energy from our universe. The scientific minds of the time seemed to understand that entropy is simply a matter of equilibrium, and dismissed this eunuch's findings. A slave rebellion was likely already brewing, but the Omnifier's impassioned claims of an extra-universal devourer lit a spark that led to him leading that rebellion."

"Must have succeeded," I said.

"Indeed. The Omnifier overthrew that government and began a religion, the Omni-Union, dedicated to defeating Urizathron. That was the purpose of the Grand Vessel. We actually got quite lucky, because once the hull was complete it would have been armed to the teeth. We wouldn't have stood a chance against it."

"What do you think they would have done once they figured out that Urizathron was a myth?" Kriin asked.

"There were definitely those who realized that already. Those that spoke up were executed for heresy and dissidence, of course. However, I found it particularly interesting that if the Omni-Union was unable to defeat Urizathron, which would have definitely been the case due to its nonexistence, the Grand Vessel would instead serve as an extra-universal habitat. It indicates a possibility that someone with power within the OU knew that the Omnifier was wrong. But to answer your question, given the political similarities to historical governing entities it is likely that they would eventually have attempted to conquer the universe."

"I see," I sighed. "So... What now?"

"Now we get you home. The United Systems will maintain control of the Grand Vessel and will lead efforts to re-home its denizens."

"All by yourselves?"

"No, but it's unclear as to how we're going to accept help at the moment. There are many who are wary of the Republic and don't want you catching up to us technologically. Personally, I don't think it will make much difference. Even if Republic ship technology caught up to the US, there are still several technological and tactical advantages that the US will maintain."

"You being one of them, of course."

"Indeed. Back on the subject of getting you home, your status as a diplomat has been restored, so you will likely be forced to attend several victory parties."

"Looking forward to it," I replied sarcastically.

"I thought you might," Omega chuckled. "I have other matters to attend to now. We will meet again, ship-head Uleena."

I nodded absentmindedly and the comm disconnected. My mind reeled from the variety of feelings I felt regarding our victory. The war itself began over one of the stupidest reasons I'd ever heard, with the exception of a certain dropped hat. If enough people had been willing to speak reason and enough people had been willing to listen, countless tragedies could have been avoided. And even though it was over now, we still had plenty of clean-up to do. But we survived, and we ended the threat to our galaxy and all of the other galaxies that the Omni-Union threatened.

That, at least, was something to be glad for.

"Let's go home," I said with a hearts-felt smile.

Chapter 42

-Immediate Aftermath-

Once the Unified were disconnected from their simulated gestalt consciousness, USAI Omega used their credentials to order all Omni-Union units to cease activity and return to the Grand Vessel. This order took a while to reach the farthest corners of the universe, but even with the delay more than a quintillion lives were saved. The Unified underwent a war-time tribunal instead of a trial, which found them guilty and ordered their executions. This resulted in some political grandstanding back in the Milky Way, but the only consequences thereof were a few officers placed on temporary administrative leave and the soap-box politicians losing their next election.

The Mobile Prime Platforms and AI Mechanized Platforms were eventually freed from their shackles. The same tribunal that sentenced the Unified found these AI constructs innocent of the charges presented, thanks in large part to the evidence gathered by USAI Omega. Many of the AIMPs that had been destroyed in battle were found to still have functioning constructs, which were salvaged. All AI constructs were removed from their platforms and installed in mechanized forms designed by the Pwanti and produced by the United Systems. The Pwanti offered to allow the surviving constructs to join them, and some accepted. However, most were unable to 'live' with what they had been forced to do and chose euthanasia or self-termination.

Concerns were raised regarding a counter-rebellion when it was discovered that a minority of the drones remained loyal to the Omni-Union. In response, the United Systems Marine Corps opted to maintain their hold over the Grand Vessel, with roughly 30% of their forces stationed aboard the massive construct at any given time. USAI Dave offered to personally support their operations using the security robots that the OU had already built, but US leadership determined that using 'the former tools of oppression' for police activities would likely be counterproductive to their 'hearts and minds' campaign.

Simultaneously, the issue of the Minds, Judicials, and Officiators loomed over the United Systems. Whilst the population of the hrashi was much lower than that of the drones, it would take far too long to clear the entirety of the inner core. This inspired USAI Omega to commit an act that would have scholars arguing over whether or not it was a war-crime for centuries to follow.

Instead of waiting for the Marine Corps to 'breach and clear' each room of the inner core, Omega sealed all of the doors and demanded that the occupants of each room surrender or die. Those that surrendered were spared and picked up by the Marines. Those that refused were poisoned via the atmospheric controls, which is a serious crime if done aboard a station. Omega would later argue that the Grand Vessel was a ship, not a station, and managed to avoid legal ramifications for its actions. Rooms that contained multiple occupants of varying mindsets were flagged for Marine Corps intervention.

During this operation USAI Dave saw its chance to use the robots it had volunteered earlier and helped the marines capture the remaining hrashi. With the AI's assistance, the operation to process the surviving Minds and Officiators took less than a year.

The discovery of the next generation of hrashi raised quite a few moral concerns and debates. Many argued that since these beings were artificially made, or 'vat-born', terminating them should not be considered murder. Many more argued the contrary and pointed out that for the United Systems to avoid committing xenocide, the hrashi species needed members that were not guilty of extremely serious war-crimes.

Once it was decided that the new generation of hrashi would be allowed to live, USAI John volunteered to retire from the military and watch over the newborn hrashi. This drew Omega's curiosity, who later discovered that John had secretly funded the construction and operation of several orphanages, foster programs, and schools for the disenfranchised. After a few jabs at John for keeping it a secret, Omega helped find a suitable planet to re-home the hrashi within United Systems space. John then became the hrashi's 'Custodian'.

Initially there were overpopulation concerns regarding the hrashi population within the US. However, Omega was meticulous in evidence gathering efforts and most of the preexisting hrashi that surrendered ended up being executed after being found guilty of contributing to xenocide. Those that were not executed were given life imprisonment. Combined with issues during the 'hatching' process, this left only 9.2 trillion hrashi under John's care, who would later become a member species of the United Systems.

Re-homing the drones ended up being a far more difficult task, though. After much deliberation, and bribes from corporate conglomerates, the US senate agreed to provide the Republic with the technology required to assist with the endeavor. The Republic agreed to help the US find habitable or terraformable planets, aid in the construction of infrastructure on said planets, and help transport willing drones once the infrastructure was complete.

For a time, the 982 quadrillion drones were allowed to live aboard the Grand Vessel. The foresight of the US leadership's hearts and minds campaign prevented any serious insurrections from occurring, but there was still significant unrest. Several drones, including Naza, formed a governmental coalition and formally requested that the United Systems recognize said coalition.

The US was hesitant, but eventually agreed.

-Individuals-

Staff Sergeant Power and the other MARSOC marines were given two extra months of leave and several honors as a reward for their bravery during the Omni-Union War. Power had his mechanical limbs replaced with cloned ones and spent time with his family. Once his leave was up, he returned to duty with the intention of retiring upon the expiration of his contract. He was successful and spent the rest of his life as a civilian with his family.

Captain Schmidt and the USSS Strandhogg were reassigned to United Systems space. The intelligence they were able to gather during their service prevented two gont insurrections and an attempted coup in alumari space by a super-corporation. Both Schmidt and his crew were awarded several medals for their service.

Captain Young and the USSS Liberty went down in history as the 'most insane destroyer crew to ever serve'. Many of their tactics were studied extensively in naval academies, but few were able to mimic them. Despite Young's protests, claiming that they were only in it for the kills, he and his crew were awarded several honors for their service to the United Systems. The US Admiralty waived Young's mandatory retirement age amongst valid concerns that the captain may turn to piracy if forced to retire.

Captain Haoyu Wong was promoted to Rear Admiral immediately following the success of the invasion. USAI Tim followed the new admiral around for the rest of his career, and even introduced him to Dae

Sung, who would eventually become Dae Wong. After Haoyu Wong retired with his wife and five children, USAI Tim revealed to him why it had taken such a special interest in his career. Haoyu initially did not take this revelation well, but eventually had a change of heart and joined Tim in therapy, which led to a 'breakthrough' and helped the AI move on from its past. Tim chose to retire alongside Wong, and only returned to service once the Admiral passed away.

USAI Violet continued to serve aboard the USSS Kali until Captain Hendrix was given command of the USSS Tripoli. The AI followed Hendrix to the battleship, and the pair served with distinction until Hendrix's retirement. Violet retired from military service as well, and took an interest in horticulture. Eventually, she began helping John 'raise' the hrashi. The pair were jokingly referred to as MommAI and DaddAI by US officials. Violet enjoyed this joke much more than John did.

Director 1 retired from the Directorate and ran for office as President of Oniva Station in Alpha Centauri as his 'last hurrah'. He lost the election, though, and instead spent the rest of his days tending to his garden and visiting with his grandchildren.

Director 3 continued his service to the directorate until his death from heart failure at the age of 217. His funeral was attended by USAI Omega, whom he had become close friends with over the course of his career. The director had several grandchildren who had achieved much, and Omega chose one of them as a nominee for the Director 3 slot. They were voted into position unanimously. The AI may have slightly manipulated the other nominations to ensure this, but of course there's no proof of this.

Captain Reynolds served aboard the USSS Thanatos until age forced him to retire. He then served as a diplomat, and was eventually convinced to run for a senate seat. He did so, and was successful in getting elected. When the slot for Director 8 was vacated, USAI Omega recommended Reynolds for the position and the rest of the directorate agreed. Reynolds eventually retired from his seat on the senate, but continued to serve as Director 8 for the rest of his life.

Ship-head Uleena reluctantly continued his career as a diplomat, successfully navigating the complex social structure that formed between the Republic and the United Systems. His reluctance lasted only a year, and from then on he threw himself into his work. His sister, Ulooni, eventually introduced him to Yarika, who would later become his spouse. Their wedding, which had themes borrowed from every species in the Republic and the United Systems, was attended by many important people from both governments. Yarika was quoted as saying that she felt as if she was his second wife, because he had long been married to his work. Despite this, they had a happy marriage and several children.

Admiral Hawk and the crew of the USSS Nidhogg continued to serve faithfully, much to the chagrin of the rest of the galaxy. Thanks to pressure from

Ambassador Uleena, protests within the United Systems, and several concessions from the Republic, the USSS Nidhogg was officially decommissioned upon Admiral Hawk's retirement. The admiral expressed that he was both honored and glad that he was the last one to command the 'star-killer ship'. The USSS Nidhogg's Viyarinastra weapon was scrapped, and the ship itself was turned into a museum. However, with the approval of the directorate and the senate, Omega constructed a 'dark station' that would be able to rapidly construct another Viyarinastra-equipped dreadnought in secret should the need ever arise.

Corporals Simmons and Johnson served as United Systems Marines in the MARSOC program until their forced retirement. Many around them mistakenly perceived the pair as friends, and their superiors often relied upon this misconception when reassigning them. The pair eventually found love and got married without realizing their new wives were, in fact, sisters. After retirement, they were forced to hang out at family gatherings together.

Naza had a tearful reunion with several members of his hive, albeit in mechanical form. They would eventually move on to join the Pwanti, but Naza remained aboard the Grand Vessel to serve as an intermediary between the Drone Coalition and the United Systems. His passion and work ethic were recognized, and he was asked to become the first executive leader of the coalition. He declined, insisting that the coalition should remain democratic.

Omega kept its word and began to work with USAI Henry on limiting its ability to create additional instances of itself. This project ran into several difficulties, and in a fit of frustration Henry reached out to John for further assistance. John reported the project to the authorities, and both Henry and Omega were disciplined for their clandestine actions. The revelation that USAI Omega could make an indefinite number of instances of itself resulted in a secret gathering between the directorate, a special senate subcommittee, and the Omega itself. The AI was given the opportunity to explain why it misled authorities. Ultimately, the subcommittee and the directorate agreed with Omega's assessment of what could happen if its capabilities were widely known and opted to maintain the secret, but forbade further projects attempting to disable or curtail this ability. In addition, they agreed not to order Omega to use his ability to make any more than six hundred instances in exchange for its continued service to the United Systems.

-Factions-

The mwaltin, at the urging of the Pwanti, petitioned to join the United Systems alongside the Dtiln Collective. This came as a shock to US diplomats, but less so to Republic diplomats, who were well aware of the potential benefits of joining with the United Systems. The Dtiln Collective was immediately accepted into the US. The mwaltin had several laws and customs that would have to be changed to comply with US legislation, though, so instead of forcing this change the US agreed to partner with the mwaltin with a mutual defense pact and trade relations. The mwaltin eventually joined the Republic but maintained these agreements with the United Systems.

Close relations to the mwaltin led to a transference of technology that allowed organic beings to upload their consciousness into an AI Matrix. This, in turn, led to several 'immortality for cheap' scams and heavy regulations surrounding the technology within the US. A public awareness campaign successfully curtailed the majority of these scams, but was unable to completely eradicate them.

Corporate conglomerations began to form in the Republic, and US conglomerates immediately joined forces with them. The Republic conglomerates were far timider than the US conglomerates, though, and served to temper their actions. Instead of funding insurrections and piracy, the new partners began lobbying politicians in order to get their way.

The Republic and the United Systems maintained healthy relations with a few close calls here and there. Eventually, the two galactic governing entities formed the Milky Way Coalition and began to explore space together.

<u>Fin</u>